DREAM RELIC

VELVET DAVIS

Velvet Davis
www.velvetdavis.com

This book is a work of fiction. Names, characters, places,
and incidents are products of the author's imagination or are used fictitiously and not to be construed as
real. Any resemblance to actual persons, living or dead,
events, organizations, or locales is entirely coincidental.

Cover design by Damonza.com
Book design by Damonza.com

First printing: 2020
ISBN: 978-1-7321042-2-8
E-ISBN: 978-1-7321042-3-5

For my grandmother, Naomi Chandler, who will always be my favorite storyteller.

PROLOGUE

REBIAL HELD ONTO the dangling roots until an unfamiliar ache plagued his muscles. He savored the feeling, before swinging into the underground cavern. His knees buckled on landing and hit stone. Pain racketed up his body and momentarily disoriented him. This was not a normal height for a man to fall from, he remembered now.

The forest would stop sustaining him eventually. He had experienced a touch of this earlier, though at the onset the reason was unclear. Now he knew why. The woman with the mark had removed the prophecy from its resting place beneath the tree. He'd been able to cling to its power long enough for his redemption.

He staggered to his feet and started moving across the cold, damp stone. Darkness came as he furthered himself from the rift. Soon he could barely see, but nothing could hinder him now.

When he entered the first passageway, traces of the forest, that had interwoven through his skin and bones, stayed behind. His unquenchable anger stayed with them. He was flesh and blood again in totality. Thoughts formed easily and regained logic more fitting for a man. A crushing sadness overcame him at the realization of what he had lost.

Whom he had lost. She was gone forever. Or was she? Ages had passed. She should be dead. Yet they had performed the ritual. She had insisted it would work.

Bits of prophecy ingrained within his mind allowed him to recall an ending. The memory was obscure, yet clarity thrived deep within his subconscious. If only he could draw it out.

Her presence, invisible yet strong, haunted the tunnels as it had haunted his soul. He ran in hopes of finding her. The map she'd left for him had embedded into his mind during his bond with the forest. His heart pumped faster the quicker he ran. He had forgotten this feeling, the mental high from swift movement, but now it propelled him onward.

His physical presence faded as time mingled with distance. He shouldn't be alive, he knew this, and soon his body was no more. Its absence caused him to move like the wind. Only his mind persisted, searching and calling for her in silence. He would roam these tunnels until he found her. And if he never did, then he would roam forever. It was an existence he was unaccustomed to after so many years of hateful waiting, but it was also an improvement. He had survived in a halfway state before.

Chapter One

THE PRISTINE, SILVER room was vast and circular, yet it contained just four occupants. Its round shape was supposed to enhance the meeting room, invite an open-minded way of thinking, but today it only exaggerated that the conversation was moving in circles. Ceera could barely keep her thoughts from spinning along with it.

It was dizzying really: the room, High Service's interrogation, Draevik's intense and heavy stare. It would be much easier to relent and depart than continue subjecting herself to such scrutiny. But she couldn't concede to such a personal injustice. Not after what she'd been through.

"Tell us again"—Draevik prodded, his dark eyes gleaming—"what the inscription says needs to happen to the relic."

He'd asked the question several times already. Ceera's frustration with the sphere seven, supposedly the wisest of officials, was nearing a climax. This would be the third time she explained why the relic had been placed beneath the tree. His dismissal of what she deemed far more interesting—its claims to promote longevity, the map, not to mention Rebial—was borderline infuriating. Was he dense or attempting to demean her intelligence by having her repeat herself?

His hawkish gaze, complemented by his graying hair and heavy brows, suggested the latter. Given the chance, she was sure he'd sink his talons in her. A headache threatened her temples.

"It says," she stated again, "that once the relic is separated from its originator, then it is to be returned, or all will revert to the way it should have been, and its transcriber will die. This is the reason why the transcriber returned it to Rebial by placing it beneath the tree. Presumably, this was to be its final resting place. And so it was done."

And thankfully, she thought, *for this meant the relic's originator, who also happened to be the strange woman infiltrating her dreams, had lived.*

It still bothered her that this woman, seemingly a scribe like herself, had been the only one whose life was in jeopardy.

"So the prophecy was fulfilled," Draevik responded, "and we are left with nothing more than an interesting artifact." Looking satisfied, he crossed his arms over his chest and leaned back in his chair.

Did he really believe that after all they had learned? They'd determined the relic was a prophecy pertaining to a past age, but they'd never figured out why it had resurfaced. Or more specifically, why her dreams had led her to it. The relic was still an object of mystery in many ways, and she couldn't expect the officials to care how it related to her. Especially since she'd kept some of her connection a secret.

Risa and Karnen, though dressed in signature High Service silver attire, said nothing. In contrast to their status as officials, they observed more than they participated during these sessions.

"Not exactly," she said reluctantly. "There's still the questions of why the relic resurfaced after all this time, where the map leads, not to mention what happened to the past civilization after they followed the inscribed directions. Plus, the relic claims—"

"Rubbish." Draevik shooed her concerns away with a flick of his wrist. "Those are irrelevant things of the past. There is no way to answer them. All we can do is speculate, and speculation rarely evolves into solid truths."

He paused as if he were choosing his next words carefully. "It seems," he said, "that your study is nearing an end."

The room spun faster in her mind, along with everything else. Ceera gripped the arms of her chair tightly. She had risked her life to acquire the relic. Her eyes locked with his. "Excuse me?"

"High Service," Draevik continued, "feels it's time you returned to your scribe training."

Risa and Karnen glanced at each other, eyebrows raised. As servants to the public, High Service officials were supposed to rule as a group, so their silence was troubling.

"But I—"

"Surely you can't get much satisfaction from rehashing the same information. You've clearly been repeating yourself these last few sessions." The condescending smile on Draevik's face dared her to say otherwise.

Ceera's mouth opened, but a retort fell short. Stunned, her gaze strayed to Risa, the official who had been the most supportive during their earlier interrogation sessions.

The woman was the picture of serenity in her fluttery gown and swept back hair. "It's true, dear," she said gently, "you haven't discovered any new information for some time."

The comment, though spoken mildly, felt like a slap, and heat buzzed Ceera's face. The reality was she hadn't been allowed to seek any new information. Draevik had told her what to focus on, thus controlling every aspect of her study. Anger dashed her aching temples, but she refused to let it affect her composure. It was important to remain calm.

"We know it will be difficult for you to go back to your scribe work," Karnen said, "after all the excitement of your travels, and then the transcribing of what we assumed to be an important artifact, but all good things must come to an end."

Ceera avoided their eyes by staring at her hands. The birthmark on her thumb stared back. The protector of the forest, Rebial, had tried to kill her when she entered his territory to search for the relic. After recognizing her birthmark, he'd protected her from Falken, a villainous spy, and allowed her to take it. Based on his reaction, she suspected the woman who'd left the relic beneath the tree also had the mark, which would mean she was Ceera's ancestor.

Yet Ceera's connection to the relic and this past civilization, birthmark related or not, was still unexplained. Rebial had vanished into a rift to 'face the end' as he'd stated, so she only had the relic to glean information from. And they were taking it away from her.

"I still haven't figured out why I was the one singled out," she said with forced restraint. "Why the dreams came."

High Service didn't need to know her birthmark had something to do with it, not until she knew it was safe. She couldn't place herself in jeopardy once again.

Draevik nodded briefly at Karnen, who said, "Perhaps you should find comfort in the fact the relic existed at all."

His stern gaze reminded her that if she hadn't found the relic, they would've had her committed. Dassius Rucien, her traveling friend and perhaps more, had clued her into that truth. Dreams were not supposed to merge with reality. Yet her dreams, aided by the strange woman's apparition, had foretold of a relic in a mysterious forest.

When she'd learned a newly discovered forest had wrecked the sanity of the AT installers working near its remote location, the coincidence compelled her to act. She'd revealed to High Service that the forest was using her dreams to summon her. She'd then demanded to accompany Dassius to help unravel the mystery.

It had been a harrowing venture, one she hadn't the training or skill to partake in by herself. They'd had to visit the Archaics—dangerous demi-gods who mastered the elements—for advice. Their aid had ensured she and Dassius were able to resist Rebial and, ultimately, acquire the relic.

And now the officials had decided that their journey had been for naught. Her connection to the relic, though clearly paramount to her entire existence, meant nothing to them.

She swallowed loudly, unsure of what to say. Defiance was not something she was well practiced in. The trio waited expectantly, although Draevik's eyes held a mocking glint. She would earn nothing by arguing her point. That much was clear.

"I suppose," she said in a measured voice, "that I shall take your advice and check in with my mentor."

"Very good," Karnen responded. "Drusilla will be glad to have you back."

"We do appreciate your help in the matter," Risa said warmly, but her words did nothing to console Ceera.

In the past few months, Risa had disappointed her the most. The woman had undergone a disturbing transformation from role model to ineffectual leader. The change had been gradual, something Ceera kept convincing herself wasn't really happening. But now, like so many things, and in defiance of her mounting headache, clarity prevailed. Ceera's respect, the last remaining shreds of it, withered away. Risa had changed, High Service had changed, and she couldn't put her finger on why.

She stood and turned to leave.

"Don't forget"—Draevik's casual tone betrayed an underlying threat—"the importance of keeping your findings confidential."

"Of course," she said softly, gripping the door handle. "I will waste no one's time by telling them about my trivial discoveries."

She refused to give him the satisfaction of a backwards glance as she left the room, just like she refused to accept the fact that he had won.

⁓

The sword's blood-stained blade swung toward him, and Dassius whirled between two trees to avoid it. His attacker was taller by about a foot, with rough skin and a distorted, craggy face.

A giant bird flew down from a tree, a predator, evident by its clawed feet and curved beak. His opponent made another effort to strike. Dassius dodged the sword, took a mild jab in his shoulder from the bird, and swung an arm outward. He stabbed the bird in the underside before his knife arced to plunge into his main opponent's chest.

The two attackers stopped moving, yet pulsed accordingly, as their fate was decided. But Dassius already knew the answer to that. He had defeated them.

Only when the two images faded entirely did his arms fall slack. The glass doorway, now apparent since the forested scenery had also disappeared, opened, and he stepped out of the simulation box. The main room contained a bench, a shelf with towels, and a large sim-control unit. His trainer handed him a towel, and he wiped his face.

"Thanks," he said. "That was my first practice in weeks."

"You're welcome, Mr. Rucien. Glad you enjoyed the Sim."

"Where's Sidorn?" Dassius asked, tossing the towel into a bin.

Normally, his clairvoyant ability would clue him into such things, but he must be out of practice, for it offered him no possible solutions.

"He's on assignment."

Dassius frowned. What assignment? But he knew better than to ask. Assignments for the Sci-Defense team were on a need-to-know basis, and since it wasn't his assignment then he didn't need to know. He hadn't seen his friend in weeks though, was anxious to partake in some real-time combat.

"Do you know when he'll be back?" he asked.

"No," the trainer responded. "Shall I program you another simulation?"

"Sure," Dassius said, trying to hide his disappointment. "And good idea to throw in that raptor. I can see you've been reading my profile."

Though his training was scientifically designed to teach him to master adaptation and survival, Sci-Defense was a new discipline and thus ever evolving. His last assignment had been a complicated venture that had pushed the boundaries of this training. After returning, he had requested his simulations contain dual attacks by different opponent types. He was pleased his request had been taken seriously. He had almost lost someone special over it: Ceera Kestlyn.

The trainer smirked before motioning him back inside.

Dassius hesitated before stepping back into the Sim box, wishing he could instead practice with Sidorn. His friend was a skilled fighter, had vied for the same assignment Dassius had recently returned from, almost beating him to it.

Sidorn had been glad to see him upon his return, yet this happiness dwindled as Dassius's fame grew. Or so he had sensed, for his teammate was hard to read. Though the argument they'd had before he'd visited his parent's settlement proved the tension was real. They were close in skill level, which was ideal for combat practice, but also came with its own set of problems.

❧

Ceera said goodbye to the guard standing at the entrance to the Aurora as she left. She received an efficient nod back, devoid of eye contact. A low sphere High Service official or attendant used to oversee the area, but apparently no more. Only guards stood there now, recruited from Order Patrol headquarters. The result was a strange blending of law enforcement boundaries and another change in High Service's manner of leadership since she'd returned to Semadon.

As she walked away from the towering Aurora, the focal point of the village, she contemplated what she'd learned from her friend Litha.

During her adventure with Dassius, Semions had claimed High Service was mishandling village affairs; most of it relating to Atomic Transport system failures, a garden fire within the CfNL's property, and the suspicion that officials were not being forthcoming with information about she and Dassius.

The Council for Natural Law and the Council for Advancement riling up their constituents hadn't helped matters. The former claimed the tainted forest's mysterious appearance signaled that the CfA was undermining nature with its weather enhancement project. The latter had sent Falken Grihne after Ceera and Dassius to ensure they did not uncover anything proving this claim.

As a result of all the disfunction, Semions had resorted to protesting outside the Aurora. Perhaps that was the reason for the added security, although both councils remained unusually silent. The CfA had been forced into a leadership change, which was still in disarray, and for the time being this meant the CfNL had no one to argue with. Semadon was peaceful for once, but considering her recent experiences with High Service, the peace was misleading and hid a deeper problem.

She wound her way around the orbit that ringed the high circular buildings within the town's center, ignoring the passersby who looked at her with interest. Still. She and Dassius had been treated like minor celebrities upon returning to Semadon. It was a burden, albeit a flattering one. When she wasn't in the mood, like now, she walked quickly and diverted her gaze to avoid interaction.

They would no longer crave her attention anyway once High Service announced they'd relieved her from studying the relic. No longer being interesting to the public was the only advantage to her dismissal.

Deep in thought, she almost stepped on the orbit cleaner inching along the walkway. Implemented by the most famed inventor in Semadon, Hegliod Avatus was both genius and eccentric, and apparently spent too much time staring at the streets. Either that or he'd needed a break from all the space travel innovations he was rumored to be involved in. Normally, his inventions were more groundbreaking than ground sweeping. And soon would be ground leaving, if she believed all the talk.

Her mentor's office was around the curve. The brick building, marked *Mentoring Headquarters* above its rotating door, was tall and housed mentor offices of all disciplines. She entered and strode to the elevator. Having been a mentor for many years, Drusilla's office was on the top floor. Ceera stepped inside, chose level ten, and waited as the circular frame ascended.

The door chimed and opened. She walked around the hall to Drusilla's office and knocked hesitantly on the door. She hadn't spoken to Drusilla much since returning to Semadon and wasn't sure whether the older woman would be accepting of her re-entrance into scribe work. Still ruminating over what could be done about her dismissal, it seemed best to follow along with the plan, for now, in case High Service checked to make sure she'd followed orders.

Drusilla opened the door, her astute face unreadable. "Ceera, what a surprise to see you."

Her mentor held out her arms, and they hugged briefly. The hug was not warm, rather stiff to say the least, but Ceera had not experienced many over the years. Her mother had died when she was very young, and her father had given her up shortly after. Drusilla's rare hugs, coupled with Litha's, were the only ones she'd shared until recently.

Unlike most men who'd ever tried, not that there'd been many in her twenty years of life, Dassius Rucien had managed to garner her affections during their recent travels. Her hopes to further the relationship had discontinued when he'd left to visit his family's settlement. She hadn't seen him in weeks.

"High Service dismissed me from studying the relic,"

Ceera said with little emotion. "They ordered me to continue my scribe work. I hope to complete my time in transition."

Everyone was required to undergo time in transition—a supervisory period with a mentor—before practicing their work independently. Even before her journey to the forest, Ceera's time in transition seemed to be taking longer than her peers.

Drusilla took Ceera's hand, ushered her inside the office, and shut the door. The room contained minimal furniture: a desk, two chairs, a shelf, and a filing cabinet. One of the few adornments was a small, squatted cactus on the shelf, symbolic in many ways of Drusilla's prickly nature. The office was orderly and spotless, without a speck of dust or clutter. It matched the woman's work ethic and how demanding she was of her students.

"I'm relieved," Drusilla said. "I was worried things would turn out differently."

Tears pricked Ceera's eyes. Drusilla had always played the part of surrogate mother, no matter how strained their relationship could be. "You were?"

"I wasn't sure if High Service would give credence to your dreams," Drusilla said carefully. "I hear the relic thus far has been a huge disappointment."

Ceera's mouth clamped shut before she spoke. "That's what High Service seems to think."

"And with your past, I wasn't sure they'd be forgiving."

Suspicion seeped into her awareness. There were two very different things Drusilla could be referring to, one much more serious than the other. "What do you mean?" she asked. "What past?"

Drusilla's eyes flitted away for a moment. "You haven't been the model scribe, though I've always defended you."

Ceera was certain this was not what Drusilla had meant. The woman was usually unflappable, but the eye flutter suggested she was implying something far more controversial than Ceera's intermittent probations for PID idleness. Skilled in keeping her mouth shut lately, she pretended not to notice. She looked away, her gaze resting on the filing cabinet in the corner behind Drusilla's desk. The label on one of its drawers read *Transitioning Scribes*.

"When can you resume your duties?" Drusilla asked.

"Anytime."

"Excellent. How about tomorrow you go to the library and get up to date on your PID viewing? The day after, I shall meet with you there, and we'll discuss your next assignment."

"That would be great," she lied, knowing the Public Information Device would surely contain current events about her own life.

As they said their goodbyes, Ceera's focus remained on the filing cabinet. Though it looked locked and thereby inaccessible, she wondered what it contained about her. Did the past Drusilla mentioned have anything to do with her mother being crazy? And if so, had Drusilla been the one who had tipped off High Service? Needing to know whom she could trust, she was determined to find out.

Chapter Two

HETIA GATHERED WITH the other officials in the spacious meeting room, mere minutes after Draevik's unexpected summoning through the intercom system. He sat at the head of a large round table with the sphere sevens, slightly frowning as he examined paperwork. Hetia was used to seeing that frown.

"Good afternoon, Hetia," Fresdin said, taking his chair beside her.

"Hello," she responded, glad to see him even though lately they weren't seeing eye to eye. Fresdin was pleasant enough, but sometimes she required a bit more than pleasant to find someone interesting.

"What special insight do you think Draevik has in store for us today?" Fresdin asked.

The question would have amused her had it been laced with sarcasm. Unfortunately, Fresdin was serious.

She wrinkled her nose. "I tend not to get my hopes up anymore when Draevik is concerned."

Fresdin lifted his eyebrows in surprise, then pursed his lips to shush her. "Insolence is not becoming on you," he said quietly.

She scowled.

"Neither is that," he hissed.

Before she could come up with an adequate retort, Draevik began speaking.

"Fellow officials," he said, "I have good news."

Draevik smiled, triggering Hetia's suspicions. His smile was not the same as other smiles. It did not emit joy, but instead radiated danger, like it belonged on a snake or a cougar.

"Today we relieved Ceera Kestlyn of her duties."

Draevik paused as if he deserved admiration or praise, but Hetia was only dismayed. Surely others felt the same? She glanced about. No, even Fresdin stared intently, clearly mesmerized and hanging onto every word. She was not above wading in dangerous waters when justice could be found there. But the others had grown complacent lately.

"What this means is—"

"Excuse me," Hetia said, unable to remain silent.

Everyone in the room stared at her, some in apparent horror she would interrupt a sphere seven, even worse for it being Draevik Warlyn: the magnificent one who was blindly revered. Some gazed at her curiously, which Hetia took as a good sign. It meant all was not completely lost.

Draevik gave her a look that she sensed was supposed to make her cower, but Hetia was not the cowering type.

"Who is 'we'? I thought we"—Hetia stood and gestured around the room—"were 'we'. Yet we have not been consulted on the matter. Why was this decision not made as a group?"

Fresdin sucked his breath in slowly, though other officials nodded.

"Because there was nothing to discuss," Draevik said. "I, Karnen, and Risa decided prior to our meeting with Ms.

Kestlyn that if she had nothing new to say then we would be finished with her."

"Is this true?" Hetia turned to Risa and Karnen: Draevik's newly anointed sidekicks.

As most officials had raised a sphere level recently, the pair were now sphere sixes even though their leadership skills now lacked this distinctive quality. They had become Draevik's followers, a new yet dangerous development in High Service's system of governing.

Risa and Karnen exchanged glances, although Hetia suspected there wasn't much independent thought between them. If there was, then they should have noticed the misstep. Why was no one else questioning the misstep?

"Yes," Karnen said. "We decided it was appropriate since we were the ones meeting with her daily."

"I thought we were to vote on such things?" Hetia looked at Risa who lowered her gaze, a telling reaction.

"We vote on matters of importance," Draevik said. "Not matters of an obvious nature."

"I would have liked to speak with her about her findings before she was dismissed," Hetia insisted.

"There were no findings, which is why we made the decision. Now since *that* has been explained, I shall continue with more relevant news." Draevik glared at Hetia. How dare she put a damper on his announcement, his look seemed to say.

Disappointed, Hetia decided to let it be. With no one defending her, there wasn't much she could do without causing more of a scene. And based on the rigid posture and unnatural breathing sounds coming from her companion, Fresdin may have a heart attack if she were to continue.

"Our study of the relic can now move forward," Draevik

said. "Society will no longer be held back by Ceera Kestlyn's delusional dreams."

Hetia cocked her head and observed the other officials in the room. It was apparent that no one shared her thought process, for their expressions remained passive. Draevik's ambitious project moving forward, just like Ceera's dismissal, had not been decided together. And yet no one pointed this out.

She would incur Draevik's wrath by mentioning it, and her instincts told her this would be a dangerous game. Hetia only played games when she knew she could win. And for the moment, she wasn't exactly sure what the game was about.

Ceera wound her way home, thinking about Drusilla's filing cabinet. She had a right to know what was on file about her, especially if it labelled her as potentially crazy. But how to access her file without Drusilla's permission? Though her life had taken a turn in the last few months, she was not one to snoop around.

Her father might know. Back when he'd arranged for Ceera's scribe schooling, he may have told Drusilla about her mother, using it as an excuse to send her away. It could have impacted Drusilla's decision to accept Ceera into the scribe program. Not many children from settlements ended up living in Semadon. Unless they tested well for a High Service program as Dassius had managed to do, and thus were recruited for specialized training.

Settlements produced goods for society, so children were needed as helping hands. Ceera, however, had not been needed by her father. This hurtful truth she'd come to accept.

She was in an unusual position and perhaps undeservedly so. Yet if Drusilla had taken pity on her, thus accepting her into the scribe program, would she betray her now? She might if Ceera threatened to make her look bad, which was not something Drusilla would have predicted back then. Drusilla might think it better to betray her than risk future embarrassment. And Ceera and her mentor had repeatedly been at odds with each other as she failed at times to meet rigid expectations.

Or her father may not have told Drusilla about her mother at all. Which would make all her speculations a distraction from who was really to blame.

She walked up her dwelling's stone pathway. Weeds poked out from her flowerbeds and guilt pricked her conscious. She'd had no time for gardening lately. She whispered an apology to the flowers and passed by to input the code on the keypad beside her door. It swung open, and she stepped inside.

Her home was small but comfortable, containing a main room with a blue couch that curved around her global update, which she hadn't turned on in months. The kitchen branched off to the side, and a small hallway linked to her bedroom and bath. Her communication orb was positioned on the table near her couch, and she sat down to call her father.

He answered after the fourth hum. "Yes?"

"Dad," she said. "I mean, Father. It's me, Ceera."

"Hi there," he responded, almost too casually.

Had he been expecting her call or was he faking interest? Since he'd abandoned her years ago and reinstated himself in her life only recently, trusting him did not come naturally for her.

"I went to see the AT Installers speak the other day," he continued.

"How was it?" she asked, remembering that the trio were now traveling the planet to relay their experiences installing cylinders.

"Interesting to hear them talk about the forest. The place sounds strange, just like I figured. How's your study of the relic going?"

"There wasn't much to study," she said. "I'm back to regular scribe work tomorrow."

"Oh?" His tone was doubtful. "I thought since you'd found the forest, unlike your mother, you could finish whatever this dream thing was."

"Mother looked for the forest before she died?" Ceera asked.

"She did," her father replied, sounding uncomfortable. "The problem was it didn't exist yet."

Ceera did have that to be thankful for. When the dreams started for her, there was actually a forest to go to. Endlessly searching for something that wasn't there, as her mother had done, did seem a burdensome obsession. And if the impulse never lifted, couldn't even be resolved, then it made sense how one could go mad.

"High Service is putting an end to my study," she said bitterly. "They think the whole thing was a waste of time and energy."

"They do? What does the birthmark mean then?"

"What?" she asked, now distracted from the reason she'd called. "The birthmark has something to do with the dreams?"

Her father had just revealed a clue he'd apparently not intended to part with, for his pause was infuriatingly long.

"Yes," he said finally, "only those with the birthmark, like your mother, have the dreams or sometimes evens visions.

Depends on the person which one, though nothing ever came of it until you."

Ceera contemplated this, remembering her sole vision preceding the dreams. "How come you never told me this before?"

Another long pause. "I thought you knew."

"How would I know? I didn't even know Mother's diagnosis until you told me."

"I guess I didn't think about it," he said defensively. "I'm not used to talking about this. It's difficult for me."

Ceera gritted her teeth. "Tell me this then. Was Drusilla aware of our family situation when she took me in as her apprentice?"

Momentary silence again, before her father said, "That I can't tell you."

"Why not?" She leaned closer, picturing his face on the orb.

"Because, frankly, I don't know."

Her mood sank into disappointment. "I see."

"Is there anything else?" he asked. "I'm still not finished with today's work."

His indifference shook her confidence. "No, I"—she stumbled over her words—"don't think so."

"Then I'm going to let you go. There's only a few hours left of daylight."

"Okay," she said softly.

"Bye now." The orb clicked off.

Her father's abrupt ending of the call stung. And she was back to being vulnerable, otherwise known as his unimportant daughter. She even felt more conflicted now. Why had he not revealed this information about her birthmark before?

She already knew all the females in her lineage had the

mark, but not that they suffered from the dreams as well. This knowledge added another layer. It meant her relatives had a connection to this past civilization. Yet knowing this still didn't address the reason why it was happening. It only deepened the mystery and indicated she had unfinished business with the relic. But what? All its instructions had already been carried out.

On a selfish whim, she tried calling her father back to find out if the birthmark correlation meant that all the women who'd come before her were crazy too. But after five minutes of listening to his orb hum, she hung up.

She needed someone to talk to and options were sparse. Litha would lend an ear, but Ceera didn't want to impede on her friend's perpetually good mood. She wouldn't know how to help anyway. Plus, Ceera would have to reveal more about herself than she felt comfortable doing.

The answer came easily after a moment of thought. Of course, Dassius should have returned from his family's settlement by now. At least that's what he'd said last time they'd spoken, almost three weeks back.

An attraction had formed during their travels to acquire the relic, and her intention had been to keep her distance. Relations with her dad made her skeptical of men. Yet it'd been several months since they'd returned to Semadon. She had expected his interest to wane. Instead, every encounter since, though brief, had increased her desire. Whether it be a secret look of longing, an understanding smile, or a light in his eye, every moment spent in his company left her wanting more.

But it almost seemed that High Service was intentionally keeping them apart. They had allowed Dassius several trips to visit his family and kept him busy when he returned.

Despite their time together being sparse, something was left unquenched. She believed he felt it too, otherwise his attentions would have transferred to someone more readily available, someone who wasn't playing pawn to High Service. And unless he had met someone at his family's settlement, he hadn't had time for anyone else either.

She called his number eagerly only to be greeted by his voicemail stating he was unavailable. She left a message that sounded scripted even to her, then glumly set the orb down and placed her head in her hands. Feeling alone was not unusual for her, yet solitude was a heavy burden to bear on top of everything else. And there was a lot of everything else.

Still bothered by her fellow officials' complacency at the meeting, Hetia decided to get a second opinion on the matter. Someone other than Fresdin. Though he disapproved of her challenging Draevik, she didn't think she was over-reacting. Yet why was she the only one to question? Had the disorderly turn of events in recent months caused the officials to lose their ability to govern, thus making them susceptible to Draevik Warlyn deciding to rule instead of lead? How had he managed to cast such a spell on them?

Hetia knocked lightly on the door to the sphere seven advising room, hoping his voice would not be the one answering back. If so, she would have to face him, for she wasn't the type to shy away from confrontation. Though surely the encounter would be premature, for she was certain nothing would be resolved.

"Come in," came the faint response, a welcoming female one.

Glancing about the empty hall, she opened the door and

slid inside. Sadra sat inquisitively at the desk. The elderly woman's face evoked both wisdom and compassion. Relief consumed her as she shut the door.

"I'm pleased to catch you on your shift," Hetia said, taking a seat before the desk.

"Why is that?" Sadra raised an eyebrow. "Are some sphere sevens not up to your standards?"

"I'm starting to feel at odds with one of them."

"Oh?"

"Yes, and he's making me question the integrity of High Service."

Sadra eyed her knowingly. "It is good to question. It makes you an asset to our cause."

"But not all sphere sevens believe it is good to question."

"I don't refute it. A shift has occurred within High Service."

Sadra's recognition of the problem caused most of Hetia's anxiety to subside. "What happened to Draevik? Why is he so power hungry?"

"This happens when a leader suffers from imbalance. He has been without his companion for several years now. Before his own illness even."

"Is that really why?"

"Ah yes, when Jesra's heart stopped, so did his."

Hetia paused, considering. "So you've noticed it too. Why do some not notice?"

"Some leaders are so effective that those who follow do so blindly."

In their younger days, Draevik and Jesra had stifled a revolt of the settlements with cunning negotiation and tact. This was no small feat since the settlements had desired to start their own system of government over the unfair distribution of goods to Semadon instead of regionally. But something had changed since Draevik's illness. And diplomatic was no longer a word she'd use to describe him.

"But his effective leadership is a thing of the past," Hetia said.

"Officials don't easily forget what has made them strong in the past."

"He's made two decisions without the consent of High Service, and no one except me points this out. Not even the sphere sevens stick up for me."

"Sphere sevens are advisers and must stay true to their sphere level. You are correct that Draevik is overstepping the boundaries. It's up to the lower spheres to handle it."

"I still don't understand. How can you sit idly by?"

"If I were to intercede, how does that teach? Besides, I don't think I'm being idle when I advise you. It's better to allow someone else to rise up. I can see the determination in your eyes. If I can ignite the fire within you, to act, then I have done my part."

A burning motivation rushed through her, along with something less desirable. It could only be called fear. "And if I fail?"

"High Service's success lies in the capabilities of its officials. If you fail, then High Service deservingly fails too."

Hetia gazed at the old woman solemnly. "I cannot create an opposition by myself. I have already openly refuted Draevik and received no support. No one would even speak to me after the meeting, besides Fresdin. And he offered no praise."

"A man who belittles those who question him is not someone most wish to cross. The fact Draevik has appointed guards to watch over High Service speaks largely, don't you think?"

The uniformed guards replacing the attendants had bothered Hetia. "I do fear his intentions. But how do I win support?"

"Sometimes the best way to integrate change is through quieter channels. Boldness can gain attention, but cleverness will keep it."

Sadra clearly wanted her to come up with the plan herself. "Do you know if anyone else is on my side?"

"I gather you are not the only one with reservations. Use your intuition to determine your allies."

Hetia nodded. "I will begin my search tonight."

"What of your companion? Surely it would be best to start with him."

Hetia's mood deflated. She had stormed away from Fresdin's lecturing earlier, too proud to listen and too annoyed to argue back.

"Fresdin? I don't even know if I can trust him."

"You may need him to help lead your cause."

"I need no one to help lead," Hetia replied.

"A strong woman is more likely to be considered a martyr than a saint."

"They will label me the victor before it's all over," Hetia promised.

"I admire your spirit," Sadra said, "but think about what you're saying. Are you not in the same league as Draevik when you award yourself absolute rule?"

Hetia's cheeks burned.

"A leader should be both strong and humble. And asking your companion for help does not reduce your role as the catalyst for change. In fact, it's quite the opposite, for it is much easier to divide than unite."

After her humiliation dissipated, Hetia realized Sadra was right.

"Thank you for that, Sadra. I will search among my peers for others to join my cause. And I will start with Fresdin."

"There you are. Logic has always been your strong point."

Pleased and properly motivated, Hetia bowed her head and slipped from the room.

CHAPTER THREE

DRAEVIK SAT AT the desk inside his office and tried to shake away his rage at the lowly sphere three who had questioned his authority at the meeting. So brash to assume her own inexperience was a match for all the years he'd been a High Service official. Yet Hetia was so confident. Ironically, she reminded him of Jesra.

Draevik lifted the picture from his desk drawer and stared at his late companion's face. It felt like ages since he'd laid eyes on Jesra, years too long. Not to mention the last time he'd seen her, she hadn't looked so young and pretty. Dark brown hair fell in waves around her face. Deep green eyes stared back at him, gleaming with intelligence. Such a clever woman.

The shock of her being gone squeezed his insides, and he slumped over his desk and held his head in his hands. He would never get over the shock.

He had brushed against death several months after her passing. Or rather, it had brushed against him. The sickness had come on so slowly that at first, he was able to ignore it. So gradual it was that when the dangerous effects took hold, it seemed sudden. One moment he was carrying on with everyday life, the next moment he was clinging to it.

That's when he'd missed her the most, for it reminded him of her downfall and the hopeless sensation watching her slowly die had brought with it. Had she been there, his own demise would have been easier to bear.

He recovered without her. She had always been the stronger one, something he had never admitted to anyone, yet he was the one who had lived. An iron will had taken over when he had found out about the relic. And he would ensure immortality became more than just a fairy tale. He would do this for her.

It was a pity she would miss this advancement by mere years, the true shame being her strength and knowledge would be gone forever. It always seemed a waste when a sphere seven passed, their superiority unmatched within Semion culture. Some officials never reached such heights.

Normally, those who contributed to society could expect a statue erected, a monument exalting their greatness. A few adorned the Aurora's lawn. As for himself, there was no need. His impending achievement ensured he would be alive forever now: a living statue. As long as he kept enforcing what needed to happen and prevented officials like Hetia from interfering.

Intimidated by his previous achievements, most officials let him dictate what needed to happen, assuming they, too, would benefit. Since space on the planet was finite, he had already decided immortality would not be extended to all. In the future, once the Semion culture began to inhabit other planets, the privilege could be awarded on a wider scale.

Even if space did become limitless, such leniency was idealistic. After all, did everyone truly deserve to live forever? No, they should have to earn it, which meant High Service would need to come up with guidelines to determine who would be eligible. And once his ambitions proved fruitful and became scientifically feasible, he would be revered to a level none had graced before. Thus, he should determine these guidelines: only the most ambitious, the most strong-willed, the most intelligent would be considered.

Draevik stared at the photo of Jesra nestled within his palm. She would have made a magnificent companion during the enactment of this feat. Which was why he was fierce in his stance that no one as deserving as her would ever suffer such a wasteful end again. The strong should live forever to rule. Only the weak should perish. Life would no longer be a gamble, but a privilege.

Someone rapped on Draevik's office door.

"Come in," he called out, tucking the picture back into the drawer.

The man who entered was tall and formally dressed. Short, dark hair curled around his head in regal fashion. He eyed Draevik speculatively. A tidily trimmed beard accentuated his serious expression. A bright red sun ring, the CfA's insignia, gleamed on his finger.

"Glad you could make it, Glavin," Draevik said. "I wasn't sure if you would come."

Glavin nodded, picking up the marble sphere on the nearby shelf to study it. "What with all the talk around the orbits, I did consider not coming."

"But your quest for knowledge inspired you to come."

"Maybe only my curiosity brings me here."

"Same thing," Draevik retorted.

"Are you going to tell me why you called? Or shall we continue to dance around the subject?" Glavin placed the sphere back on the shelf.

"Please sit down." Draevik motioned to the chair across from his desk. "I called on a matter of great importance."

"I'll be the judge of that," Glavin said, settling into the chair.

"Immortality." Draevik emphasized each syllable with grandeur. "How does it sound?"

Glavin raised an eyebrow. "Like a mere word. An impossible dream."

"What if I told you we have uncovered a way?"

"I'd like to laugh, but to be fair, I'll wait until after you explain yourself."

Draevik smirked. "Do you know who Ceera Kestlyn is?"

"Who doesn't?" Glavin asked. "She destroyed the CfA's reputation when she returned to Semadon with her relic. What does *she* have to do with it?"

"Her relic has something to do with it. Its inscription boasts of this power, that whoever possesses the relic will prevail over the passage of time."

"That doesn't sound like science to me."

"Yet the relic is in pristine condition, unnatural for an object subjected to weathering. Plus, the root structure beneath the forest remained intact all those years."

Glavin stroked his chin. "How do we know that's true?"

The CfA member had conveniently forgotten that the mystics had advised High Service on the matter. No surprise, since the council's fixation on progress meant they were in complete denial of the enchanted entities' outdated existence.

"The mystics may be unnecessary," Draevik replied, "but they never lie."

"My council doesn't believe in the mystics," Glavin replied with a frown. "Or the Archaics for that matter."

"Belief is not required for their existence to be real. They can be touched, can they not? They can be seen with one's own eyes?"

"When you've been conditioned to think something," Glavin said, "even your own eyes can't convince you otherwise."

"Sounds like the leader may be more open-minded than his base," Draevik said. "Do they know this?"

Glavin's frown turned deadly, but Draevik took no heed.

"Besides," he continued before Glavin could object, "there was also a man."

"What man?"

"The man who killed your fellow councilman."

Glavin's hard expression wavered with uncertainty. "Falken Grihne died in the fire. Not that he's missed, but it's the truth we've been told."

"It was the safer explanation"—Draevik allowed his comment time to settle before continuing—"but the truth is Falken burned in the fire after being killed by this man. Keep in mind due to the nature of this information, the man's existence is highly classified."

Glavin's gaze drifted away and then back again. It was evident to Draevik that he had finally cracked the man's composure, and the advantage was now his.

"How to begin? Based on the information we received, this man had melded with the wood. This immortal wood, or at least it was until the relic was removed. We know Luma's fire ravaged it after. At any rate, there's no explanation for the man's existence. We checked our records. No one has come up missing. We had order patrols check every settlement. Everyone was accounted for."

"Oh? High Service's record keeping must be flawed."

"I can assure you that it's not."

"Someone was born then without a record."

"No one," Draevik said in a severe tone, "is born without a record."

Glavin narrowed his eyes. "Then who was he and how does his existence prove anything?"

"We determined he was ageless, born before we started keeping records, some sort of forest dweller or tree nymph whose existence relied on the relic remaining in the forest."

"How did you come to that conclusion?"

"Because once he gave the relic to Ceera, he said he was going to face the end. Or in other words, die. Which correlates with what the relic says in its inscription."

"Then why did he kill Falken?"

"Falken's threat to seize the relic was not well received by the forest man. So he killed him. Apparently, he was as unimpressed with Falken as the rest of us."

"That's an interesting story, really it's quite intriguing, but Ms. Kestlyn's abilities as a scribe may have propelled her to take on more creative aspirations. Perhaps she is making it up to elevate her own importance."

"Dassius confirmed it, and they both underwent polygraph tests. The only thing the two were not one hundred percent honest about were their true feelings for each other."

"Spare me those details, please." Glavin rolled his eyes. "What is your objective? Surely you realize science doesn't mix with nature's whims."

"I do; however, what we have in our possession is a tangible object. We can study its composition."

"Study it for what purpose?"

"So we can extend this immortality property for all."

Glavin shook his head. "That's a huge order. Magic and science don't play well together. And for that matter, there may not even be any science to play with. This is sketchy terrain."

"Yes, our study may have to cross a few boundaries. But I'm not intimidated by the grandiose."

"Intimidation has nothing to do with it."

"No," Draevik said slowly, "but sometimes intimidation reaps the best results."

Glavin eyed him shrewdly. "Haven't you already played that card with me? I lent you Wyman, isn't that enough?"

"You lent me Wyman for a project you agree with."

"Getting society to agree with it is another matter. Not to mention all your meddling caused my companion to resign."

"You didn't like Garia anyway."

"She was efficient if nothing else. By the way, where is she?"

"Garia is out of the public eye. Which means she's safe"—Draevik paused meaningfully—"and soundless."

Glavin's expression darkened. "What's it made of?"

"It's leather bound. The pages are made from bark. And there's an odd design on the front cover made of an unknown substance."

"Not much we can do with that."

"How about blood?"

Glavin cocked his head. "Surely the blood has degraded to the extent that it's no longer—"

"We speculate it could be the man's I just mentioned. Since he apparently was protecting it."

"You can't study a stain."

"I'd think someone in your position would want to be involved in case we do uncover anything planet shattering. There could be rewards for those who cooperate. And consequences for those who don't. Ask Garia. Oh wait, you can't…" Draevik said no more, letting temptation and implication do what it did best.

Glavin tensed. "You should have been more direct at the onset."

"Do you have anyone up for the task? I want the best this time, not another reject one step up from Falken Grihne."

Glavin stared into the distance with focused attention. "Baclus most likely. He's our most promising scientist and tests on the level of genius. You can borrow him on one condition."

"Which is?"

"That this study will in no way harm the reputation the CfA has built back up. The public has still not fully recovered from their perceived betrayal of our two former leaders."

"It won't, and you leave the public to me."

"Are you recruiting anyone else?"

"I'm rounding up a small team of scientists."

"How small?"

"As small as two."

"Who's the second?"

"Another genius. The very best. He's the perfect match. Someone who can be trusted to keep his brain active and his mouth shut."

"Sounds perfect," Glavin said, standing. "Send word when you want Baclus to begin."

"That I will."

When Glavin exited the room, Draevik retrieved Jesra's picture from the drawer. Such a pity his former companion would not reap the benefit of the immortality extraction. If she were still alive, he would place her first in line, even before himself.

Chapter Four

HETIA KNEW SADRA was right about confronting Fresdin. He was, after all, her companion. They had been paired together at an early age. They understood each other better than anyone. Yet this meant Hetia recognized how difficult it would be to sway him. Fresdin was bright but not the type who questioned things. And she'd always wondered if he regretted being paired with someone like herself.

High Service officials were supposed to remain without personal attachment and thus not marry or have children, but sometimes this led to affairs between companions. She and Fresdin had never partaken in such activity, yet there was an unspoken attraction to each other that bordered on fondness and something more. It was inevitable, with pairs working close together, but that didn't mean this behavior was accepted. It did, however, mean the dynamic could become quite heated.

The mystics had determined long ago that leadership was only complete when both the male and female led together. This was the governing model society used and was probably, as Sadra had suggested, the reason for Draevik's unnatural manner of taking charge.

And High Service was letting him, another atrocity she would have to point out.

"I wondered if I'd find you here," Hetia said as she approached Fresdin tending to some plants in the Aurora's garden. Gardening was a hobby he enjoyed, not a task he was assigned to as an official.

In contrast to the healthy plants surrounding him, Fresdin gave her a withered look. "Why? So you could stomp away from me again? Is once not enough for the day?"

Hetia was surprised at his level of sulkiness, usually her companion behaved most appropriately. "Are we taking turns being insolent? Or can you accept my apology?"

"I suppose I can accept it," he said begrudgingly. "Though I'm not sure what's gotten into you. And I doubt you'll clue me in."

"I may clue you in," Hetia said, "if you'll walk with me."

Fresdin stood. "You'd better," he said, brushing the dirt from his hands.

They walked silently at first, as Hetia considered how to approach the subject. It would have to be done carefully to avoid more strife.

"Well?" Fresdin said. "Are you going to say something?"

"Tell me," Hetia said as they rounded a path lined with clusters of yellow and purple flowers, "what you think of High Service's new way of ruling."

"I don't know what you mean," Fresdin said. "I know you're unhappy, but I don't understand why."

"Sure you do. Never before have we allowed absolute rule by one. And without a companion to balance him out."

"High Service rules as an entity. And though Draevik's companion has passed, there are still plenty of female officials."

"Then why has Draevik been making all the decisions? What happened to the vote?"

"Who would refute the opinions of Draevik Warlyn? I mean, besides you," he said with a sideways glance. "He's the backbone of High Service."

"The backbone is supposed to consist of the lower spheres. As a sphere seven, his role is adviser not dictator."

"Dictator? That's a harsh word."

"His actions deserve harsh words."

"You better keep that thought between us," Fresdin said, "before you get locked up for treason. And stop causing such a scene at meetings."

Hetia decided to focus on the positive. "There is an understanding between us? I can trust you?"

"Of course you can. I can help you sort out this nonsense swirling in your head."

Hetia bristled. "I don't need your help, though I think you may need mine."

Fresdin faced her. "Why?"

She forced a smile. "How do you expect to ever rise a sphere level if you resign to being a follower?"

"You raise a sphere level through cooperation."

"Not based on what I've been learning from the sphere sevens."

"Which one? Draevik?"

Hetia sighed. "There are more sphere sevens than Draevik. To raise a sphere level, to deserve it anyway, one must make a stand for justice."

"What if justice is already being served?"

"I asked this same question," Hetia lied. "The adviser said justice is not a constant. It needs to be fought for continuously. It's when people get complacent that injustices creep in."

"Such philosophy," Fresdin replied. "What are you trying to attain?"

"Isn't it obvious? Justice."

"So where is this corruption?"

Hetia knew better than to try and convince him. When someone was as brainwashed as he, it was best to allow the revelations to form within.

"That's what I thought," Fresdin said. "Let me know when this corruption occurs. I'd like to raise a few sphere levels myself."

"I can do that," Hetia replied, "but I would need your absolute loyalty."

"Who better to trust than your companion?"

"There is no one better to trust. And that goes both ways," Hetia replied as he followed her around the bend.

❧

Ceera's mind raced for a semblance of direction. She couldn't silently abide by High Service's wishes, not when she needed answers. But where to start?

She needed to see inside Drusilla's filing cabinet. Only then could she determine whom to trust. She was tired of guessing such things.

But how could she gain access without her mentor's permission? She worked the options in her mind. The solution wasn't difficult, but did she have it in her to be deceptive? A memory of her fear inside the forest surfaced, when Dassius told her High Service had planned to commit her.

Suddenly she knew she did have it in her. She had to

stick up for herself, even if that meant doing things she never would have considered before.

She picked up her communication orb and called her mentor. She pictured Drusilla carefully putting down her dinner spoon and patting her mouth clean before striding over to her orb.

"Yes, dear," Drusilla finally answered with a touch of weariness.

"Sorry to bother you," Ceera said pleasantly, "but can we meet tomorrow to discuss my new duties? I'd rather not wait another day."

"Of course." Drusilla sounded delighted. "Shall we meet first thing in the morning? At your PID? Say nine o'clock?"

"That would be great. I'll be looking forward to it."

After they hung up, Ceera racked her brain for the perfect lie: one that would excuse her from missing their meeting because she would instead be rifling through the filing cabinet. Since she had never been a model scribe—somewhat disorganized and lacking focus—the excuse came easily. She'd tell Drusilla she'd thought the plan was to meet at Mentoring Headquarters. And since that was exactly where she planned to be, it wouldn't be too much of a lie.

Pleased, she set that issue aside and replaced it with a different concern. Several hours had passed, and Dassius had not returned her call. Was he avoiding her? She sighed deeply, trying to rid herself of paranoia, but it clung tightly to the worries in her mind.

She went to bed still obsessing over the day's problems. Despite tossing and turning, she eventually fell into a deep slumber.

A familiar image formed inside a dream: a woman with long, dark hair; a tan dress; a beaded bag dangling at her side. This was the woman who had alerted her to the relic's existence. The woman she suspected Rebial had mistaken her for after seeing her birthmark. The woman who had evaded death by returning the relic to Rebial.

A forest stretched behind this woman, a giant vegetative mass atop a maze of interconnecting roots deep beneath the soil. The relic lay within, beating life into every tree through the snaking roots beneath their trunks.

Hands—perhaps her own—now reached for the relic and removed it from behind the brittle roots. Their cries were audible through a rippling, crackling effect coursing through the root system. Dust settled where the relic had once been.

A gnarled stump aged with many growth rings came into view. The woman knelt to trace her finger around the thin grooves. Over and over her finger swirled until Ceera felt induced into a trance, aged even, compelling her to remember that time was embedded between the lines. Days and weeks stretched within fractional amounts of space.

Her hands removed the relic again, this time in slow motion. Roots cracked as she pulled it free. The stump came back into focus. The woman placed her finger between two growth rings, pointing to the small distance they encircled. Her finger moved outward ever so slowly but stayed within the rings. Then the roots in the soil around her withered and decayed.

Ceera bolted upright in the darkness, breathing heavily. It had been awhile since the dreams had come, possibly because she hadn't been sleeping well. This one, like some from the past, was accompanied with a sense of foreboding, which meant something was still not right. Her instincts had suggested this, and she had spent the day mulling it over, but now proof existed, if you considered dreams proof of anything. Based on her recent experiences, Ceera did.

She swung her legs over the bed and staggered into the kitchen for some tea. The woman from her dreams was again trying to tell her something. She considered this as she boiled lavender tea leaves inside a teapot on her stove.

Why relive herself removing the relic from beneath the tree? It had seemed an insignificant action at the time. The real importance was having it, not taking it, though the relic had impacted the forest and even Rebial.

Ceera poured a cup of tea, absently took a sip, and burned her lip. The dream's meaning was clear enough. Removing the relic from the roots had triggered the woman to trace the growth rings. And growth rings literally represented the age of a tree. And something else coincided with age: time.

Suddenly a line from the ancient manuscript came to the forefront of Ceera's mind.

Once the manuscript is separated from its originator— which she had always interpreted to mean the dream woman—*then it must be returned.*

According to Rebial and what her past dreams had shown her, the woman had done this; she'd returned it to Rebial. But sometimes words had multiple meanings, and her dream implied she may have mistranslated. She and High Service had assumed the final resting place was beneath the tree since Rebial had claimed ownership of the relic, but maybe they were wrong. Perhaps the relic still needed to be returned.

She could check what she'd transmitted onto the PID, since this is how she'd been studying it, but she may have missed something in the original pages. The relic was stored in a private room at the library, preserved in a locked case that needed High Service's permission to be opened. Surely, they would no longer grant her this privilege. Ceera took another drink of tea, this time more carefully.

She had no choice. It had to be done. She had to figure out what it meant within a certain amount of time. The woman had pointed to a small space between the growth rings, signifying less than a year. Perhaps only a few months. High Service was ready to end the study entirely. She needed to access the relic as soon as possible, with or without their approval.

Tomorrow would be a day of deception twice over, and Ceera didn't know whether to be proud or terrified of whom she had become. But at least she was no longer a pawn.

Chapter Five

CEERA ARRIVED AT the library minutes after it opened. Instead of heading toward her PID station, she walked confidently toward the main desk. The librarian wasn't supposed to allow anyone usage of the key except High Service officials, yet Ceera knew luck was on her side when she saw who was on duty.

The woman was younger, fresh out of transition, and had taken an interest in her ever since she'd returned to Semadon with the relic. So she took advantage of the woman's admiration and garnered the key with a smile and a promise to stay quiet.

The relic was in a room deep in the library. To reach it, she passed rows of arched bookcases and many statues of various sized Semions reading books.

The relic's small enclosure contained the case and a flat top desk similar to the one at her PID station. She unlocked the case, unlatched the clasp, and lifted the glass lid. Then she put on special gloves and delicately pulled the ancient manuscript free.

The spiral on its cover glittered in its unusual way, so arresting she paused with it in her hands. She laid the relic gently on the desktop, glanced to make sure the door was still shut, and stared at its perplexing cover. Power emanated from it, even more noticeable than when she'd first brought the relic to Semadon. How could High Service deny this? It was peculiar that they did.

She opened the book slowly, making sure the map was still tucked into the fold inside the cover. Its thick pages emanated the musty smell of dirt.

The first passages described an end time that was strangely reminiscent of what the Archaics had told her and Dassius during their visits. According to the relic, the planet would become unlivable, and the relic's people were supposed to regress underground to avoid the dangers above. It disclosed what signals nature would use to warn them.

Equally cryptic and fantastical, the relic's portrayal of reality read like myth. She and High Service hadn't known what to make of this, so they'd determined it referred to a lost culture from a past age.

The Caretaker of Ancient Affairs had even been consulted, and since the relic aligned with what the Archaics said, the message was accepted but relegated to the status of legend. They also speculated the story was symbolic of something in the past, as opposed to a literal representation, since the Semions had no record of any other culture.

Carefully turning past these pages, she came to the section pertaining to her recent dream. She reread the words ingrained within her memory, her attention lingering on two spots within the passage. The symbols had evaded her notice before—they were barely a few scratches—but now she couldn't drag her eyes away.

She gasped and pulled off a glove to stare at the mark on her thumb. The match was unmistakable. Her birthmark had always puzzled her, when she took the time to think about it, but until recently she had never fathomed there to be a reason for its existence. At least not until Rebial had noticed it and decided not to kill her. Now she knew why he'd refrained.

Her face flushed with anticipation. How she'd missed the connection amazed her. The scratches must not have fully transferred onto the PID.

The marks were part of the sentence she apparently had never fully comprehended. She read the ambiguous words again.

Once the manuscript is separated from its originator, the sentence began.

As she had contemplated the night before, words could have dual meanings, for *originator* was interchangeable with *origin* which could also mean *roots*. Her dream, portraying the relic being torn from the roots, confirmed she had chosen the wrong one.

Once the manuscript is separated from its roots, it must be returned by (the marking), *or all will revert to the way it should have been and the bearer of* (the marking) *shall die.*

She had always glossed over the spot containing the marking, assuming the barely visible scratches were the remnants of words lost over the course of time. Had she noticed them previously, she still may have associated the marks with the woman. But now, based on her dream, she knew these scratches, this marking, meant her.

What High Service had been quick to dismiss as a colorful imagining, was now a matter of life and death. And she had proof to show them. Her intuition about concealing the birthmark correlation until the right moment was now justified. For if she'd mentioned beforehand the woman probably had the mark as well, then she'd have a hard time convincing them these marks referred to her.

Since the meaning of this passage had changed, Ceera focused on the one directly before it, the one relating to the past civilization who'd been instructed to regress.

Those in possession of this manuscript shall prevail over the passage of time and not suffer the passing of a generation, until the time has come to re-emerge. This marks when these words should part ways with the people.

Throughout the text there were times when the relic referred to itself as a prophecy, a manuscript, and even as a compilation of words. This had been her greatest difficulty as the translator, determining whether these different words were used for specific reasons. And with the added stress of High Service's interrogations and manipulations of her focus, she supposed she shouldn't be too hard on herself for blending the meanings.

Now that her original translation was no longer valid, was there more to consider in what before had seemed inexplicable? If the relic's return coincided with these people's re-emergence, did this mean they were still underground? They hadn't possessed the relic, so the original people should be dead, but what about their descendants? Would Ceera's completion of the task liberate them from the planet's depths? And if she failed to return it?

All will revert to the way it should have been.

Her own culture would suffer greatly for its negligence.

She leaned back in her chair and cupped her chin in her hands. The last pages described the way things would come to be and implied that the mystics and Archaics had been included in an exchange. The two entities were part of a new age, as explained within the passage. The relic even stated this past culture would earn special powers, but what these powers entailed remained unclear.

Regardless, the Semion culture was now thriving on the planet and also part of this new age. Could it survive without these entities it had learned to rely on? Would High Service believe her? She had no choice but to find out. Keeping such things to herself could be fatal. And she was finished allowing fate to have its way with her.

Someone knocked heavily on Hegliod's door. The knock was unlike his apprentice's. Annoyed, he looked up from his desk. No one had scheduled an appointment. Not that he would have agreed to one, for he was busy. Unannounced visitors were a bother, but really, so were the ones who made appointments. Perhaps if he ignored the knocking then the perpetrator would leave.

As he waited, he considered how to prevent visitors altogether. He could place something undesirable on his doorstep. Replace the door with a wall even? His mind relaxed, despite knowing he was being unreasonable. Then the sharp knock broke into his thoughts again. With a sigh of defeat, he trudged over to the door and flung it open.

The official standing on his stoop was not one he'd seen in some time. He'd heard, unwillingly of course, since gossip was such a useless distraction, that the elderly sphere seven had spent most of the year in the hospital, very sick with pneumonia. He looked recovered, although there was an unhealthy gleam in his eye that made Hegliod bristle. Not a sickly gleam but a conniving one. Aside from that, he looked as if he wanted to come in.

"Draevik, what a surprise," Hegliod said. "I wasn't expecting you."

"It's good to see you too," Draevik replied. "May I have a moment of your time?"

Instinct begged him to deny the request; however, rudeness was not compatible with his station in life. "I suppose if you must, please come in." Hegliod stepped aside.

Draevik entered and waited for Hegliod to gesture toward the couch. Only then did he sit down.

"What can I help you with?" Hegliod asked, hoping the drawings and open books covering his desk would signify he hadn't time to be of any help at all.

"Have you heard about the ancient manuscript we uncovered?"

"Yes. What of it?"

"We need a scientist to study it. One with superior intelligence."

"You want me to study it for what purpose?" Hegliod asked, in too much of a hurry to feign modesty.

"For the betterment of society," Draevik responded in a haughty tone.

"Can you be more specific?" Hegliod hated delusions of grandeur.

"We think the manuscript is several thousand years old."

"Oh?" Hegliod asked with mild interest.

"Yes." Draevik leaned forward conspiratorially. "Many years older than what should be possible."

Hegliod leaned away from him, as it seemed the most natural thing to do.

"This information," Draevik continued, "coupled with the longevity of the forest, or at least its root structure, has stirred our interest."

"In what way?" Hegliod asked.

"We wonder how such a thing could exist. Does the manuscript have a property that prevents it from biodegrading? Did this property affect the forest?"

"And if it had?"

"Then we can figure out how to extract this property from it."

"Again, I ask, for what purpose?"

"Don't play dense, Hegliod. Imagine if society could control its own longevity. You know how often a good life runs short."

Hegliod studied the official skeptically. "Are you telling me you wish to capture the essence of immortality? From an object?"

"That would be the ideal result."

"Ideal but not very likely."

"High Service will be the judge of that," Draevik said.

"So now you are scientists too? You do realize this study would end up destroying the manuscript, no matter the result?"

"An unfortunate trade, but a necessary one."

"What of the young woman who discovered it for you?" Hegliod asked. "Doesn't she have some sort of connection to it?"

"A fragile one to say the least," Draevik responded. "The manuscript belongs to High Service."

"Doesn't it belong to the Semion culture?" Hegliod huffed. "At least if you are keeping it from the girl."

"The girl is in no position to appreciate what we plan to do with it."

"More like she'd be in your way," Hegliod said. "Why not ask her permission?"

"High Service does not need permission to do things."

Draevik's tone distracted Hegliod from what he'd previously been doing. His mind now fully present, he said, "Ah, you've changed, Draevik. And not for the better."

"A near death experience will do that to you."

"At your age, you should be happy death didn't come closer."

"Don't remind me," Draevik said bitterly.

"Where is the righteous-minded youth I went to school with? Why all this underhandedness?"

"You haven't answered me," Draevik said wearily. "Are you in?"

"I am not in," Hegliod said emphatically. "I have my own pursuits."

"We're not getting any younger. Doesn't immortality interest you at all?"

Society was aggravating enough during the time he'd already been alive. The last thing he wanted to do was endure it forever. "Not if I have to share it with you."

"Do you dare mock me?"

"It was a joke," Hegliod responded, using a tactic he'd seen others use to get away with unseemly responses.

"Not a very funny one," Draevik snapped.

So this was going to be the way of the conversation. Time to end it then. "I am already immortal."

"Really?" Draevik said unconvincingly.

"My inventions will carry my name into eternity."

Draevik's mouth twisted in distaste. "Any suggestions of who can assist us then, since you're above such trivial desires?"

"Try Cafold Brine."

"Your apprentice?" Draevik scoffed. "Isn't he the one you

took on after the AT system malfunction? How is the project going to be adequately served with a mere apprentice? One still in transition even."

"I came up with important discoveries when I was in transition," Hegliod replied.

"And you think Cafold Brine's intellect is a match for your own?"

"His potential is unmatched," Hegliod said benevolently. "Besides, as my apprentice, is he not the next best candidate after myself?"

"I suppose if you put it like that."

"Trust me, he'll serve you well."

"And he can consult with you if the need arises?" Draevik asked.

"If the need arises, of course."

"We appreciate your help," Draevik said coldly.

"Good luck to you. May your quest for eternal life be short-lived."

Draevik gave him a nasty glare before exiting the dwelling. The door slammed shut, rattling the diagrams framed on his walls.

Relieved, Hegliod returned to his desk. There would be no guilt rolling through him if he could influence Draevik's project through Cafold. His apprentice was young, trustworthy, and would fight for what he believed in. Pleased to have unburdened his conscience, he focused again on his work.

Ceera had one more thing to do before she confronted High Service. Even if it would only satisfy her curiosity, she had to seek the truth. So she placed the relic back into the preservation case, returned the key to the doting librarian who agreed to keep their encounter private, and left. Again, she dashed around the orbits to avoid encounters with others because she was already running short on time.

It didn't take long to reach her mentor's orbit, and she slowed as she approached the building. Making sure no one was watching, she crouched behind a bush near the entrance. She felt ridiculous, and her legs burned while she waited, but she'd undergone far less comfortable situations in the past few months. Even so, it took forever for Drusilla to exit the building.

When she finally emerged, she strode briskly to the orbit. Drusilla had perfect posture in the most mundane circumstances, even when hailing a travel pod. Ceera's own twisted and ergonomically challenged position made her somewhat bewildered by this. If Drusilla were ever inclined to spy on someone, surely she wouldn't stoop to compromising her carriage. Within minutes, a travel pod came to a halt and whisked Drusilla away.

Ceera stood self-consciously and headed to the back of the building. Then she walked around it to the entrance, stifling her shame. It wasn't her fault life had prompted her to take such measures. She'd much rather be in a position to trust her mentor and High Service.

After entering, she took the elevator to Drusilla's office. The door was unlocked as she'd expected it to be, since there was no reason to lock it during the day. Ceera slipped inside, closed the door and did lock it, hoping no one would come calling for her mentor.

Drusilla valued punctuality and would only wait for her in the library for fifteen minutes. So with the shortage of time now a theme in all respects, she scrambled to the filing cabinet and examined the lock. It was a typical lock, nothing extraordinary about it. She dug a small piece of cloth from her pocket and unwrapped a pin. Then she stuck the pin in the keyhole and wiggled it around, wishing luck would come to her aid, but nothing clicked in response.

Flustered, she now needed to figure out where her mentor kept the key. Drusilla wouldn't have taken it with her, for she was methodically precise. This was the woman who'd reprimanded Ceera once for taking her recorder to an event she wasn't recording. It wasn't practical to take a key to the library where it had no use. Losing it would cause Drusilla great embarrassment.

She approached Drusilla's desk and opened the drawers quickly, as if speed lessened the severity of her actions. She examined the contents: basic office supplies, writing utensils, paper, an old recorder cord. Another drawer held extra recorders. The third drawer contained a ledger with assignments and corresponding names.

When she saw her own name on the list, she wrinkled her nose. Drusilla had assigned her to record a meeting in which the CfA planned to discuss the recent resignation of their head chairwoman. Hopefully, there'd be a scribe in the library ready to take on the task Ceera would not be present to receive.

Nothing of interest was hiding in Drusilla's desk drawers. Her mentor was neat enough that this was obvious right away. So where would a woman like Drusilla hide something? Or would she hide it at all?

Ceera desperately scanned her surroundings, noticing a small wooden box sitting on the same shelf as the squatted cactus. It looked out of place in an office with minimal decoration. And Drusilla was not the frivolous type. She approached the shelf and carefully shifted the cactus away from the box by its base. Then she picked up the box and lifted the lid.

Three keys lay on the tan felt, and her heart raced as she removed them. Placing something sharp beside something valuable was classic Drusilla. Pricking a finger would be a fitting consequence of putting one's hands where they didn't belong. Drusilla exposed herself by her restrictive nature.

Ceera tried turning a key inside the lock, but it wouldn't budge. The second key jammed inside the hole. She spent several minutes trying to pull it free without breaking it. Sweat formed on her face, and she shook her head in agitation before trying the last one. The key slid inside after a moment of uncertainty. The cabinet clicked open.

Her hands flew to the files. She searched through them, reading the names and pausing briefly when she came to people she knew. Then she found the file displaying her own name.

It was thicker than the rest, something she found troubling. She opened the front flap.

All her recent life events were listed on a chart in brief, emotionless ways: *fidgety and restless at her PID, insubordination for PID idleness, daydreams profusely, not transitioning as smoothly as her peers.*

Ceera bit her lip upon reading *suffers from hallucinatory dreams* followed by *validity of dreams still pending.* That's where Drusilla had left off, and she wondered what description would be placed there next.

She flipped through more pages, skipping what appeared to correspond with her middle years, until she reached a page near the back.

In painful short phrases it described her entrance into scribe work: *deceased parent, donated by father*—Donated?—*solemn child- should be fit for scribe work.*

Thoroughly disturbed now, she flipped to the last page and beneath her age and height, she found what she'd been looking for: *family history of mental illness*. This confirmed her suspicions about the dreams in relation to the birthmark. And why had her father lied about telling Drusilla about the family situation?

Tears threatened but she forced them to stay back. Over the heightened sound of her own breathing, footsteps sounded down the hall. Panicked, she crammed the file back in place and locked the cabinet shut. Thrusting the keys into the wooden box, she stood and placed it back on the shelf, pricking her finger on the cactus's greedy spine. She unlocked the office door just as the handle turned.

Her mentor stared at her in surprise.

"I've been wondering where you were!" Ceera said, diving in for a hug to hide her face. "You're never late."

Her mentor placed robotic arms around her and continued to stare when Ceera pulled away.

"You had me worried." Ceera tried to smile.

"Young lady, we were supposed to meet in the library," Drusilla stated in a strained voice.

It was evident she wanted to scold but refrained. Perhaps Drusilla was relieved that Ceera had not stood her up as she had undoubtedly thought.

"We were?" Ceera released all the tension bottled up inside her. "I'm so sorry," she gushed, certain she looked distressed.

Drusilla relaxed at this. "Yes, well," she responded as she took off her hat, "it is like you to start off poorly."

Ceera looked down at her hands clasped together. Blood seeped from a finger. With Drusilla turned away to hang her jacket, she raised it to her tongue before her mentor noticed.

"I see you've picked up a nervous habit," Drusilla remarked as she swung back round.

"I—" Ceera began, removing her finger from her mouth.

"Don't bother defending yourself, dear. You've been through a lot, I know this. Just remember nail biting is disgusting. You'll need to squash that habit if you wish to complete your time in transition. Now please sit down. We have much to discuss about your future."

CHAPTER SIX

AFTER SPENDING A few tortured hours listening to Drusilla prattle on about expectations and impending assignments, Ceera headed to the Aurora. She'd told Drusilla that she needed to meet with High Service to wrap things up. The truth was, she hoped the meeting would put a hold on any future scribe work so she could focus on the relic.

"Ceera, my dear, what a surprise." Risa's face was colored with shock when she met her in the waiting area. "Did Drusilla have nothing scribe related for you to do today?" She led Ceera into the room where Karnen and Draevik awaited them.

"She did," Ceera responded tightly. "But I have news. Somewhat disturbing news." She sat gracefully at the forefront of the table.

"Please," Draevik stated curtly, "enlighten us."

Though it required revealing her recent disobedience, she decided to be as forthcoming as possible. "I had a dream last night," she began, "so I went to view the relic one last time."

Draevik's glare cut across the room at her.

"And I noticed," she continued, "something that didn't

transfer over to the copies I've been studying. A marking that matches my birthmark."

She held her thumb up, and the officials leaned forward to get a better look.

"Interesting marking," Draevik said, squinting.

The other officials murmured agreement.

"The relic states the person bearing the mark, my birthmark, needs to return it."

"We've already determined that was taken care of," Draevik said.

"We did, but the mark proves our interpretation was wrong," she replied. "This still needs to happen."

"And you expect us to let you have it so you can throw it away somewhere?"

Risa gave Draevik a warning look and placed her hand on his arm, but he shrugged it off.

"Not throw it away," Ceera said, "but return it. Like it says."

"Return it where?" Karnen asked.

"I'm not sure," she replied uncomfortably. "But I suspect the map leads to the place."

"I thought we determined the map led to an underground cave," Karnen said. "One that no longer exists."

"There's no reason to believe it doesn't exist," Ceera said. "That was speculation on Draevik's part. And speculation rarely evolves into solid truths." She couldn't resist using Draevik's own argument against him after he had mocked her at their last meeting.

"I didn't say it didn't exist," Draevik said. "I pointed out there's no way to determine which cave. And this planet has thousands of them. It would be a blind start to an uncertain race."

Frustrated, Ceera bit her lip.

"If we allow it," Karnen said, "it'd be a good time to try out Hegliod's new—"

"Yes, Hegliod," Draevik grumbled. "So helpful."

Risa glanced at Draevik before speaking. "Now you say 'return', does that mean the relic originated in this cave and doesn't belong to Rebial? Because you said it did."

"I don't know," Ceera said. "I was going by what he told me."

"You've also claimed the relic has long been separated from its originator," Risa said, "which should have set in motion back then what needed to happen."

"My dream showed the relic being removed from the tree roots repeatedly. I think the word 'originator' was supposed to mean 'roots'. And my removal of the relic from the roots was actually the trigger."

"There's too much uncertainty," Draevik said, "with no viable reasoning to back any of it up."

"But my dream—"

"Your dream is not evidence," Draevik interrupted.

"I'm certain it was trying to tell me something," she insisted.

"How are we to take you seriously," Draevik said condescendingly, "when you keep changing the meaning of things?"

After taking a deep breath, she said, "Don't forget what will happen if the relic's instructions aren't carried out."

"What now?" Draevik tilted his head at her impatiently.

"The Archaics and mystics will be gone. And I will die."

"Nonsense," Draevik said, a fiery look in his eyes. "I will have none of this tainting our study."

Anger burned inside her. They had mentioned nothing of an alternate study. They had lied.

"A study?" she asked.

"It's obvious," Draevik said, "that you're reluctant to go back to your scribe work and are, quite literally, reading into things."

She ignored the insult and said, "But my life depends on you believing me. I can even show you the passage—"

"Enough!" Draevik erupted.

The other officials looked taken aback.

"Draevik," Risa interjected, "Ceera is only relaying her opinion on what she discovered."

"She's confusing this opinion with fact," Draevik replied.

"Risa," Karnen barked, "you know better than to question Draevik. High Service would be nothing without him."

Shock collided with her anger. Karnen reprimanding another official, his own companion, was something that she had never seen before in all her dealings with High Service.

"We," Risa said firmly, her cheeks aflame, "will evaluate Ceera's discovery as an entity, together as High Service." She turned to Ceera. "Meet us back here tomorrow morning at the same time. We need to discuss this."

Her own death was a matter of discussion? Not to mention the fate of the Archaics and mystics? Was she that inadequate at relaying her findings, or was Draevik's opinion so important nothing else mattered? They hadn't even considered examining the relic with her.

Ceera nodded and stood, bewildered by this display from High Service. Perhaps word around the village was true. High Service was lacking in integrity lately. And the leader of this betrayal scowled at her as she exited the room.

❧

With nowhere else to go, Ceera decided to spend the afternoon doing what was expected of her. Or at least pretend that she was. This meant she sat disinterestedly in front of her PID at the library.

For the first time in her life, besides when she'd traveled in dangerous areas with Dassius, she contemplated her own death. Surely High Service wouldn't let her die, would they? Could Draevik be so heartless? And what of this new study? They must have decided the relic was important and that she was not. Therefore, her death might even be convenient to them.

The scribe sitting nearby cleared his throat. "How about doing some work?" he said rudely.

"How about minding your own business?" she retorted.

Unlike the librarian who'd been attempting not to stare at her, there were some within the scribe profession who had not taken kindly to her adventures with Dassius. This Semion was apparently one of them.

"Too important to be a scribe now," he muttered. "You were never good at it anyway."

Not too important, she thought, *just too close to death for it to matter.*

"Sorry, I've been busy. Maybe you should read up on it." She clicked off her PID and stood. It was clearly time to leave since she wasn't fooling anyone. Some things never changed.

As she walked around the orbits, the feeling she was being watched surfaced. While this happened often enough anymore, this felt different.

She stopped at a fruit stand and glanced backward. Someone ducked behind an AT cylinder, a fleeting image of gray clothing and black hair. So she was being followed. She purchased a few peaches, thinking it better than picking fruit alone in the highly foliaged garden near her dwelling.

Not much to see here, she mentally told her pursuer as she headed home through the crowded orbits. She should be worried, scared even, and part of her was. But danger seemed to be closing in on her no matter what she did. This depressing reality numbed her fear.

Reaching her dwelling, she quickly entered and locked the door behind her. Her communication orb hummed as she neared. She eagerly pressed the button to listen. Her heart sped up when his voice filled her ears.

"It's me," he said, rightly assuming she would recognize his voice. "I got your message and would be happy to meet up. Call me. I may be in training, but leave a message with the time and place, and I'll be there."

She tapped her finger against her chin. If High Service had been trying to keep them apart, they wouldn't like them conspiring alone. Meeting him out in public would minimize any suspicions. She made a decision that surprised even her, left a return message, and started getting ready.

Hetia sat in the meeting room, curious as to why Draevik had called them together again. Fresdin sat beside her, looking eager. She sighed. There was so much work left to do on him.

"Thank you all for attending," Draevik began. "Since this is an unexpected meeting, one you can thank Risa and Karnen for reminding me of its necessity, I will get straight to the point. Ceera Kestlyn has intruded once again in the business of High Service. She's convinced she must take the relic to a cave in order to carry out its instructions."

"What is she basing this on?" Asfin asked.

"What do you think?" Draevik snarled. "Her dreams of course."

The officials exchanged worried glances which told Hetia that Draevik would not be further challenged. This meant she would have to be the one to speak.

"Ceera's dreams have—" she began.

"Yes, I know," Draevik interrupted. "They've had some merit. But we can't stop our study because of them."

"I don't see why not," Hetia replied, "if what she says is true."

Fresdin cringed.

"For how long should we give credence to one woman's dreams?" Draevik stood and leaned over the table in a threatening manner. "Long enough to destroy something that could benefit our culture?"

"It's unclear whether this benefit will even come into fruition," Hetia retorted, unfazed by his audacity.

"When you have the best scientists working for you, it's clear they will succeed," Draevik said.

"I thought Hegliod refused to participate?" asked Leynin.

Hetia was relieved someone else was questioning Draevik, although the innocent expression on Leynin's face lacked defiance.

"He recommended someone take his place," Draevik said, "and has opened himself up to consultation through this person."

"Ceera also mentioned," Risa said, "that if we don't comply, then the Archaics and mystics will cease to exist as we know them."

"The Archaics!" Draevik scoffed. "Tell me what purpose they serve?"

"Well"—Risa faltered—"they did help Ceera and Dassius in the forest."

"Apparently for their own gain so they could find the relic and dispose of it. Why should we forfeit our immortality for theirs? The continuation of their powers has no advantage to us. They are living myths, interesting but unnecessary."

"And the mystics?" Hetia asked. "They are just as inconsequential?"

"Our people can't even come to a consensus on whether they're still needed."

"Only the CfA doubts their value," Hetia retorted.

"Has everyone forgotten we value progress?" Draevik said. "We need to leave behind the things that weigh us down."

"The mystics clued us into the forest being the reason for the abnormal energy reading," Hetia continued.

"Could we not have traveled there and figured this out ourselves?"

Hetia pressed her lips firmly together and folded her arms across her chest.

"The mystics and Archaics have become obsolete. It's time we take charge of our existence and move on. I have dreams, too, and they don't revolve around the fanciful like Ceera's."

"There is one more thing," Risa said hesitantly. "Ceera mentioned her life would be in danger if she didn't fulfill the instructions."

"In danger by whom?" Draevik asked. "The only thing to fear is the destruction of something that will benefit our culture."

"It seems a valid concern to me," Hetia said.

"Does anyone besides this lowly sphere three dispute my logic?"

No one spoke. Hetia fumed in silence.

"Very good then. We shall proceed as planned. And if the young woman refuses to cooperate"—Draevik made a point to glare at Hetia—"we shall devise a way to silence her."

Draevik settled in his chair, signaling the meeting was over.

Hetia rose and leaned over the table now. "And just what would that be?" she demanded.

"I believe I have adjourned this meeting, sphere three," Draevik said in an icy tone. "So be on your way."

The other sphere sevens nodded meaningfully at her, so she left. Walking around the hall, she realized it was time to try a different tactic, more indirect perhaps. Let the bully rule their meetings like a dictator. She would figure out how to take control of everything else.

CHAPTER SEVEN

DESPITE LITHA'S REOCCURRING invitations, Ceera rarely frequented The Helix, mainly because the club bludgeoned her with sensations. Coping with the spinning, flashing lights; loud and obnoxious voices competing with fast paced music; and mingling odors of alcohol and strong perfumes, was a challenge.

Still, she found her way to a corner table, ordered a drink, and watched the entrance. The smoky haze obscuring it dissipated every time someone entered, only to replenish from the room's interior once the door shut.

Ceera sipped her drink slowly: a sweet, blue concoction that tasted like candy with a jarring bite. She drank to blend in, not because she wanted to feel the effects.

Her drink did not share her caution. The colorful surroundings buzzed with an energy she had not noticed upon arrival, and her mood soared despite the troubles prevalent in her mind. Music blared ruthlessly into her ears, and the circular dance stage, shaped like the club's namesake, rotated endlessly up and within itself. Each platform was congested with dancing Semions. If only she had come to dance the night away.

When Dassius appeared at the entrance, the haze cloaking his figure gave him an aura of mystique. The reason she'd asked him to come wavered in her thoughts. His eyes met hers instantly, and she could hardly suppress her smile. Of course he knew exactly where to find her. He grinned and strode with confident steps to her table, gaining the attention of several females he passed. Their eyes lingered on him longer than she deemed necessary, but he ignored them.

"Sitting in the corner by yourself?" he teased.

"I was waiting for you," she responded. "I'm only here to see you." She traced the condensation on her glass.

"Good." Flashes of light hit him from various directions, accentuating the contours of his face. His midnight blue eyes glistened. He tucked a dark curl behind his ear. The alcohol in her intensified every move he made, but even his good looks couldn't distract her from what was really on her mind.

She leaned in close. "There's something I have to tell you."

Dassius's broad frame hunched over the table, and he rested his warm forehead against hers. It stirred her emotions, but she painstakingly ignored them.

"Then tell me," he said.

"I'm being spied on," she said flatly. "Don't turn around, but he's to your left, sitting at the bar, in the gray coat."

Dassius immediately stiffened and drew back from her. The playfulness dropped from his face. "I had a feeling, but I assumed it was because of our newfound popularity."

"It's because of my controversial translation," Ceera said. "High Service doesn't like it. They're acting strange. Something's up."

"If there is," Dassius said, "then they won't like us meeting. They'll think we're discussing it."

"That's why I chose here, hardly the place for heartfelt

communication. Plus, you're the only person I have to talk to about this."

"And I'm not saying I don't want to be. But it might get you in more trouble."

Facing the bar counter, her stalker snuck glances at them over his shoulder. But it was the stocky man only a few paces away, elbow leaning casually against the counter, who stole her attention with his brazen stare. After making eye contact, he smirked and sauntered over.

"I'm not sure that's even possible." She lowered her gaze. "Someone's coming up behind you."

"I know." Dassius briefly touched her chin and winked.

The man gave Ceera a mischievous look as he roughly swatted Dassius on the back.

Dassius turned, a wide smile playing on his lips. "Sidorn, isn't it past your bedtime?"

Sidorn's eyes crinkled, and he took a swig of the brown syrupy liquid in his frosty cup. "It's never past my bedtime," he responded good-naturedly.

"This is Ceera Kestlyn." Dassius gestured at her. "I know you've heard of her. Ceera, this is Sidorn, my teammate from the Sci-Def team."

Sidorn eyed her in a way that made her uncomfortable, but it wasn't because he was sizing her up as a female. She knew this right away from her interactions with Dassius. Sidorn was looking deep into her mind. Or trying to. She adjusted the front of her shirt and fidgeted with its hem.

Dassius put his arm around her shoulder. "Take it easy," he warned.

"Sorry," Sidorn said lightly, "just a habit." He held out his hand, and she took it tentatively. "It's nice to meet you." He pressed her fingers to his lips.

Surprised, she glanced at Dassius, who was shaking his head.

"What can I say? My friend is a flirt."

"It's nice to meet you too," she said slowly, reclaiming her hand. "I think."

Sidorn's gaze traveled past her.

"Ceera, what are you doing hogging all the attention?" a familiar cheery voice said as its owner joined their table.

"Litha," Ceera said. "I wasn't expecting to see you."

"Why didn't you tell me you'd be out?" Litha feigned annoyance. Her face had been painted rather skillfully, enhancing the shape of her eyes and her lips, the cleft of her cheeks. A glossy black dress hugged her figure.

Ceera tried to think up an excuse.

"Oh, don't mind me"—Litha nudged her gently with an elbow—"I'm glad you're here." She then angled her face and smiled sweetly at Sidorn, who looked at her with interest.

Ceera glanced down at her own modest attire, efficient but not attention getting. She caught Dassius watching. His face wore amusement, and she shrugged.

"Litha," she said, "you know Dassius. This is his friend, Sidorn. We've just met."

Sidorn eyed her intently, and Litha's eyelids fluttered back at him. Ceera wondered how many drinks her friend had already consumed. When he reached for her hand, Litha gladly complied. His lips stayed longer on her fingers. Litha's eyes shone, and she giggled. Ceera looked at Dassius helplessly. Their meeting was now officially crashed unless she could figure out how to distract them.

"Sidorn," Ceera said, breaking his gaze from her friend. "Perhaps Litha would like to dance?"

Litha perked up eagerly and Sidorn's mouth quirked into

an appreciative smile. "I'm up for it," he said, downing his drink and placing the empty glass on the table.

Litha set her own drink down carelessly, the glass wobbling precariously on its stem before settling upright. She grabbed Ceera's hand. "You have to come too."

"No," Ceera said, "we don't want to intrude."

"Intrude? Don't be ridiculous," Litha said. "Besides, how often do you get out and have fun anymore?"

"Same to you." Sidorn nodded at Dassius. "Too good to hang out with the commoners now?" The question came across as a challenge.

A moment of tension followed as the men stared at each other, speaking without words. It was an odd thing to witness since they'd been friendly at the onset. Finally, Dassius broke the tension with a grin.

"There's nothing common about you, friend," he said, "and there's not much good about me."

Sidorn laughed.

Sensing Dassius had just made an agreement of some kind, Ceera caved as well.

"Yes, fine. Let's dance."

With a pained look on her face, she allowed Litha to lead her toward the stage. Sidorn draped his arm around Litha's shoulder, and Dassius followed. The rotating lights were dizzying as they climbed onto the stage, and Ceera waited until Dassius placed his hands on her waist, before swaying to the music along with him. Litha and Sidorn tangled together in a mass of flailing arms and rotating hips.

"First chance we get to sneak away," she whispered into Dassius's ear, "let's take it."

He stared at her knowingly, and Ceera felt a flutter in her chest.

Her drink was having more of an effect on her than she'd intended.

⁓

Hetia sat beside Fresdin in their small office, silently evaluating settlement progress reports. The tension between them had not waned since the recent meeting, though they stewed for separate reasons. Finally, Hetia could stand the uncomfortable silence no longer. Besides, they weren't getting anything done.

"How do you feel about Draevik's plans?"

Fresdin sighed. "Unlike you, I value Draevik's decision making and don't think he has ill intentions. He's aggressive, but only because he's a victim of his own high standards."

Hetia refrained from gritting her teeth. "What do you think he'll do to silence her?"

"He'll probably tell her if she doesn't keep her findings confidential then disciplinary action will be taken."

"You don't believe what she says? That her own death is imminent?"

"Ceera is not a mystic. I side with Draevik here. She's just overreacting." Fresdin gave her a long look before turning back to his report.

Hetia knew he included her in that assessment. Yet he had also unwittingly prompted her to come up with a defense tactic. "Overreacting? That's an interesting choice of words."

"Why?"

"I side with caution. I think Draevik is the one overreacting."

"In what way?"

"In an obvious way, if you take the time to think about it."

Fresdin threw up his hands, causing his report to flutter onto the table. "Tell me why I shouldn't disown you as my companion. You're bound to stir up trouble."

"Do you remember what our mentor said to us when she paired us together? She said my independent thinking makes me deserving of High Service. Do you remember what she said about you?"

"Yes, but—"

"She said you'd be wise to listen to me, because you are destined for great things too, but your mind works best at strategy. She said we'll make a successful pair."

"You're minimizing what she said to me so that you sound more important."

"Wrong. I know what needs to be done, but I need your help in achieving it. How complimentary is that?"

"I see your point," he conceded. "But I'm still not fully convinced—"

"I would like to offer you a test. If circumstances proceed as I suspect they will, then it would give you reason to start seeing things my way."

"It might," he replied tentatively. "But it would depend on your prediction."

"Remember what High Service planned on doing to her when her dreams started? When the relic's existence was in question?"

Fresdin shrugged. "Yes, but she found it. There's no reason to commit her now."

"You agree that doing so would cross the line?"

"I do."

"I think Draevik will do something as unjust. If I'm right, will you promise to try and see things my way?"

He frowned. "I suppose you would deserve it then."

"But that would require one more thing."

"What?"

"That you take your blinders off."

"Blinders? Seriously Hetia—"

"Prove to me you're not brainwashed. That's all I ask."

"I'll prove it." He resumed studying his report.

"I believe you," she responded sincerely.

She was certain Draevik would continue to rule with ruthless authority. Soon this would become evident even to Fresdin now that she'd prepared him for what to expect.

&

The cold air felt good after being surrounded by sweaty, dancing bodies all evening. Dassius had walked her home, and now they stood by her front door, reluctant to part.

"Sorry we got interrupted. Can we talk tomorrow?" Dassius's arms were around her waist.

Sidorn had kept buying them drinks throughout the night, and the liquid had washed away any plots to escape. It felt good to be carefree for once. Yet now, standing on her stoop, she wasn't so drunk as to think the sensation would be permanent. Or that what was happening now was what she'd originally been trying to avoid.

"You could come in," she suggested hesitantly. Meeting in private no longer seemed like such a risk.

When he didn't argue, she led him inside. As she closed the door, his hands made their way to her stomach. "Dassius," she said softly as he twirled her around to face him. But then he was kissing her, and words seemed a hindrance.

"It feels like forever," he whispered in her ear, "since we've been alone together."

"It has been," she replied. Shyly, she met his gaze and felt heat rising in her cheeks.

She wasn't sure what had kept them apart, High Service or life circumstances. Conflict of interest perhaps, one was busy when the other was free. Plus, he had left Semadon to visit his family on several occasions. She felt a pang of jealousy, for she had not been offered a vacation, nor had her father invited her to visit, but the resentment faded when he kissed her again.

"We went from being together every day to always missing each other's calls," he said, sliding his hands down her arms.

"Yet here we are together now." She smiled, her heart beating quickly.

She had vowed not to fall prey to his charms. Seeing his friend's behavior earlier in the night could either justify her hesitation or prove to be an unfair comparison. The intensity of his gaze was electrifying though. Her body pulsed with desire.

"You said before you wanted to take things slow," Dassius said. "Has it been slow enough for you?"

His hands on her waist, he pressed gently into the skin near her hip bone. Her breath caught in her throat.

"Slow is good," she responded, draping her arms across his shoulders.

"I haven't seen you in weeks." He stroked her back lightly, giving her goose bumps.

She unbuttoned his shirt, her fingers brushing against his solid compact chest. He fiddled with the hem of her shirt, but she twisted away.

"One thing at a time," she whispered. As his shirt dropped to the floor, she turned off the light.

He took that as a cue to take off her shirt and she allowed it, pressing against him. His hands traveled from her rib cage down to her waist. Through the dark, they made their way to the couch. He sat and pulled her into his lap.

She sat there breathlessly, feeling eager yet anxious, but somehow this reminded her that she had something to tell him. And it was far more important.

"This is good," she said, hitting the dimmer on the wall behind him.

It was enough light to make out the firm muscles of his arms and chest, the dark hair framing his glistening face. He looked her over in return as she removed his hands from her hips and clasped them between her own.

"Can we talk now?" she asked, ignoring her desire to do otherwise.

Fleeting gratifications had never been worthwhile to her. Tonight had been an anomaly. What good would passion do her now if she were dead tomorrow?

The twinkle in his eyes faded, yet he still seemed wrapped in the moment. "You've had my attention all night."

"Maybe the club wasn't a good idea," she said.

"It was your idea," he pointed out.

"I know, but I didn't think we would end up like this."

"What's wrong with this?" he asked

"It's not what I had in mind."

"You don't think about us like this?"

"No, I mean, sometimes," she said. "Just not lately."

Dassius frowned. This wasn't going how she'd planned.

"I can't think about us being together when I'm scared for my future," she said soberly.

Concern etched his face. "What do you mean?"

"I'm scared."

He drew her close. "Of what? Do you honestly think High Service will punish you over a poorly received translation? How is that even your fault? Don't you just relay what it says?"

"Draevik Warlyn hates me. He belittles everything I say. He opposed the translation. I don't like it either, but ignoring it would be bad for us all."

"I do sense conflict brewing. What does the relic say?"

"I can't tell you," she said. "I've been ordered to keep silent."

"If you feel strongly about your translation then don't back down. I trust what you have to say, and Draevik should as well. You weren't dragged into this for nothing. And if you need me for anything, all you have to do is ask." Dassius hugged her tightly and kissed the top of her head.

"I may need you," she replied, then added softly, "I do need you. I'm sure of it."

"Well, I'm here," he said, as if she weren't conscious enough right now of that.

"Stay with me," she said, brushing her lips against his. "All night. Please."

"You don't have to plead." He kissed her. "I want to stay with you."

Grabbing his hand, she led him into her bedroom. Curled together in bed, she felt safe for the first time in days.

Chapter Eight

HETIA ENTERED THE meeting room and pressed the emergency button on the wall panel. She didn't like using it for a meeting that should have been scheduled, but she couldn't count on Draevik allowing it. Plus, her guest would be here soon.

The recorded words sounded on the intercom, "An emergency meeting will convene. All officials gather at once." They would repeat until Hetia pressed the button again or set the timer. Not wanting to immediately reveal she had called the meeting, she set the timer for five minutes and sat in her normal seat.

She'd spent the past evening devising a plan to expose Draevik's intentions to Fresdin. The trick was stalling his intentions for Ceera at the same time. Of course, Draevik's plans may not even come into fruition if Ceera agreed to back down, but the moral repercussions of allowing that to happen were too large for Hetia to bear. Especially if the poor girl's life was indeed in jeopardy.

How her fellow officials could ignore this, she had no idea, but hoped it came from their faith in Draevik and not lack of compassion. Since Hetia did not revere him like the others, she had little faith. And so she'd acted accordingly with some success. Although Ceera had unfortunately not answered her communication orb.

Other officials entered the room. They looked at her curiously as they took their seats, probably wondering where their beloved Draevik was, who hadn't yet arrived. She could see it on their faces; only he would have something important enough to say that would justify an emergency meeting.

Hetia gave them her most professional smile.

Fresdin slipped into his chair. "Where's Draevik?"

Hetia took a long, deep breath before responding, "If he follows protocol, he will arrive here shortly."

Fresdin raised his eyebrows at her. "Did you…?"

She nodded. "I did, so please pay attention."

"To what? Why?"

Draevik burst into the room. "What's the meaning of this?"

The remaining officials filed in. Risa and Karnen looked at Draevik quizzically as they passed.

Hetia went to turn off the intercom, pleased the officials had congregated before the five minutes had ended.

"I appreciate your prompt attendance," she said. "I've called this meeting on a matter of dire importance."

"You called this meeting?" Draevik studied her resentfully.

"Thank you for reiterating that," Hetia responded. "Now if you'll please take a seat?"

Draevik continued to glare at her. The room was as silent as it had ever been, but that only widened her stage.

"It is within an official's rights to call a meeting," she reminded him. "Article 57B."

"State your purpose then," Draevik commanded, taking his place at the head of the table.

"During our last meeting, in which we discussed Ms. Kestlyn's translation and minimized the importance of her life," Hetia said, unable to keep the bitterness from her voice, "it occurred to me that High Service was being unfair and not properly evaluating all factors. And since I value Draevik's motives so greatly, I've called the Caretaker of Ancient Affairs here so we can discuss the purpose of the Archaics more thoroughly."

"So thoughtful," Draevik said insincerely.

"In fact"—Hetia glanced at the clock—"he should be here already. Guard?" She motioned to the guard standing at the entrance.

He obediently opened the door.

The Caretaker hobbled into the room and settled in the chair that Hetia rushed to pull from the table for him. Then she sat in her seat nearby.

"Thank you for coming," she told him. "Your input is vital."

Draevik muttered something across the table.

"I'm not used to being called here," the Caretaker said, gazing about as if the room held some mystique.

"This is a room that usually houses problems of a more immediate nature," Draevik responded with a hint of condescension.

The Caretaker's gaze rested upon Draevik, but he said nothing in return.

"Now—" Hetia began.

"As you mentioned," Draevik interrupted, "this meeting is about my own plans which means I have the right to conduct it. Article 63Y."

Hetia's anger level soared to new heights. She should have known he would use her own tactic against her. Beneath the table, Fresdin placed a hand on her arm. For once he wasn't squeezing it, which she took as a good sign.

"Tell us," Draevik asked, "what purpose the Archaics actually serve."

The Caretaker screwed up his face. "You mean, you don't know?"

"Would I be asking the question if I did?" Draevik responded.

"Perhaps," the Caretaker replied as he studied the high-ranking sphere seven. "I think perhaps you would."

"What you think has no bearing on any of this," Draevik snapped. "Please answer the question."

"I'll answer your question," the Caretaker replied, "and stifle mine, which is how could an entity that controls public proceedings lose sight of such an important matter? Surely that ancient manuscript isn't blocking your memory."

"High Service decides what's important around here. And the relic has nothing to do with this."

"I'm surprised someone your age doesn't recall it." The Caretaker's lips curved into a tiny smile. "Surely it was taught in schools when you went through them."

Draevik slammed his fist down on the table. "Must I have you incarcerated?"

Hetia tensed, feeling again Fresdin's gentle tapping on her arm.

"For evading questioning?" the Caretaker said. "No. The answer is obvious, to those who pay attention. The Archaics make the planet safer."

"Safer? They are dangerous entities," Draevik said. "How do they make it safer?"

"By providing the planet with an outlet for its pent-up

aggressions. You do realize a ball of pressurized heat resides at its core?"

"Of course I know that," Draevik said.

"Since the planet's stability is driven by its core," the Caretaker continued, "the Archaics, in turn, stabilize the planet for its inhabitants."

"I'm still not grasping the correlation," Draevik said.

"The Archaics temper the planet's volatility by absorbing it, so society doesn't have to. Or at least they control and lessen the effects. This why they are so edgy. Since they have Semion tendencies in manner and physical likeness, they act humanely. Only a deity could endure such tribulations for the benefit of others."

"Lovely," Draevik said.

"They are servants of the planet," the Caretaker continued. "Although they do release this aggression at their whim, usually it's at a lesser extreme than would have happened if exerted by the planet itself."

"This is verging on plain ridiculous," Draevik said.

"Call it what you will," the Caretaker replied, "but the truth is the Archaics are a gift from the planet. Why the sudden interest in them?"

"That's none of your concern."

"I forgot," the Caretaker said slyly, "that a man in my position exists solely to inform."

"Please don't forget it again," Draevik replied with a glare.

Hetia could withstand the abuse no longer. The Caretaker had succeeded in making his point.

"Thank you, Caretaker," Hetia said. "We appreciate you consulting with us."

The Caretaker stood slowly. "I'm always happy to help."

He shambled toward the door. Was it her imagination or had his gait weakened since she'd last seen him?

"Guard, please escort him," Hetia said.

Draevik's glare swung her way, and Fresdin tugged at a fold in her gown. Again, it was subtle in manner.

"You forget who is leading this meeting, sphere three," Draevik said.

"I didn't forget," Hetia responded, calmly sitting down before he could order her to do so. "You, however, did forget your manners."

Tension circulated throughout the room. Draevik trembled in anger.

"He is close to one hundred years old," Hetia stated. "A respected elder."

"I am your elder too," Draevik retorted, "and four spheres higher. If you show disrespect to me again, I will have *you* escorted from the room. And it won't be because you need help walking."

Hetia returned his glare with one of her own. No one else defending her, not even Fresdin, told her what she already suspected. It would ruin her career to stand up to Draevik Warlyn. But if she didn't stand up to him, he would ruin everything else.

"I understand how the Caretaker's news could inspire fear for our safety," Draevik said, now addressing everyone. "But don't forget about our planetary stability monitor. It will alert us to the planet's aggressions. And a prepared society is one that will advance. Which is why I stand firm that our study shall proceed as planned. Immortality will allow us to reign victorious and not be pawns of the planet."

The clapping of many hands at such a statement further bruised Hetia's soul.

❧

Ceera woke with a foggy headache and the pleasing sight of Dassius lying ruffled nearby. On her way to the kitchen, she noticed a voice message on her communication orb from the day before. A High Service official named Hetia had requested that Ceera return her call before the night ended. Odd since she had an appointment with High Service later that morning. It was too late now to call Hetia back, but her curiosity had been piqued.

She cleared her headache with a cup of tea and made breakfast. After, she and Dassius held hands on her stoop, not ready to part. She wished he would attend the meeting with her. She dared not ask, for it would get him in trouble if he accepted. And she knew he would.

He invited her to meet him later for dinner. She was sure it had a joint purpose, so she could tell him about the meeting with High Service. And perhaps for a more personal reason as well. Time apart had enhanced their time together. The light in his eyes had not faded. She was certain her own eyes shone back.

Ceera now sat in the lobby inside the Aurora, waiting to meet with the officials who would decide her fate. She fidgeted nervously, curious as to whether Hetia would be present. Though she wanted to believe the officials would decide in her favor, she had her doubts. After all, their favor would have to comply with Draevik's, and she was certain he had no special regard for her. She hoped the severity of her claims was apparent so they could at least work out a deal. Denying her claims outright was not an option she was willing to accept.

Amid those concerns, images of her night with Dassius

flashed through her mind. They had slept intertwined all night. It'd felt like torture leaving the safety and comfort of his arms.

The door opened slowly, squashing those thoughts, and Draevik stood at the doorway.

He motioned her inside. "We're ready for you."

Her stomach dropped. Feigning confidence, she said, "Thank you," and followed him into the room.

Karnen and Risa sat at the table. Ceera reluctantly took a seat opposite them. Draevik remained standing in the background. His refusal to sit signified the discussion would not take long.

Risa wouldn't meet her gaze. "Ceera," she said quietly, "a decision has been reached on your proposal."

"Yes?" Her voice came forth as a whisper.

"We've decided your translation is misguided," Karnen stated plainly, not sharing Risa's reservations.

Draevik watched the two lower spheres with a disturbing sparkle in his eye.

"I understand your position," she said, "but if you would let me explain further—"

"We've already decided your involvement is finished," Draevik said forcefully.

Ceera took a quick, shallow breath that did not calm her nerves.

Risa frowned at him, and Ceera felt a flicker of hope.

"Draevik, you promised to let us handle it," Risa said.

"But you're not doing a very good job of that, are you?"

Ceera's hope dissipated, and she stood, feeling the urge to run far away from Semadon and these monsters who called themselves servants to the public. Hearing sounds behind her, she glanced back. Two guards now stood at the door, blocking her from a quick exit.

"You can't keep me from the relic," she protested, "when I'm the one who found it for you."

"We think your involvement has taken a toll on your health," Karnen said.

"My health? I'm perfectly fine. What do you mean?"

Risa struggled to maintain a neutral expression. "Your travels have left you mentally drained," she said in a rehearsed tone. "Some time alone might help you recover."

Why was Risa saying something she herself did not believe?

The guards edged closer. Panic rose in her chest. "Time alone? In my dwelling?"

Risa cast her gaze downward, refusing to acknowledge the question.

"We like to call it an institution of the mind," Karnen said, as if eloquence could lessen the reality of where they were sending her.

An awful pain wrenched in her chest. Her worst fear had been realized. They were committing her. After everything she had gone through for them. After finding the relic. Her relic. Draevik's eyes gleamed with approval and satisfaction. At her expense.

"I have plans later with Dassius," Ceera said, voice shaking. "You can't do this to me."

"Oh yes, we can," Draevik said emphatically.

She turned to leave. Draevik made a motion to the guards. One of them sprang forward and injected something sharp into her arm. She struggled in vain while her surroundings turned as black as Draevik's soul.

❧

Hetia sat beside Fresdin in their office. They were sorting through paperwork again, but she couldn't focus. He hadn't said much after the meeting, and she was dying to know whether Draevik's behavior had impacted his opinion yet.

"How did you feel about the way Draevik treated the Caretaker? And while we're on the topic, how do you feel about the way he treated me?"

"It was disappointing," Fresdin admitted, looking up from his report. "I can only come up with one reason for his behavior."

Hetia bit back disappointment. She'd been certain he would be on her side now. "Which is?"

"What he hopes to achieve is so important that its delay is causing his patience to wear thin. I heard other officials discussing it after the meeting. It makes perfect sense."

"So you're letting group think rule your logic?"

"What's wrong with being unified with High Service?" he huffed.

"When has conforming ever been synonymous with leadership?" she asked.

"Draevik is our leader," he said.

"Draevik is our ruler. He no longer exercises the vote."

"He strives for the betterment of society."

"His plans are selfish and destructive," she said. "Undermining the way society governs, at the people's expense, should not be pursued when things are not broken to begin with. And for something so unreachable."

"How do you know immortality is unreachable?"

"Because only nature can allow such things. The fact the relic needs to be returned, per its own instructions, makes that point obvious. Draevik's desire to live forever will destroy the Semion culture."

Fresdin stared at her. "You think so?"

"I do," Hetia replied, "and you'd see it, too, if you weren't so blinded by his reputation. Draevik plans to immortalize society at the expense of everyone's safety. You heard the Caretaker, the Archaics losing their powers will make our culture susceptible to natural disasters. Draevik's end goal is in direct dispute of itself."

Despite her frustrations, Hetia managed to keep her voice level. Blowing up at Fresdin would achieve nothing. Instead, she rose and looked out the window to sort her thoughts.

"I can't dispute your logic," Fresdin said, "but you always put such a negative spin on things."

Hetia watched two guards jog down the walkway, carrying something between them. Or someone, she realized, catching sight of a shoe poking out from underneath a blanket.

"Fresdin," she said imploringly.

"I know you're set in your opinion, but can we at least discuss the pros and cons—"

"Come here," she demanded. "Hurry."

He rushed over. The guards were now stuffing the person into a parked travel pod on the roadway. Semions hurried past, fitfully glancing at the display and pretending not to be interested.

"Who is that?" Fresdin wondered. "What are they doing?"

The blanket folded over and exposed a female's face, answering his question.

"Resorting to extreme measures," Hetia said tightly. "Draevik's orders I presume."

"I didn't think…" he said, backing away from the window in disbelief.

"But Fresdin," she said softly, "I did. And I was right."

A range of emotions crossed his face before his expression settled on grim. "I guess you win then. I owe you an apology."

"I knew you'd come around," she said.

His demeanor had fully changed. "Now that I'm here, I'll make sure I'm a useful addition."

"What do you have in mind?"

"I will no longer be deceived." Fresdin's eyes radiated intensity. "I will be watching the guards, assessing their loyalties, looking for anyone we can conspire with to stop Draevik from his tyrannical ways."

Hetia's eyes widened, surprised by his sudden virility.

"But only when the time is right. Until then, we wait."

She nodded, glad she finally had Fresdin, the tactician, to balance her brash assertiveness. Together they would accomplish what needed to be done.

CHAPTER NINE

THE SEAT OPPOSITE Dassius at the crowded restaurant remained empty. He took a few gulps of his drink and checked his watch. Ceera was late, possibly because her meeting had been rescheduled. Or she might have been assigned some scribe work with a strict deadline. Despite these potential causes, worry hovered in the back of his mind. He couldn't determine the reason, but his suspicion that neither of his excuses for her were correct did his concern justice.

Silverware clattered against plates. Smells wafted over, causing his stomach to growl, but hunger seemed a petty desire.

He'd spent the day in heavy Sim training, so his instincts would have missed her despair grazing his awareness. Normally, he wasn't expected to train so hard in the middle of the week. For whatever reason, they usually scheduled the most demanding days of training for the beginning and the end. Perhaps they were mixing things up. Or perhaps not.

Dassius took another drink of his beverage, knowing if he asked for something that could tame his anxiety, his mental abilities would decrease. If it came down to it, he needed to figure out where she was, not hide from the truth.

He fidgeted with the small package in his pocket. It

contained a ring he had bought for her when he'd returned from his family's settlement. Not an engagement ring, but a promise, an acknowledgment that they were a couple. He'd been waiting for the right time to give it to her. After they'd rekindled their relationship last night, he knew the time was right. But where was she?

His outlook dimmed as time passed. Laughter from other tables mocked his apprehension. Drinks clinked together as Semions talked animatedly between bites of food. The frequent glances in his direction were starting to annoy him.

Ceera was now twenty minutes late. He considered that they hadn't been on many dates. The bulk of their time together had been spent journeying to find the relic. She might have a punctuality problem. Except, last night she'd arrived at The Helix before him.

He motioned for the waiter.

"Are you ready to order?" the waiter asked.

"No, I'm still waiting for someone. I'd like a refill on my drink."

"Certainly," the waiter replied and whisked his empty glass from the table.

Fifteen minutes later, his drink had returned and was already empty again. The chair across from him was still empty as well.

She wouldn't stand him up, would she? She'd been primarily unenthusiastic about their relationship, a side effect of having been abandoned by her father when she was a child. And she had been nervous last night when they had been intimate. Did she regret their intimacy? He decided to go to her dwelling to make sure she hadn't succumbed to any reservations.

He motioned for the waiter again.

"Ready to order now?"

"No, I'll take my bill please."

The waiter removed a small notepad from his shirt pocket, scribbled on it briefly, and handed it to Dassius.

Dassius placed his money on the table and left the restaurant.

A dusky gloom pervaded the streets, enhancing his anxiety. He walked briskly to her dwelling, clearing his mind to make way for any fleeting insights regarding her whereabouts.

When he turned onto her orbit, a man who'd been lurking beneath an oval streetlamp came walking toward him, a man he vaguely recognized. Yet it wasn't the man's dark hair and round face that jostled his memory, it was the feeling they'd been in the same vicinity before.

The man was clean-shaven and dressed proper, in slacks and a long, gray coat. "Dassius Rucien?" he asked in a gravelly voice.

Dassius stopped moving, his body now tense. "That's me."

He focused on the knife attached to his hip, ready to reach for it, if need be. Criminal activity in Semadon was rare, but it still happened. The man didn't look likely to have a weapon, but his demeanor was cold and shifty.

"I have a message for you."

"What?" Dassius said unkindly.

"It's from the woman who lived in that dwelling." He pointed to Ceera's dwelling.

The man's usage of the past tense did not go unnoticed by Dassius. "I know her," he replied.

"She got called to her father's settlement. He's ill. She left to take care of him. And the news of his condition upset her so much that she couldn't remember where she was sup-posed to meet you."

Dassius stared blankly at the man. Was this true?

"She's not expected back anytime soon. In fact, due to the severity of her father's illness, she may not return at all."

Dassius nodded stiffly. "I see."

"Said something about only having scribe work to come back for and didn't seem enthused about it." His lukewarm smile portrayed no hint of friendliness.

Dassius did not smile back. The words stung even though they couldn't possibly be true. His instincts knew better.

The man began to walk away. Dassius held out his hand to stop him.

"That's all I know," the man said sharply.

"Tell me how you are acquainted with her."

"I'm an old friend, a good one. One she entrusted to tell you the news."

Jealousy ripped through Dassius. He suppressed his desire to show the man how it felt with his knife.

"Did she not tell you about me?" The man smirked and swaggered past.

Deception stained his thoughts. But whose? The man's or his own misguided opinion of who Ceera really was? Surely she hadn't befriended this odious bearer of news, and if so, for what cause? How long had he known her? Long enough it seemed. She claimed to distrust men, yet sometimes trauma caused Semions to do unnatural things.

The lights were off in her dwelling. He knew without knocking that she really wasn't home.

He walked to his dwelling, carrying the weight of the planet on his chest. He couldn't use his clairvoyant ability to pursue the truth under this much stress, but his emotions were too strong to brush aside.

She'd made no mention of an ailing father. In fact, she'd had but one concern, and it had terrified her. But to whom could he voice his suspicions?

High Service would never reveal what happened to her if they were the reason behind her disappearance.

&

Ceera awoke in a dimly lit room, her grogginess exceeding what she'd endured that morning. The realization she was not in her own bed broke through the mental fog. The mattress beneath her was too stiff. The blankets tucked around her were too thin, resulting in little warmth, and their white material starkly contrasted her flower-patterned blankets back home. Bare walls surrounded her. To the left was a chair and a bulky machine lined with silver on a wooden cart. The machine looked ready to be hooked into someone. Probably her.

A sense of dread compelled her to sit up quickly, where she was greeted by a splitting headache. Resigned, she sank back down and burrowed her face into the flat pillow. Tears flooded her eyes and soaked her pillow. So this was her fate after all.

The door opened and a woman peeked in.

How did they know she'd woken up? Did they have her on camera?

"Good evening," the woman said as she stepped into the room. "I wasn't sure if you'd be awake yet." Her attire, a white uniform replete with a matching cap that tamed her brown curly hair, indicated she was a nurse.

"Feeling okay?" the nurse asked.

Ceera shook her head. Speaking would make the situation more real.

"You've slept all day. You must be hungry. Do you want to eat your first meal in your room or the cafeteria?"

When Ceera said nothing, the nurse continued, "We expect you to eat regularly in the cafeteria; however, we like to give you time to adjust to your new environment. The first day here can be a shock. Have you a preference?"

Ceera rolled away and closed her eyes. If she refused to participate in what had to be an alternate reality, it might go away.

The nurse sighed loudly. "Very well, I'll assume you want to dine alone."

Something rolled through the doorway. It stopped between her bed and the wall.

"Here's dinner. Please empty your plate in the garbage inside the cart when you're finished. Enjoy."

The door clicked shut.

The food's thick aroma wafted over, inspiring a wave of nausea. Her thoughts reverted to the meeting room and the injection. She lurched upright, leaned over the bed to grab the garbage can, and emptied the contents of her stomach into it.

She wiped her mouth and lay back down. The vile taste on her tongue tainted her thoughts. The fight was now over. Being here, inside this room, was what she'd been headed toward her whole life. She meant nothing to the outside world.

It had started when her mother passed; her father had given her away to authorities. Drusilla had punished her for not excelling at being a scribe. She thought she'd finally found her place in the world through her involvement with the relic and the forest, but High Service would rather let her rot than do something meaningful with that connection. Even if it meant something better for society. Being important enough to matter had inconvenienced High Service so much they had banished her.

She was tired of fighting. The best revenge would be to go with the flow. She may end up dead but so would important aspects of Semion culture. Draevik would suffer for it eventually.

This last thought helped her drift back to sleep.

Chapter Ten

LIGHT SHONE THROUGH a tiny window, waking Ceera from her slumber. Hunger pains ravaged her insides. Her head had cleared, leaving behind a fury that had vanquished her self-pity from the day before.

They may have figured out a way to silence her, but she was still alive. So much to dwell on, yet first she needed sustenance.

Watching Draevik suffer for his actions, or even seeing disappointment brush his features, was further motivation to get moving. She sat up, noticing the food cart had been removed. A newly bagged garbage container had been placed beside her bed. Not having to deal with the leftover smell was a good start to the day.

She pushed her blankets aside and swung her legs over the edge, pressing her toes onto the cold floor.

The ominous machine remained nearby on its cart, and she leaned forward to examine it. Four silver interlocking circles decorated its bottom half, shining as if they had recently been polished. The wires protruding from the machine's side attached to a flexible pad covered with small metal disks. The machine's top half contained a panel with different colored buttons. Above them was a blank oval screen.

Its composition made her shudder. She stood and instinctually turned away, telling herself the machine was probably a fixture in each room.

Her thin, white gown barely hung past her knees. Everything here was bare and sparse. It was enough to drive anyone crazy, especially someone like her, with so much red swirling inside.

She cracked open the door and peered out. More doors lined the hall, most of them shut. Someone was moaning from behind one. Another door separated the hall from a muffled commotion, but she couldn't make out the source.

A woman sat at the nurses' station, not the nurse who had brought dinner the night before. She didn't acknowledge the disturbing noises, so Ceera decided to ignore them as well.

In defiance of her white gown, Ceera approached with shoulders back and purpose in her step. She was, after all, quite sane and undeserving of being here.

The nurse's head jerked up from the paper she'd been studying. "Good morning," she said tentatively, her hand moving slowly toward a red button on the wall.

"You won't need to press that," Ceera said assertively. "I only want breakfast, then access to a communication orb so I can make some calls."

The nurse's eyes lit with amusement. "Breakfast is a yes, but I cannot allow any calls."

Ceera took a deep breath. "Why?"

The nurse looked her up and down appraisingly. "I've been given strict orders not to."

Unwilling to show any hint of frustration, which would give them more fuel to condemn her, Ceera asked, "Where's the cafeteria?"

"I'll show you." The nurse stood and led Ceera around the hall.

She refrained from asking about the strange machine in her room, not wanting to remind the nurse it was there. A similar device might have something to do with the disturbances coming from the other rooms.

The cafeteria was half occupied with other patients, long-faced and emotionless, eating quietly. A nurse tried to feed an empty-eyed woman, who kept batting her food away.

"Now Garia," the nurse said as some of the food fell to the floor, "you usually love your veggies."

The name prodded Ceera's memory as she headed to the buffet. As a scribe, she reported on current events and was exposed to many names. But this name she'd heard recently. And she hadn't been doing scribe work recently. She filled her plate with veggie toast and sausage cakes.

The realization came as she reached for a cup of juice. Her fingers brushed against the cup during her shock, almost spilling it.

Garia had been the CfA chairwoman who'd recently resigned. The meeting to discuss her short term had been the one Ceera had evaded having to record. But had Garia willfully resigned? Why was she now in the mental institution?

Ceera glanced at the former CfA member. Food dribbled down her chin. She'd went from leading one of the most influential councils in Semadon to being force fed in an institution. If she'd had an accident, the CfA wouldn't have needed to discuss the resignation. They'd just vote for a new leader. Garia's downfall was too extreme to ascribe to chance.

Suddenly, the machine in her room with all the metal wires broke into her thoughts.

She grabbed the cup of juice. Trying not to look again

at Garia, she found an empty table. A cool breeze wafted at her then from inside the kitchen, soothing her anxiety and restoring her mettle.

The nurse who'd escorted her to the cafeteria now chatted with another nurse near the entrance. They openly observed her, but Ceera paid them no attention. She took a large bite of toast. Let them talk about her. Unlike Garia, she wouldn't be here long.

&

Dassius sat uncomfortably in the waiting area, wedged into the tiny chair. He was taking a risk coming here, but his safety was secondary to Ceera's. He had to know what happened to her. Even though he doubted they would tell him, he may be able to garner a clue from the conversation. He had to try.

Knowing his capabilities, High Service would make every effort to not give him any clues at all. He would pretend like they'd succeeded.

As a Sci-Defense member, who trained to serve and protect society, rebellion against authority was not something he'd ever envisioned for himself. Yet Ceera, despite being his girlfriend, or at least that's what he'd hoped to establish at dinner, was a member of the society he had pledged to protect. Thus, his status did not make him a game piece of High Service. This was the correct point of view, though it could be considered blasphemous by some.

They were making him wait an unreasonable amount of time. It was their way of trying to shake him. Or they could be coming up with something to tell him. He had to be careful during the exchange. Though he was skeptical a handful of guards could take him down, it was possible.

Hours passed. Longer than he had waited for her at the restaurant, but he would not let the officials kill his motivation. He had hardly slept the night before, if at all, but could stay awake on the upwards of seventy-two hours. Of course, it would never come to that.

Finally, the door swung open. Draevik and several officials exited the room.

"Oh"—Draevik paused, feigning surprise—"You're still here."

Dassius nodded grimly. What was there to say?

The other officials eyed him curiously, but Draevik waved them away.

"Be off with you," he said graciously. "I will speak with Mr. Rucien."

They traipsed past, giving each other worried expressions that did not go unnoticed by Dassius. He stood, attempting to appear smaller than his oversized body. It would be best for him to appear nonthreatening. He didn't want to cause any friction, though his muscles were tense and itched to do just that. His instinct begged him to grab the smug old man by the throat. He slumped over a bit so this truth wouldn't be obvious.

Draevik gestured for him to enter the room. Dassius complied, all too aware of the guards standing attentively around the room.

"Have a seat," Draevik offered. He sat neatly at the main table, looking at Dassius with contrived interest.

Dassius sat. "Do you know why I'm here?" he asked, intending to broach the subject in a non-accusatory way.

"Not really," Draevik said offhandedly.

Dassius changed positions in his chair, noticing the guards shuffle a little closer. "I'm concerned for a friend of mine."

"Oh?"

"Ceera Kestlyn."

"Who?" Draevik pretended be thinking.

Dassius looked at him reproachfully. "I went with her to the forest."

"Ah yes, of course. You'll have to forgive an old brain like mine." Draevik cast him a look of appeal. "The memory is the first to go, and High Service encounters many Semions. But she was here often for a span of time. I remember now."

Dassius maintained a neutral expression to convey that the official's disingenuous behavior was not offending him. Surely Draevik didn't think he could trick a member of the Sci-Def team, one trained to read people and situations better than most read books. He had expected the run around, but not one so obvious.

"Were you aware of her disappearance?" Dassius asked.

Draevik pretended to be stunned. "Now wait one moment. I do recall her father fell ill, and she left to tend to him. Did she disappear from there?"

Dassius stifled his frustration. "I think she never arrived."

"Never arrived?" Draevik repeated.

There would be no straight talk from Draevik Warlyn. It would be game after game.

"Do you know where she is?"

"Young man," Draevik said, "all I know is what I've been told. Have you tried to contact her at her father's dwelling?"

Dassius shook his head.

"Then there may not be a problem after all," Draevik said lightly.

"Do you have her father's number?" Dassius asked through clenched teeth.

"It's against the law to give it to you. A privacy thing."

"Never mind," Dassius said as he stood.

His personal space shrank as the guards inched closer.

"You do realize," Draevik said sternly, "that it may have been her wish to go away quietly. Her whereabouts could truly be none of your business."

Dassius sensed the underlying threat. He nodded despite the glare forming on his face. "Yes," he grumbled, "I'm bothered she doesn't want me to know." An explanation for his glare.

"You're a talented member of the Sci-Def team," Draevik's words slithered from his lips, "well-trained and competent. Don't waste your time fretting over someone who fails to give you the same thing in return."

"Thank you for your time," Dassius said, turning to leave.

"The pleasure was mine."

The guards' watchful gazes followed him to the door. His insides were on fire as he left the Aurora. Ceera's fears about the man running High Service were valid. He would have to figure out why, not to mention where they were hiding her, and try not to get implicated in the process.

Chapter Eleven

CEERA SPENT THE day brooding in her room. The nurses had suggested she play games with the other patients, but she'd refused. Keeping her spirits up was a trial around the other patients. Not to mention her pity for Garia mingled with an uneasiness that told her she'd be next.

In the cafeteria, those she'd at first thought sullen and detached had made their true nature apparent. Some talked to themselves in random outbursts, and others blurted out strange sounds. The combination blended into a cacophony of background noises that made for an unsettling breakfast.

One patient had violently grabbed onto his nurse escort and had to be held down by two others, who'd given him an injection before carting him away. The situation was awfully familiar, and a dark, sinister cloud now hovered in her mind and enhanced her dread of the machine alongside her bed. The nurses' stony indifference to the events, implying such things were common, made everything worse.

The bitter truth that her own mother would have belonged in such a place added to her misery. At least no one here was rambling about a forest.

At some point, she remembered she had stood Dassius up. How long had he waited for her? Did he know where she was? What if he had tipped off High Service? Her recent confiding in him could be considered treason. And perhaps he'd hoped to take advantage of her before High Service put her away.

She huddled on her bed and wrapped her arms around her knees, refusing to cry. There were enough tears falling in this building.

Stop it, she scolded herself, *doubting Dassius makes no sense.*

But keeping a straight head confined in these white surroundings was difficult. Nothing to look at, nothing to do. Her mind kept trying to fill the bareness with thoughts, most unwelcome. Why were there not scenic pictures on the walls instead of all the ugly, empty space?

Escape was not an option. All the doors and windows she'd noticed so far would set off alarms if forced open. A high stone fence surrounded the expansive yard around the building. The large oak tree out back wasn't close enough to the fence to be useful. She had scoped out such things on the way back from breakfast, all the while ignoring the sobbing she'd heard as she passed closed doors.

Her only hope for rescue was from an outside source. But who, besides Dassius, would come for her? Her father probably wouldn't notice she was gone for months, maybe even years. Litha would be just as clueless since she'd never confided her predicament. All the other scribes were jealous of her and would probably revel in her absence.

Drusilla had seemed concerned, but what about the incriminating information she had about Ceera hiding in her filing cabinet? Would Drusilla have told High Service about her mother, giving them the perfect solution for how to get rid of her? Relief swelled inside her because this would mean Dassius had not betrayed her. But she already decided he hadn't. She sighed in frustration.

Worry gnawed her logic. Dassius had protected her before. She could count on him. And why would Drusilla reveal the information about her mother? The woman may be stern, but she was also smart. She would have known it could cause Ceera to be locked up.

And really, she was wasting time. High Service didn't think she was crazy anyway. They just didn't want to deal with her anymore.

It was time to go over the facts. The only Semion she knew for sure wanted her locked up was Draevik. And if she didn't fulfill what the relic said to do, she'd end up dead whether she was locked up or not. Which meant if she did somehow escape, she'd need to steal the relic from the library. Since she had struggled at unlocking a mere wooden box in Drusilla's office, this seemed unlikely. And even if she succeeded, Draevik would have order patrols find her and incarcerate her again. The longer she thought about it, the more she came to accept she truly was stuck. Which left her one conceivable option.

She would conjure a mystic. Only with one's guidance could she determine whether her situation was futile. But she would have to wait until the nurses thought she was asleep. During the day was too risky. She just hoped the enchanted beings would, unlike High Service, still give her the time of day.

⤚

Ceera pretended to be asleep when the nurse entered her room that evening. Clutching her blanket tightly under her chin, she dared not flicker an eyelid. Her breaths were slow and calm as she had practiced.

The nurse stood over her an uncomfortable amount of time. "Your last real sleep," she muttered.

What was that supposed to mean?

Struggling to breathe evenly now, Ceera persevered.

Then the floor creaked near the doorway. The light dimmed, and the door clicked shut. The sound of the nurse's footsteps faded down the hall.

Feeling especially motivated after the nurse's statement, Ceera counted to one hundred before opening her eyes. She watched the clock on the wall, waiting for fifteen minutes to pass. Then she sat up slowly, to avoid the bed creaking, and crossed her legs in front of her. She turned the dimmer beside her bed to its lowest setting. Her palms pressed together near her chest.

Time passed slowly as she conjured. She stretched her mind out, seeking and inviting. A panicked thought that mystics were forbidden to join with one in a mental institution jabbed at her concentration. Before it could poison her invitation, she banished the thought.

Hope and patience melded together in her awareness. She held them there and did not waver, allowing their union to consume her. Through half-closed eyes, she watched a shape form in the chair beside her bed. The shadow refused to fully materialize, but she breathed a sigh of relief that the mystic had bothered to come at all. She would take what she could get. Knowing she may only have a matter of minutes, it pained her to keep silent, but it was impolite to speak before the mystic.

"Invitation accepted," the mystic finally spoke in a scratchy voice.

"Thank you for joining me here," she whispered.

"You reek of desperation." The words were not accusatory but spoken as fact.

"Yes," she replied. "I won't deny it. I've uncovered something controversial in the relic I found at the forest, the one your kind made us aware of several months back. High Service was displeased, decided to silence me. They've locked me away here, and I need your help on what to do."

"This controversy, what is the nature of it?"

"High Service plans to have the relic studied, by whom and for what purpose, I don't know. Its inscription says it needs to be returned to a cave, by the one bearing the mark. This mark." Ceera held up her thumb to the mystic, who viewed it through hazy eyes framed with wrinkles.

"And if the one bearing the mark does not return it?"

"Then I will die. And the Archaics will lose their powers. And"—she faltered—"the mystics will cease to exist."

The mystic seemed unaffected by the prospect, though the light in the room did flicker. She hoped the flicker wasn't evident through the cracks in the door.

"Now obviously if I carry this out, then the relic cannot be studied. They banished me here to keep me from telling the public."

The aura around the mystic undulated slowly. His expression remained unchanged.

"Perhaps," she whispered, "they would take advice from a mystic."

"Mystics only come when called, by the person in need. High Service has made no move to conjure us."

Ceera's body deflated, and she slumped forward.

"The Archaics will help you. They are of a worldlier persona and live to suit their own purpose, which coincides with yours. It would be wise to involve them."

"How do I involve them? I'm locked in here and am closely monitored."

"Call them to you."

"Call them? How? They're spread out across the planet. There's no way to contact them."

"You are thinking on your own terms. To call them, you must think on theirs." The mystic's outline grew fuzzy, signifying his impending disappearance.

"Wait," Ceera said quickly. "Tell me what I should do!"

"Plan by design. It will not fail you."

The mystic's words made no sense, so she tried a different tactic. "Doesn't what I've discovered worry you?"

"Worry is for Semions, not mystics."

"But you'll cease to exist!"

"On many planes and levels," the mystic said faintly, "existence is open to interpretation."

He faded like a breath of air, though his ambiguous words tucked themselves away in her psyche for future consideration. His chair was now disturbingly empty.

Ceera's heartbeats filled the silence. How could she possibly call the Archaics from an insane asylum? Mystics were one thing, existing between the planes of reality which could be accessed from anywhere. But the Archaics existed on the same plane as her and were many miles away. Yet according to the mystic there was a way; she just had to think like an Archaic. Or had the mystic assumed it was possible? Did mystics make assumptions? She'd never heard of such a thing.

She revisited her time spent with each Archaic. They had not deemed her significant. A few had even attempted to kill her, on accident, so they said. How could she possibly convince them to come when she had only succeeded in conjuring the shadow of a mystic? And she still had no idea how to call one. No one had ever done that before.

Her gaze fell on the forbidding machine with the silver rings. She would soon be enduring its torture if she didn't figure out how.

Chapter Twelve

CEERA DISCOVERED THAT being free from everyday tasks allowed solutions to come easily. Or perhaps it was natural to think crazy thoughts when trapped in a mental institution. A memory came to mind as she rinsed her toothbrush the next morning, words spoken by Anemona, the mischievous child who had caused a monsoon of trouble during her and Dassius's visit.

Anemona had mentioned that when Oc~ea, her mother, stared at the water, it revealed information. The other Archaics should also have this ability, in their own special way. Thus, Ceera could use the elements to communicate with them.

Since she was being monitored, her window of opportunity was sparse. One at a time was too risky, for it would prolong the delivery of the message. The Archaics would have to be reached simultaneously to ensure the task was successful. But how? Envisioning them all together brought chaos to her mind. The encounter would be turbulent and stormy. A spark ignited in her brain, and she grinned for the first time in days.

She would transmit her message through the coming storm.

During breakfast in the cafeteria, she'd watched on the global update that the planetary stability monitor had predicted a late afternoon storm. It was to be Semadon's last storm before several weeks of calm weather, so she would have to capitalize on the moment. The planetary stability monitor had already impacted her life when it had alerted the public to the forest's existence. It seemed fitting it was about to weigh heavily on her future yet again.

She'd also experienced a bit of luck, overhearing the kitchen aids complaining about having to close the window before the storm hit. Apparently, the room had poor ventilation and became quite warm with the stoves on. Their ability to open the window told her that it wasn't linked to the alarm system.

Feeling encouraged, she'd pretended to be helpful by taking an empty food tray from the buffet to the kitchen. As she handed it to the kitchen aid, who seemed pleased by the gesture, she peeked in to gauge the size of the window. She'd need to climb the sink but would fit through easily.

Dassius had once said luck was only a misconception. If her plan worked, and she made it successfully out that window, Ceera would have to disagree. She had yet to devise how to sneak from her room but did have recent experience doing similar things. And the nurses, though stern, were not Drusilla. Nor were they order patrols.

She spent the rest of the morning in her room plotting how to send a message through the storm. As the mystic advised, all she had to do was think like an Archaic. It had worked for her earlier in the day. Oc~ea would be reachable through rain, Baric by something organic, and Atmos through wind. But how would she reach Luma, the demi-god of fire? And most importantly, how would she convey the message? Should she scream for help during the storm and hope they'd hear? Swirl the word *danger* in the mud?

Suddenly her revelation to use the storm seemed less clever.

She glanced around the bare room, her gaze catching once again on the ominous machine. Its metal adornment attracted her attention like nothing else in the room. Whatever the nurse had meant the night before had not come into fruition…yet.

She was tempted to destroy the machine before it did but couldn't risk getting into trouble before she'd had a chance to call for help. The four silver rings on its exterior were so shiny, she could see her reflection on them. She wondered why there were four of them. Were they integral to the machine's purpose or just part of a design—

An idea born from coincidence came then, a correlation two-fold. She peered closer and verified the silver adornment was, in fact, a design and could be easily pried off. The mystic had told her to plan from design, and a design now stared at her with her own face.

More specifically, four faces reflected at her, which meant each ring could be altered to represent an Archaic.

If she were to modify this silver design and take it outside, would it be enough to gain their attention? Would they find it as eye-catching as she did? Could it draw lightning from the sky and thus attract even Luma's attention?

Ceera leaned against the wall, shocked by her reckless ambitions. Attempting such a thing was dangerous. But the mystic's advice was now clear, and what other choice did she have?

There was no sure way to control lightning. The silver design would look small from above. Though if she placed it within the prominent knot jutting from the giant oak growing near the fence, the tree she'd originally considered useless, it might have a chance at being seen.

It was a crazy idea and attempting it would frighten the nurses if they caught her. But did it matter? They'd already deemed her crazy, so why disappoint them?

With her mouth set in a straight line, she readied herself to explore the public areas for supplies. The building had to contain something depicting the Archaics, and she was determined to find it.

∽

Cafold followed the Aurora's guard, headed toward his doom with grim acceptance. His mentor recommending him for Draevik's corrupt project was both infuriating and flattering. The last thing he wanted to do was divide his attention now that he had finally been accepted as Hegliod's apprentice. Yet his mentor claimed Draevik's plan would cause their own space travel projects to be cast aside. Not to mention destroying the relic for fruitless research was immoral and bordering on criminal.

Hegliod had expressed so much faith in his ability to impact the project for the better that he couldn't refuse. And literally, as an apprentice, he couldn't refuse. His standing was limiting in many ways, yet Hegliod had been very direct when he'd said:

You'll do what you can to control the situation.

Cafold would certainly try. But so far in his life, he hadn't been able to control much.

The guard motioned him into the meeting room. It contained a small table and a handful of chairs. A scientist he shared an acquaintance with, Baclus, was the room's only other occupant. They nodded at each other, but Baclus's interest was fleeting. He looked away, resuming the same stony expression owning his face upon Cafold's arrival. He recognized that look. It was the look of a Semion who, forced to be polite, was disgusted at being paired with someone beneath them. Baclus had likely graduated from transition at least five years prior.

Nevertheless, Cafold walked across the room and sat beside him. He folded his hands on the table. How long would he be expected to wait? Baclus was not the type of Semion he wanted to spend much time with, but he supposed he had better get used to it.

Draevik Warlyn strode into the room with the force of a brisk and unsettling wind. He smiled at the two men in a way that caused Cafold to inwardly shudder.

"I see you've made it. Excellent." He sat across from them. "Since you were both recommended by your superiors, I don't expect to be disappointed."

For some reason, the statement seemed more like a threat than a compliment.

"I'm told you're quite the genius." Draevik nodded at Baclus whose bland expression transformed into a look of pride.

"I aspire to greatness, yes," Baclus replied.

"And you"—Draevik turned his attention to Cafold—"recommended by the top inventor in Semadon, the best that's ever existed."

"He does me a great honor," Cafold said, holding rigidly still to hide his intense discomfort.

"Before we begin though, I must ask, how does it feel?"

Cafold blinked. "How does what feel?"

"How does it feel to be the chosen ones? Both of you, the cream of the crop or"—Draevik cast a shadowed look at Cafold—"floating near it somewhere, at any rate."

Cafold couldn't tell whether Draevik was being condescending or genuinely complimentary.

"It feels natural," Baclus replied. "Like I should be here."

"Very good," Draevik said before turning to Cafold. "And you?"

"It feels precarious," Cafold blurted out. Actualizing immortality was not something that seemed to align with job security, but perhaps truthfulness was not in his best interest.

Draevik frowned. "What do you mean?"

Baclus gave him a wary look, though Cafold was unsure as to whether this was aimed at him or the discussion they were being forced to participate in.

He scrambled to cover his slip of words. "In a society like ours," he said, "it's difficult to stay at the top for long. Although the threat of defeat can bring out the best in a man." He smiled. "Even a young one like me."

"I see what you mean," Draevik said, slightly narrowing his eyes. "In your case, let's hope it does."

Cafold exhaled slowly.

"Has either of your superiors mentioned why I've asked you to come?" Draevik asked.

"Yes, Glavin was straightforward about it."

"Hegliod was as well," Cafold said.

"Good. Let's discuss the importance of this task. It will elevate our culture to new heights; thus, your involvement means you'll reap great rewards. Brilliance," Draevik said emphatically, "will be awarded generously in this future I foresee."

Cafold wasn't used to hearing High Service officials using the word 'I' in such grand terms. Or for that matter, being addressed by an official outside of a group or without a companion. The whole encounter was strange in many ways.

"Just the future you foresee, sir, or one foreseen by all of High Service?" he asked with an innocent expression.

"Hegliod surely is rubbing off on you, young man.

Which could be both good and bad…" Draevik surveyed him as if assessing whether he was truly worth the hassle.

Cafold imagined his own youthful face, not hardened or experienced. Surely it was not one to fear.

Apparently agreeing with Cafold's unspoken assessment, Draevik continued, "Let's just say High Service has followed my pursuits eagerly. My goals are indeed also theirs."

Cafold nodded, his heart beating rather quickly.

"Can you elaborate on these rewards?" Baclus said.

"When your success becomes a reality, then I will reward you with long lives. Eternal lives to be exact." Draevik eyed them speculatively. "Are you both on board?"

"I would be honored," Baclus said.

"As would I," Cafold agreed with forced enthusiasm since he hadn't lived long enough to worry about his own mortality yet.

"Good. Now come with me, and I shall introduce you to the specimen. I'm sure it will become as much your obsession as it is mine."

The comment was off-putting. No one should be that attached to a material object. Yet Cafold followed the two men as if he, too, couldn't wait to be enamored of its glory.

Instead of escorting them to the library where Cafold had heard the relic was being stored, Draevik led them to an elevator. He gestured them inside, then pressed the button to the basement.

"We set up a special laboratory for you," Draevik said, "since the study is confidential."

Cafold had never heard of High Service conducting its own research within the Aurora.

Validating his private thought, Baclus stated, "This is new territory for science. Doing research in secret. What if we need something we don't have in stock?"

"Then let me know, and I'll acquire it for you."

The elevator door opened, and they followed Draevik around the hall and into a room.

The ancient manuscript was the focal point of the room, atop a pedestal encased in glass.

"Here it is," Draevik said fondly.

The spiral design on the leather exterior sparkled in a captivating way. But what was it? From outside the glass it was hard to tell.

"What's that design on the cover?" Baclus asked.

"That's part of the study. First, though, you'll study the composition of its pages."

"There's not much to study inside paper," Baclus said in a monotone voice.

Draevik wrinkled his nose. "Such negativity."

"As a scientist, I relay facts," Baclus replied. "Still, we can try. We'll need to extract several samples."

The tension left Draevik's face. "That's more like it. And besides, I wasn't finished. There's dried blood on it too."

"That does increase the likelihood of finding something interesting," Baclus conceded, "though only marginally. Depending on its age and a multitude of other factors such as temperature and—"

"The age is the most relevant factor here. Start with the blood and then continue your studies from there. Of secondary interest is the design on the cover. I want to know what it is."

Cafold was again put off by the singular pronoun. "If we do any of that," he said, "we'll have to destroy it. We'll need multiple samples for multiple tests and would never be able to refer back to the pages again."

"Doesn't matter," Draevik responded. "The end result is all I care about. Tell me what tools and equipment you need, and I'll have them stocked."

Baclus rattled off a list of items with no reservations. Cafold had been under the impression they would work in a public laboratory. Working in a secret location felt treasonous in a society that portrayed itself as transparent.

"What about you?" Draevik turned to Cafold.

"I'd prefer to work in a public laboratory," Cafold said. "They contain everything."

"That won't be arranged. You knew secrecy was involved; I'm sure Hegliod told you."

Draevik pointedly turned away to make further arrangements with Baclus, who seemed almost bored. Perhaps he knew this was all a waste of time, at least in the grand scheme of what Draevik expected. But if he did, why was he going along with it?

Then he remembered Baclus was a member of the CfA. The relic had destroyed their council's reputation upon discovery. It was doubtful Baclus cared about keeping it safe. Cafold would be on his own.

⤜

After scheduling a time for his scientists to return, Draevik went back to his office. He'd spent so much time orchestrating the onset of the immortality project that he hadn't spent enough time considering the effects of it.

The Caretaker's news had presented a problem he'd not yet considered. And like a pro, he'd managed to come up with a method of countering it right on the spot. Yet not even the meddling sphere three had noticed the shallowness to his solution, which was mainly that the planetary stability monitor could only forewarn but not correct disturbances. He'd have to spend time mulling over this problem, because you can't immortalize people who are dead.

Unless the Caretaker was making a big deal over nothing. After all, the Council for Advancement didn't even believe in the Archaics. Perhaps they weren't as powerful as the Caretaker claimed?

He pulled Jesra's picture out for motivation. So inspiring were her eyes, her smile, her lips. Then he remembered a topic they had talked about long ago, back when they were still transitioning together, something she had brought up as a joke, yet the discussion had lasted well into the night. So late their senses had escaped them, and they had shared their one and only kiss.

Guilt coursed through him for enjoying that moment. Intimacy was against the rules. But their kiss had been inspired by Jesra's revelation that one day there would be a sphere eight. She had insisted society would continue to advance and what then? Would it operate in the same way? Would accordance to custom be good enough?

At the time they had laughed at such a thing, since it was unlikely either of them would see this advancement come into fruition. But now…

Now he was primed to make sphere eight a reality. Jesra had been right, with immortality in the picture, they couldn't proceed the same as before. Immortality was deserving of its own distinction, its own special realm of importance. And what better distinction than to call the officials undergoing it sphere eights?

Certainly not all the sphere sevens automatically

deserved this privilege. Even they had not noticed the flaw in his solution at the meeting. And a High Service official would need to prove their worth and advance through the rankings like a normal Semion to be worthy. Which brought him to another disturbing prospect. If the privilege were only offered to sphere sevens, how could it be offered to the public? And what would be the deciding factor?

Had he been thinking too generously before? Was the public ready for such a privilege?

Although, in theory, she would never bother him again, Draevik envisioned Ceera frequenting the Aurora on a regular basis for the next one hundred years. Trying to manipulate society with her dreams. Gaining the sympathy of low sphere officials, resulting in meeting after meeting to discuss whether her concerns were valid. The thought repelled him.

Perhaps the public should be content with what they had and just be thankful their competent leaders would forever be leading. Or else such offerings needed to be awarded strictly, with only the sphere eights deciding who and when.

They could use the same strategy they used to determine who deserved to graduate from transition: testing. But something more thorough than answering questions, something more revealing, something without the propensity to lie about its source.

The most fundamental component in every being was its DNA. Yes! Genetic testing could be used to determine who was deserving of such an honor. And while they were at it, indicate to High Service who didn't deserve to be a member of society at all.

Chapter Thirteen

CEERA PACED HER room in nervous steps. She'd eaten dinner hours ago. The sky, though ashen and bleak, had yet to produce a storm. If the weathermen turned out to be wrong then life was perhaps too cruel, for her plan had developed nicely.

During her exploration of the public areas, she'd discovered a worship room barely larger than a nook. Along with pictures of the planet, the solar system, and various constellations, the room contained miniature wooden effigies of each Archaic arranged around a candle on a table.

The find surprised her, considering the CfA's efforts to rid society of its reverence for the Archaics, but apparently this building was behind the times. The effigies were the right size for attaching to the silver design. They even had holes drilled into an appendage protruding from each head, as if they were crafted to be worn as a necklace. With a glance over her shoulder to ensure no one was watching, she snatched them up and tucked them within the pocket in her gown.

Next, she'd stopped at the arts and crafts room, which strangely contained no scissors, and swiped a small ball of twine.

Back in her room, she'd bit through the twine and carefully threaded it through the appendages on the effigies. Then she'd placed both them and the leftover twine beneath her pillow since she'd need to wait until the last moment to attach them to the metal design. She couldn't risk a nurse noticing her handiwork beforehand.

After dinner, a dull knife joined the collection. Adversity was certainly impacting her morals.

It was nearing bedtime when the first drops of rain finally drummed onto the rooftop and fogged the glass of her window. Knowing the nurse would be in shortly, she hid an exercise outfit she'd found in her dresser beneath her blanket. Then she lay down and shut off the light. The plan was to sneak outside when the nurse checked on other patients. If they discovered her in the hall, she'd claim to be on her way to the bathroom and decide how to proceed from there.

The door creaked open after several minutes, but instead of staring at her in the darkness like before, the nurse flicked on the light.

"How can we ever start therapy when you go to bed so early?" the nurse complained loudly.

Ceera felt her shoulder jiggle. She opened her eyes. The nurse was rolling the machine closer to the bed.

"What therapy?" she asked.

"Your dream therapy," the nurse responded.

She sat up and edged away. "Who signed for that?" she asked, terrified to learn the answer. There were only two people who could legally do so: her father and Drusilla.

"No signature is needed when a procedure is ordered by High Service."

The storm outside rattled her window, signifying her plan was now in peril. There wouldn't be another storm for weeks, and in the meantime, how many of these so-called therapies would she have to undergo?

"That sounds illegal," she ventured.

"My hands are tied," the nurse responded without emotion. "I will have to inject you with something if you don't cooperate."

Fear fluttered through her chest. An injection would knock her out for an unspecified amount of time, and time was something she already didn't have. The dream therapy though, what was it?

"What does it do?" she asked.

The nurse sighed. "It will make you stop having those troublesome dreams. Or any dreams. Now please lie down and let me fit this on your head."

Ceera hesitated for that sounded like a terror she'd been hoping to avoid. In response, the nurse placed her hand on a needle that had materialized on the cart. The treatment could be harmless. She didn't have to fall asleep and be subjected to it. She could still slip out…

She lay back down obediently.

"I knew you still had your wits about you." The nurse attached the flexible pad with the metal disks to her scalp. "There you go. Now it should only take a minute."

"What should?" Ceera asked, alarmed, as the scenery blurred. The disks felt cold and heavy on her head.

"Falling asleep, of course."

Those were the last words she heard before a dark void overcame her.

⤙

Dassius paced his dwelling, focused on figuring out Ceera's whereabouts. His worst fears had come true. His skills faltered in her presence, when his feelings for her were strong. And he couldn't let go of his anger that High Service would do something so dishonorable. Ceera did not deserve such treatment, especially after everything she had done for them.

The storm fed his fury, violently shaking his windows and doors as if to purposely provoke him. Let it storm throughout the night. For some reason he desired this.

His confidence was supposed to be an asset not a weakness. He was disgusted with himself for not seeing the severity of her problem. He had probably even caused her more trouble by telling her to stand up for herself. Or perhaps if he had gone with her to the Aurora…

And why hadn't he? Because he hadn't realized High Service was straying from its purpose. All the time he'd spent at his parent's settlement, visiting family and old friends, had distracted him. Was this intended? It was an interesting possibility. And during his studies, he'd learned coincidences were rare. Most actions by those in charge of other people were orchestrated to cause desired results.

The box containing her ring sat on his table. The few weeks he'd spent with her had brought out the best in him, gave him someone to focus on besides himself for once. He'd thoroughly enjoyed it, even though during their journey he had not mastered every challenge. But he'd developed a craving to protect her. The craving grew the more he learned about her. She had experienced a troubled childhood. And then there had been the High Service issue.

They had planned to commit her if she didn't bring them the relic. An extreme reaction, yet somewhat logical because Ceera had come out of nowhere with her dream claims. She'd been a scribe in transition who said she saw things, an oddity in Semion society. He hadn't questioned it at the time, but it did clarify High Service's position as leaders, that they would not tolerate irregular behavior. Yet they were willing to allow her the opportunity to prove her claims. She just had to follow through and back them up.

So Ceera's dreams had been correct, and she had found the relic. But now they didn't like what she was saying about it. Was this such a crime? It was if her theory threatened their motives. And what was the best way to handle crimes that were not really crimes? Asking someone to stay quiet was a gamble. Forcing someone to stay quiet was not.

Suddenly he knew where she was. It was that simple. His fists clenched while his blood boiled even hotter. So much power inside him, but what could he do with it? How could he impact the situation without making things worse? She might even be safer in the institution for the moment, until he could figure out the root cause of High Service's mishandling of the situation. He would kill Draevik Warlyn if he had to, but Dassius had been taught that killing was the last resort.

Something told him time would answer the question for him. He was okay with that, for now, but it had better hurry up.

Ceera resided in a dark slumber, in a dream world without pictures. Devoid of recognizable images, her thoughts were locked inside a mental vacuum in which nothing could break through to activate her awareness. Except that something did.

It began as a nudge, barely discernible in the darkness. Once and then twice, until persistence caused a wrinkle so subtle the void did not yet realize the invasion. The wrinkle rippled slightly. One undulation turned into several fluctuating black threads. Pictures formed from these threads with only dark and darker defining their edges.

An almost indistinguishable speck of light appeared and expanded, in defiance to the void's sudden recognition of the takeover. Nothing tried to grow back. But the light had already won the battle, for it is difficult to thwart the momentum of what is gradual.

Fingers poked through the gap and into a void no longer barren. They wrenched a massive hole. Though still unconscious, this triggered Ceera's awareness, for the action caused a dreamlike pain. A familiar figure appeared within the damaged darkness. This woman, who had shown her where to find the relic, was stamping out the remaining blackness and beating it with her fists.

Ceera wanted to cry out in pain, but the woman held a finger to pursed lips, and suddenly her comprehension solidified. Not only was this the oddest dream she'd ever experienced, but she now remembered that this dream shouldn't be happening at all.

Her eyes shot open. The clock on the wall said ten pm. She'd been asleep for two hours. Rain still beat against the window, telling her she still had a chance.

She removed the flexible pad from her head and placed it on the cart. She didn't have time to think about what had happened to her, how the dream woman had burst through her mental void induced by the machine. She had to enact her plan before it was too late.

She turned the dimmer on low and removed the wooden effigies from beneath her pillow. Using the knife she'd stolen from the cafeteria, she pried the silver design from the machine. It came off with minimal effort. She placed the metal decoration on the nightstand and tied each effigy within a circle, making sure the knots were tight.

Then she put on the outfit she'd hidden beneath her blanket. Placing her creation inside a pocket, she tiptoed toward the door. She turned the handle slowly and peered out through the crack.

The hallway was dim. The nurse on duty stood at a patient's door around the hall. Opening the door a bit wider confirmed the hallway was otherwise vacant. A loud cry prompted the nurse to fully enter the other patient's room. Ceera slipped from her room and carefully shut the door behind her. Then she crept in the opposite direction, the commotion growing quieter as she rounded the hall.

The hallways were deserted, as she'd expected them to be during the evening, and she hurried through their depressing interiors.

The cafeteria doors remained propped open. She entered quickly, navigating around the tables in the darkness and into the kitchen. The window glowed above the sink. Leaning across the porcelain, she opened the window. Wind blasted her face. Heaving her body onto the sink, she climbed backward through the oval opening and into the wicked outdoors.

Rain pounded down mercilessly, drenching her clothes in an instant.

At the far end of the yard stood the giant oak with the convenient knot in its trunk. She rushed toward it with rain blurred vision. As she wedged the design inside the knot, a clap of thunder sounded.

She moved back across the yard, distancing herself from a potential ground current in case the metal drew lightning as intended. Standing a good distance away, she focused on the tree knot's shimmering design.

She pressed her hands into mystic conjuring pose and visualized the Archaics joining her in Semadon. She imagined her plea coursing through the water, cascading over her body, and soaking into the soil. Some of this water would replenish the plants around her. Some would travel deeper into the ground and meet an underwater channel. Some of it would join rivers and streams and eventually flow into the ocean.

If it didn't reach Oc~ea quickly, all her efforts would be in vain.

Alerting the rainwater would extend her message to all water, for it was one entity after all, whether here or there.

The water soaking into the soil would alert mycelium and the roots of nearby trees, thus communicating her plea to Baric. During her imaginings, she recited the relic's warning. The wind picked up, stealing the words from her mouth and whipping them away. She envisioned the wind carrying this warning to Atmos.

She focused so intently in those mere minutes that she did not hear someone approaching. A hand roughly grabbed her upper arm, breaking her trance.

"Playing in the rain like a child," a nurse scolded, yanking her backward, "when you should be in bed."

As the nurse pulled her toward the building, she remained fixated on the glimmering design positioned in the tree knot. She focused intensely on the Archaics themselves: their physical images, their powerful auras, their inseparability with the element each represented. The mystic had told her they could be called, that if she planned by design it would not fail her, and mystics were always right.

As though commanded by her will, a flash of lightning erupted from the sky and struck the tree. The tree cracked and groaned from the impact, it's trunk now obscured behind a cloud of smoke. Temporarily blinded, though vindicated, a smile grazed Ceera's lips.

The nurse cried out, "Our tree's been struck!" Her shock turned to disgust when she noticed Ceera's smile. "It's your fault, isn't it?"

Ceera said nothing as the nurse dragged her inside, past another wide-eyed nurse who now guarded the door. She kept her focus on the outdoors: the flow of the water, the power of the wind, the powerful lightning striking the tree and thus transmitting her message.

The nurse forced her into a bathroom and stripped her down to nothing. Then she reached inside the glass shower to turn on the water. "You could have been killed," she said, before shoving Ceera inside.

The hot water slammed onto her skin, enlivening her, and she began to laugh.

The nurse peered at her through the glass door. "What's so funny?"

The irony of Ceera's plight was now paramount in her mind. Death was a prospect for her even when it came to saving herself.

The nurse, having no idea she'd committed a serious blunder, said, "Stop laughing and clean yourself."

But Ceera continued to laugh, tracing swirling letters onto the fogged-up glass encasing her, the word *Help* over and over until the nurse tired of her display and turned off the water. As the remaining droplets trickled lamely from the spout, Ceera's laughter waned with it. A harsh reality struck her. She had either solidified her status as a crazy person or secured her escape.

Lightning hitting a tree meant nothing if the message hadn't been received. Time would determine her fate. And so far, it was working against her.

Chapter Fourteen

WHEN CAFOLD ARRIVED at the secret laboratory, as he'd resigned to calling it since it reminded him of mad scientist stories in books, he and Baclus greeted each other with begrudging politeness. They had no reason to hate each other, but it was uncomfortable being thrown together with someone you barely knew and given the task of moving mountains. Or capturing the essence of immortality, same thing.

Using gloves, they carefully examined the manuscript to find the blood spot. Oddly enough, it was in the shape of a smudged thumbprint, oblong and circular. Baclus began to gently tear the page from the manuscript, but Cafold stopped him.

"Do we even have the proper solutions on hand?" he asked.

Baclus yanked his gloves off. "I doubt it. And I didn't think of it yesterday since we were ill equipped with even the basics." He rummaged through their meager supplies.

"Would be nice if our scientific study had been scientifically planned," Cafold said.

"Tell me about it." Baclus sighed. "I'll go find Draevik and tell him what else we need." He stalked out of the room.

Alone now, Cafold decided to take a closer look at what he considered the most interesting aspect of the whole study: the substance on the cover. It was odd. He likened it to an oozing radiance. Liquid feeling to the touch, soft, squishy in a barely there kind of way; handling it was like trying to touch light itself. Or some in between medium. Yet light needed to have a source and liquid needed to be contained.

The substance was very mysterious, and it perplexed him that a bit of dried blood was hogging the spotlight, even though there was the slight potential to examine DNA. This odd design though, who knew what it truly was.

And why should he waste time with Baclus away? He slowly closed the manuscript and loaded it onto a large microscope. Then he centered the design beneath the lens and hunched to look through the eyepiece. Light flashed, blinding him, and he staggered backwards. The microscope slid toward him.

Cafold's eyes refocused, confirming he was not blind, and that he had better save the equipment which balanced precariously at the edge of the table. He rushed forward to scoot it back to safety.

He had never been nearly blinded by looking into a microscope. Disoriented, he verified he was still the only person in the room. Had anyone witnessed the incident, Cafold's skittish reaction would have reeked of inexperience. A mark of being in transition for sure.

He leaned forward cautiously now to get another look, squinting because of what had happened prior, or in this case, what he saw but didn't see with his own eyes. It was no fluke as far as he could tell, but there had been lots of strange things happening lately. Another flash of brightness endangered his pupils, this time controlled by him, for he merely peeked before withdrawing.

One more time to eliminate any doubts. He adjusted the magnification to the lowest setting and peered through the eyepiece again. Still, a blinding brightness in return. Cafold backed away and cupped his chin in contemplation. If only Hegliod were here.

It was obvious that whoever, or more disturbingly, whatever, had created the substance on the cover, did not want it being studied. The relic had been designed in defiance of such a thing. Which meant Draevik could be correct. Immortality properties might be present. But would he accept that the relic was not intended to be studied? Or would they have to destroy the entire thing in hopes of getting a glimmer of what they were searching for?

Being honest about what had happened would move the process along faster; Draevik would have them doing more extractions, cutting it into pieces, in no time. Lying could prolong that, though Draevik would only be easy to dupe on a temporary basis. Baclus, not so much. He could tell the former the examinations were in progress. The latter would want to see for himself.

How far was he willing to go to prevent its destruction? How far would he need to go? Baclus was only slightly interested and had expressed little hope they'd discover anything. The blood was old. They had discussed this truth earlier. Could he bribe Baclus? Or would he have to do something more conniving? At least conniving for him, someone who felt bad when his studies harmed an insect. Murder was out of the question, not even a potential solution. He shivered that the stray thought had come to him at all.

Suddenly Hegliod's voice rang into his head. *You'll do what you can to control the situation.*

Cafold had faith in that voice. And so he would.

❧

Ceera paced her room again. The small space didn't allow for much of it, but her anxiety would not allow her to be still. She hadn't slept the night before. After what had happened, it'd seemed impossible.

The so-called dream therapy machine had been temporarily removed from her room so they could analyze what it had recorded during the short time she'd undergone treatment. They'd questioned her on what had prompted her to wake up, but she'd told them nothing. Let them figure it out by themselves. The dream woman's ability to counter the machine's effects puzzled her in a way that was both unsettling and comforting. She could only attribute it to her dreams being important, though this truth offered her no favors in the real world.

She'd been scolded for defacing the machine and told a different machine would cure her disobedience. She was scheduled to meet with it later that afternoon. She hadn't the heart to ponder what that would entail, but assumed these unnamed machines were the reason for the sounds of distress coming from behind closed doors. And most definitely explained what had happened to Garia.

At any rate, if this new machine didn't finish doing the job, she would end up crazy from all her worrying. *As if to* prove her own point, she dragged her chair to the window— too small to fit a body through—and stood atop the chair. She wrote the word *Help* in the condensation, watched it disappear, and wrote more pleading words. *You are in danger.*

Constantly reiterating words of desperation was an endeavor that would also drive her crazy eventually. She sighed and pushed her chair back to its place against the wall.

Even if Dassius wasn't a traitor and he came for her, where would they go? Bliss pacified her for a moment, as she fantasized about them living together, eating together, sleeping together. Could she ask him to give up his life for her safety? She wouldn't dare. It would be too humiliating. No one had ever put their life before hers. It was a silly thing to even contemplate.

A laundry cart rolled past her door, evident by its squeaky wheels and a nurse's loud sigh. She waited to ensure they had skipped her room before pressing her ear against the door. The nurses' voices were faint, but audible.

"We're leaving that one alone for now."

"Why?"

"Didn't you hear what she did?"

"My shift just started. What happened?"

"She pried the metal design from that new dream machine and snuck outside with it during the storm. She was supposed to be undergoing treatment. No one knows how she regained consciousness. They're analyzing the brain wave recording as we speak. Anyway, she's the reason our tree got hit by lightning. The firemen found the glob of metal when they were hosing down the trunk."

"Shocking! And I was beginning to wonder why they sent her here."

"Don't bother. High Service wants us to keep a closer eye on her."

The discussion faded as the nurses continued down the hall.

Ceera climbed onto her stiff mattress and curled up

beneath the blanket. She wondered what the nurses would say if they knew about the wooden effigies, which must have become unrecognizable during the lightning strike.

The rain continued outside, each drop poking holes in her confidence, but she refused to believe the Archaics would ignore her. They were supreme beings after all. And not for much longer if they didn't comply. But had her message been clear? Or would they just decide, like the nurses, that she was crazy too?

❧

Cafold's concentration broke when Baclus returned to their laboratory. He had just developed a rough plan to stall his fellow scientist from proceeding with the study, but Baclus's confident demeanor did not seem vulnerable to excuses. Besides that, he looked annoyed.

"You won't believe this," Baclus said. "Draevik asked us to wait while he has a guard retrieve the solvent liquid. I don't know if he thinks he's being helpful or if he doesn't think we'll be quick enough."

"How insulting," Cafold agreed, in contrast to the relief he secretly felt.

"He suggested we take a break while we wait. We've just arrived for planet's sake."

"I'll go for a walk," Cafold said, "since I'm not hungry."

"It's storming again." Baclus placed his knuckles on the table, as if attempting to calm his agitation.

Rain seemed a petty obstacle in the grand scheme of things. "A little rain doesn't bother me," Cafold replied nervously.

"I'll go to the cafeteria and stare at the food. And to think I could be in my own laboratory, doing something I'm actually interested in." Baclus raised his head. "Something with a realistic outcome."

Cafold had the power to ease Baclus's frustrations. Revealing what had happened when he'd attempted to study the relic's cover would spur Baclus into a curious frenzy. But this, he was trying to avoid.

Instead he replied, "I'm with you."

Baclus straightened. "Let's get out of here."

They exited the room together and headed toward the elevator.

No need to tell Baclus where he really planned to go.

❧

The Archaics rode in on the tail end of the storm, when the wind and rain had tapered down enough for Semions to feel safe walking the orbits again. Those dodging the last remaining drops weren't the least bit pleased when the weather took a turn for the worse. The area around the Aurora suffered the most.

Heat flared up, amid a soft buzzing sound, causing everyone in the vicinity to break into a mysterious sweat. Lightning struck, depositing a fiery-haired apparition with soot highlighting her eyes and cheeks. She left no sparks in the grass, having kept them all to herself. Her dress was rubbery and coal-black with accents of red. Colorful stone rings decorated her fingers. Her gaze burned through anyone who glanced her way.

At the opposite side of the Aurora, a torrential downpour liquefied the dirt. The viscous mud oozed onto the normally well-cleaned orbits, until it reached the feet of a man with a timeless face, rounded muscles, and hair that alternated brown and gray. Or had the mud formed the man? The incident was highly debated after by the bystanders.

Rain fell like a glistening curtain in a different area, leaving behind a towering goddess with wavy, yellow hair. Her skin glistened as if it were moisturized by a product that captured the beauty of sun shining on water. Her gown flowed around her like gentle waves upon the shore. A few streaks from the puddle rushed past her feet, disappearing into a small grove of trees.

The wind careened in across the orbit, and when it died down, a frail, wispy-haired man trembled in its place. Despite the oddness he evoked, for leftover air still swarmed lightly around him, many were surprised he had not been knocked down by the dangerous gust that had blown past. Or had the wind carried him there? Who knew?

The four demi-gods gained their bearings by brushing themselves off and patting themselves dry, or perhaps rubbing things in. The passersby, fascinated, kept on their way for reasons they could not verbalize. Though the Archaics were a sight to be seen, there was something intimidating about them. Especially when they all started marching toward the Aurora at once, ignoring the travel pods whizzing by in their paths.

They met on the front lawn, unsurprised by each other's presence.

"That building can sure block the wind," Atmos said, motioning to the Aurora.

"Stone is still vulnerable," Baric replied solemnly, "over time."

"Not much isn't," Atmos agreed. "But I'd rather not stand here and prove it. Shall we venture inside?"

Luma sniffed. "If we must resort to politeness, then yes." She smoothed the soot on her cheekbones.

"Let me get the door," Atmos said.

Wind busted the door open, causing it to hang loosely off its hinges.

"Thank you, Atmos," Oc~ea said as she moved smoothly through the doorway. "So thoughtful of you."

The others followed her inside.

The frightened guard standing in the entryway said, "One moment please," before hurrying away.

The Archaics, sensing his urgent intentions, showed their appreciation by waiting. Before long, he and several other guards returned. With the utmost politeness, the guards ushered the Archaics into a large meeting room and motioned to the chairs.

"High Service has been notified and will arrive shortly. Can I get you anything?" the main guard asked.

The Archaics looked at each other.

"You?" Luma blurted out, causing everyone who was not a divine being to jump in surprise. "What could you possibly bring us that we desire?" She threw her head back and laughed.

The guard shrank away from her.

"No need to be rude, Luma," Oc~ea said softly. Then to the guard she said, "If you would be so kind as to light that candle over there, she may find it calming."

The guard rushed to light the candle. Luma's laughter died as she watched the flame, but the glint in her eyes stayed vibrant.

"Could you bring the officials something to drink?" Oc~ea continued. "I believe Semions normally have water nearby during meetings. So it has told me."

The guard nodded vigorously. "I can bring some."

"And could you crack a window?" Atmos asked.

The guard rushed over and opened a large oval window. A light breeze streamed in and Atmos sighed happily.

"Thank you," he replied. "I was getting stuffy."

"Anything else," the guard asked Baric, "before I go get the water?"

Baric said nothing for an uncomfortable length of time, at least it was uncomfortable to the guard.

He cleared his throat nervously and again asked, "Anything else?"

"That plant," Baric finally said, pointing to a drooping philodendron in the corner of the room, "needs sun."

The guard rushed over to the plant, hoisted it up, and set it closer to the window.

"No, not there," Baric commanded.

The guard whipped his head around, still bent over the plant.

"Over just a bit." Baric gestured to indicate where.

The guard obeyed and looked again at Baric, who said nothing more. He then nodded, apparently to himself, and scurried out the door.

⁂

The Archaics together in a room was like a paradox of sensations, contradictory and complementary all at once. To say High Service was overwhelmed was an understatement.

Though Oc~ea sat with calm complacency, the green in her eyes swirled forcefully around her pupils, threatening to erupt into a hurricane of emotions. Atmos's smile did not detract from his cool demeanor and frosty gaze. Baric exuded a crushing longevity, minimizing all who gazed upon him. Luma's face held such a calculated smugness that eyes glossed quickly over her. She drummed her blood red nails on the table.

"What can we help you with?" a bewildered Draevik finally spoke.

"Where is she?" Luma demanded.

The candle flickered nearby, though the breeze from the window had blown out the flame minutes after the guard had opened it.

Draevik narrowed his eyes. "Where is who?"

"The female who called us here," Luma said. "She threatened us."

"Warned is a better word," Baric said, his voice filling the room.

"I have no idea who you're talking about," Draevik said.

"She visited us recently. And just last night I felt her presence coursing through the water." Oc~ea's voice was tranquil as she reminisced. "Such a way with it she had."

"Are you referring to Ceera Kestlyn?" Hetia asked.

"If that is her name, then yes," Oc~ea responded.

"Oh her," Draevik said dryly. "She's locked away."

"She said we were in danger," Oc~ea said.

"We did not feel her interpretation of the relic regarding you was correct, for we are a scientific culture, not one that patronizes fairy tales and myths."

"Do I look like a fairy tale to you?" Luma tensed and stood, anger radiating off her face. "Don't make me show you what I really am."

None of the officials dared move.

"Calm yourself, Luma. Perhaps High Service just needs to be reminded of our importance," Atmos said slyly.

"No one is undermining your importance," Draevik

said. "The problem comes from the source. The girl is unreliable, claiming her dreams speak to her. How are we to take such a thing seriously?"

"Bring her to us. Let us decide." Baric's command shook the cups on the table.

"Of course," Draevik conceded, then turned to a guard. "Can you go fetch her?"

"Yes, sir," the guard replied, feeling a push from the empty air on his way out the door.

Chapter Fifteen

CEERA WAS IN bed staring at the ceiling when she heard loud voices in the hall. Thinking another patient was acting up again, she did her best to ignore it. But the voices grew closer and soon her door was thrust open by one of High Service's guards.

He ordered her out of bed and whisked her from the room still wearing her white gown. Had her attempts at calling the Archaics worked? The nurses stared knowingly as she passed. Maybe not.

"What's going on? Where are you taking me?" she asked as she padded alongside him on bare feet.

The guard would not respond, his expression plain and unyielding. Sweat dripped down his face. His quick, efficient steps suggested something important awaited them. He led her briskly out the front door, ignoring the nurse at the desk who stood as they passed, and helped her into an illegally parked travel pod before climbing in behind her. The driver sped away as soon as the door shut, zipping around the orbits at high speed. Ceera focused on her breathing as the scenery blurred past the oval window.

The travel pod stopped abruptly in front of the Aurora. She hid her face behind her hands as the guard dragged her up the walkway, through the entrance, and into a room she was familiar with: the large room where community meetings were held. He then gave her a slight push forward and remained by the door.

It was immediately apparent that no one from the public was involved. Instead, four strong presences drew her attention, and she waded hesitantly into the midst of their scrutiny. The Archaics gazed at her in curious fascination. She stared back, taken aback by how fully they consumed the room.

"Here she is," Draevik said, his pleased tone contrasting sharply with his vexed expression.

"You," Luma stated accusingly. "It was you who called us here."

Ceera crept farther into the room, feeling silly in her gown. "Yes," she replied, determined not to let Luma crush her confidence. "It was me."

"Why did you call us?" Oc~ea's calm demeanor strengthened her resolve.

"I found an ancient manuscript, a relic, in the forest Dassius and I visited you about. It says—"

Draevik's sharp glare gave her pause. Baric noticed as well. The tabletop shook, causing Draevik's cup to tip over and splash him with liquid. He yelped in surprise, and with his attention now diverted, she flashed Baric a grateful smile and continued.

"It says if the relic is not returned to its rightful spot inside a cave, by me, the one bearing the mark, then all will revert to how it was before, and I will die."

The Archaics stared at her contemplatively. Draevik scowled at the stain in his lap. The rest of High Service shifted nervously in their seats.

"All will revert to how it was before. Before what?" Atmos prodded.

"Before the relic's creation."

"Now tell me," Luma said, "why this was important enough to pull me away from my volcanic eruption."

"An eruption? Go check and see if we were aware of that," Draevik hissed at a male official, who scurried from the room.

"Your death," said Baric, "is not our concern if it must happen."

Oc~ea raised an eyebrow at him. Luma nodded voraciously.

Baric's words demanded careful consideration. Something told her he knew what she was about to say.

Atmos settled back in his chair with a grin. "Please finish telling us the story. And do make it enjoyable."

"Stories are for children," Draevik grumbled.

"Stories are what made the world," Baric replied.

"Go on," Oc~ea urged gently.

"The relic contains a story that claims four babies were sacrificed during the planet's collapse, the one you all mentioned in our previous encounter."

"You mean the planet's redemption," Luma interceded. "Did you learn nothing from your visit?"

"Pardon," Ceera said nervously. "During the planet's redemption."

"Let her continue," Atmos said. "We haven't got to the good part yet, I gather."

"The babies would be taught the ways of the planet," Ceera continued, "would be considered servants to it, and keep everything balanced to ensure the world would revolve smoothly for eternity. It insinuated the babies would become you."

She hoped she sounded genuine. If they didn't believe her, she was doomed. And so were they.

"That can't be," Luma protested. "We have always been."

"Not according to what I read." Ceera felt herself shrinking beneath Luma's scrutiny.

Draevik perked up in his seat.

"Liar," Luma spat out. "I cannot patronize such a ridiculous allegation."

"Why not?" Baric asked, the corners of his mouth twitching upward.

"Because it implies that we were once mortal, like them." She shuddered. "How revolting."

"Such an interesting story," Atmos said, leaning toward her. "Is there more?"

"Yes," Ceera continued, "if you go back to how you were before…" her words trailed away.

"Mortal we would become again," Baric said gravely.

"And our powers would slip away." Oc~ea's words rippled around the room.

"I would rather burn myself at a stake than suffer such a thing," Luma said defiantly.

"Wouldn't the flames enliven you?" Atmos asked, rubbing his hands together in glee. A tiny torrent of air spun between his palms.

"And before my fall from divinity, fire and I would destroy the world."

Draevik stirred in his seat. "Now see here—"

"There's a deadline," Ceera interrupted. It was time to lay it on thick before Luma's fantasies became reality. The

Archaic was already eyeing one of the pillars holding up the ceiling.

Luma froze, for some reason a disturbing thing to witness. "What deadline?"

"We only have a short time to give the relic back once it's been removed from the roots."

"How long?" Atmos asked, his eyes twinkling in excitement.

"I don't know for sure," Ceera admitted. "But I did have a dream about it."

"Dreams, dreams, and more dreams." Draevik threw his hands into the air. "If the truth is not apparent, let's ask her dreams. If only all of us could have such dreams."

Atmos gazed at him coolly. Oc~ea calmly grabbed Luma's arm, evading a reaction yet to be seen. Baric sat eerily still.

A female official stood. "Let's not forget," she addressed the officials, "that so far her dreams have been correct."

"An annoying inconvenience," Draevik muttered. His eyes flashed malice at the younger official, for once not directed at Ceera.

"Tell us about the dream," Atmos urged.

"It showed the relic being removed from the roots, then the woman who placed it there traced her fingers around the growth rings on a stump."

"How far did her fingers go?" Baric asked.

"She traced them for a bit, probably waiting for me to understand she was signifying time. Once I did, her fingers only traveled a short distance between two rings."

"How far?" Baric asked.

Ceera pinched the air between her thumb and forefinger. "Barely between one ring to the next."

"So not very far at all," Baric responded. "Which means the allotted time is small."

"And like I said, it's already been several months."

"You will let her go at once," Luma snapped at Draevik, who instantly broke into a sweat.

"We will do what we see fit," he responded, though his voice was weak and tentative. "We cannot allow her to leave with the relic based on speculation from her dreams."

"What she says is true. All of it," Baric said. "The planet shares its secrets with me."

"You knew," Luma said, her words dripping venom.

Baric's expression remained indifferent.

"Nobody knows anything," Draevik insisted.

"We're clearly at an impasse," Atmos said, a clever gleam in his eyes. "Don't forget, we haven't lost our powers yet." He released the tiny whirlwind from between his palms.

The air circulation in the room increased. Papers flew up from the table and blew around.

Luma winked at Atmos. "I see you're warming up to my earlier suggestion."

"Though some of us may come off as soft," Oc~ea said, "it is more a matter of going with the flow. You do boat often, correct?" Her question overflowed with meaning.

"How did you know?" Draevik asked in shock.

"And on a less interesting level," Oc~ea continued, "bathe daily?"

Draevik fiddled with his collar.

"There are no boundaries to what we can do," Baric said. "And don't forget the planet and I form a deep bond, at least for now. My powers against you are limitless."

Draevik shrank back from the threat.

"I'll just set him on fire right now," Luma said, focusing on the candle near Draevik. Its flames grew larger until he blew it out and pushed it away.

He turned to Ceera. "Go," he ordered. "Go now."

She looked at him quizzically. "Where?"

"On your precious journey. Go back to your dwelling and collect your things. Change out of that ridiculous gown. The relic will be ready upon your return."

"I'm to go alone?" Unease stirred within her.

"We can assign someone to join you," Risa said.

"Please let it be Dassius," Ceera pleaded, feeling brave with the backing of the Archaics. "He already knows a bit about what's going on."

"Great idea, I concur," Draevik said with a glint in his eyes that seemed out of place.

Ceera was relieved, despite suspecting she was missing the significance of something. "We'll need the map. And a travel pack containing several weeks' worth of food and drink. I'll go at once." She turned then hesitated. "Can I be escorted by travel pod? It will be faster plus less embarrassing." She motioned to her gown.

"Yes, have it your way." Draevik waved her away dismissively. "Guard?"

The guard took a tentative step forward, no longer threatening in the presence of the Archaics.

"Escort her home. Wait outside with the travel pod and bring her back as soon as possible."

The guard nodded and stood ready by the door.

"Will you still be here when I return?" she asked the Archaics.

"Oh yes," Atmos said with a grin. "I have a feeling we will remain in Semadon for quite some time."

Ceera smiled with gratitude and walked out of the room.

❧

"How long will you be?" the guard asked once they reached her dwelling.

"Fifteen minutes?" She only needed to change and pack a bag.

"The faster the better," he replied. "I'll wait out here."

Ceera hurried inside. Just as she slipped on a different set of clothes, there was a soft rapping on her back door. She rushed through her kitchen to answer.

Litha stood there, eyes wide and cheeks flushed.

"Litha!" she exclaimed. "I don't know if you're allowed here."

"I took the route behind the dwellings. I don't think he saw me. Can I come in?"

"Yes," she said, stepping aside so Litha could enter, "but this has to be quick. I have less than ten minutes. Follow me while I get ready."

"I saw you arrive as I was leaving my dwelling. What's going on? Are you in danger?"

"Not anymore," Ceera responded.

"What is *that*?" Litha asked, pointing to the white gown Ceera had carelessly left on the floor.

"I was committed," she replied, stuffing clothes into her bag.

Litha's mouth opened in horror. "Why?"

"I've since been released. Dassius and I are going on another journey. I'd explain but it's long and complicated, and I don't have time."

Litha followed her to the bathroom. She grabbed some personal hygiene items.

"How terrible. I'm so sorry. I hope you're successful on

your journey. Will the global update clue us in like last time? It didn't reveal much, but at least I knew you were safe."

"I sincerely doubt it."

"I'll have Sidorn find stuff out for me. I'll be so worried."

Ceera whirled around. "Be careful with him. I don't think he's trustworthy."

"Why?" Litha asked, crestfallen.

"He bothers me. I'm not sure how to explain."

"I think he's charming," Litha replied.

"Almost too charming. Don't forget he's an agent of High Service."

"So is Dassius," Litha reminded her.

"Yes," Ceera said. "It did take me time to trust him. But you don't know Sidorn very well. If you ask him questions about secret matters, he may turn you in."

"He wouldn't do that," Litha protested. "Sidorn has proven to be a gentleman. He won't betray me."

"I hope you're right."

Ceera looked at her friend, so innocent and vulnerable like she herself had been just months ago. She should have confided in Litha about her problems. Unfortunately, it was too late now.

"I have to go," Ceera said. "I'll let you out the back door. Stay hidden until we drive away."

"I will. Be careful!"

They hugged tightly, and Ceera held on a little longer than usual, regretful she didn't have more time with her friend.

⌘

Ceera ignored her desire to throw herself in Dassius's arms when she saw him back at the Aurora. He caught her

152

eye when she entered the room, but then his expression darkened. Why was he angry at her? Did he not want to accompany her? Maybe he'd turned her in after all, which would explain why Draevik allowed him to accompany her, since his betrayal would sabotage her happiness. She hated how her own thoughts had turned against her.

The Archaics stood around Draevik while he briefed Dassius, towering over him like god figures. His worried expression satisfied her. It was time for him to squirm for once. He had to do what was right or the Archaics would kill him. It seemed a fair predicament for him to be in.

The female official who'd stood up for her at the meeting walked over. "We found Dassius. He was already getting ready when we called."

Of course he was. "He looks angry."

"A few days ago, Draevik lied to him about your whereabouts."

Draevik continued briefing Dassius while the Archaics observed. Luma eyed Dassius seductively, but he ignored her.

"Why does Draevik have such an influence over High Service?" Ceera dared ask. "I have never known it to function this way before."

The official gazed at her appraisingly. "These are tumultuous times. Draevik's past has caused many to revere him more than he deserves."

Ceera was surprised at the official's tone. "You're Hetia, the one who left me a voicemail before Draevik had me committed. Why?"

"I was hoping to give you a chance to speak before High Service. *All* of High Service."

Ceera smiled. "Thank you for that. I regret not seeing it in time."

"It's a shame it didn't work out; however, thanks to your clever thinking you're again in charge of your destiny."

Ceera was appreciative of this official for giving her hope for the system, despite Draevik's tarnishing of it. "If I don't return the relic in time, and the mystics cease existing, who will choose the next officials? Will High Service be forced to dismantle?"

"Good question," Hetia said, "but I wouldn't worry about it if I were you."

"Why not?"

"You wouldn't be here to witness it."

Ceera took a shallow breath.

"You've risen to the occasion before. Have confidence in yourself." Hetia patted her arm before stepping away.

Draevik waved her over.

"Dassius has been briefed about the journey," he said as she approached. "We even had time to go over the map."

Dassius nodded slightly, an expert at acting indifferent.

"I have some exciting new equipment to share." Draevik opened his palm. "This is a roamer. It's similar to a communication orb, except it can be used remotely."

The flat device was curved and black with a small circular metal grid on both sides.

Draevik held it up to his ear. "We've done testing and it works well above ground. We're eager to see if it maintains contact below."

Dassius took the device. He pushed a button and it beeped accordingly, then he pressed it to his ear. "What powers it?" he asked.

"A heat-core modified for long-term use," Draevik responded. "Which is why underground testing will be useful. Please keep in contact for as long as the device allows."

His words sent a trigger of alarm up Ceera's spine. Devices didn't allow things. They either worked or they didn't.

"Now, on to your route," Draevik said. "Dassius thinks he has determined where it begins."

"Oh?" Ceera was surprised. "Where?"

"It begins in the forest. The one you've just returned from."

Ceera reeled in shock. Dassius grabbed her arm to steady her.

"Don't worry," Luma said smugly. "I left some of it there for you."

Chapter Sixteen

"HOW LONG DO you think this venture will take?" Draevik asked, once Ceera pretended to recover from her shock.

Inside she was still panicking, but having experience lately in the art of deception, she kept it carefully contained. Even though she and Dassius had safely returned, hiking the forest had been a terrifying venture. It had possessed a mind of its own, one that contradicted itself, simultaneously helping her find the relic and keeping her from the relic. Whether this had to do with Rebial's presence, she did not know.

As for Rebial, he should be dead, which both saddened and relieved her. Yet if anything, she'd learned from the relic that things were not always as they seemed.

"I'm guessing a few weeks," Dassius said. "Shorter if Ceera could stay awake as long as me."

"I could probably skip sleep tonight," she said hesitantly.

But her offering seemed to perturb Draevik, who turned to Dassius and said, "Make sure she's well rested so she can carry out the task."

"Of course."

"Don't push yourself," Draevik said to her. "You must keep up your strength."

Ceera nodded, once again inclined to think Draevik's

concern was disingenuous. Especially since he had recently ordered the tampering of her dreams.

"I'm on your side now," he added, placing his hand on her arm.

Dassius's posture stiffened, but he said nothing. Hetia claimed he was mad at Draevik, but he also seemed mad at her. What had she done? He couldn't possibly be upset she'd inadvertently stood him up.

A guard holding a familiar bundle rushed up.

"You can pass that to Ceera," Draevik said.

When the guard handed her the relic, an uncertainty came over her, perhaps derived from Draevik's satisfied expression.

"What's wrong?" Dassius asked.

"I don't think this is the same rope binding it when I found it," she said. "Not that it probably matters, but—"

"Open it and see what's bothering you," Dassius said.

"Wasting time," Draevik said, "when you could be on your way."

"Better to waste time now than waste away later," Baric replied.

Remembering another study had been in progress, Ceera unwound the rope. She opened the manuscript and knew immediately what was off. "A page is missing," she said coldly.

Everyone turned toward Draevik in an unfriendly manner. He had the grace to blush. "Let me retrieve that from my scientists," he said before scurrying off.

Ceera strapped the relic to her chest. She wore the same outfit from her previous venture into the woods, as it seemed most suitable for travel. Dassius had chosen his same outfit as well. Besides the unspoken tension between the two of them, the Archaics also seemed to be harboring volatility amongst themselves. She had never experienced a silence so uncomfortable.

Draevik returned shortly with the missing page, along with Risa and Karnen. He handed the page to Ceera, and she placed it gently in the book. The Archaics continued to glare threateningly at Draevik, but he seemed distracted.

"Risa and Karnen will accompany you to the cylinder," Draevik said. "I have some unexpected business to attend to."

He watched while they set off together but was already gone when Ceera glanced back seconds later. The Archaics followed them out of the Aurora and down the walkway. There was no fanfare this time, though the group received many curious looks from passing Semions.

When they reached the main cylinder, Karnen opened its door. Ceera and Dassius stepped inside.

Baric placed his weathered hand on the door's edge before Karnen could shut it. "Pay attention to your surroundings," he said. "The map will show you the way, but the stones speak and will guide you to understanding."

Ceera let his words sink in, though their meaning was unclear.

"Anything else?" Karnen asked. When the other Archaics didn't respond, he said, "Okay, be on your way then. And be careful." He shut the door.

Finally alone with Dassius, Ceera opened her mouth to speak, but he held up a hand to silence her. Then he turned abruptly to press buttons. When the coordinates flashed, he reached for her, pressing his lips to hers as the transfer began. They faded into the atmosphere, undulating through it as one.

When she regained consciousness, Dassius had already pulled away. He'd always transferred better than her and had probably felt it inappropriate to continue kissing her motionless body once they had materialized. Thank the planet for that.

"I can't believe you didn't tell me," he said.

"Tell you what?" she murmured, still feeling faint.

"That your life was in danger."

"I told you something was wrong," she said, standing slowly to prevent a headache from forming. Anger surfaced instead. "Besides, what was that? How dare you kiss me during a transfer? Who knows what could have happened."

"I knew nothing would happen," Dassius said simply, with less conceit than he would have expressed a few months back.

Still, his recklessness upset her. Clairvoyant or not, it was no excuse to take risks.

"There was no need—"

"Don't change the subject. The AT system has been working fine," Dassius responded. "You told me High Service was upset with you. Not that you'd die if they didn't believe you."

Surprised at his outrage, Ceera bantered back. "Does it matter? They had me committed. You never would have seen me again anyway."

"No." Dassius shook his head firmly. "That wasn't going to happen."

"How can you be sure?" She didn't believe High Service had any intention of ever releasing her.

"I would have come for you," he said, his expression now serious.

"And get yourself killed? Then I'd be in the same situation you're complaining of."

"If I'm going to die, it won't be because of order patrols," he said fiercely, seizing her in a tight embrace. She returned it with the same passion. Pressed against the cylinder, he kissed her, a hungry kiss that took her breath away. He gently pulled away.

"It's okay," she replied softly. "We're here together now."

"I still can't believe they committed you." He swung the cylinder door open. "I should have seen it coming, but…it won't happen again."

They stepped out and into the lush green scenery that had ingrained itself so well into her memory. The forest loomed in the distance, though she wasn't ready to give it her full attention yet.

"What can you do if they decide to commit me again?" she asked. "Ever since I admitted to the dreams and found the relic, I've been their pawn. Just like Falken said before Rebial killed him, except he had the game leader wrong."

"Draevik's causing tension within the ranks," Dassius said quietly, as if he feared someone was listening. "I sensed it today, and not everyone's on his side. Anything can happen."

Ceera shivered. "I'd rather civilization not crumble before our eyes."

⌬

Draevik scurried down the winding, rickety staircase, his panic increasing as he descended. Life had taken a disturbing turn. He berated himself for underestimating Ceera. She took herself way more seriously than anyone else, something he decided to never overlook again. And the Archaics, how would he sabotage her endeavor with the four of them lurking about?

His dim surroundings, though he carried a flashlight, enhanced his desperation. There was only one way to defeat them, and he would soon find out if it was possible.

As he neared the door rimmed in light, his most trusted guard at his heels, he was thankful neither the public nor the Archaics were aware that such a place existed. It housed a project he'd been eager to implement for some time and had finally gotten the other officials' agreement a few months back. Perhaps because they'd had reason to fear for their lives when the protesting had started. You never knew when you may need to use force to tame an unruly crowd.

He hadn't recruited the best minds to begin this project. Weapon creation, though frowned upon, was not complicated. Destroying people was much easier than improving them. He had pondered this irony much in his earlier years, before accepting the former was a more superior way of accomplishing things.

When it came to implementing change within the masses, he'd long ago given up that there was both a humane and efficient way of doing so. The mind always took the path of least resistance, whether it be the minds of the people or their rulers. And to a ruler, what benefit was there to being civil when the desired result could be achieved at a faster pace? Pride and integrity were overrated and slowed progress.

Even Jesra had claimed pride to be an emotion not worth pursuing. And he wanted to abide by Jesra's way of thought.

"Here at last," he said to his guard, as he knocked on the battered, metal door.

The door opened, exposing a sallow faced middle-aged man with baggy eyes. "Good day, Draevik," he said, the corner of his mouth quirking upward.

"How's the project coming, Wyman?" Draevik and the guard stepped into the musty room. Sketches of equipment hung on the walls; gadgets covered a wide desk.

"Very good. The kinks we've discussed have been resolved. We're now beginning production and have a small set of weaponry ready for choosing."

"Ready for using?" Draevik asked hopefully.

"I said choosing. We need your approval before we can finish production of the pieces."

"Of course you do," Draevik said, wishing for once that someone besides himself had some forethought, even if it meant ignoring the rules. "How long will it take to finish them?"

"A few days at least," Wyman responded, an unpleasant smile grazing his lips.

"That's unfortunate," Draevik said. "We could have used these weapons sooner than later."

"If I hadn't been sidetracked by those tests you had me run on the relic—"

"Can you put a rush on production once I decide?" Draevik was in no mood for Wyman's smug accusations.

"Of course. Come this way."

Draevik followed Wyman deeper into the weaponry unit, passing through darkened halls. "Tell me," he said, "do you have anything that will be useful against those of a divine status?"

Wyman inclined his head. "Whom do you mean?"

"The Archaics are here, causing problems, and I was hoping—"

"It's doubtful," Wyman interjected, "that any of our weapons could harm an Archaic."

"And why is that?"

"Because the Archaics are immortal."

A slap in the face, ironic even, but it was what he'd been expecting. "And you're sure you can't have anything ready within a few hours?"

"Quite," Wyman responded without hesitation.

Draevik considered the setback. It meant he would have to recruit someone more powerful than a regular guard, someone who would be a match for Dassius Rucien. The solution came with a slight risk.

He turned to his guard. "This is as far as you go."

The guard stopped obediently but raised an eyebrow.

"I need you to set up a meeting for me."

❧

As they neared the forest's outskirts, Ceera's sense of foreboding returned.

"So where is this cave?" she asked, dread mingling with her curiosity.

"Near where you found the relic."

Their entrance into the cool, dark woods seemed to magnify his statement.

"Are you sure?"

"Would we be here if I wasn't sure?"

If he didn't have a point, she would have found his cockiness annoying.

The trees seemed less twisted and gnarled than before. They emitted a healthy vibe that the forest lacked on her first visit. Though still, out of the corner of her eyes, she saw traces of movement. Small animals or insects could be causing the subtle visual, but she was taking no chances.

"Wait," she said, coming to a standstill.

She retraced their steps and peered through the vegetation dangling from the trees framing their entrance. The cylinder was still visible in the distance.

"Not like last time," she said. "We can still leave."

"Much more pleasant in here without Rebial skulking about."

Ceera said nothing, for she was still conflicted about Rebial. He had tried to kill her yet had allowed her to leave with the relic after recognizing her birthmark. Now she knew the relic wasn't really his as he'd claimed, unless she'd misunderstood something, which was possible. She shouldn't be running into him again, he should be dead, yet…

"We may be following him down into the ravine," Dassius said, interrupting her thoughts.

She hugged the relic to her chest. "How do you know?"

Taking the relic where Rebial had gone vastly confused things. It was illogical, and she was glad Dassius had not mentioned this to High Service.

"Because when he descended, he said he was going to face the end. It just seems fitting."

"But we thought that meant he was going to die." Rebial no longer being in possession of the relic would support this.

"I still do," Dassius replied. "But his death seems to imply the end of something. And you need to finish something. I told you how I feel about coincidences, right?"

Ceera didn't want to get into that discussion. "But we have two different agendas. You and I are following a map he no longer has access to, so we can return the relic. Who knows where he went."

"Didn't he tell you the woman left the relic so it would bring him to her? He must have memorized the map."

"But she didn't have the relic, so she should be dead," Ceera said tentatively, and though she believed it, she also wondered how this woman could reside inside her dreams. "And if the map leads to her, then she could have just returned the relic herself."

"Does that mean she also has the mark?" Dassius asked.

"I assumed she did after Rebial mistook me for her, but the truth is, I don't know," Ceera admitted.

Something didn't make sense, but she couldn't pinpoint

what it was. Plus, it did her no good to continue keeping what she knew from Dassius. It could be dangerous even. So she told him.

§

Hetia was shuffling papers at her desk, unable to stifle her giddiness. She had felt especially light spirited after watching the Archaics bully Draevik. It was most fitting. And with Draevik knocked from his pedestal, maybe she'd be so lucky that he would stay there. The sun shining through the window complemented her mood, and she hummed softly as she stared blankly at her paperwork.

Fresdin swiftly came in and shut the door. "You won't believe what I've just heard."

"You do know shutting the door will cause our peers to whisper about what we're doing in here," Hetia joked.

Annoyance edged his features. "I don't think you'd be joking right now if you knew."

Hetia's cheerfulness dissipated as she realized then how weighed down he looked. His expression in sharp contrast to the sun's rays, he was a male version of her mirror image earlier today. "Sorry, please relay it."

"I overhead Draevik tell Risa and Karnen that he plans to send a crew down after Ceera and Dassius in an attempt to overtake them."

Hetia's remaining joy crumbled. "How is that possible with Dassius being so skilled?"

"It will be one against many. And he plans to send one of his scientists."

"Whatever for?"

"To keep the relic safe during its return to Semadon," he said.

"Does he not fear the Archaics?" Hetia asked.

"He has fear but no respect. His plan is for the crew to stay in the cave with the relic until the Archaics' powers have faded. His plans for Ceera and Dassius are less clear."

"You see! I told you he was conniving and reckless!" She burned with the knowledge that she had been sitting there wasting precious time, clueless and unsuspecting of how right she continued to be.

"Stop with your arrogance. We don't have much time. Draevik left the Aurora for who knows what reason and will be back shortly."

"Is there a way to warn Dassius through the roamer?"

"Only Draevik has the number."

"What should we do then?" Hetia asked. "Alert the Archaics?"

"No, I fear they'll react in a way that will harm the innocent. Remember Luma's threat? We need to play Draevik's game to stop him. Gather a small crew of our own. And we need to do it quickly."

"But how to rally support without knowing whom we can trust?" she asked.

"Don't forget. While you've been focusing on Draevik, I've had my eyes on everyone else."

"Teacher was right. We fit together perfectly, like a puzzle."

"I have an idea," Fresdin said quietly.

Hetia smiled. "I was hoping you would."

Chapter Seventeen

DASSIUS HAD LISTENED attentively to Ceera's information about the relic. The dream therapy had angered him, though he was intrigued by her resistance to it. Afterward, they'd trekked through the woods in silence. Confiding in him had lifted some of the burden, and she appreciated allowing her thoughts to still, knowing he continued to mull it over. Perhaps when he was ready to talk about it, he'd add insights she'd overlooked.

They headed toward the sound of rushing water and soon stood at the river's edge. Across it was a depressing sight: a fire ravaged forest, thanks to Luma.

"Falken's pathetic canoe is gone," Dassius said.

"It must have floated away," Ceera replied. "Or rotted away."

"You up for wading?" he asked.

"It's not like we have other options."

They stepped into the river and glided through. The current was more peaceful than she remembered. Of course, last time she'd been in this waterway, Rebial had tried to kill her. She didn't have to worry about that anymore.

Dassius held her hand. His firm but gentle grip helped her relax.

"What are you thinking about?" he asked.

"Rebial again. It's hard to think of much else here."

"You could think about us."

"What about us?"

"How glad I am to be the one escorting you."

"Who else would have escorted me?"

"One of my peers. There are five of us. And Sidorn is just as skilled as me."

Uncomfortable at the thought of being alone with Sidorn, she said, "He hardly seems serious enough."

"Sidorn plays the joker when it suits him, but he's also clever. He and I went back and forth during our testing. One day I was on top, the next day him. I'm not sure why they chose me when we were so evenly matched."

"I'm glad they did," she responded. "He rubs me the wrong way."

"We used to be close, but I think it bothered him to be passed up. To make matters worse, we got into a heated argument before I visited my parents. We haven't really restored our friendship yet."

"What kind of argument?"

"I'd rather not say."

"I'm worried Litha may have fallen for him."

"I wouldn't worry. I think Sidorn enjoyed her company."

"That's exactly what worries me," she said. "What if he hurts her?"

"You don't trust men at all, do you?"

"Only you," she said, "and that took a while. You know, life and death experiences may have impacted it. And even sometimes still…"

"What?"

"Negativity taints my logic."

"In what way?" he asked.

"When I was in the institution, I feared you'd betrayed me to High Service."

"I can't believe you'd think that." His hand fell limp.

"Yet I knew I was being unreasonable." She coaxed him to forgive her by squeezing his hand.

"I'm capable of interacting with a female without playing games. I expect Sidorn is the same."

"He hasn't dated much?"

"He dated another Sci-Def member once, but she wasn't his type, so they split. He's more devoted to his discipline than you give him credit for. He wants to make a name for himself."

Ceera let the words sink in, deciding the only thing she could do was wait and see. Upon returning to Semadon, she would know how the relationship between Sidorn and Litha had panned out.

"What about you? Have you dated much?" she asked.

"A little, but no one has interested me like you. I had to completely reorganize my brain once I fell for you."

Ceera laughed. "So did I. In fact, don't take offense, but it's a work-in-progress."

"I don't think I'll like meeting your father," Dassius said.

"Who said you'll meet him?" Ceera asked, surprised by the assertion. "I've barely known him my entire life."

"He'll come into the picture," Dassius said. "I just can't figure out when."

Ceera gave him a curious look but said nothing. After all, she had no idea when she would see her father again either.

"And based on what you told me," Dassius continued, "about the birthmark and dream correlation, I suspect he knows more than he lets on."

She couldn't argue with that, yet if he were keeping anything else from her, she'd have to question his reason for coming back into her life at all.

⁂

Draevik returned to his office and sat restlessly at his desk. It bothered him the weaponry would be unavailable for another few days: a mere scrap of time to someone striving for immortality. Now he would have to test the loyalties of a stranger. His whim of a plan would have to work.

A knock sounded on his door, causing him to straighten in his seat.

"Come in," he called out with more authority than he deserved. Though not everyone had witnessed his ungraceful submission to the Archaics, he still had to bear it himself.

His guard entered and bowed respectfully.

"Did you find out where the Archaics went?" Draevik asked.

"To the CfNL's garden."

"Good, that's far enough away. Did you bring whom I asked?"

"Yes, should I let him in?"

"Please do."

The guard opened the door and gestured inside, exchanging places with the new arrival before leaving the room.

Sidorn made the door frame behind him appear small. He looked around as if he were taking it all in—the room, Draevik, what could be seen outside the window—before venturing a few steps farther inside. Best not to let one from the Sci-Def team ponder for too long.

"Thank you for coming on such short notice." Draevik motioned to a chair.

"I didn't have much of a choice," Sidorn said lightly.

"Do you know what I'm about to propose?"

"Hopefully nothing that will tie us together for life. I'm not one for commitment." Sidorn gave him a mocking grin and took a seat.

Draevik bristled. "Do you think this is a matter of playing games? I am your superior."

"At your command." Sidorn gave an exaggerated salute.

Draevik narrowed his eyes. Perhaps he should try a different approach. "Before I reveal why I called you here, may I ask how it felt playing second fiddle to Dassius Rucien during the Sci-Defense team's last big assignment?"

Sidorn's smile faded, the crinkles around his eyes moving to his forehead. "I wasn't happy about it. He was my friend, but I still wanted it to be me."

"All the fame he acquired could have been yours."

"Yeah"—Sidorn lowered his gaze—"he gained a lot of attention after that."

"And your feeble attempt to help him and Ceera during their time of need. I'm sure you were hoping such a failure wouldn't follow you around forever."

Sidorn's gaze shot back up. "The AT system was down."

"Yes," Draevik said sadly. "Too bad."

Something brewed in Sidorn's eyes, the light in them now gone.

"Yet Dassius got to prove his worth to society and not only that"—Draevik paused—"he was able to have time alone with that scintillating young woman."

Sidorn eyed him in a manner Draevik could not determine and said, "She's interesting."

"Tell me, how has your friendship been since he's returned?"

Sidorn leaned back in his chair. "Sporadic. Not really a friendship. He's been busy. I see him around."

"Like at The Helix the other night?"

"I saw him there."

"Did you plan on meeting him out?"

"Nah." Sidorn placed his hands behind his head. "It was just a coincidence. A possibility that came true." He winked.

"He has surpassed you yet again," Draevik said.

Sidorn's eyes dimmed. He looked away then back again. "How?"

"He's been asked to accompany Ceera on another errand. A fallacious one this time. Have you noticed who's in town?"

"The Archaics. I sensed them. I've never met them, but it's easy to tell."

"Yes, you never did meet them, did you?" Draevik's tone was sympathetic.

Fire burned in Sidorn's eye. "They're here because of this errand."

"Such a sharp mind," Draevik said, "so far put to waste. But don't take offense; you're correct. They bullied us into letting her go."

"Go where? Why?"

"Where an outdated map directs them. They plan to dispose of the relic they worked so hard to collect. Ceera convinced the Archaics it's the best thing for society."

Sidorn was expressionless.

"Although society won't be so thrilled this time. Unless someone has the courage to stop them."

Sidorn nodded his head slowly. "That someone would be me."

Draevik smiled. "I was hoping you would make the connection. It's time for you to replace Dassius as the hero."

"It's always been time," Sidorn said. "I can do whatever you need me to do."

"Very good, because matters could turn dire. He is convinced Ceera will die if he doesn't help her."

"Oh?" Sidorn raised his eyebrows. "Is this true?"

"That remains to be seen. But what if I told you one death could prolong the lives of many?"

"Huh?"

"There's a secret property to the relic, one that hasn't been revealed to the public."

"I gathered that. Otherwise I wouldn't be here."

"The relic contains a property allowing it to persevere longer than scientifically possible. This trait extended to the forest. And a man who resided in it. We cannot allow the relic to be destroyed."

"There was a man?"

"Did Dassius not confide in you?"

Sidorn's eyes narrowed.

"Gone now, but yes there was a man. Some sort of forest dweller who couldn't die. We think his blood is on the relic."

"So you want me to follow them and take the relic back?"

"Yes. But there's more to this task than just that."

"What else?"

"We'll have to wait until the Archaics lose their powers before we openly defy them. Plus, we can't have Dassius coming back and complaining to society about Ceera's misfortune. Do you understand what I mean?"

"You want me to kill him," Sidorn said grimly. "So society can live like this man who couldn't die."

"That's exactly what I'm asking you to do," Draevik responded.

Sidorn's expression was just as blank and indifferent as

Draevik hoped it would be. Then a smile crept on his lips. "I'm really going to enjoy this," he said.

"You have every right to enjoy it, for your actions will enable Semions to enjoy the benefits of immortality. You'll be famous forever. Alive to see it even. A living legend."

"Sounds like the opportunity I've been waiting for."

"I'm glad you see the value in it."

"I was trained to see it that way," Sidorn responded. "I do what's best for society. So they can thank me when it's over."

"And they will. I'm in the process of gathering a crew. You will lead them."

"I'd be glad to. And I promise," Sidorn said, an intense gleam in his eye, "that I'll do what needs to be done."

"Yes," Draevik said, "I can see it in your eyes. Failure is not probable for you anymore."

Chapter Eighteen

CAFOLD AND BACLUS returned to their laboratory to find the solution they'd requested sitting unopened on the table. The manuscript, however, was no longer in the room.

"Where—" Cafold began.

"Obstacles, so many obstacles," Baclus interrupted. "This relic gets harder to study by the minute." He placed the cup he'd brought from the cafeteria on the table and said, "I'll go find Draevik again."

"Hopefully, we don't get blamed for this," Cafold said. "We weren't told to lock it up. And since we have a secret laboratory, why would we?"

Baclus mustered an appreciative smile before stomping into the hall.

Perplexed, but with no time to dwell on the relic's disappearance, Cafold pulled a small vial from his pocket. He poured its contents into Baclus's cup and carefully stirred to dilute the specimen. The stirring was more for his own benefit, calming his thoughts. He'd never had to resort to deviant behavior before. Yet Hegliod had been clear in his directions. And he was the mentor. Cafold had to do what he could to stall the program. And scientists usually stayed home when contracting the flu.

He placed Baclus's cup back in its original spot and turned around. A High Service official stood in the doorway. He nearly jumped several inches at the sight of her.

"I was just—" Cafold paused, trying to come up with a good explanation.

"Quenching your thirst? Are Draevik's rules so strict they deprive one of basic necessities?"

"No." He smiled. "I'm Cafold Brine."

"Hetia, sphere three."

They shook hands.

"Are you here to check on our progress?"

"Yes, and a bit more," Hetia said hesitantly.

This signaled something unusual. High Service officials were normally straightforward. He had seen some unnatural behavior lately, but this felt different.

"Draevik mentioned one of his scientists had expressed reservation in the experiment." She stepped closer. "He also mentioned that Hegliod wasn't pleased with it either."

"Yes," Cafold responded. "That's true."

"I can say with certainty at least two officials share the same reservations."

Hetia was careful not to reveal too much, but Cafold sensed her intent. "And you're wondering whether this scientist will collaborate with those two officials."

Hetia's expression revealed neither assent nor denial.

"I can say with certainty he will," he said.

Hetia's expression sharpened. "We don't have much time."

"Yes, on two counts, for Baclus will be returning shortly."

"I can't relay all the details then. Just be aware Draevik will be asking one of you to join a task force. Accept. Make sure it's you. And demand a roamer." She slipped a piece of paper in his hand and walked toward the door.

He stuffed the number sequence into his pocket. Baclus entered the room, greeting Hetia with a nod.

"I'm glad your study has begun," she said to Baclus. "I was just asking your partner about the details."

"Thank you for your interest," Baclus responded, taking his place at the table and lifting his cup to his lips.

Hetia wrinkled her brow and looked at Cafold.

He looked back at her nervously. "Harmless," he stammered, "but necessary. Just stalling really."

Baclus squinted. "What?"

"The study, I mean." His words made no sense, but what could he do? If she suspected poison…

"Strange choice of words," Baclus said. "I would go with idealistic yet slightly possible, potentially groundbreaking. And yes, it's been taking too long to get started."

"Great minds," Hetia said with a smile, "are working together in this room." She retreated into the hall.

Baclus took another long swill of the liquid, hopefully enough to infect himself with the virus. It shouldn't take long for the first signs to show.

He then gave Cafold a look, as if the younger man were a pup learning the ways of the world, and said, "Draevik wants to meet with us."

⧫

The door to the CfNL's headquarters rattled in place. Marvus, the head chairman—who happened to be passing by the entryway—startled at the noise and crept toward it cautiously. Paint peeled near the handle, curling into strips that dropped onto the floor. The door groaned and shuddered, as if someone were trying to rip it from its hinges. Thinking a vandal was causing mischief on the stoop, he flung the door open.

Instead, his idols stood there, creating such a frenzy within him that all he could do was gape in a fascinated ecstasy. Sweat dripped from his forehead, and the urge to pass out threatened, but before he could submit to it, the four Archaics pushed him aside.

"Marvelous grounds you have here," Oc~ea said as she passed.

Marvus strained not to get caught in the flow of her movement. He grabbed onto the green, tree emblem on his necklace to steady himself.

"We'd like access to your gardens." Baric made no eye contact as he followed Oc~ea.

"We'll *have* access to your gardens," Luma said with an unnerving coyness.

"But thought we'd come in through the front door to be polite." Atmos winked.

Speechless, though a response seemed unnecessary, Marvus followed the Archaics through the entryway and onward, his knees shaking and heart pounding. Was he seeing things again? What would Desnia, his co-chairperson, say?

The Archaics strode through the hallway toward the room of the statues. Upon entering, he was relieved the statues were in their usual positions. The Archaics gave their likenesses looks of approval as they walked past. Then he followed them outside and into the garden Desnia had inspired to grow wild.

Plants edged the pathway and trees hung over it, emulating a tunnel of vegetation. Its aura of remoteness defied its location near the center of town.

The Archaics stopped in a clearing. Marvus paused as well, unsure of what to do. Nervousness rattled his composure and he couldn't find the right words, if right words existed for such a moment. Thankfully, or not, the Archaics seemed uninterested in him.

They faced each other, the air between them charged, almost visibly, with an electrical current. Then Luma marched up to Baric and slapped him violently across the face. "How could you," she said darkly, "keep such a thing to yourself?"

But Baric remained as still as a statue, not reacting to the slap at all, which had sounded like a thwack against stone not skin. Luma flapped her hand as if to shake away pain.

Baric's mouth twitched to one side, no hint of redness on his stony face. "Back off," he said, causing the ground to rumble.

Luma stumbled but was clearly undeterred. A ball of fire erupted in her palm.

"I could burn you to the ground with this," she said threateningly.

A wave of nausea rolled through Marvus's gut. "No fire, please," he said weakly. "No fire in the garden." But his protest went unnoticed. Had he turned invisible? The experience was very surreal.

"Try it," Baric replied just as threateningly, "and see whom the ground prefers."

A thundercloud formed above them, giving the dueling pair pause. Oc~ea eyed Atmos appreciatively.

Luma threw the fireball at Baric. Atmos whipped up a wind with a flurry of hand gestures that blew it off course. Marvus fell to his knees. As Luma's fireball hit a tree, Oc~ea motioned for rain to fall onto the igniting sparks. Baric smirked convincingly and the ground beneath Luma crumbled. She sank swiftly through the dirt. The soil hardened over top of her, muffling her screams.

"Peace at last," Baric said.

The ground rumbled again and buckled, protruding upward. A caldera formed. Luma stepped out of its mouth.

A giggle fell from the branches of a tree, followed by a guffaw of laughter. Marvus jerked his head upward in surprise. Two children sat atop a branch. The young girl had yellow hair and appeared to be dressed in seaweed. The teen boy wore both an obstinate expression and scaly green pants. The pair looked terribly familiar. They resembled the child statues that appeared near Oc~ea's statue from time to time.

I knew it, thought Marvus, *I knew they were real.*

"Must we partake in such childish games?" Oc~ea sighed.

"You always have your secrets," Luma said passionately to Baric. "But what if it came true?"

"It's not our place to alter the course of events," Baric said.

"Listen to him"—Luma turned toward Oc~ea—"acting like it's no big deal."

"He's steady as always," Oc~ea agreed.

"Does mortality not repulse you?" Luma demanded.

"It has yet to be," Baric replied, "and perhaps never will."

"Do you know what will happen?" Luma asked.

"The future is ever changing. That's why it's best to focus on the present so we can mold the future into something ideal. That's why we're here."

"Here? How will we coexist in this hole in the planet?" Luma said distastefully.

"I imagine this place is bigger than it looks," Atmos

said with a gleeful twinkle in his eye. "You've already started decorating your section." He gestured to the caldera.

Luma gave it a once over. "It does have some appealing aspects."

The caldera rose higher, forcing Marvus to walk around it to keep his vantage point.

"Just remember," Atmos continued, "that it'd be best if it remained inactive."

"I suppose I must accept the mundane if I live among those who obey its prison." With a huff, Luma slipped behind a flank.

"Come, Waive and Anemona," Oc~ea said to the children. "There must be a pond somewhere."

"There's not, Mother." Anemona shimmied down the trunk while Waive jumped to land nimbly on his feet. "We've already checked."

Waive smiled and shook his head at his younger sibling.

"Nonsense." Oc~ea took Anemona's hand. "The water is calling me."

"Contain it please, no flooding!" Marvus pleaded, but no one even glanced his way.

Mother and children wandered past the trees and out of sight.

The last two Archaics departed without ceremony. Atmos faded to mist and disappeared amid the foliage. Baric leaned against a trunk. He crossed his arms and soon blended with the bark, the tree becoming gnarled and disfigured with his shape.

Marvis blinked, clearly alone, though his skin prickled as if he were being watched. He backed away slowly before hurrying into the CfNL's headquarters to find Desnia.

⚡

Cafold followed Baclus into the meeting room and sat at the table, certain he would soon learn about Draevik's task force and mystified as to what it would entail. Draevik entered the room like a man on a mission. Baclus coughed during Draevik's passing and took several seconds to clear his throat. The virus was working.

Draevik stood before them, radiating anger in his stance. "There's been a change of plans. The relic is no longer in Semadon."

"Was it stolen?" Baclus asked. "We weren't told to lock it up during our breaks."

"No," Draevik replied. "Though we ordered Ceera Kestlyn to resume her scribe duties and leave the relic alone, she decided to instead interpret it in a most inconvenient way. Her interpretation also involved the Archaics, who came to Semadon and rallied to her cause." He slammed his fist onto the table.

Cafold jumped and dared to ask, "What cause is that?"

Draevik's eyes lit with aggression. "Let's not concern ourselves with the fallacies of that young woman's mind."

Cafold swallowed and nodded dumbly.

"While it's important to appear cooperative, we cannot let their skewed interpretation affect our studies."

Cafold screwed up his face in thought. What was that supposed to mean?

"How can we study it when it's no longer here?" Baclus asked.

"You will follow them," Draevik said with a sidelong glimpse to where no one was sitting. "And study it inside the cave where they are taking it. I will enlist a crew to assist you."

Cafold felt an uneasiness rising inside him. "What about the Archaics?"

"They won't be tagging along. You need not concern yourselves with them."

"But when we get back?" Baclus asked.

"By then they will no longer have powers."

Cafold found this very concerning. "Why would their powers—"

"I said you need not concern yourselves with them."

The resulting silence spoke of dire implications.

Still, Cafold felt the need for more information. "How can we study it inside a cave?"

"Right," Baclus said, clearing his throat. "We can't carry all our equipment with us."

"It won't be so much studying," Draevik said, "as it will be making sure it's kept in a state of preservation. I can't leave such a delicate task to guards."

"How long will this take?" Baclus asked.

"A few weeks, maybe," Draevik said vaguely.

Cafold and Baclus exchanged a quick glance. Had they been friends it would have been more revealing. Instead, Cafold felt confused and skeptical all alone, and wondered if Baclus felt the same.

"I'm asking for a volunteer," Draevik continued, "someone who can bring the relic back safely."

The statement rubbed Cafold the wrong way. "Why can't Ceera bring it back safely?" He wished Draevik would be more forthcoming.

"Ceera," Draevik said sadly, "may not return. Poor thing has been feeling rather unwell."

Cafold and Baclus said nothing for several minutes as Draevik gazed at them with a sternness that didn't match his false concern.

"I'll go," Cafold blurted out. "I'd like to venture outside Semadon for once."

"As would I," Baclus said, "despite my many other projects. But I'm feeling rather unwell myself."

"That's a shame," Draevik replied, for once seeming genuine as he stared at Baclus's drawn, pale face and red-rimmed eyes.

Baclus did look decidedly ill. The virus was taking him down quickly, causing guilt and relief to wash over Cafold simultaneously. He hadn't chosen a virus that normally took lives, but still.

"When should I be ready?" Cafold asked, hoping he had time to confer with Hegliod beforehand.

"As soon as possible," Draevik replied. "Or perhaps even sooner than possible."

Cafold ignored his apprehension and stood.

"Is there anything you need?" Draevik asked.

"Yes." Unlike the last time Draevik had asked this question, Cafold requested a list of items.

"Anything else?"

"I'll need a roamer to communicate with you. And Hegliod, too, if need be."

"Sidorn will carry one. You can use his."

"Who's Sidorn?" Cafold asked.

"The Sci-Def member who'll lead the crew."

Cafold wondered if Hetia knew about Sidorn. "Don't you think it would be better to have a backup?" he persisted. "In the event Sidorn's breaks? I assume he's going because he's a skilled fighter and fights are unpredictable. I'd hate to think of you being left in the dark."

"Very well. I will retrieve your items. You hurry home to get your personal belongings." Draevik left the room.

"You do look unwell, Baclus," Cafold said. "I think you should go see a doctor."

Baclus gazed at him with hazed over eyes.

"Shall I escort you on my way home?"

Chapter Nineteen

LITHA EXITED HER dwelling, not expecting to see Sidorn coming toward her up the walkway. She'd been headed to the library for scribe work but would gladly spare a few minutes beforehand. Sidorn may have information about her disturbing encounter with Ceera. She'd been worrying about it all afternoon.

"Hi beauty," he said during his approach.

She lingered on her stoop and smiled. "Hello."

He smiled back, but something marred his expression.

"What's wrong?" she asked.

He responded with a quick kiss on the lips. "That's my line."

"Maybe I also have special powers," she said coyly.

"I bet you do." Sidorn kissed her again. "I'm here to say goodbye."

Litha's smile fell. Perhaps Ceera had been correct; she'd been a fool to believe in this man.

"You've barely said hello," she said with a choked chuckle.

"Don't take it personal. I have to go on assignment."

"Oh." Her voice felt small. "I was hoping you would be around to tell me how Ceera and Dassius were faring."

Sidorn's expression hardened. "How do you know about that?"

Litha opened her mouth to tell him but thought better of it. "How about I prove to you I'm good at keeping my mouth shut?"

Sidorn's expression relaxed. "It's easy enough to guess how. Anyway, even if I knew how they were doing, I could get in trouble for telling you."

"Only if someone found out. Where are you going?"

"Also a secret," Sidorn said.

Litha sighed. "I'm tired of all these secrets."

"Secrets are part of my job."

"Can you tell me about it when you get back?"

Sidorn shrugged. "Hard to say."

"How long will you be gone?"

"As long as it takes," he replied, humor now absent from his face.

It was the first time she'd seen his expression so solemn. "When will you learn to trust me?"

"I do trust you," he said, "but I've been sworn to secrecy. I don't want to endanger you."

"So now you're protecting me?" Litha asked skeptically.

"More so than you know," Sidorn replied, "because when I get back, I still want to date you."

"You always have a way of twisting things around."

"Everybody twists reality into what they want it to be."

"So for you to continue dating me," Litha said, "you have to keep secret the purpose of your mission?"

"That's right." He grinned.

"And keeping your secret from me keeps our relationship safe?"

"Yep, you got it."

"I can live with that. I have a question though."

"What?"

"If I can't know about your assignment, I want to know how a man so good at keeping secrets says goodbye."

"He says it like this," Sidorn said, drawing her close and pressing his lips firmly onto hers.

And just like that, Litha knew she would wait.

❦

After walking Baclus to the medical clinic, where Cafold grabbed an immune-boost pill for himself just in case, he headed to his dwelling. He packed some necessities and made a few quick calls to family before hurrying to his mentor's.

As always, it took Hegliod an unfathomable amount of time to answer his door, and he tapped his foot to endure the wait.

When he finally answered, he smiled in his typical Hegliod fashion—a practiced expression that had grown more natural lately—then looked perplexed at the sight of the bag slung over Cafold's shoulder.

"Can I come in?" Cafold asked. "It's important."

"Certainly," Hegliod responded, his forehead still creased, "but why are you carrying a bag?"

Cafold followed him inside. "It's my overnight bag—"

"Why bring that here?" Hegliod interrupted.

"I'm not planning on staying. I'm leaving Semadon because of that assignment you recommended me for."

"Ah." Hegliod relaxed.

"But I'm worried," Cafold said. "Draevik wants to go against the Archaics and—"

"Cafold, slow down," Hegliod said. "Start from the beginning."

"Ceera thinks she needs to take the relic into a cave. Dassius is going with her, and the Archaics are in Semadon to make sure Draevik allows it."

Hegliod nodded. "And what is Draevik asking of you?"

"I'm to keep the relic safe. Our group includes a member of the Sci-Def team, and we're to follow Ceera and Dassius into the cave and steal it back. I'm not sure what I can do to thwart his plans."

"What are you getting at?"

Cafold knew Hegliod was not the consoling type, but his frustration was growing. "I have no weapons—"

"There's your flaw in logic."

"What?"

"You have a weapon more powerful than any." Hegliod tapped the side of his head. "Your mind."

"But I don't know what to do."

"Sometimes you must stop forcing the mind to comply. I've learned such a thing myself. The mind works best when it's not awash in desperation."

Cafold said nothing as he struggled to understand.

"Give your mind a break. Let logic prevail. It will serve you better than any weapon ever could."

Leave it to Hegliod to sidestep a meaningless pat on the back with a meaningful pep talk. Feeling calmer, Cafold asked, "Have you a roamer?"

"My dear boy." Hegliod smiled widely this time. "Of course I do. I invented them."

Cafold threw his hands up in the air. "When? When did you invent the roamer?"

"It was an idea that came and went. Then came back. I created it just prior to you becoming my apprentice."

His mentor would never cease to amaze him.

"That's convenient," Cafold said, fingering the paper in his pocket. "Can I use it quick?"

⮞

Hetia had not been trained for clairvoyance, but if anything she was flexible. She needed to size up the leader of Draevik's charge, see if he could be swayed. Every avenue had to be explored. She had no choice but to be vigilant.

Sidorn glanced up before she was even near enough for him to hear her, as if he'd sensed her approach. She'd expected this, knowing quite well what those on the Sci-Def team were capable of doing.

She kept her posture straight, her expression non-accusatory. Remaining cool and aloof would combat suspicion. Although with a man in his profession, all her efforts could be in vain. She tried to think positive and mask any traces of apprehension with an unyielding confidence. She cleared her mind, drawing on her meditation practices. It was similar to conjuring a mystic, in a backwards kind of way.

"So you've been assigned to lead the charge," she said in a neutral tone as she joined him.

"Yep, I'm Sidorn," he replied. "Nice to meet you."

"Hetia, sphere three," she said, watching in distaste as he grabbed her hand and pressed her fingers to his lips.

"Do you greet men the same?" she asked, reclaiming her hand and wiping any traces of his saliva down her pant leg.

He looked surprised. "No, why would I?"

"It would be less sexist." She shook her head at him in dismay. "It's ignorant to assume a woman always desires to be charmed."

His eyes betrayed amusement. "Sorry I offended you."

Hetia sighed deeply, annoyed her brief time with the man had so far been spent on frivolities.

"I gather you're not here to discuss my charm?"

"Correct, or lack thereof," she replied, ignoring his frown. "I came to discuss the mission."

"I've been given strict orders by Draevik not to discuss it with anybody. Even you," he added, then more contemplatively, "especially you."

"And does Draevik dictate all your actions? Does he rule over you the way he does High Service?"

Sidorn gave her a look of discomfort. "Not all of my actions. And no, he does not rule over me. He's just the boss."

"Do you always bow to those in charge?"

"Probably about as much as you do." Sidorn's gaze was both guarded and alert. "Maybe."

Was his statement a hint or a warning? "I can see you are a man of honor then. Maybe." A smile could insinuate an understanding between them, but someone like him may interpret it as a flirtatious gesture, so she refrained.

"I'm a man who gets results, for the betterment of society." His gaze flicked past her. Then he stepped back and nodded to someone in greeting.

"I see you've met Sidorn," Draevik said, sliding between them.

Hetia cursed herself for being so focused on Sidorn that she'd stopped paying attention to the rest of her surroundings.

"Yes," she responded. "He seems capable."

"What are you implying?" Draevik asked, narrowing his eyes.

She flushed, having forgotten she wasn't supposed to know.

"News travels fast," she said shortly. "Especially when you discuss your plans loudly in the hall. But I assume you'll hold a meeting to officially discuss them?"

"Yes." Draevik scowled. "Now, if you'll excuse us." He turned his back on her and began speaking quietly to Sidorn.

"Of course," Hetia responded to the back of his head. She walked calmly away, angry at herself for revealing that she knew.

The encounter had not gone as planned. Besides her mistake, Sidorn was entirely too tricky. She couldn't decide whether he was patronizing her, evaluating her purpose so that he could tell his boss, or whether he was the one doing the grilling. His eyes were on her even now as she rounded the hall.

She would have to rely on her less powerful ally within the group. Cafold was weak in body but not of mind. He was a scientist after all. And he had already made himself useful by calling her to reveal Sidorn's involvement. He would have to be good enough.

⸙

The sun shone on Ceera and Dassius through bare treetops, drying them once they emerged from the river. They walked between the blackened trunks and past the deep rift in which Rebial had fallen after recognizing Ceera's birthmark.

The once lush forest was desolate, ravaged by Luma's fire.

"I wish the CfNL would come here," Ceera said. "And rejuvenate this place like they did their garden."

"I'm sure their hands are full," Dassius responded. "The Archaics plan to camp there."

They walked faster now, as if their previous trip to the forest dictated their present speed. Both ventures to and from the gigantic tree had not been leisurely for different reasons. On the way there, they'd hoped to evade Rebial. Luma's fire chased them on the way out, after allowing their passage through the flames. Their venture was also much quicker without the forest's trickery disorienting them and leading them astray.

When they reached the enormous tree, under which she'd found the relic tangled in roots, she was once again amazed. The tree stood with an aura of vitality, even though it now grew from a patch of land in a precarious position. The rift separating it from the larger land mass had caused it to sink lower since last time they'd been there. Rambling roots kept the tree and its land patch from breaking away entirely.

Oddly enough, the land separation had benefitted the tree, for it had suffered minimal, if any, effects from Luma's fire.

The massive trunk with its expansive canopy still held a commanding presence. Even more so now that the nearby trees had been damaged by the fire. The roots parted at its base had allowed her the entrance she'd needed to crawl beneath and retrieve the relic.

"It's around here somewhere," Dassius said as he surveyed their surroundings.

Ceera carefully averted her eyes from the spot where Falken had died, even though his body had been eaten by the forest dwellers. Any leftover parts should have burned after that. It was disturbing to think about. She peered into the rift instead.

"Do you think we should climb down there like Rebial did?" she asked.

"No, I think we're looking for an actual cave." He wandered away from the giant tree and past several blackened trunks, to where the ground slanted upward. "According to the map, it should be here. Ah, there it is." He pointed to a narrow opening, partially exposed by burned vegetation.

Ceera eyed the fissure warily as she approached. "How far in do you think we'll have to go?"

"Quite a way," he said.

Seeing the fear in her eyes, he put an arm around her. "You'll be with me, remember?"

"How could I forget?" she responded.

He kissed her gently on the lips. "I'll keep you safe," he promised.

Ceera gave him a brave smile and together they ventured into the dark opening that was little more than a crevice outlined with jagged stone.

Standing on the back lawn of the Aurora, Cafold packed the supplies Draevik gave him into his bag. After the handover, the sphere seven's focus shifted to Sidorn, who was readying to speak to the crew. Cafold joined the group of well-built guards, feeling out of place with his slender and wiry frame.

Draevik dug his vulture-like fingers into Cafold's shoulders. "This is Cafold," he told Sidorn. "He's been assigned to tag along and keep the relic safe. Which means you will keep him safe as well."

Cafold bristled at the thought of his life only being worth guarding because of a possession. Sidorn's stare added to his discomfort.

"He'll be at the top of my list," Sidorn said with a wink aimed at Cafold, "of things worth protecting."

Cafold stiffened, all too aware that Sidorn's comment

was disturbingly similar to his own thought. He knew Sci-Def members had mind reading abilities, especially when it came to strong emotions, but also knew their ability was dependent on the person being read. Which meant he was so far an easy target and would need to put up mental walls. Because if, well, it was important to think plainly. Starting now. Keeping the relic safe was the goal. It was, in all respects, the root of his motivations.

Sidorn gave him another glance before he addressed the crew. "Now that we've all met, let's get going. We need to move fast since we've lost hours on our targets. I hope you all got a good night's sleep because we may be skipping one tonight."

Cafold hadn't considered the actual grueling and laborious aspect of the task. He hoped he was in good enough shape for this.

"Remember," Draevik whispered in his ear, "that much hangs in the balance. Don't cause the scale to tip in the wrong direction."

Cafold tensed considerably from the threat. "I would never—" he started to say, but Draevik was already walking away.

Chapter Twenty

AS CEERA AND Dassius descended through the sloping tunnel, darkness seeped toward them from the cave's depths. Before it hampered their sight, Dassius fumbled in his pack and produced two headlamps. He handed one to Ceera, and they each put one on.

The ragged tunnel was composed of rock, possibly limestone. Smaller rocks littered the ground. Ceera had flashbacks about the cave they'd traveled in to find Baric. His cave had consisted of dirt tunnels that led to a mystical room filled with crystals and minerals. This cave matched pictures she'd seen in books. It seemed more natural. Still, she had her doubts it was where they should be headed.

"Are you sure about this?" she gasped to Dassius, feeling the effects of the physical exertion. Her job, until recently, involved sitting in a chair after all.

"I am, but there's always a chance for human error. Small possibilities impact reality, no matter how unlikely they are to be true."

"Forget I asked," she replied as her foot slid on a rock.

Dassius quickly turned and braced himself against the tunnel to keep her from falling.

Facing him now in such tight quarters, she appreciated

the proximity. Dassius apparently did too, for he leaned to give her a quick kiss. Their headlamps clinked together and now his feet were sliding, but he caught himself with expert reflexes.

"Kisses are too dangerous," he said, turning around to continue their descent.

"This tunnel is growing smaller," she said. "Does it bother you?"

"Nah, I've been in all kinds of tight spaces. My trainers think of everything."

They continued a few more paces before Dassius stopped abruptly to peer over something. "I'll need to lower us into that cavern."

She waited while he reached into his pack and began knotting the thin yet strong rope that would aid in that endeavor.

∽

Hetia waited in the back garden outside the Aurora, hood raised to keep the evening chill at bay. The wind blew past, but she refused to shiver, instead she dwelled on something else entirely. Would he come? And just as importantly, had he recruited any allies?

Perhaps she'd been a fool to trust Fresdin. Sadra hadn't thought so, but she didn't know him like Hetia did. They'd grown up together. His intelligence was a different kind than hers. He was smart about what could be found in books and strategic planning. While she, too, was privy to facts and information, her strength was in big picture thinking and the need to feel integral in what happened around her.

It was difficult to stand by and wait for her time to come. Elevating a sphere level had seemed like an accomplishment once Ceera and Dassius had returned to Semadon with the relic, but now something more was at stake.

Not alerting the Archaics was a risk. She hoped she hadn't erred by agreeing to it. A small part of her was even suspicious of Fresdin for making the suggestion.

Footsteps rustled the grass behind her. She would now know for sure whether he truly was on her side.

"I brought company," he said grimly, gripping her shoulder.

His tone perplexed her. Had he brought friends or foe? She turned. A small group of guards stood before her. They donned no uniform, which meant they hadn't come to arrest her. She relaxed and smiled politely as Fresdin introduced her to them.

"I'm glad to meet you," she said with genuine appreciation. "Are you sure you weren't followed?"

"That was the first priority," Fresdin said. "We didn't travel together. We met a short distance from here."

"Excellent. Since you've come," she addressed the group, "I assume you're ready to take action."

"The brainwashing hasn't affected us like it has our peers," Bidlyn spoke up.

"There may be others," Nespi said, "but the delicacy of the situation makes us cautious."

"Caution is necessary. You do well to be suspicious. Draevik's ideas have managed to infect even those with the best intentions."

"Are you the only officials who oppose him?" Bidlyn asked.

Hetia bit her lip. "Presently, but as you say, there may be others who feel the same. Our gathering suggests the possibility of more. We may not have his numbers, but our secrecy can be advantageous."

Her words were met with silence, no signs of fear evident on their faces. Apparently, such a declaration came as no surprise.

"Where do we begin?" Nespi asked.

"I need one of you to access the guards' information center so we can figure out Draevik's plan of attack."

Bidlyn stepped forward. "It would be easy for me to do this. I work there."

"Then you it shall be. Trust no one in your endeavor except those present today."

Looking pleased, Bidlyn nodded.

"Next, we need someone who can access the copy of the map. I'm aware the cave is in the primeval forest, but that is where my knowledge ends."

"I know where it's kept," Nespi said. "I can make another copy."

"How soon can you do this?"

"Within the next few hours, during the shift change."

"Please bring the copy to me or Fresdin."

Nespi nodded and stepped back into the group.

"Lastly, we need a leader," Hetia said. "Someone who can guide the charge once Nespi provides the map."

"I have experience leading a crew," Xyria said. "I can do this."

"Who will assist you?"

Hetia waited patiently while several volunteered to join Xyria's crew.

"You'll need to figure out how to track Draevik's crew without being discovered," Hetia said. "How do you propose to overtake them with so few of you?"

"The only one more skilled than us is Sidorn," Xyria said.

"How do you plan to overtake him? His intuition could detect you before you're ready."

Xyria crossed her arms over her chest. "Let's hope Dassius takes care of him first."

"You plan to wait until the last moment?" Hetia asked.

"Sidorn's distraction will be our gain."

"I like how you think. So now would be the time to ask, does anyone have access to Dassius's roamer number? If you could join forces beforehand, all the better."

"Only Draevik has access to that," Nespi said, "and probably the two officials who follow him around."

Hetia met Fresdin's intense gaze. So far, it didn't seem likely they could infiltrate the trio. Still, she said, "Fresdin and I will do what we can to try and get Dassius's number. It's possible Risa or Karnen may turn. And the same can be said for your own peers. Observe them closely. If anyone seems fit to join our cause, please tell Fresdin so he can interrogate them."

"How will you explain our absence to High Service?" asked Xyria.

Hetia paused as she considered.

"We'll tell them we sent you to investigate a disturbance in a settlement," Fresdin spoke up. "Hetia and I monitor complaints so this will seem believable."

"Fantastic idea," Hetia said, thrilled by his cunning, "which allows us to begin this very hour. May justice prevail."

And so it had begun. A tiny shiver worked its way up her spine. There would be no backing out now.

After some handshakes, the group dispersed, leaving Hetia and Fresdin alone. The stars emitted bits of light, subtle yet effective. They symbolized what the crew may be able to attain, despite being small in number.

"You did well," Fresdin said.

"Thank you for bringing them," she replied.

"Bidlyn brings up an interesting point," Fresdin said. "Are we truly the only officials who don't agree with Draevik's tactics?"

Hetia smiled. It wasn't so long ago that she'd convinced him, and yet here he was, conspiring with her. She had underestimated him.

"Besides Sadra, I truly don't know."

Fresdin stroked his chin. "Which makes sense since you're always busy countering Draevik. But I have an idea."

"Tell me."

"At our next meeting, you debate Draevik as usual, but instead of me watching you, I'll watch the other officials' reactions. I'll especially monitor Risa and Karnen."

"That's brilliant," Hetia replied. "Although I think I make the other officials uncomfortable whether they agree with him or not."

"You do," Fresdin agreed, "but I'll watch them more closely. All the while pretending to be appalled myself."

"And I'll try and say things that will inspire reactions."

"Just don't get yourself arrested, please," Fresdin said with a chuckle.

"Ha, well. At least Draevik has not resorted to such measures yet."

❦

Ceera hung onto Dassius's back, her face pressed against his neck, as he lowered them into a large, cold cavern.

When her feet touched down, she ascertained their colorful surroundings. Stalactites hung from the ceiling like jagged teeth, and stalagmites jutted from the ground in odd-shaped towering columns.

"This place looks enchanted," she said, digging through her pack for her jacket.

The dazzling environment—dripping blue, purple, and green—seemed a fitting precursor to the important task she had yet to fulfill. It enlivened her sense of purpose, both to herself and to her culture, and evoked just how magical it was that her dreams had led her to this moment.

"I'll leave the rope." He gave its knotted end a swing. "We'll have to climb back up eventually."

Several imperfectly shaped passageways led out of the cavern room.

Dassius was already staring at his copy of the map. "I prefer to use intuition," he mumbled, "but it seems a waste of resources when we have a map." Having apparently concluded something, he tucked the map into his pack.

Motioning for her to follow, he headed toward the middle passageway. They walked across damp stone to reach it, weaving between peculiar yet alluring formations that were slimy to the touch.

"Do you think situations like this," she said, "with multiple possibilities, are like decisions of the mind?"

"What do you mean?" he asked.

"This cave will explain my connection to the relic if we make the right choices."

Dassius gave her an interested glance.

"And now as we enter this passageway, I wonder, are all the answers within me already if I just choose the right path of thought?"

"Your perspective intrigues me."

They smiled at each other before continuing into the passage, leaving behind the fairy tale setting for a dark tunnel.

"Do you know where the map leads?" Dassius asked.

"No," she admitted. "I've had no time to dwell on that mystery. Escaping the institution was my primary focus."

"Now that you're safe with me," Dassius responded, "let's figure this out. Who or what controls the Archaics, the mystics, and whether you live or die?"

"I wish I knew. I think we'll find out."

"I'm glad you're the one who's been given this task."

"Why? I can't even protect myself," she said with a laugh, remembering Dassius's complaints about dealing with her on their first mission.

"Because you're genuine and purpose driven. Even when you doubt yourself."

His compliment prompted another smile. "All this time I've thought the relic belonged to Rebial and the forest. I can hardly fathom anything else. Unless where I'm taking it involves the people who are still underground."

"Why do you think they're still down here again?" Dassius asked.

She explained her theory, which ended in her triumph of liberating the relic's people. It would be a good reward for all her struggles. She assumed they would, like Rebial, recognize her birthmark. And they might even appreciate her, unlike her father, Drusilla, and High Service.

Dassius frowned. "You think you'll be taking it to them?"

"Not exactly. I think they might show me to this unknown entity, and I can lead them out after."

Dassius nodded slowly as he digested her reasoning. "What does High Service think about this?"

"I never told them," she said. "Draevik only cared about the relic."

"Why is he against returning it?"

"He thinks it's nonsense, that the relic has no bearing on society today."

"What could he achieve by holding onto it? So far the negatives outweigh the positives."

"There was a study. They never let me in on it."

They rounded a curve and the temperature dropped further. She raised her hood over her headlamp.

"What was on the page Draevik tried to keep from us?" Dassius asked.

"The passage that said the relic needed to be returned, which hardly seems like something he would want to hold onto."

"Then there's something else besides that."

"There was a blood stain."

"Whose blood?" Dassius asked.

"We presumed it was Rebial's."

"So their interest lies with him."

"Yes, they didn't know where he came from or how long he'd been alive." She placed her hand over her mouth, before uttering a sheepish, "Oh."

"So they planned to study the blood to make sense of Rebial and his existence."

"When Draevik first started interrogating me," she said, "he'd just recovered from an illness that almost killed him."

"I see where you're going with this."

"He was fascinated with the longevity aspect," she continued, "at least originally. Afterward, he decided the relic's claims were outdated and bogus. His sudden change of interest didn't sit right with me."

"So he thinks the relic contains something that promotes longevity. What is every person's dream?"

"To live forever," Ceera whispered, feeling the cold air against her lips.

"Maybe the relic was safest all these years with Rebial."

She shivered. "And I hope to prove that he made no mistake when he gave it to me."

Cafold's legs already hurt and the group hadn't even reached the cave; they were still within the shadows of the wood. A wood he'd never, until recently, thought he'd ever have reason to visit. Fire ravaged trunks evoked monster-like shapes. The unnatural lack of vegetation added to the creepiness.

Unhindered by the darkness, Sidorn tracked Dassius's whereabouts with an ability Cafold likened to a wild animal. He banished the thought before Sidorn noticed. He had no idea when the Sci-Def member was reading him. He remained focused on the relic but tried not to think too specifically about it. Everyone had the same goal here; they just had different reasons for attaining it.

As they walked, the guards took turns glancing back with amused expressions. Their flashlights illuminated them from the chest up, giving their faces an evil glow. He deduced they mocked him since he straggled so many paces behind. It wasn't the walking that hindered him, it was the uphill spans, the stepping over and between randomly placed felled trees.

Sidorn turned to make eye contact with Cafold. "Need to hop on?" he asked, thumbing a gesture to his back.

The other guards chuckled.

Annoyed, Cafold strained to compose himself. "No," he responded.

"Then no lagging behind. We need to gain ground, not lose it." Sidorn turned back around.

Cafold ignored his aching legs and struggled to keep up. He could have sworn they moved faster now, just to spite him.

Chapter Twenty-One

CEERA FOLLOWED DASSIUS through another dark passageway. Fatigue was wearing on her, perhaps inspired by their earlier discussion about Draevik. The perpetual darkness, headlamp or not, didn't help.

"We should set up camp," Dassius said, probably sensing her discomfort.

"Fine," she agreed.

While he readied their sleeping bags, an eerie sensation crawled into her mind. As if eyes watched them from the shadows. The invasive feeling reminded her of an experience she'd had in the forest. The one that had almost destroyed her.

The memory caused a shudder.

"What's the matter?" Dassius asked.

She shook her head dismissively.

"I wish you wouldn't keep things from me," he said.

"Something isn't right."

"This cave does feel spooky."

She hesitated before saying, "You noticed?"

"The feeling comes and goes."

Just like before, except without the sound effects, and suddenly she knew.

"It's him," she whispered.

"Who?" Dassius asked.

"Rebial."

His expression dimmed while he fingered his knife handle. "How is that possible? He claimed he was going to die."

"I don't know," Ceera said. "There's nothing in the relic suggesting it brings back the dead."

Dassius slowly looked around. His headlamp lit various nooks and crevices in the stone, but was too weak to penetrate every shadow. "We could be near his remains."

Ceera had never visited a dead body, but his suggestion made sense. "We must be."

"Let's set up camp elsewhere." Dassius wasted no time rolling their sleeping bags into an untidy bundle. He held them to his chest as they walked farther into the passage.

She ignored the hazy darkness lining the stone. Rebial's remains could stay hidden.

By the time Dassius chose another spot, the feeling had subsided. They turned off their headlamps and lay together in the darkness. But as she tried to sleep, the unwelcome feeling crept back and hovered at the blurred edge of her consciousness.

⋟

The bonfire raged into the night, a tall mass of writhing flames. The Semions, who'd only been paying enough attention to keep the fire lit, now huddled around it for warmth. Their tents were scattered in the distance, waiting to be occupied. Once the reveling ended, they'd drag their tired bodies inside.

The fire crackled loudly, and something within the

blaze stirred. Those nearest peered closer. A figure, somehow unscorched, crouched inside the curling flames. Hair that matched the blaze fell around her body like a shawl. Her skin was almost translucent.

A scream broke the stunned silence, triggering a frantic search, as each Semion ensured friends and family were accounted for. After determining everyone was safe, the Semions stood around the fire and gaped.

The figure stood, yawned, and stretched. The fire continued to dance around her, though strangely it refrained from ravaging her person. Her pale skin remained unmarred, her hair long and flowing. Despite this, someone poked a hefty stick into the flames to help her, but instead of grabbing onto it, she snarled and swiped it away. Then, unattended, she stepped out.

Her blood red hair whirled lightly with the breeze, no longer covering her nakedness. Only soot covered her female parts and rimmed her eyes and cheeks. She wiped delicately at her arms and legs as if to rid them of the heat still swarming her skin. A swirling rubbery gown, that had gone unnoticed before, lay in a heap nearby.

"Have you no sense of decency?" A mother spat out while shielding her child's eyes.

"I should say the same about you," Luma retorted as she swooped down to pick up her dress, "for having the indecency of watching me bathe."

She slung the gown over her shoulder and with a backward glare walked away and into the trees.

⁓

The sky was just beginning to lighten when Cafold and the others reached the cave. One by one, the men squeezed inside the narrow opening. Soon he was the only one left. He did not have to slide sideways like they did when he maneuvered his way inside. Down the tunnel, Sidorn's headlamp lit the path ahead. The rest took this as a cue to strap on their own, and there was a brief time lag as they did so.

During their slow descent through the tunnel, Cafold slid on some scree. He took out two unsuspecting guards, who cursed loudly as they landed on top of him, wedging him into the rocks in a painful way that hindered his breathing.

They climbed off him with no regard to his comfort, jabbing at his ribs and gut, still cursing. Feeling abused, Cafold had little motivation to move.

"Get up," one of them demanded.

He carefully stood, hoping his bones were still in place and that rocks hadn't torn through the fabric of his pants. Luckily, his pain did not increase with movement and his limbs still worked. A fist grabbed him by the collar.

"Watch your step," the guard threatened. "If you knock me down again, I'll—"

"Let him go," Sidorn ordered from somewhere up ahead. "No threatening the help."

"He's clumsy," the guard complained, releasing him. "We should make him go first."

"Or you could watch your back better," Sidorn retorted.

The guard glared at Cafold before proceeding downward.

Cafold swallowed loudly and followed, watching his feet as he had never done before.

§

The woman was a solitary figure in the hazy realm of Ceera's dream. Her long, black hair and beaded bag gleamed accents of light. Walls with blurred edges confined her within the small space that she paced.

Ceera knew she was dreaming. Within dreams more mundane, this awareness would trigger her to wake. But instead she watched intently, waiting for the woman to reveal a clue to guide her.

Instead, the woman did something she'd never done before; she raised her head to acknowledge Ceera. They stared eye to eye within her mind. Ceera tried to back away, mentally, but was trapped within this shared consciousness.

The woman began pacing again. This time she did not avoid the blurry walls. With outstretched hands and arms, she purposefully collided with the walls and rebounded between them. Their rocky edges deepened and refined as she did this. Grief tore at her face. Ceera continued to watch, fixated, as the woman beat at the walls with clenched fists, realizing she was trapped inside the pocket of a cave. Terror and frustration bled into Ceera's mind, vibrating chaotically, as she continued pounding on the walls.

Tears pouring down her face, the woman stopped and pointed to a dusky corner that shaded a gaping hole. As Ceera gazed into it, she passed farther and farther into its interior, like a mouse scurrying through a dark tunnel. And what she saw within its depths made her scream.

Her eyes flicked open. Darkness stared back.

Dassius rolled quickly overtop her. "What's the matter?"

"Another dream," she said. "Of the woman again. Except this time she was pacing around. Inside my head."

"Is that all?"

"Inside my head," she repeated. "As if she were trapped there."

Dassius stared at her, patiently waiting.

"Then she pointed to a corner in my mind. There was a hole, and I went through it."

"What was inside?"

"I don't remember. It was terrifying."

"No pressure. Dreams are fickle."

"Not my dreams," she said. "The woman only appears when she has something to say."

"What do you think she was trying to tell you?"

Ceera remembered the desperation on the woman's face. She'd been flippant before, but perhaps the woman truly was stuck there. She reiterated this to Dassius.

"How could that be?" he asked uneasily.

"Ever since we discovered the forest she's been coming and going through my dreams, keeping me on the right track. Breaking through during the dream therapy. In this dream, we even shared the same consciousness."

Ceera didn't like the look Dassius was giving her. He cupped her face. "I think you should let this one go."

Tears welled in her eyes. "I have to know what it all means."

"What if there is no way to know?"

"This cave, I see it as my mind hiding secrets I have yet to uncover. And now this woman, who I suspect once roamed this cave, is real inside my dreams."

She wondered if the dream therapy had tainted her, affected her in reverse, and made it so she could no longer separate the real world from her dreams. It had, at the very least, provoked the woman. Wouldn't that suggest the woman was real, in some way, if she were able to negate Ceera's treatment?

Suddenly, words from a mystic entered her mind.

On many planes and levels, existence is open to interpretation.

Was the woman existing in a plane of reality that resided only in her mind? Were there planes of reality within the mind? Is that what dreams were? She trembled from the weirdness of such a thought.

"That sounds like what you were saying about the cave earlier. So what happened in the dream could be a product of your imagination."

"No," she snapped, "I went to sleep thinking about Rebial." Then, seeing the hurt on his face, she added, "I'm sorry."

It would be best not to worry Dassius by revealing she still felt traces of Rebial lurking in the shadows.

That she was being haunted both inside her head and out.

Dassius's expression softened. "Maybe," he said gently, "you should focus on the main goal and the rest will come later. Your mental health is at stake."

"I suppose you're right," she responded.

He drew close to kiss her. She wished his kiss could erase her worries, but it only gave her fleeting satisfaction.

She pulled away from him. "I want to get moving. I don't think I can fall back asleep."

If shadows could talk, she was certain murmurs of assent would rustle from the darkness. The reason for this deranged thought remained elusive. Much like the cause for her lucid dream.

❧

Cafold's descent into the large cavern had been humiliating. Sidorn's obnoxious grin had been bad enough when he'd discovered the dangling rope at the cliff's edge, but then Cafold had to sweat it out while each man climbed down.

It gave him time to remember that back in school, rope climbing had been his nemesis. And he'd thought this embarrassment was behind him, something he'd never have to endure again. But here was the same challenge, and this time he'd be the only one displaying a lack of mastery.

Except, as Hegliod had foreseen, his mind had served him. Because he'd thought to bring gloves. He put them on during the wait.

When his turn came, he crouched at the cliff's edge and carefully grabbed onto the rope.

"Don't worry," Sidorn hollered, "we'll catch you if you fall."

The resulting laughter suggested the words had not been spoken benevolently.

"Yeah, thanks," he muttered.

He inched his legs over the edge and hung there, muscles tensing, preparing to climb down. Instead, his glove's slippery material submitted to his weight, and he slid down the rope as if it were a pole.

His descent ended abruptly when he landed awkwardly on something sturdy.

"Good thing you have a strong grip," Sidorn grunted, having borne the brunt of Cafold's landing.

The Sci-Def member had caught him just as he said he would.

Sidorn let go, allowing Cafold to drop the remaining few feet, and stepped away to join the crew. Cafold's knees shook even though his feet were now firmly on the ground. He peered at his tattered gloves. His hands would be just as shredded if he hadn't worn them.

This disturbing reality hung over him as Sidorn led them past a series of mineral deposits and into a passageway. As did the jokes about him sliding down the rope like a child at a playground.

After several hours of tramping through tunnels, Sidorn said, "We break here."

Cafold watched their surprised reactions.

"Thought you said we'd skip sleep tonight," a guard said.

"We're making good enough time. Besides, I can smell the fatigue on that one." Sidorn nodded in Cafold's direction.

Mortified, Cafold watched all heads turn his way.

"I'm doing fine," he said, but Sidorn clearly wasn't interested.

"Two hours max is all you get. Use it wisely," he said darkly as he tossed his pack down and propped his large body against it.

Sidorn's relaxed posture proved who was the tired one, but none of the others shared Cafold's skepticism. As he was getting used to, they glared his way before following Sidorn's actions.

Cafold, the fatigued one, was the last to lie down, and due to his overwhelming discomfort, was sure he would get the least amount of sleep.

Chapter Twenty-Two

ANEMONA SAT WITH Waive on the shore by the bay, watching the boats drift in the gentle current. She had suggested they wager on the fishermen's skills, cause the waves to flow more unpredictably to see who could keep their boat from capsizing, but Waive had shrugged her off.

"Nah, too obvious. Mother would get mad."

Anemona frowned, toying with the green shell hanging from her necklace. He always acted like her ideas were beneath him, as if she were too young to be useful.

"Wait here," he said, before diving in after a boat.

He was always telling her what to do, never trusting her to tag along. She dug her fingers into the sand in frustration.

Waive was supposed to be watching her, as if she still needed protection. Anemona was certain she did not. Her skills with the water increased every day, but she never had anyone to practice them on, besides her mother and brother, who were both more advanced. Waive was not as advanced as he thought, but he was still ahead of her by several years. And she had tired of watching him steal the fisherman's catch.

Anemona was distracted from her thoughts when farther down the coast a girl ran to the water's edge. The girl's face expressed pure delight, so unlike her own. She had never seen a child her size before, not this close anyway, and Waive had always been that much bigger.

The girl wandered into the water up to her calves, bent over, and paddled her arms to splash around. Anemona understood this pleasure yet also pitied the girl if that was the extent of the game. She considered joining to aid in the fun. She could show the girl so much. But her mother's words have been clear.

Do not interact with anyone. Semions are afraid of those different from them. And fear can turn people into monsters.

Still, her mother didn't realize how skilled she had become. She could ward off any attack. Her bond with the water would protect her.

Anemona sighed as the girl ran laughing along the shore. The light tinkling sound reminded her of raindrops spattering. A deep longing fluttered within her chest. Perhaps she could play too, just from afar.

She concentrated on the tranquil water and a slight wave responded, undulating toward the shore. It splashed at the girl's knees, causing a gleeful giggle.

Anemona smiled. Such fun they would have if she could play too.

She concentrated harder and another wave came forth, splashing up to the girl's chest this time. Entranced, the girl stepped further into the water up to her thighs.

Anemona understood the pull, the magnetic draw, that the girl was feeling. Excited now, she concentrated on producing one mighty splash. Its power would endear the girl to the water forever.

The wave rose and cascaded over her like a miniature tsunami. Feeling proud, Anemona leaned forward and peered closely, trying to see if she had also impressed the girl. Except, where was she? The water rippled calmly, and the girl was no longer in sight.

&

Dassius's headlamp swung from side to side as he evaluated their choice of tunnels. His light caught on something, drawing Ceera's attention. She'd been trying to avoid staring into the shadows, but the sparkle was too unlike anything else in their surroundings to be ignored.

She walked up to the small, round object perched on the wall's narrow protrusion and picked it up. She rubbed at the dirt until more colors gleamed through and the tiny holes at either end were visible.

The small bead reminded her of someone, and a feeling of validation came over her. This was the first tangible evidence they'd come across proving the dream woman had actually walked these tunnels and wasn't just a product of Ceera's imagination. She hadn't realized Dassius suggesting it had bothered her, but now she had a feeling of accomplishment. Like they were on the right track. Like she could erase the doubts that had recently crept into her thoughts and instead enjoy her moment.

"Look at this," she said, raising it between her fingers.

Dassius squinted and peered closer. "A bead," he stated simply, "from a time long past I gather."

"It belongs to the dream woman. She carries a beaded bag."

"It could have been dropped by anyone."

"It wasn't dropped. She placed it here," Ceera said, pointing to the dusty ledge.

"Why put it there?" Dassius asked.

"To show me the way."

"Why would she leave beads when there's a map?"

"To be sure I wouldn't get lost," she said. "To let me know I'm on the right track."

To let me know that she was real.

She wondered how the woman had known to place it there so long ago. Perhaps if she had another dream in which they shared the same consciousness, she would ask. And most importantly, ask why she had entrusted Ceera to return the relic and thus liberate a people who'd been forced to endure the ages in this bleak and meandering cave.

A cave whose shadows stalked you. And lingered in the cracks between your thoughts.

The screaming grew louder as Oc~ea neared the bay. Her pace quickened, though to the passersby it appeared she floated faster, for Oc~ea did not walk but moved swiftly like a current.

Semions crowded the shore, shielding their eyes from the sun as they surveyed the bay. Some were emerging from the waves, shaking their heads and showing their empty hands to the gathering spectators. A woman still screamed hysterically within the tight huddle at the water's edge.

Oc~ea sighed, then noticed her daughter peeking out from behind some large rocks.

"Anemona," she said sternly. "How could you?"

"She was having so much fun," Anemona said, lip quivering. "We both were."

"I told you not to interact with anyone. Where's Waive?"

"He followed a fisherman…" Anemona's voice trailed away.

The screaming intensified.

"Watch and learn, dear child, and hope that water will not punish your actions as severely as I will."

Anemona bowed her head in shame.

Oc~ea left her daughter behind the rocks and stepped boldly into the chaos. Semions parted as she approached. A woman with a tear-streaked face emerged from the huddle, grabbed onto her sleeve, and shook it aggressively. Refusing to be affected by the woman's screaming, Oc~ea calmly loosened the Semion's grip. She stared out at the bay and half closed her eyes.

The water swirled in tiny currents. Far away, one grew into a whirlpool that rose and drew a figure from its depth. The body was limp, overturned, hovering atop the water as if it were a bed. Then a mighty wave carried the child to the shore and brought her to rest near Oc~ea's feet. The girl's face was blue and unmoving. Oc~ea sighed again.

Someone felt the need to state the obvious. "She's dead."

"Drowned in the wretched bay," a woman said in a hateful tone.

The distraught woman shrieked louder and fell to her knees. An equally distraught man stroked the woman's hair as she did the same to the motionless child. Angry voices rose with accusations.

"There wasn't supposed to be a tide today," a man said, casting a glare at Oc~ea.

"The water just reached out and grabbed her!"

The Archaic was in no mood to be trifled with. She had her own daughter to attend to.

"Step aside," Oc~ea ordered, causing everyone to shuffle backward several steps. Then she knelt and placed a hand on the child's chest and pushed in one swift motion. Water gurgled out the girl's mouth, and her small body lurched from the pressure.

"Stop her," the distraught woman yelled, but thunder rumbled overhead, distracting the Semions who had moved to detain her.

Oc~ea leaned over and placed her mouth on the child's frozen lips.

She shared her breath, felt the coldness leave the girl's lips as they softened. The blueness faded from her face.

"Come back to us," Oc~ea said gently, warming the child's hands between her own.

The girl's chest began moving. Her eyes opened slowly, though her pupils were glassy and unfocused.

"She's alive," the distraught man shouted.

The girl coughed violently then, and as the remaining water and algae escaped her mouth, Oc~ea stood.

"Respect the water," Oc~ea said while the girl sputtered, "for it gave you back your life today."

Color returned to the girl's cheeks and the once dis-traught woman knelt to console her. The tears flowing now were happy ones. The crowd gathered around the heartfelt scene while Oc~ea floated away to find her own daughter.

Anemona still crouched where Oc~ea had left her. Her daughter's mouth no longer trembled but had twisted into a strange smile.

"Know your strength," Oc~ea said, "and never fall prey to such carelessness again."

"From now on," Anemona said, "water will be my only playmate."

Oc~ea took her daughter's hand and led her away, though she took one last look at the shrinking scene behind them. The water raged in the distance, angry it had to give back one it had rightfully taken, but Oc~ea turned away and for once moved most efficiently, refusing to be swayed.

&

Hetia and Fresdin entered their office with a composure that belied their bottled-up emotions. Having suffered through the most outrageous meeting Hetia could recall, and lately there'd been many, they were beyond ready to discuss.

"Not one official questioned his motives," Hetia gushed after Fresdin closed the door.

"They were distracted by what the fisherman reported," Fresdin responded. "And the fact a child almost drowned. I won't mention what happened with Luma."

Hetia gave him a look. "Yes, please don't."

She sat at their desk, watching him pace. "Those events needed to be discussed, of course," she continued, "but Drae-vik just admitted he sent Sidorn and his crew down after Ceera and Dassius, and *no one* seemed bothered."

"Can you blame them? Draevik's smart. He presented it by way of insurance. Right *after* we discussed the questionable behavior of the Archaics. They hardly acted like protectors of the public today."

"Oc~ea did save the girl."

"Yes, but for show? There were bystanders who saw the wave pull her into the bay."

Hetia shook her head in dismay.

"You did your best," Fresdin continued, "challenging Draevik like always, but there's nothing we can do if the Archaics continue to impact things in a negative way."

"They should have left Semadon," Hetia said glumly. Then she perked up. "Did you catch any dissent from the other officials? Anyone who would have access to Dassius's number?"

"No, Draevik timed it perfectly. He's a master of manipulation."

"That he is," Hetia said. "And he even got the majority's support to deny the public a meeting."

"After he suggested that revealing the truth would jeopardize our safety, what did you expect?"

"Someone other than us to see through it all. Does he think the public will accept our refusal to meet with them? They have no idea why the Archaics are even here."

"If the so-called advocates of Semadon's citizens won't support them," Fresdin said, "then why would anyone else?"

"If only Risa and Karnen could be turned," Hetia mused.

"That would be helpful, but it's not like we're doing nothing, thanks to you." Fresdin smiled.

"Yes, but I feel helpless as a fly. I can't even check in with Cafold to see how close they are to Ceera and Dassius. It might alert the others to his loyalties."

"At least we know our crew is gaining on them."

She had been impressed with their crew so far. Nespi had provided a copy of the map as quickly as she'd promised. They'd given it to Xyria, who had set out with the rest of the crew before daylight. As a result of their scheming, Hetia had barely slept, which explained the heightened anxiety she was experiencing.

"Their proximity is a relief. And the rope they found proves they're on the right track. Speaking of that, they're not the only ones I'm impressed with."

"Oh?" Fresdin looked puzzled.

"You are a master yourself, Fresdin, of evading suspicion.

When your roamer started beeping during the meeting, I was certain we'd be found out."

"Because you didn't think I'd have an excuse ready for such an occurrence?"

"I didn't think to have one."

"It didn't take much thought. We did supposedly send those same guards to check on a settlement. It would make sense we sent them with a roamer for updates."

"Still," Hetia said. "It was brilliant."

"I appreciate the compliment."

"I appreciate the effort."

"Let's just hope our efforts are enough," Fresdin replied pragmatically.

❧

Glavin felt an ominous sense of dread as his attendant led Draevik to the seat across from his desk. He'd thought the official would leave him alone now that Baclus had returned to the CfA headquarters, sick as a dog and just a tad warier. Wyman was still busy and apparently knee deep in training assignments of the sinister persuasion. But no, Draevik kept materializing like a bad habit. Someone else's bad habit.

He twisted the sun ring on his finger, taming his fury, while the older man settled into the chair. How much more blackmail could he endure?

"To what do I owe this displeasure?" Glavin asked once his attendant had left the room.

"Such a negative attitude," Draevik said, wrinkling his nose.

"What do you expect?" he retorted. "Our council is in limbo because of you. I still have no companion—"

"Hush now," Draevik said. "No need to get defensive."

Glavin refrained from spouting off, knowing if he didn't keep his temper, Draevik's guards would keep it for him. And he was too vain for that.

"What if I'm here to end this limbo?"

Glavin's intuition and cynical nature stifled any naive hopes. Draevik couldn't create a new companion from thin air, one that could automatically be voted in. "Are you?"

"Our ambitions have aligned. I think you'll be pleased."

"What does that mean?" Glavin found Draevik's indirect manner of speaking to be quite tedious.

"How would you like to begin implementation of your weather enhancement project?"

These had been the words the CfA had been waiting to hear for the upwards of a year. And yet…"Move forward without a companion? You alone can authorize this or has all of High Service agreed? What about the public's consent? Are you saying we can bypass meetings with the CfNL even?"

"The CfNL can no longer be trusted. They've allowed the Archaics to reside in their headquarters and are not keeping tabs or control over their actions. You've heard what's been going on?"

"I have," Glavin said, uncomfortable, then for the benefit of Draevik's guards added, "the Archaics are compelling actors." Since his sense of reality had been shaken, he said it with less enthusiasm than he would have just a week ago.

Draevik gave him a knowing smirk. "You have to stop denying their powers. Especially now."

"Why?"

"Because even though their powers are strong, they're also fleeting, and that's where you step in."

Draevik's words enlivened Glavin's ominous sense of dread. "Is it now?"

"Your weather enhancement project can save us."

"Can you be more specific? The Archaics, or whatever they are, have never claimed to be the instigators of the weather. It is a self-correcting mechanism of the planet."

"But the Archaics are servants to the planet, balancers of this mechanism, and thus keep the public safe."

Glavin shrugged. "If you say so."

"That's what the Caretaker says and based on their display of powers since they've been in town, we have to take his warning seriously."

"What warning?"

Draevik relayed the news with an unnerving callousness that Glavin found more disturbing than the news itself. Not to mention the official had missed the mark yet again, more so than he'd done with his vision of the relic.

"I'm sure Baclus filled you in on the latest developments concerning the relic," Draevik continued, "so you're aware Ceera and Dassius are unlikely to complete their task. Which means soon the Archaics will be as powerless as your followers believe them to be."

"What exactly are you asking me to do?" Glavin asked through clenched teeth.

"I want you ready to combat any planetary disturbance."

"How—"

"Haven't you been working on enhancing the weather for years?"

"Yes, but our project is about altering it," Glavin said bluntly, "not overriding planetary disturbances. The CfA cannot combat the planet."

Draevik straightened in his chair and smiled slyly, his guards hovering just that much closer, and said, "I think you better try."

Chapter Twenty-Three

AFTER DASSIUS AND Ceera exited another bleak tunnel, a clear pool of water awaited them. Orange stalactites hung from the low ceiling, enhancing the visual that looked too perfect to be real. They stopped to admire the water's still and glassy image, gazing at their reflections staring back.

Dassius put his arm around her shoulders, liking how it looked there. She smiled at him, then bent over to scoop some water into her thermos. He gestured for it when she stood to take a drink.

"I forgot," she said, "it may be contaminated."

But they couldn't pass up a chance to drink from it if possible. Their own water supply wouldn't last forever. Dassius dipped his thermos into the water before squeezing a purifying solution into both his and Ceera's. They waited several minutes while the solution did its work, then drank languidly to quench their thirst.

"Delicious," Ceera said. "Maybe we didn't need to purify it."

"We can't take any chances," he replied.

They stuffed their thermoses back into their packs and continued into the adjacent tunnel. The passageway lit up before them.

Strands of glittering light hung from the ceiling, giving the impression of the night sky.

"It's beautiful," she breathed.

"It is," Dassius said, but there was something else about it too.

"What's wrong?" she asked.

He shrugged. "What is it?"

"Something pretty. Can we set up camp?"

Dassius frowned. "You want to sleep here?"

"Just a short nap."

There was a gleam in her eye, as if she were keeping something from him. But he didn't ask.

"Alright, you rest and I'll keep watch."

"You're not going to nap with me?" she asked.

"I'm not tired," he said.

She arranged her sleeping pad and lay down. Dassius leaned against stone and tried not to stare at her.

He hadn't slept well the past few weeks, or even at all. His worry for Ceera when she'd come up missing had snowballed. And then he'd been asked to accompany her. Anxiety kept him awake during the night they'd spent so far in the cave.

His apprehension waned the longer he gazed at the twinkling splendor. For the moment, all was fine. He closed his eyes. A few minutes of sleep was all he needed.

❧

"Speak your purpose," Draevik snapped at the guard who'd entered his office, annoyed to be disturbed from his moment of peace. The Archaics making life easy on him had been a surprising yet welcome development, but the guard was evidently about to put a damper on his good mood.

"The Archaics plan to speak on the global update soon. Through the CfNL."

His anger solidified. "Who told you this?"

"I saw their program added to the listings." The guard clicked on Draevik's global update sphere and stepped aside.

Marvus and Desnia appeared on the screen. Though standing in the background, the Archaics overshadowed them.

"An unprecedented situation plagues us," Desnia was saying, "and the Archaics have honored us with their presence. They've been called to Semadon by Ceera Kestlyn, who, as you know, has recently left the village again. Strangely, High Service has not relayed the reason for her sudden departure, have even denied the public a meeting, yet the Archaics are not so secretive, for this reason involves them as well. They've revealed the relic contains secret information. It prophesies something High Service intends to hide."

Draevik scowled at the screen. "Go to the control center and cut the program."

"What reason should I give them? The CfNL has broadcasting privileges."

"Tell them I said to do it," Draevik said, "to avoid the unrest their speech will stir up. Go!"

The guard backed away and fled. Draevik turned his attention back to the screen.

Marvus was now speaking. "So Ceera must return the relic to a cave. If she fails, then she will die and the Archaics will lose their powers."

Draevik shook his head in disgust. Why had his guard not reached the controls yet?

"And why," Marvus continued, "is High Service behaving disingenuously? What compels them to be so secretive?

Why are they failing to serve the people and endangering the life of young Ceera and the cherished entities we've come to rely upon?"

Baric moved forward to the microphone. Trembling with surprise, Marvus stepped aside and clasped his hands together anxiously. Unimpressed, Draevik drummed his fingers on his desk and waited for the image to disappear. Did one not have to run fast to be a guard?

"There is even more at stake," Baric said gravely. "Parasitic creatures live inside the planet, creatures not unlike yourselves yet altogether different, transformed by time and circumstance. They slipped through the cracks, long ago, when your forest became what it is."

Curious, Draevik perked up. What news was this?

"Some of you dare think the Archaics serve no purpose," Baric continued. "That we only exist as otherworldly beings to fear. But I'm the one who keeps these creatures from reaching the planet's surface. I keep the cracks sealed. Today I felt the ground shift, indicating our future is uncertain. And it is an Archaic's duty to protect. If I lose my powers you become vulnerable, for these creatures seek to kill and will come upon you most voraciously."

The global update screen turned black at that precise moment. The guard had finally completed his task, but the timing dramatized Baric's warning. The public would now need consolation, and Draevik grimaced at the task of smoothing over such a declaration. And what was this warning? Truth or manipulation? He would have to set up a meeting with the Archaics to find out. A most unsettling prospect, and not something he wished to subject himself to.

Even if the warning were true, that a band of parasitic creatures would soon come upon them, what did the people have to fear? With his weapon program in the works, his guards could keep them at bay. Even if they moved as slow as turtles.

⁓

Dassius snapped awake, jerking away from the cold stone. Ceera was no longer lying on her sleeping pad.

"Ceera?" he called out.

His senses led him to her. She stood around the bend, fixated on the glowing threads that she'd immersed herself between. The sight of her amid such splendor was breathtaking. But nature could be deceiving.

She reached out to touch one of the glittering diamond-like strands.

"Don't!" he yelled.

But her hand had already grazed the strand, and she paused, a confused expression on her face. She pulled her hand away, but the strand stayed glued to her fingers. She flung her arm outward, causing more strands to bond with the first.

"Stay still," he commanded.

Ceera's arm tensed and lifted upward, entangled within the rising strands. She met his eyes as her body rose. Looking upward, she screamed.

A transparent beetle, or was it a worm—too large at first for his eyes to believe—had aligned its slimy body with a strand and appeared to be reeling her in. Its back end glowed, and its protruding eyes gleamed in the lethal splendor it had created. From the creature's size, it was easy to deduce it ate well frequently. Which was both horrifying and puzzling to say the least.

"I'm coming," he said, carefully weaving between the strands.

But as he neared, he realized close proximity would do him no good. How would he reach her? He couldn't climb the strands when they were so sticky.

He backed up, stuck his knife's blade between his teeth, and began scaling the wall.

"Dassius," she screamed.

"Don't panic," he shouted. "I'll be there soon."

He zeroed in on the nearest strand. The trick would be swinging with one hand and cutting his way with the other. Speed and timing were essential. It reminded him of a test he had undergone during his training. He'd never imagined how it would be used in real time. It was now or never.

He sprang from the wall. His hand wrapped around a sticky strand. He swung, maneuvering between others. As his swing widened, he cut the strand above his hand and reached for the next.

Nearing Ceera's squirming body, he wrapped an arm around her. They were now intertwined several feet beneath the giant glowing creature. It awaited them with its slurping mouth, swaying from their combined weight. She clung to him. He hacked the strands they were attached to.

"We're too high up!" she exclaimed.

But he had a plan. As they plummeted, he grabbed onto another strand. It absorbed some of their fall even as he cut it, allowing them to fall a short distance. He did this bit by bit until they were only several feet above the ground.

"Hold on tight," he said.

Then he cut the final strand.

He minimized the force of their fall with momentum. Landing on his feet, he quickly fell to his backside and then his pack. Ceera landed on top of him. Since he'd cut all the strands in the nearby vicinity, they had space to stand. Glowing globs still clung to their palms, as if they were gods holding power instead of two Semions in need of a good cleanse.

"Do you think it will come for us?" she asked.

"If it were capable of pursuit, it would have been down here already. It has devised a pretty clever way of capturing its prey."

He glanced upward again. A growing mass of shadow crept toward the beetle, which had retreated to the ceiling. He narrowed his eyes, searching for another beetle within the darkness, or at least a reason for the visual. But then Ceera buried her face in his chest, distracting him.

"Thanks for rescuing me," she said in a muffled voice.

He refrained from touching her. "I thought you wanted to sleep?"

"I did," she responded, "but then I couldn't…"

Since she sounded upset, he let it go. "Let's wash off in the pool," he said, leading her toward it.

"Giant cave beetles?" she said. "How could such a thing exist?"

"They must have large and abundant prey," he replied.

An understanding formed in her eyes. "Creatures our size? Not the people I'm here to save!"

Dassius winced. "Whichever. Someday I need to teach you how to use a knife."

Reaching the pool, they knelt to swish their arms in the water.

"Someday our lives might not be in danger," she said with a forced chuckle.

"That's the life for you, not for me."

Despair rode across her face. She must have forgotten why the Sci-Def team had been implemented in the first place.

⤜

After the cave beetle incident, Ceera tried to rest, mainly to pacify Dassius. They moved farther down the passage, but even the renewed distance away from the creature did nothing to ease her worries. She tossed and turned, unable to feel safe despite Dassius sitting wide awake this time nearby.

The disturbing feeling that the shadows hid more than empty spaces returned as well.

After a restless few hours, she propped onto her elbow. "Are you going to tell High Service?"

Dassius's gaze rested on her face. "About the fact you almost died?"

"Don't make Draevik's day, please. I'm talking about the creature."

"I owe them nothing," he said flatly. "Not after what they did to you."

"But it doesn't impact the relic. They should know such a thing exists, for the sake of science at least."

He shrugged, still looking unconvinced.

"Besides, you promised," she added, "to keep them informed."

"Are you trying to make me a good person?"

She laughed. "You already are, though we could probably add that you're a stubborn person."

"I'm being loyal to you."

"Then please reconsider. Remember, you said there was tension in the ranks. Not everyone in High Service is named Draevik Warlyn."

"Fine, I'll tell them," Dassius conceded. "But I can't fathom why you care." He reluctantly dug his roamer out of his pocket.

"Because it's the right thing to do," she said simply. "An official named Hetia tried to help me. She gave me a bit of a pep talk before we left."

But he already had his roamer pressed to his ear. "Dassius speaking. I have news."

He described the creature in great detail.

"We think it must have a very large food source," he continued, then paused, listening. "I guess that's possible. Any other news? …Okay then. Goodbye." He clicked the roamer off.

"What did they say?" she asked.

"It was Draevik," Dassius said with a deliberate frown. "He said life is uneventful in Semadon. That he'll inform about the creature, but we shouldn't worry about it. He thinks it was just an anomaly."

"Of course he does," Ceera said, feeling like a fool.

"Yeah," Dassius said, sliding his roamer in his pocket, "so much for science."

⌇

"Get up." Something slammed into Cafold's shoulder.

He opened his eyes. A guard scowled down at him, apparently having been given the task to wake him up. With his foot.

"I let you sleep long enough," Sidorn said, glancing up from his roamer. He raised it to his mouth and stepped away.

The guard cocked his leg again.

"Knock it off," Cafold barked. He hadn't thought he'd fall asleep, but so he had.

The guard chuckled and went to stand with the rest of the crew.

Cafold's stomach rumbled. He rummaged in his pack for a snack.

"Wrap it up quick, men," Sidorn said when he returned. "You too, Cafold."

Cafold took another bite of his vegetable bar, annoyed but somewhat resigned. His treatment was getting old, though not to the men whose jeers continued as enthusiastically as they'd been from the start. Which was an oddity in and of itself.

Semions had a code of conduct. It wouldn't be unusual for a stray guard to be unpleasant, but the whole lot of them? Had standards dropped so drastically within the last few months? Draevik's manner of leadership and apparent disregard for anyone who opposed him may have rubbed off on his personal guards, but Sidorn too? Usually those involved in social programs held themselves to higher standards, but Sidorn was the instigator here.

He glanced at Sidorn, who was zipping up his pack. The large man paused to look his way.

"Evil breeds evil, kid. You know that."

Cafold flushed. "I—"

"And remember, sometimes evil's just a matter of opinion." Sidorn winked before turning away.

Sometimes it's sitting just three feet away from you, Cafold thought inside his mental walls.

Chapter Twenty-Four

HETIA HEADED TO the meeting room, feeling as if she'd just left. They'd already held a meeting that went deep into the night over Baric's speech and had decided to resume first thing the next morning. Which had been a good decision in retrospect, due to what she'd witnessed out the Aurora's window that morning.

Risa and Karnen looked especially troubled, which didn't surprise her, since they were undoubtedly overwhelmed with complaints from Semadon's citizens. She was glad the public was not bowing to submission. Of course, now that they feared for their lives, why would they?

Draevik, also not to Hetia's surprise, looked perturbed. Last night, the other officials had overturned his decision to conceal their weapon program from the public. He had insisted it was too soon, but the other officials had wisely determined the admission was necessary now that the public had been told their lives would soon be in danger. And Dassius had relayed news supporting the validity of this claim. They had yet to decide how to inform their citizens about the weapon program, but that was to happen this morning.

"The public have demanded another meeting," Karnen said once everyone was seated, "because of Baric's news."

"They are frightened, and rightfully so," Risa added in a severe tone.

"We already guessed they would be," Draevik said.

"But we did not guess they would congregate outside the Aurora first thing this morning," Risa replied.

"They've organized themselves overnight?" Draevik seemed shocked, having apparently not looked out the window yet.

"The tension never died from before," Karnen responded. "Baric's speech induced panic."

"Which reminds me of a more important matter," Draevik said contemplatively.

"What could be more important?" Risa asked, exasperation creasing her forehead.

"I've enlisted the help of the Council for Advancement, in preparation for the Archaics' impending demise."

The following silence was imbued with shock. The other officials were beginning to realize the ramifications of Draevik's actions. He hadn't stated this was his hope, just that he had recruited Sidorn as a backup plan. Now his intentions were obvious.

Hetia pressed her lips together into a firm line, choosing to pick her battles carefully.

"Back to this childish rebellion. It's annoying and begs a question," Draevik said. "How do we gain the public's sympathy after being villainized by the Archaics?"

"Very delicately," Karnen said, "so we don't incur the Archaics' wrath."

"We must appear to be on the Archaics' side while simultaneously defending ourselves," Draevik said. "It's a most trying conundrum."

"What do you suggest?" Karnen asked.

"When I address the public today, I will use my speech to our advantage."

"You will manipulate them at a public meeting?" Hetia asked incredulously.

"There will be no meeting," Draevik replied.

"But you agreed to—"

"I agreed to address them, and I will. From the upper balcony. Well out of range of any of their outrage. It's more controllable that way. And I can still ease their fears from above."

"But—" Hetia began again.

"This is a compromise," Risa interrupted. "Remember, Draevik had not wanted to address them at all." She gave Hetia a look of warning. Or was it annoyance? Perplexed, Hetia considered the meaning behind that look.

"Thank you, Risa," Draevik said. "It's nice to know someone has faith in my plans."

Risa's gaze flitted between Draevik and Hetia.

"Now, let's adjourn," Draevik continued. "I have a speech to write, one that will both console and influence our people."

"Some will not be so easy to manipulate." Hetia couldn't refrain from speaking up. "They will see through your attempts to deceive them."

Draevik sniffed. "Some will always stay firm in their opinions, no matter how insensible they are."

"Disregarding the Archaics could cause society to crumble." Hetia ignored the frowns aimed at her from other officials. She kept her focus on Draevik, trusting that Fresdin was scoping out their peers.

"It's the way of the world. Evolution always causes the demise of *some*," Draevik said, glaring at her.

She gazed back with complacency, for it was also true that evolution was not ruled by Draevik Warlyn. It would cause the demise of whomever it deemed unfit.

&

Ceera and Dassius wandered the dark passageways again. They'd given up on sleep after their disappointing call to High Service.

In a state of weariness, Ceera discovered another bead on a narrow ledge gleaming in their dismal surroundings. When she picked it up, her headlamp shone on words etched onto the wall in reddish dye.

> *Our flesh and bone have dissolved. So it seems. We walk as ghosts who need not. All my desires have waned but for one. That is you. How long before you seek out your tribesmen? How could you allow me to leave you behind? What do you have to live for now besides hate and death? Funny you choose death. Life grows in my belly while hate thrives in your heart. But perhaps you have learned to respect the prophecy and are on your way.*

"Dassius," she said excitedly. "Baric was right, the stones speak."

Dassius stood beside her, reading for himself as she scanned the words again.

"So going underground somehow dehumanized them," he said. "And whoever wrote this is mad at their lover."

"The woman wrote it," Ceera said, showing him the bead, "and she's addressing Rebial. He said she left the prophecy so it would bring him to her. Apparently because she loved him."

"Yet he chose to stay above ground," Dassius said. "He turned his back on her."

"And she was with child," Ceera spoke softly. "Do you think he knew?"

"He didn't seem to care about much," Dassius said dryly.

"He told me he saved the forest," she said. "He made it his duty to stay above."

"Let's not give him any credit. Especially since we're the ones finding the beads and not him."

Jealousy sprang up inside her. Heat rose in her face.

"I knew she'd left them for someone," she said, roughly stuffing the bead into her pocket.

But instead of being disgusted with Rebial, she was upset that the woman had not left the beads for her to find. She'd left them for her lover, suggesting he hadn't always been a monster trapped in the wood. But it also suggested something else.

Ceera looked down at the relic strapped to her chest. The woman she suspected had transcribed it was embedded in her mind. And Rebial, who had wanted nothing to do with the relic, was prowling her, watching from the shadows, if not in real life then in some medium similar to the woman in her dreams.

On many planes and levels, existence is open to interpretation.

Something else was at stake down here. And it needed to be fulfilled.

Wyman, looking paler than usual, opened the door to Draevik's persistent knocking. Being cooped up beneath the ground was starting to have effects on the man's complexion. Not that it was glowing to begin with.

"I wondered if you'd be back today," Wyman said by way of greeting. "I do get global update reception down here. Perilous things, those vermin." He flashed a smile that reminded Draevik of a weasel.

"Your suspicion was correct," Draevik responded. "I need training to begin immediately."

"That can be arranged. How many will undergo this training?"

"A couple hundred order patrols, though I'd like them trained in rotations since we'll need some to remain at Semadon. A group will meet you here shortly and escort you to the location by travel pod. It's several miles past Semadon, remote enough that you won't have to worry about any interference from the settlements."

"When you're holding a powerful weapon, you don't worry."

"I'm talking about snoopers, not viable threats," Draevik chided.

Undeterred by the scolding, Wyman said, "I'll ready the weaponry."

"How long do you think this training will take?"

"Not long. There's not much skill involved. All you need is good aim and the ability to press a button."

"Have you anything for keeping Semions in line? In case we need to inject fear as opposed to death?"

"Threats work. Especially once a person sees what happens to a target."

"Then make that part of the training," Draevik said.

Wyman smiled in his disturbing way again. "Of course I will."

⌘

Sidorn's crew had been pleased to find the pool of water. Until they saw what floated in it.

"I'm not normally a queasy guy," Sidorn said, "but that's disgusting."

The guards murmured in agreement.

Cafold, catching sight of the slimy mass, clutched his stomach to keep from heaving.

"Mr. Scientist," Sidorn said. "What is that?"

Cafold frowned at being put on the spot. "I would have to do testing."

Sidorn looked unsurprised, which irked him since it meant the Sci-Def member had probably read his mind.

"No time for that," Sidorn said. "Let's go."

They trudged forward and Cafold followed, pausing to stare at the nasty glob.

Sidorn stopped abruptly after entering the nearby tunnel. "There's our answer."

The men voiced sounds of amazement. Cafold peered around them. Glittering strands hung from the ceiling, more eye-catching than the gelatinous glob in the water.

"I got a call about this earlier," Sidorn said, his tone betraying a note of puzzlement. "But no one told me there'd been a casualty."

As the men inched forward, unblocking Cafold's view, he saw what Sidorn was referring to. Splattered unceremoniously on the ground was the remains of a creature, some sort of Arachnocampa, it's insides trailing away from its body.

"Don't touch the strands," Sidorn said, as the men moved closer to the creature.

Cafold gaped at the creature's face. Though insect-like, it was as big as his own. He instinctively grasped his roamer in his pocket, wanting desperately to consult with Hegliod.

"Odd," Sidorn muttered, "that Dassius murdered it."

"Why is that?" Cafold asked. "It appears they were covered in its mucus."

Sidorn grimaced. "That thing wouldn't have outright attacked them. It probably just got a little hungry."

He wondered why Sidorn, whose own integrity was lacking, would bother to question Dassius's actions. Not that hypocritical didn't align with other adjectives he'd use to describe the Sci-Def member.

Then one of the men shoved another into the glowing strands, and Sidorn charged forward like an angry parent to put a stop to the rough housing.

Chapter Twenty-Five

CEERA AND DASSIUS hadn't traveled far from where she'd found the last bead, when he held out a hand to stop her.

"Stay here," he said, slinking past and rounding the tunnel.

She waited, lips curling downward. Headlamp or not, she didn't like standing in the darkness by herself, unable to see him. It was unfair of him to put her in this position.

Tiptoeing after him, she peered around the bend. A strange sight met her eyes in an alternate passageway.

Her headlamp illuminated a group of creatures Semion-like in stature but noticeably smaller, even from a distance. Their hunched backs facing her, they seemed to be gathered around something.

It occurred to her that these could be the ancestors of the relic's people. Time had not been kind to them. Her sympathy rose at their brutish appearance—long, scraggly hair and dressed scantily in rags—for surely they had waited too long for their liberation.

Excited now, she inched closer. Several creatures slowly turned with blank expressions, revealing the totality of their tragic history. Her heart went out to them as she neared.

They were ugly, scabby creatures with pale faces worn and drawn. In place of eyes, they had sunken crevices, yet seemed to know exactly where she stood.

"I've come to free you," she said, holding up her thumb. "I have the relic and bear the mark."

As she continued around the bend, she saw what they'd been focused on—a scuffle—and realized these were not a people awaiting liberation.

Dassius thrashed within their inner circle. They reached for him in ruthless fashion, tugging at his clothes, clawing at his skin. Blood gushed down his arm. He fought them off with a flurry of arms, stuck his knife through one of them. Its scream echoed through the tunnel.

A creature broke away from the others and slunk toward Ceera. She backed away as it advanced, shadowing her movements, and she wished she'd learned to use a knife like Dassius said.

❧

Draevik stood above the protesting Semions, atop the balcony in the Aurora. Watching their ridiculous behavior, if he'd had any reservations about genetic testing to determine who was worthy of immortality, they would have fallen away. Instead, he felt more vindicated.

Guards worked the crowd, pointing up at him like he'd asked, so the citizens would shut their ungrateful mouths. Only then would he address them. When the noise finally died down, he spoke.

"Semions," he began, "I want to calm the worries that have recently disturbed our peaceful society. The CfNL had noble intentions by informing you of the plight of Ceera and the Archaics. Rest assured, Ceera is on her way to returning the relic, and we hope she prevails. But I want to explain High Service's hesitancy in allowing this to occur, for the relic contains an important property that has not yet been disclosed to you, even by the CfNL."

Draevik paused. Passive aggressive tactics were always more successful when given time to manifest. The doubt must be allowed to surface naturally.

"We did some carbon dating on the relic and discovered it was of ancient origin, which I'm sure you all suspected. Something you don't know is the relic's material should not withstand this duration of time. This suggests it has some sort of longevity property. We planned to study it in hopes of duplicating this feature for the benefit of society. This is why we held back from allowing its removal from Semadon."

Draevik looked down on his people with a sorrowful expression.

"But alas, the Archaics came and we complied with their demands. It's easy to understand their desire to remain immortal, for they have always been, and we've only just had this possibility at our fingertips. It is most fascinating. Who doesn't marvel at the concept and wish it for themself?"

Draevik stared into the distance with a glint in his eye that he hoped would spur desire in his audience. If they could see it from so far beneath him.

"We all do," he continued, "and most urgently, we now fear for our immediate future. Baric has relayed news of the vermin, creatures of death who are coming for our lives. But"—Draevik held his arms out to his people—"I assure you there's nothing to fear, for your safety has always been our greatest concern."

His audience was so still and attentive that it was hard to differentiate them from the statues on the lawn.

"This is why," he said, "we began a project soon to be carried out by our loyal order patrols and guards. We will supply them with weapons, or as I like to call them, safety machines. Once equipped, they will kill these vermin and thus ensure your protection."

Rumblings from some, a shifting in stances, but most remained silent.

"High Service," Draevik said dramatically, "has always had your best interests at heart."

He paused into the stillness, a generous act since it allowed for a rebuttal from the crowd. None came within the seconds that followed. Yet silence could also be dangerous when it spurred reflection, and this thought prompted his next words.

"Now, in order to prevent anymore unwarranted concerns," he added, "I am making it illegal to conjure any mystics, for I daresay they may also inject us with their fears. And I think you can agree, there is no reason to wallow in a misery we are striving to avoid. Anyone caught conspiring with a mystic will be fined or worse. We can't have society affected any further."

A heavy whispering resounded from the crowd. A mix of exasperated and aggravated expressions formed among the faces. Some made inappropriate gestures, while others tried to tame them with words too soft to hear and waving hands.

Draevik bowed his head and walked back inside to where the other officials stood.

"You said nothing about the mystics at the meeting," said the voice he'd expected to hear.

"It was a spur of the moment idea," he said condescendingly. "You might try having one yourself someday, instead of complaining about everyone else's."

Hetia's face turned bright red, a most satisfying reaction, and Draevik reveled in it.

"Besides, the mystics won't be around much longer. May as well get used to it." He walked past, the rest of the officials falling into step behind him, signifying where their loyalties lay.

But the crowd at his heels also reminded him that he'd intended to thin the herd at some point. And he'd better move forward with that before he started tripping on his followers.

⌘

Ceera screamed as the pale creature reached for her. Dassius spun away from his attackers and in three quick strides was beside her. Clawed hands reached for him, but Dassius was too fast. He stabbed her attacker just as she'd turned to flee. Its death cry chilled her bones.

"In there," he said, pointing to a tunnel. She obeyed and he followed, slashing his knife at creatures that neared.

The creatures' nails scrabbled against the rocks as they pursued, their moans echoing in a grotesque chorus. Fear kept her from looking back.

"They must be the beetle's food source," Dassius shouted. "Let's not become a brief link in their food chain."

He helped her scale a rock formation alongside the tunnel and climbed up after her.

The creatures kept coming, their loud moaning preceding them.

Dassius fell behind as she scrambled higher atop the uneven stone. She glanced down; a creature had hold of his foot. He yanked it away, but another grabbed on. He swung his knife at them, but his arm could only reach so far.

Looking around frantically, she noticed a jagged stone perched on the ledge. She pressed against the wall and bent to pick it up. She raised an arm and aimed. The stone crashed onto the attacker's head. The creature slid down the rock, taking out several beneath him. She breathed a shaky sigh of relief, feeling helpful for once in the realm of attack. Dassius took advantage of the opportunity and joined her. But he wasn't content to linger and ordered her to keep climbing.

"You're getting better at this," he said. "That was good aim."

"Survival was on the line," she said. "Yours."

The crest of the rock formation joined with a narrow opening. With nowhere else to go, they crawled inside and continued through the burrowing tunnel on hands and knees until more tunnels, just as confining, branched off.

"Let's stop here," Dassius said.

They waited, panting, to see if they'd be followed. The space was too tight for fighting, and she wondered if the creatures would approach them one at a time.

A creature dipped its head inside, spoke words in a strange language over its shoulder, and disappeared from view.

"I could have killed them all," Dassius said.

"You were outnumbered," she responded.

"They're not skilled fighters."

"Your arm is covered in blood," she pointed out.

"They become more vicious after the first cut."

She shuddered. "Why did they stop chasing us?"

A sound rustled down the tunnel behind them.

"That's why," Dassius said.

A giant arachnid scuttled toward them on a blur of legs, its many glossy eyes bulging larger than her own. She fled into an alternate tunnel, banging her knees on stone. Not hearing Dassius behind her, she whirled around.

He crouched, waiting with knife ready, for the spider to approach.

It scuttled faster, the sound of its many legs tapping the stone.

When it came within range, Dassius inserted his knife beneath its exoskeleton, resulting in a moist, slicing sound. Its legs stiffened.

"If you don't have one of these," he said, removing his blade to wipe the juice on stone, "then it would be much harder to defend yourself."

More rustling sounded behind her. "Dassius," she said. "There are more of them."

"Move," he ordered, shrinking to the side to allow her passage back through.

Ignoring the dead creature inches away, she quickly obeyed.

The spiders skittered toward them.

"I'm going back the way we came," she said. "Those other creatures can't still be waiting for us."

"If they are, let's show these spiders to their next meal."

She hurried back to the original opening and crawled out. Dassius pulled his large body out beside her. They climbed onto a rock jutting above the entrance.

Several pale creatures still lurked below. The spiders emerged and crawled down the cliff straight toward them. The creatures screeched and ran, the slowest meeting an unlucky end by fangs. The spider rolled its victim in white threads before scurrying after the others. Dassius was digging in his pack for something.

More pale creatures came from the adjacent tunnel. Smarter than the others, they had timed their attack more strategically. "I see them," he said.

But then, darkness etching the cave's walls transformed into a shadow. The creatures shrieked as it edged toward them.

"Dassius," she said, voice trembling.

He looked up; his arms fell slack.

The shadow man was a trickery of the eyes and sensibilities, roughly sketched and unrefined.

Still shrieking, the creatures ran as a giant mass back into the tunnel. The dark silhouette followed, slow yet menacing, melting back into the shadows once the creatures scrabbling could no longer be heard.

She had seen many strange things over the past few months, but this was the hardest to accept. A shadow had come to life, and she had a feeling that she knew whose it was. Or at least whose it had been.

"I would have saved us," Dassius said.

"I know that," she replied. "But Rebial did not."

&

Hetia and Fresdin headed back to their office, talking in low murmured voices. She was trying to pretend as if Draevik's words had not bothered her, repulsed that his insult was taking precedence in her mind over the larger problem: the illegality of conjuring a mystic.

"There's nothing we can do about it," Fresdin said, "and it's not like Draevik can keep tabs on everyone. If someone conjures a mystic, how will he know?"

"One should not have to break the law to gain valuable advice," she retorted. Then she recalled what Fresdin had been doing prior to the speech.

"Did you speak with her?" she asked quietly.

He raised a finger to his lips and motioned to their office. They went inside and shut the door.

"I did," Fresdin said, "but it's not clear whose side Risa is on. She's disturbed by Draevik's actions, but her loyalties are still with him and Karnen."

"How did you glean all this without outing us?" Hetia asked, impressed.

"Very carefully," Fresdin responded. "Although Risa is not the cleverest sphere six."

Disappointed, Hetia turned to the spherical screen to check on the settlements. "I was hoping we'd have Dassius's roamer number by now."

"Has Cafold checked in?" Fresdin asked.

"No," she replied in frustration. "Though Xyria called to confirm they passed the giant beetle we warned them about. Sidorn's crew killed it."

"That's reprehensible," Fresdin said. "Though I shouldn't be surprised. At least we know they're close behind."

"There is that," she agreed, skimming the screen. "Check out these complaints rolling in." She bit her tongue, reminded again of Draevik's insult.

"Anything besides reactions to Draevik's speech? Not much we can do about those."

"Actually." Hetia's tone grew serious. "There is. Look at this!" She moved aside so he could access the screen.

He skimmed the complaint. "This is news!"

"If this doesn't open up the eyes of the other officials, I don't know what will."

Ceera and Dassius hurried away from the tunnel where they'd encountered the pale creatures and Rebial's ghostly shadow.

With distance between them, she felt safe, though there was no reason to believe they were truly in the clear. Their safety could change without warning. And the thought of Rebial defending them didn't comfort her like it should. It confused her. He'd also protected her in the forest when he'd killed Falken, but this time felt different, and the implications were bothering her for reasons she could not yet explain.

Even more difficult to bear was that, once again, she'd been wrong in her interpretation of the relic. And the error had almost killed her.

"I hate to say this," Dassius said, putting his now bandaged arm around her, "but I don't think those creatures are the relic's people."

"They must be somewhere else," she said half-heartedly.

"Ceera," he said, facing her, "why can't you see that the relic's people…they're us."

Blood drained from her face as her world stood still. "But High Service—"

"Has been steering you in the direction that best suited their agenda."

His expression, a mixture of pity and concern, indicated in a painful way how blind she'd been to the truth.

Her sense of reality now shaken, she asked, "But why?"

"Because they thought you would go away quietly? And they wouldn't have to answer to society if word got out that the relic was a cultural artifact."

Memories filtered through her mind then, how she'd been forbidden to speak with the Caretaker once they'd concluded the relic's people were from a lost age. After guiding them to that belief, Draevik had said further discussion would lead to unhealthy rumination. And hadn't they forced her to repeat this so-called truth for several weeks before dismissing her?

When she'd brought up her birthmark and they'd refused to investigate further, didn't even seem interested in the connection, this made sense now too. Why would they when they had already determined a connection existed?

Angry tears streamed down her face. Why hadn't she seen the fallacy of her own belief? She was the descendant of this woman, as evidenced by the birthmark, and was not living underground. It was as simple as that.

"I feel so stupid," she said.

"You interpreted the relic just like High Service wanted you to," Dassius replied. "Don't be too hard on yourself."

But her interpretation had relied on wishful thinking, on seeking a greater purpose than just being the person who moved the relic from one place to another. Because even though she was tasked with the responsibility of its return, she had yet to find specific meaning in that. Perhaps she still would, but after almost being ripped to shreds by the pale creatures, her hopes were diminishing.

Still, Dassius was not her enemy, so she said, "How did you know?"

"I'm clairvoyant, remember? And something didn't seem right when you told me how High Service had controlled your study."

"Why didn't you say anything before?"

"I was hoping you'd be right. I saw how important it was to you. But now, there's too much evidence otherwise."

Stifling her embarrassment, she said, "It was naive of me to think there were people down here waiting for me to save them."

"Mind control is a powerful thing. It led you to think that."

"The relic says nothing of those creatures," she said.

"Remember Atmos's story about the degenerates?" Dassius asked.

Though Atmos had given them what she'd decided in retrospect was a mind-altering tea, his story was clear in her memory. He'd spoken of a past culture that had polluted the planet and thus destroyed themselves. Since the Semions had no record of this culture either, they'd viewed his story as a fabrication of reality.

Ceera was impressed that Dassius had made the connection. "You think that's them? I assumed the degenerates died."

"Atmos never said they died. And since it happened so long ago, that would explain the difference in appearance. They've adapted to living in caves."

"But why haven't they been discovered before?"

"Semions have been focusing on space travel, not investigating the planet's cavities."

"We've done some studies on caves," she said.

"But there are so many. Not to mention this cave was hidden until recently."

"That's true," she conceded.

"The greatest mystery is that we haven't found the remains of their above ground civilization. Unless it's buried beneath years of sand and dirt."

"It could have been whittled away by mushrooms," she said.

"Huh?"

"They break down and digest things. Usually, they pop up where they're most needed."

"How do you know all this?" Dassius asked.

"My father is a mushroom farmer. Part of his farm is used for recycling."

"That's interesting, but mushrooms couldn't have kept the degenerates inside the cave."

"Agreed. I have no answer for that."

"Rebial may have kept them in check," Dassius said bitterly.

"You hate him."

"He tried to kill us in the forest."

"That was before he saw my birthmark. Then he saved us from Falken."

"I should be the one protecting you," Dassius said, his voice now gruff.

Perplexed, Ceera said, "Would it be so horrible for him to protect me too?"

"Is he doing it for you though? Or for the relic?" Dassius asked, bluntly clarifying what had been bothering her about Rebial.

His protection was disingenuous if he was using her. This blow she should have seen coming. Despite his complicated relationship with the relic, it still mattered more than she did. She couldn't fathom why he cared after all this time.

"He defied the relic, remember?" she said.

"He did," Dassius said, "but he came down here to die. Instead, he's running around a shadow of his former self. You say the relic doesn't bring back the dead, but it does have someone's blood on it, which you assumed was his. This connection could still be sustaining him."

It was impossible to know whether Dassius was correct; however, it was easy to distrust Rebial and his motives. At least in relation to her.

"That settles it then," she said quietly. "Rebial's not protecting me to be kind. He's doing it for his own benefit."

"I don't want you putting him on a pedestal. He has an agenda. Maybe you need to finish your part so he can finish his."

"It's ironic," she said, "that the relic is a burden to some and an asset to others."

"That's probably why it needs to be returned," Dassius said ruefully. "It's a paradox."

Ceera's emotions were now fighting a paradox of their own. Staying motivated to help those who were using her as a tool to accomplish their own agendas was difficult. Yet not returning the relic would allow Draevik to selfishly do with it as he pleased, which would alter Semion culture. This conflict seemed irrespective of what was best for her, at least if she took her own life out of the equation.

Baric stood at the outskirts of Semadon's village park, leaning against a nearby tree. He was called there because the grass had a difficult time growing. He knew this instinctively, felt the plants struggle as if it were his own. Those less observant could even glean this, hence the *No Parking* sign.

He was pondering how to help, when a Semion drove his travel pod onto the grass and lowered it to park beside the sign. Baric sensed the grass weaken beneath the pressure. The man stepped from his pod and looked around, as if aware that someone was watching him. Baric remained camouflaged by the trees, unconcerned as the man's eyes grazed past. He failed to notice the Archaic and strode away.

Baric swiftly nodded in the direction of the travel pod. Skinny pale caps protruded from the dirt atop thin stems.

"Quickly now," Baric muttered. "You must work fast."

The pale caps opened like tiny umbrellas and began engulfing the travel pod.

"Faster," Baric insisted. "The grass depends on it."

The vehicle disintegrated as the mushrooms broke down the materials composing it. Before long only the fungus remained.

Baric's eyes gleamed with satisfaction. "So versatile and useful."

The Semion returned soon after, carrying a bag of items he'd purchased from a nearby store. He stopped short, puzzled by the disappearance of his vehicle. Mushrooms withered nearby, and he kicked at them in disgust, causing Baric to materialize from the patch of trees.

"Careful," he warned.

"Did you see what happened to my pod?" the man barked, then did a double take upon realizing whom he was speaking to.

"The one you left by the *No Parking* sign?" Baric replied.

"It was only for a second," the man protested. "What did you do with it?"

"Seconds are like blades of glass," Baric said, "numerous, yet still important."

The man's temper was in apparent conflict with his logic. His mouth opened but no words came forth. Frightened now, he wisely took a step back.

Baric maintained his serious expression. Then he frowned, noticing a chunk of pod remained. The mushrooms had not obeyed him in totality if they were leaving things behind.

The man noticed it now too. He grumbled something, wrongly assumed it went unheard, picked up the leftover chunk of pod, and walked away.

Chapter Twenty-Six

SINCE MOST OFFICIALS now viewed Hetia as a martyr, just as Sadra had predicted they would, she allowed Fresdin to relay the complaint at the meeting.

"We received disturbing news from the Aturin settlement," Fresdin said. "And Semions are linking this issue to current events."

"Well, get on with it," Draevik said, with less annoyance than if Hetia were speaking.

"Our main heat-core facility has malfunctioned. Aturin's citizens are no longer receiving power from the source."

Draevik's forehead crinkled. "Don't we have energy in storage?"

"We do, but laws state that stored energy can only be used for public buildings and not personal dwellings."

"I'm sure if Aturin sits tight this inconvenience will be over shortly."

"Since this has never happened before, Aturin is blaming the outage on High Service," Fresdin stated.

"How is it our fault?" Draevik asked.

"They say our slow handling of Ceera's plight has put our culture in jeopardy. Some suggest High Service continues to interfere with her progress. They claim our mismanagement of affairs could also be the cause for the outage. Your recent speech has them suspicious of our motives."

"What do we care what a few farmers think?"

Beside him, Risa frowned.

"They threaten to march upon Semadon," Fresdin said.

"For what purpose?"

"To keep an eye on our proceedings."

Hetia wasn't sure whether she should later applaud or rebuke Fresdin for his dispassionate presentation. She supposed it was why they had chosen him to do the speaking, but a little more urgency couldn't hurt.

"Bold claims indeed. What is the population of that settlement?" Draevik asked.

"Around three thousand."

"And probably less than half are able-bodied men or women. We have our guards."

Risa's frown deepened, which Hetia took as a good sign.

"Aturin has demanded a meeting to discuss what we can do to aid Ceera and Dassius."

"There will be no meeting," Draevik said. "Everything rests on whether they can find this mystery spot."

Hetia could hold her tongue no longer. "But their demands are forceful!"

"Then we shall return the force," Draevik snapped, "with the aid of our new weaponry program."

Several officials gasped.

"But the weapon program was not instated to use against the people," Hetia protested. "It was developed to protect us during space travel, and more recently, we agreed to its implementation to thwart the vermin."

"I have directed Wyman to train the guards to both kill the vermin and threaten the people if they continue to riot."

"But that's unconscionable—"

"Only a foolish government would allow itself to be vulnerable to its people. If they continue to challenge us, then we have no choice but to test these weapons on them."

Troubled expressions around the table indicated not all were on his side.

"These are tumultuous times," Draevik said. "If any of you wish to engage the people on more peaceful terms, I assure you my guards won't interfere." He threw the threat out idly, as if he were truly being helpful.

No one responded.

"Anyone?"

Still silence.

"Alright then, we shall proceed as I suggested."

"What if the people turn to the Archaics when their government uses force against them?" Risa asked quietly.

Hetia perked up. Could this woman truly not be wavering in her loyalties?

"That is a worthy point, but the Archaics are not living up to their role as protectors, which makes them vulnerable to distrust. Just before this meeting, in fact, a man came here claiming we owed him a travel pod—"

Draevik's attention shifted mid-sentence when the door swung open. A guard poked her head in and spoke quietly to the guard inside the meeting room.

"What's the meaning of this?" Draevik sternly asked.

The guard rushed to stand full in the room and held up a hand to excuse herself from the intrusion. "I have news," she said. "Who is in charge of the Wakovian settlement?"

Asfin and Leynin gestured, but Draevik said loudly, "You can bring that to me."

The guard walked the silver envelope over to Draevik,

who snatched it from her hand. She withdrew into the background.

The unusual disruption brought with it a sense of foreboding that Hetia found unbearable as Draevik opened the envelope and examined the contents. His expression was inscrutable while he read, then he passed the pages to Asfin and Leynin and cleared his throat.

"There's been a welcome turn of events," he said, in contrast to the look of horror forming on Asfin's face as she began reading.

Hetia waited, confused, for what came next.

"The planetary stability monitor has detected a storm capable of producing a tornado that will hit the Wakovian settlement tomorrow."

Hetia's heart sank amid the other officials' worried murmurs. Storms were common but tornadoes were rare. They preferred wide, open spaces where no one lived. One predicted to impact a settled area bordered on natural disaster.

"Some of you may consider this news unfortunate," Draevik said, "but I am not so negative. This proves the Archaics' powers are fading and that we'll gain the upper hand."

"But what shall we tell the Wakovians?" Asfin asked, glassy eyed. "Surely the global update is alerting them this very moment. They'll need an immediate plan of action."

"We'll have them evacuate."

"But to where?" Leynin asked.

"How about Eslan? Isn't that their sister settlement?"

"That would be easiest," Asfin mused. "It's only five miles east."

"Well, we can't give them sanctuary here," Draevik said. "Especially since we have a group from Aturin headed our way. It could cause an even larger rebellion and increase the likelihood of our guards having to use force against them." By his expression, Draevik seemed to know he had backed them into a corner.

"But what about their homes?" Leynin asked. "Plus, the Wakovians grow many of our crops. What happens to them will affect us all, not to mention decrease our already dwindling reputation."

Draevik brightened. "I'm glad you asked. We will save their homes and livelihoods with the CfA's weather enhancement project. Its success will paint us as masters of civilization. Who would dare rise against us after that?"

"You have that much faith in the CfA?" Leynin asked.

"They've been working on this project for years. Letting them unveil it will elevate us all. Now, let's decide which guards will help enact this feat groundside, shall we?"

Hetia watched disdainfully as Draevik and the others began compiling a list of preferred guards. Fresdin patted her hand beneath the table, and she clung to that small comfort. But she couldn't remain silent, her temper flared too vibrantly.

"You act like this is all a game," Hetia said. "What if the CfA fails?"

"They won't," Draevik said.

"Then you forget about the Caretaker," she said between clenched teeth. "He could reveal the truth about the Archaics, and the reason why we were susceptible to a tornado at all."

"And now you have also made a worthy point, Hetia," Draevik said.

She shivered at the compliment, aware she'd made a grave error.

Draevik turned to his guard. "Please escort the Caretaker to a nice, musty cell. We can't have him swaying public opinion."

Hetia's world spun then, gravitating around Draevik's smug look. Fresdin squeezed her hand, telling her without words to shut her mouth or she'd be next. The others not disputing Draevik's decision, whether out of agreement or fear, confirmed there was nothing she could do.

❧

Cafold followed the men though the tunnel, worried thoughts bouncing frantically inside his mental walls. There'd been no opportunity to alert Hetia of how close they were to Ceera and Dassius, as evidenced by Sidorn's gloating face. Nothing could slow Sidorn down, it seemed, and Cafold wondered whether there was anything he could do.

Darkness lining the tunnel took shape before them. A shadowy image came forth, teasing empty space with its rough edges. He shivered, not a reaction he was accustomed to when confronted with the unknown. The other men kept walking, oblivious to the anomalous freak of physicality farther down the tunnel.

But the dark presence would not be ignored. It crawled stealthily within their midst. Glimpses of an outraged face and clawing hands stabilized briefly within its form. The men reached for their knives, but the presence was unperturbed, as if it knew their weapons were made to hinder flesh and bone, not traces of something barely there.

"What is that thing?" someone yelled as it slunk past.

"Can you see it?" Cafold said, though they all clearly did. "The face? The hands?"

Not as spooked as the rest, Sidorn stood still while he

analyzed the phantom. "It can't hurt us," he finally said. "It can only scare us."

The guards dropped their weapons uncertainly.

"Just ignore it," Sidorn commanded. "Let's go."

The group moved forward, and the presence faded back into the darkness. Cafold sensed it following along the wall's edge and tried to ignore the fact that science had no explanation for what he'd seen with his own eyes.

∽

"You want me to do what?" Baclus asked with his normal smug-laced arrogance.

Glavin reiterated the task before them. Baclus's smug look transformed to incredulity when he realized Draevik's demands were not a joke. Glavin was disappointed to see this unusual expression on his comrade. Sometimes smug arrogance could be an asset if it inspired one's ambitions. Baclus's expression told him there was no reason to keep up pretenses.

"This is what happens when politics mingles with science," Glavin said bitterly. "Ignorant officials make unrealistic demands. Just yesterday I was told to be ready with no target goal identified. How does one even prepare for that? I barely slept trying to figure it out."

"What did you figure out?" Baclus asked.

"Nothing. It was an impossible task." Glavin paced the room. "Our weather enhancement project since I've been in charge was attainable. We weren't changing the weather, we only planned to redirect it. Now we've been given the task of playing god."

"You believe in god?" Baclus asked, surprised.

"Don't misconstrue," Glavin snapped. "We need to create

a wind strong enough to counter the rotation of a tornado. We'll all have to believe in god to attain that."

"Our wind controllers were designed to blow a storm off course, ideally before a tornado forms. And we've been unable to test their capacity since High Service suspended the program several months ago."

"You think I don't know that?" Glavin hissed. "Try telling that to Draevik Warlyn."

"I'd rather not speak to him ever again."

"You'll be doing that and more if you don't at least try. Our reputation depends on it."

Baclus suddenly looked pale. "To achieve accuracy, we'd have to calculate the exact location of where the storm begins. Only then can we impact it at the right moment and direct it elsewhere with precision. That's something we haven't mastered yet. Scientists are still arguing over what to consider the point of origination—"

"Gather all the information we have on this topic. I want to examine every experiment, every calculation we've made. I want you elbow deep in this, along with everyone else. We only have a short time to come up with a plan."

"May I ask why you're so intent on obeying Draevik's orders? Can't you just tell him it can't be done?"

Glavin paused. Did he want to tell one of his fellow council members, one lower than him in standing, that he, the leader of the CfA, was being threatened? Did no one else wonder what had happened to Garia?

"He gives me no choice," Glavin muttered.

Draevik's fellow grays ambled into the room with timeworn grace. They settled into position around him, wrinkled and shrunken versions of their younger selves. It disgusted him. Why hadn't immortality been discovered while they were still youthful looking?

"We're surprised you called us," Sadra said.

"Thought you were enjoying ruling the spheres all by yourself," Harnol said with a slap on the back.

Draevik cringed from the familiar contact. Harnol was someone he didn't predict would score well. In his younger years, Harnol was a clever sort, but traces of dementia had set in. Immortality would not cure it, and what then?

Although the chances vastly improved for age reversal technology to be discovered when one lived eternally, he couldn't rely on hope when it came to repairing brain function. False hopes could end up amounting to a lot of impaired Semions milling about the planet.

"We thought you'd never come around!" Zivan said, grinning at Draevik as if he'd finally seen the light.

He had, but not in the way that they assumed. "I haven't called you here for advice," he said, "but to send you off for testing."

"What kind of testing?" Sadra asked.

"The kind that will determine whether you are suitable to become a sphere eight."

Their looks of confusion produced more wrinkles.

"I know I'm not as sharp as I used to be," Harnol said, "but I don't recall there being a sphere eight."

"There is no sphere eight," Zivan retorted, "unless you count death."

Draevik scowled. Could they not put two and two together?

"Doesn't the manner in which we've already lived count for something?" Sadra asked with a frail smile.

"In some ways," he said, "but we're talking about immortality and forever is a long time. If you've nothing to offer for the long term, then…" He was surprised at not being able to finish his own sentence.

"We're adequate for the present but not forever? How does that make sense?" Sadra asked patiently.

Obviously, this one still had her wits, at least on the surface. Which is why he'd gathered them in the first place, to find out what was going on within their skulls.

"The testing will determine whether any degeneration has set in. If it has, then it may be wise to let it run its course."

"I can assure you that our faculties are fine," Sadra said firmly.

"And our minds are still performing great feats of wisdom," added Zivan with a wink.

Here is where Draevik disagreed. They'd allowed him to rule without their consent, sticking to tradition as advisers instead of transitioning with the times and taking on more active roles. Not that he could blame them, for he was gifted at persuasion, but this only validated his position. Jesra would never have conformed to this degree. There were even sphere threes who were thinking on a finer level.

For some reason, this truth inspired a ruthless decision, even for him.

"Then perform them during the tests," he said with little emotion. "Your longevity as even a sphere seven depends on it."

Then he bowed his head, and with a flourish, motioned for the guards.

Chapter Twenty-Seven

"I'M TIRED AND cold," Ceera said to Dassius when they emerged from a particularly dismal tunnel. "Let's take a break."

Leftover grievances from their earlier discussion would not fade. Perhaps sleep would clarify things, because at present, her mind contained too many puzzles, and she was finished trying to slide the pieces into place.

"Want me to build you a fire?" Dassius asked.

"Is that safe?"

"It'll be temporary, to warm you up. This area's pretty wide open so we won't have to worry about oxygen. And if those creatures come back, it may scare them off."

"That sounds wonderful," she said.

Without further consideration, she followed him to a spot alongside the wall with a rocky overhang. She laid down her sleeping pad and burrowed into the blankets, watching with bleary eyes as he started the fire nearby using matches and a small bundle he'd retrieved from his pack.

After it started to blaze, he said, "I'll let High Service know about those creatures."

He relayed the news through his roamer. Again, his conversation was brief, as if Draevik didn't care to be bothered with their problems.

"I've about had it with Draevik Warlyn," he said, after shutting off the device.

As the heat warmed her, Ceera drifted and fell asleep, wishing she'd have a dream that would speak to her. But dreams never did come by command, whether they were frivolous or life altering. They only came on their own accord. Or when you wished that they would stop.

❧

Hetia stared listlessly at the screen as she typed *Request for meeting declined due to security reasons.* The excuse felt empty, much like her desolate mood. She couldn't believe she'd put the Caretaker in danger with her foolish, naive comment.

"There's nothing you could have done," Fresdin reminded her again.

He hadn't left her side since the meeting, making every effort to comfort her. But he couldn't keep Draevik's guards away from the Caretaker. And he wasn't addressing the fact that if she'd kept silent, their elder would be safe.

"Those words do nothing to console me," she said.

He was silent for a moment, then said, "I alerted our crew about the potential vermin encounter."

She'd heard him talking on the roamer earlier, but nothing had registered in her mind.

"Thank you," she responded, not looking at him, but instead at the replies of outrage scrolling across the screen.

"What are they saying?" He leaned in curiously.

"What do you think?"

He read the complaints. "They'll be marching upon us in no time."

Hetia had a reckless thought. "I should warn them about Draevik's plans."

"You'd put yourself in danger," he warned.

"But I have to do something. Especially after failing the Caretaker." Never would she admit that something would be tears if she didn't act. Instead, she came to a decision. "I'm doing it."

Fresdin didn't argue with her as she'd expected.

"I won't dissuade you," he said. "But if Draevik finds out you did this, and something happens to you, I'll still need to lead our cause. I just ask you wait ten minutes."

"Why?"

"It gives me time to have an alibi," he replied. "I'm going to make a visit to our most wishy-washy official and see if she's changed her mind."

"Be careful," she said.

"You do the same," Fresdin said. "It's the only thing we can still control."

☙

"Time for another break," Sidorn said, unexpectedly.

Though Cafold's thoughts remained on the shadowy presence from earlier, he had maintained his assumption that Sidorn wouldn't stop until they found Ceera and Dassius.

Relief won over his surprise, and he crouched to dig through his pack.

The other guards didn't protest this time. They unrolled their bedding and arranged them certain distances from each other. Cafold did the same, though he contemplated sneaking off and making a call on his roamer.

"You, Cafold," Sidorn said. "Sleep in the middle of the group."

Cafold stopped unrolling his bedding. "Why?"

"It'll be safer that way," Sidorn replied.

"Like anyone will be keeping an eye on me while they sleep," Cafold retorted. He begrudgingly tossed his pad into the center.

"There are more eyes in this cave than you realize," Sidorn responded with a yawn.

Cafold plopped down on his pad and buried his face in it, trying to ignore the ambiguous statement, and at the same time remember whether the odd shadowy creature had eyes. Hideous body odors wafted his way from the surrounding men.

Frustrated, he stuck his fingers in his pocket to feel for Hetia's number, as if touching it would create the opportunity to use it. But all he felt was empty space, and, upon further inspection, what could only be a tiny ball of lint. His mental walls came crashing in on him then, and he scrambled to repair them so he could figure out what to do.

∾

Ceera woke to her body being thrust away from its warm nest. A loud crash followed. She screamed, terrified the creatures were attacking them. But it was Dassius who held her, and his expression was furious.

"I passed out again," he said between clenched teeth. "The fire cracked the rock. It fell and almost killed us."

In shock, she clicked on her headlamp, and gazed at the dust cloud hovering in the spot where she'd lain. Rubble and debris covered her bedding.

"How could this have happened?" she asked.

"I've been so worried about you, that I..."

"You what?"

"I didn't see it coming."

"Your feelings for me distract you?"

"Yes, no." Dassius ran his fingers through his mussed hair. "I'm really tired. Please forgive me."

Her heart still pounding, she said, "I forgive you. But I no longer feel safe."

Dassius slammed his fist onto the stone wall, causing bits of rock to fall from the ceiling. Then he stood and staggered to the fire, silently working on putting it out. Staring at the dying flames made her think she'd been too hard on him.

"It's my fault too," she said. "I'm not helpless."

His arms stiffened. "You have enough on your mind."

Ceera pondered what else she could say to make him feel better, but she'd been interrupted from a deep sleep. Unfortunately, she'd had no insightful dreams.

She knelt behind him, gently massaging his shoulders.

"How many days have you been trained to stay awake?" she asked.

"Three," he retorted, his muscles relaxing beneath her fingers.

"How many has it been?"

"I haven't had a good night's rest since you disappeared."

"Then give yourself a break," she said.

"But you said you no longer feel safe."

"I was being unfair. You came through in the end."

"How so?"

"Because we're not under there." She pointed to the debris. "And the fire could have kept the creatures away. You could be more on top of things than you realize."

Dassius gave her a weak smile. "I want to give you something to protect yourself with in case we get separated."

"That's not necessary," she started to say, but he cut her off with a swift gesture of protest.

"I have an extra knife," he said, rummaging through his pack. "Or I could give you a fire bundle so you could light a torch to keep those creatures at bay."

"I'll take the fire bundle," she said, not wanting to carry a knife but still wanting to make him feel better in some way.

He handed her the bundle.

"Thank you." She gave him a quick kiss.

Then they dug their sleeping pads out from beneath the rubble, shook them clean, and were on their way.

Chapter Twenty-Eight

SIDORN'S ROAMER HUMMING jarred Cafold from his agitated slumber. He'd fallen asleep obsessing over the many possible scenarios in which he could have lost Hetia's number. There were too many incidents to pinpoint anything with certainty.

There'd been the strenuous hike in the forest where he'd climbed over toppled tree trunks. His slip in the tunnel which had resulted in several guards falling on him. Even his slide down the rope and his awkward landing could have caused it to fall from a gaping pocket. He berated himself for not programming her number into his roamer as he'd done with Hegliod's.

He could relay a message through Hegliod, but this was less direct and seemed unprofessional for someone still in transition. Doing this would still require him to find time alone. And Sidorn would wonder why such a harmless call needed to be made in private.

The other men stirred around him, officially making it time to get moving. He now followed behind them, wondering if he would ever have a moment to himself again.

Sidorn paused to stare upward at a narrow opening atop a rocky protrusion. He'd looked especially thoughtful since talking on his roamer, more focused even. He placed his fist against his chin.

"You're not going to ask us to squeeze through that hole, are you?" a guard asked.

"Nah," Sidorn said, "but I do sense a lot of confusion. Dassius and Ceera went in and out in a hurry. Like they were being chased."

"Dassius hiding in a hole," the same guard retorted. "What a wimp."

"He was practicing for when we catch up to him," his buddy joked.

The guards snickered.

"No, genius," Sidorn shot back, "you're missing the point."

"Which is?"

"Dassius is not a wimp. You don't have to like the guy to admit that. Plus, I guarantee he's so busy swooning over Ceera that he has no idea we're pursuing them."

"Then what *is* your point?"

"We're not the only predator down here."

Cafold gulped loudly, but the guards were so distracted by Sidorn's suggestion that no one noticed.

"What else could be down here?" someone asked.

"We're likely to find out," Sidorn replied, moving past the tunnel.

Cafold ignored the violent imagery flashing through his mind and followed close behind.

⤚

Ceera couldn't tear her focus from the words written on the wall. She had to force herself to blink. She read them one more time, rolling the gritty bead between her fingers like a stress toy. It was worse than she could have imagined. Dassius gently kneaded her shoulders.

They threaten to kill me for leaving the prophecy. Except only I know the way. I will teach it to our child. She will carry the same burden. So will our descendants until it is done. Only when the prophecy is returned can our spirits sleep. Even though we've altered fate, you should have come. If I don't see you again in this life, I will love you in the next.

Here was proof that this woman, her ancestor, existed as a restless spirit inside her dreams. Like Rebial, she wasn't helping Ceera fulfill her destiny. This woman had altered fate. Put a spell on her, some ancient curse that controlled her existence. Not only hers, but her grandmother and mother. All had been crazy. Just as her file in Drusilla's cabinet had confirmed.

And now she knew why: because the woman had not carried out the task meant for herself. This unfair burden had killed Ceera's mother.

And she'd done it for Rebial. The pair weren't so different from each other. Both passionate, both defiant. Both a slave to their own passions. Both willing to abandon or burden their progeny for their own failings or desires. They were the reason she was in this predicament. It made sense now. If she didn't return the relic, Rebial would live on as a shadow, and the woman would stay trapped inside her dreams. If she did return it, they would reunite at death.

And history only repeated itself, for Ceera had suffered both betrayals. Burdened by her ancestor and abandoned by her father. Could one ever truly escape the past? She choked out a chuckle.

"What's so funny?" Dassius asked.

"I'm cursed," she said plainly. "My ancestor cursed me. If I'm not High Service's pawn, then I'm hers. She cursed our bloodline so I could finish what she failed to do herself."

"How do you know this is not just a story written on a wall?"

"Because I'm living it. I thought I had the gift of dreams, but no, they're a tool to manipulate me with."

Dassius said nothing as tears burned her cheeks.

"I exist solely to meet this end. And all because she loved a stubborn man." Ceera sank to the ground. "I must sacrifice my happiness for theirs."

"Neither seemed to have ended up happy." Dassius sat and embraced her. "While you still have a chance…"

"Didn't you read the last line? She's altered fate. They get to be together after death."

"That's a grand leap of logic."

"Is there any reason not to believe it? After all we've seen?"

"You'll get your happiness too."

"Tragedy begot me and rules me even now. I'll probably die and be separated from you. You'll find someone else."

"That's poetic," he said, "but I'm not going to let you die, and I don't want someone else."

Ceera gazed up at him, her tears giving him a sparkling persona. She placed her head against his shoulder.

"We still have time. You'll succeed. After that, you'll have the rest of your life with me: someone you may never have met if it weren't for this curse. Besides, did you really want to spend your life as a scribe?"

"Not really."

"So maybe this was the best way. Not just for your ancestor and Rebial, but for the relic. Look at how greedy Draevik has become. She may have been subjected to the same greed down here, without Rebial to protect her. The relic could've ended up in the wrong hands. You never know."

"Yes," she said softly, "and we never will."

"After this is over, you'll be a hero."

"You're the hero," she said. "I'm just a slave to warped fate."

"You're making the best out of the choices you have. Not everyone would have been so brave."

"Then they'd be dead."

"People die all the time from making the wrong choices. You made the right choice. Even more reason to be proud of yourself."

Ceera smiled, despite the fact he was giving her too much credit. "No one has ever supported me like this before. Surely not my father, who—" the words stuck in her throat. She broke free from his arms and stood, staggering to the cave wall. She pressed her headlamp against the stone.

Dassius was right behind her. "Are you okay?"

"No," she said, unable to stop trembling.

"What's wrong?"

She fell into his arms. "It was my father."

"What was?"

"It was the females in his lineage who had the mark."

Dassius stumbled beneath her, as if he, too, were affected by the shock.

⚬

Glavin observed the screens surrounding him at the CfA's headquarters, feeling more commander than head chairman. Nerves on fire, he silently cursed Draevik for putting him in this position and wished he hadn't become the dog of the most powerful man in High Service.

Baclus stood nearby, roamer pressed to his ear, exchanging status updates with the scientist stationed at the Planetary Stability Laboratory.

The storm had not materialized yet within the vicinity, but the scientist at the lab had confirmed that it was coming. They had placed several groups of guards at various points around the Wakovian settlement, several miles from the outskirts, in hopes of catching it before it worsened. But they couldn't place someone everywhere at once. And they only had so many wind controllers. So the strategy was incomplete at best.

But it was important to hit the storm at the precise moment, the correct position, as devised from their equations. Only then could they ensure predictability in outcome. It was too dangerous otherwise.

"It's here," Baclus said suddenly, "and fast moving, coming from the southwest."

"Squad three, it's behind you coming fast," Glavin barked into his roamer. He focused on their screen.

High-speed wind and sideways falling rain came upon the guards within seconds. The gray-streaked sky didn't allow him to see much else. Each guard held a wind controller, sleek cone-shaped devices capable of shooting air and redirecting storm clouds.

But they'd need to wait until it came within range.

Adjusting the screen so the settlement came into view—dwellings orbiting around taller buildings that modestly mimicked Semadon's interior—he waited nervously with Baclus and watched his crew.

The radar told him in swirls of yellow and red that the

storm was within miles of the guards. Baclus seemed to be confirming this on his roamer, but Glavin had yet to see the rotation of a tornado on the screen. Perhaps it would restrain itself until it reached them. Knowing they'd capitalized on their data, he could only hope.

"Get ready," he commanded through the roamer.

The storm intensified within a matter of minutes, adding to his stress.

He zoomed out on the screen to enlarge his vantage point. He watched the men, now miniatures, raise their wind controllers and aim them upward as the storm approached.

But it was still outside of range.

Betraying them by a mere half mile, the storm's column of air dropped to the ground. Glavin cursed loudly. Baclus stiffened beside him. The sky darkened and turned green. Hail pelted the men and their machines. The wind calmed. Then there was a treacherous, whining roar.

The giant cyclone moved closer quickly. Hurling trees about, it looked ready to demolish anything if given the chance.

Glavin had been told not to give it the chance. He waited anxiously as the cloud neared the spot marked on the grid.

"Now," he shouted grimly to the men.

Air burst forth from the wind controllers, uniting as one solid force. But instead of reaching the cloud and diverting the funnel west, it caught within the rotation. The funnel cloud swelled more ferociously now. It spun east toward the Eslan settlement, sucking up guards along with it. Their shouts went unheard above the noisy turbulence.

Glavin closed his eyes to what came next.

❧

Atmos sailed through Semadon like a subtle breeze, though some tightened their jackets as he brushed past. He'd been riding the wind all day, enjoying an occasional brief spurt that took someone by surprise, and blowing leaves from strangely tidy piles. He sent gusts through cracked windows and even flapped jarred doors, knowing this induced fear in one susceptible to nerves.

It was sporadic and fun, but really, he was biding time until the big event. A gathering had been scheduled to dispute the Archaics' credibility. Amused by this, he couldn't wait to attend.

The wind had carried these plans to him. Words came to him constantly and from all angles in Semadon. Every phrase, every motivation, traveled through the air in its own unique way. These plans had come forcefully, telling him the event was considered important.

The gathering was small, as most Semions were not so ignorant as to publicly defy the Archaics. Many held signs, which gave him an ironic idea.

The wind picked up, and the signs wavered accordingly. Some signs rightfully smacked their carriers' faces, while others blew from tight grips and flew away. Atmos ignored the harsh sounds the wind carried from these Semions' mouths. Those who attempted to retrieve their signs found the handles out of reach every time they stooped to grab them.

Atmos chuckled at the display.

Undeterred by the unruly signs, the speaker began giving his speech. So Atmos intervened further. A cool mist leaked from his skin, wafting from his pores and spreading across the lawn. Soon, the mist enveloped the entire gathering spot.

But something was wrong, for the mist thinned away. Semions pointed at him. He looked down, surprised to see his body was visible. He tried to call the mist again from his pores, but nothing happened. It was as if he'd used up all his powers. Or they had vanished into thin air without him.

Ignoring the shouts and jeers from the crowd, Atmos drifted sadly back to the CfNL's garden. Having to use his legs ruined his normally smooth glide.

When he arrived, Baric greeted him, or didn't depending on how one viewed such things, and told him of the devastation that had occurred many miles away. Baric had felt plants rip from the ground but had been unable to intervene besides saving a few trees by strengthening their roots.

The commotion in Semadon had prevented Atmos from knowing a tempest was brewing. Had the whisper of an impending tornado made it through the racket, he would have used his powers to impact it, and perhaps would have achieved mild success, but he no longer had the will to bluster. With his powers so weak, he may have broken the tornado into smaller cyclones capable of producing more widespread damage.

The thought knocked the wind out of him, and for the rest of the day he stared vacantly at his palms.

⍦

Ceera pressed her forehead against Dassius's chest, wanting separation from the real world for as long as possible.

Dassius had kindly removed her headlamp, and it lay on the ground nearby.

"I thought your mother had the mark," he said, breaking the silence.

"So did I," she replied, dutifully pulling away, "because

she had the dreams and my father said they went together. But my father's mother had the mark. I remember now, because she sewed, and I used to watch her fingers. My maternal grandmother did not have it. Which means neither did my mother. All this time I pictured it on the wrong female. My early years are so difficult to remember."

"What made you piece this together now?"

"I was thinking how Rebial abandoned my ancestor and their child, and how history repeats itself. It just clicked."

"Does your father have the mark?"

"I don't know. His hands are always dirty from working in the fields."

"Was your mother even mentally ill?"

"My file in Drusilla's cabinet confirmed it ran in the family, but it never said which side. My dad told me my mother was crazy, but the only thing I know for sure is that she's dead."

"But if she didn't have the mark then she didn't have the dreams, which would mean your dad was lying."

She shrugged helplessly. "Yes, he used my mother as a decoy. I don't know why, then again, I don't really know *him*."

"Because he thought it would lessen his involvement?"

"Great, then I'm the decoy. I'll add that to my list of aliases. So far, we have pawn, decoy—"

"Stop feeling sorry for yourself."

"What do you expect when I keep getting shafted? Life keeps happening to me instead of the other way around."

"Are you planning to do anything about that?" Dassius asked, as if she had any say in the matter.

"I want the truth. I'm tired of all these mysteries and guessing games."

"Then ask him."

"My father, the liar? No thanks."

"He might confess once he knows you're on to him."

"No," Ceera said. "I won't do it. Besides, I can't."

"Why not?"

"He doesn't have a roamer."

Chapter Twenty-Nine

IN A PLACE where silence was paramount, the sudden sound of frantic scratching down the tunnel was vastly disarming. Cafold, along with the rest of the crew, paused to listen.

"Here we go," Sidorn said from his position up front. "Weapons out."

Cafold froze as the guards obeyed, perplexed since he had no weapon. No one had suggested he bring one. The only opposition was supposed to be Dassius, and they had Sidorn for that.

Disturbingly pale and distorted creatures emerged from the tunnel. Half-naked and only several feet high, they had no regard for even each other. They came forward as one writhing, disgusting mass, trampling each other in the process. It was safe to say decency was not their strong suit. And the entire mob was coming their way.

"Vermin," Sidorn said, as if he enjoyed the sound of the word on his lips.

As the men prepared for the onslaught, fear shrank Cafold inward, as he battled with himself on what to do. The others had been instructed to keep him safe, yet not one of them truly cared. Neither did Draevik. If they found the relic, any guard could carry it back, and Baclus could carry on the experimentation when they returned. The paranoia that Draevik had recruited him to get rid of someone who wasn't working out, nagged at him.

He closed his eyes as the others engaged in what would surely be a massacre based on the primitiveness of these creatures. Hands reached for him, surely the sickening hands of a creature, and he jerked away.

"Don't stand there," Sidorn barked. "Outliers without weapons are targets. Get up on that ledge."

Relieved, Cafold nodded and obeyed, climbing awkwardly up the rocky ledge. Sidorn directed someone to stand nearby so he could take back his leadership position up front.

He tried not to watch the slaughter but was both disturbed and fascinated when several creatures started eating their own dead. It reminded him of a fish feeding frenzy, except these creatures used claws to shred flesh before dipping in to take a bite. Shuddering, he couldn't turn away. What kept these creatures from being cannibals whenever they felt hunger? Were there rules?

They seemed incapable of doing much thinking, yet had to know, at least innately, that cannibalism would slow their population. Did they only feed on the dead and unhealthy? Such a practice could explain their evolutionary demise. Perhaps the mothers had to protect their babies from being eaten like some of the larger predators above ground.

Since their eye sockets were empty slits, containing only reddened blotches, he supposed they moved by echolocation.

He couldn't wait to tell Hegliod about this. If he survived. What it would feel like to be torn to shreds tormented him.

More creatures scrambled from the tunnel. A man went

down. Cafold pointed and made an odd grunting sound when creatures swarmed the fallen guard.

"Still trying to keep our own down here," Sidorn shouted, swinging his blade through the chests of two creatures.

Cafold decided not to watch anymore. He turned away and tried to pretend that the wet, gushing sounds were anything but the sound of metal knives dragging though putrid flesh.

After what seemed like a repugnant eternity, it became silent once again.

"That's a wrap." Sidorn's words echoed through the tunnel.

He opened his eyes. The men were removing their weapons from creatures, checking on the guard who had fallen. Cafold would be surprised if he got back up.

"Good job, men," Sidorn said as he plucked his knife from a creature. "I could really use that pool of water we saw earlier, globs or not—" Sidorn's eyes grew large then narrowed at Cafold still standing on the ledge. "Don't move," he said and flung his knife at him.

Cafold froze in disbelief as the knife neared. Surely, this had been the plan all along, to get rid of him at the best moment—

But Sidorn's aim was off, for the knife veered to the side and pierced something with a squelching sound. Cafold turned. The blade had impaled an arachnid so large he nearly fainted, right between its grotesque, protruding eyes.

"Just because you're up there, doesn't mean you should be sleeping," Sidorn said, hoisting himself swiftly up the ledge.

Placing his boot on the limp body, he pulled his knife

free. "Look at the size of this thing," he said, kicking the spider over the edge.

When it landed, pale blue body fluid gushed from its death wound.

As the men nudged it with their feet, Sidorn held his knife toward Cafold. "Sure you don't want one of these?"

Cafold eyed it suspiciously. "For what?"

"In case of another surprise attack, and I happen to be busy," Sidorn said with a wicked grin. "Why else?"

Cafold stared at the fluid dripping from it, trying not to look as uncomfortable as he felt.

"You do know how to use one, right?"

"Not for killing," Cafold responded.

"You know where the bullseye spots are?"

"I'm a scientist. Of course I do."

"That's all you'll need then," Sidorn said, a wild gleam in his eye. "The little bastard won't suspect a thing if you're quick."

But Cafold had seen enough death already, and the pit in his stomach answered for him. "No, thank you."

"Just checking." Sidorn gave him a wink and hopped down.

Thoroughly disturbed for multiple reasons now, Cafold climbed down gingerly and waited for the group to begin moving again.

✧

News of the natural disaster had hit Hetia with a force she wasn't ready to bear. She liked being right, but not in ways like this.

An emergency meeting had been called, and the officials gathered with grave faces. By then, Hetia's despair had transformed into anger, but Fresdin reminded her she needed to appear compliant or she'd be joining the Caretaker in a cell. At this point, she thought that may be preferable to sitting through another meeting run by Draevik Warlyn.

"The tornado has caused hundreds of deaths in the Eslan settlement," Asfin said solemnly.

"The CfA's failure will be addressed," Draevik said. "I'll make sure of it."

"That won't lessen the devastation for the survivors," Asfin replied.

"We can soften the blow by offering them longer lives," Draevik said with a shrug.

"Do you think the survivors care or even want longer lives at this point?" Asfin said, eyebrows raised. "They've lost loved ones, not to mention large regions of their homeland are in ruin. Eslan's production of heat-cores is at a standstill and will be for months. This is serious and life altering for all of us."

"We'll send workers and provisions to aid them. Hopefully, they can restore the heat-core production sooner than later."

"Besides the tragedy itself, which you seem content to undermine," Leynin said, "Semions are blaming High Service for its occurrence."

Hetia was gladdened by Leynin's bluntness.

"That's ridiculous," Draevik said, unmoved. "As far as they know, we have no control over planetary disturbances. Why not the CfA?"

"We enlisted them, remember?" Karnen said. "The people know the CfA could not act without our approval. Although the council's reputation has now hit an all-time low."

Draevik looked annoyed. "Let's kick them while they're down then, shall we? A little deflection of blame can right things. And if Glavin needs to go so that the CfA's projects can be better implemented in the future, then so be it."

Hetia sputtered indignantly, but Draevik paid her no heed.

"Any news on the status of the Archaics?" he asked Risa.

"There was a protest against them," she responded. "It's been reported that Atmos was there employing the wind to interfere with its proceedings."

"An ironic use of time," Draevik mused, "with a tornado on the loose."

"He then failed to turn into mist after," Risa added.

Delight transformed Draevik's features. "That's the end of his powers then."

"Regardless, the people still don't trust us, and who can blame them?" Karnen said. "A vicious rumor has spread through the settlements."

"What rumor?"

"A true one, actually. They've heard High Service is considering using weapons against the people."

"Who told them?" Draevik demanded.

Fresdin stiffened. Hetia made every effort to remain calm.

"That is information I do not have," Karnen replied.

"So we have a traitor in our ranks." Draevik swung his gaze around the room. "Anyone know who it might be?"

His gaze rested on Hetia, and she focused on deflecting his intensity back at him. He would not break her down. His belittling of the other Semions' misfortune strengthened her resolve.

"It could have been a guard," Karnen suggested, "bragging about it."

Draevik's gaze flicked away from Hetia, contemplating. "Let's do what we can to distract them from this rumor."

"How so?" Karnen said.

"With another truth," Draevik replied. "You heard Risa's report. Instead of protecting the people in the settlements from the tornado, Atmos was using his powers to antagonize those in Semadon."

"But that doesn't align with what the public knows of the Archaics," Karnen pointed out. "The Caretaker has been locked in a cell."

"Well, now is the time to tell them," Draevik said. "The Archaics are responsible for the planet's doings and are not keeping it tamed like they should be."

"Can we release the Caretaker?" Hetia asked hopefully. "Since his warning can be spun to align with our position?"

"No," Draevik said lightly. "Let him rot."

Hetia said nothing, feeling a rebuttal would detract from the vulgarity of what had already been spoken. Some officials frowned with disgust, namely Asfin and Leynin, which she took as a good sign.

"Some may still turn this around on us," Karnen said, "by saying we stalled Ceera's progress."

"We need not reveal the tornado is a byproduct of our inaction. Only that Atmos's final use of his powers reveal the Archaics' priorities."

"When shall we tell them?" Karnen asked.

"Later. First I need to make sure the other Archaics are just as powerless."

His choice of pronoun, when they should be making

decisions as a group, caused Hetia to realize with alarm that Draevik was the only sphere seven in attendance.

❧

Hetia had approached Asfin after the meeting. "I'm sorry to hear about the Wakovians—" she'd started to say, but Asfin had pretended not to hear and walked away.

The insult bothered her, and now she moved like an automaton back to her office, wondering when Fresdin would join her. He spent a lot of time with the others, talking and looking for hidden meanings in conversation. She hoped he'd bring more officials to their side. And where were the sphere sevens? Why hadn't Fresdin taken her hint to meet back at the office so she could point out their absence?

A whisper sounded behind her. She turned. Risa gestured from a halfway open door. Shunned by one and beckoned by another. She stifled her suspicion and obeyed.

"Yes?" she asked wearily as she entered the storage room.

"I, well…" Risa glanced around anxiously. "I suspect you don't always agree with Draevik's decisions."

Hetia eyed her speculatively. "That should be obvious."

"It is, but would you be willing to join forces against him?"

Now Hetia was speechless. After a moment, she asked, "*Are* there forces against him?"

"Just me. I can no longer stand by. He's getting crueler by the second." Tears formed in Risa's eyes and traveled down her cheeks.

"Tears never solve anything," Hetia said, placing her hand on the older woman's arm.

"But I don't know what to do," Risa said softly.

"I knew you were too kind to follow such a man."

"It was you, wasn't it, who alerted the people?" Risa said. "I admire you for it, even though I'm several spheres above you."

Hetia stared at Risa's creased forehead, her troubled blue eyes, the lone gray hair that before now had gone unnoticed. There was only one way to determine whether her concern was genuine.

"Before I answer, I have a question for you. Where are the sphere sevens?"

Risa hesitated, then her hopeful look devolved into sadness. "Draevik sent them to the lab for testing. They are being analyzed and monitored for degeneration."

Hetia was aghast. "When will they return?"

Risa cleared her throat. "That hasn't been decided yet."

"Are they being held against their will?"

"Yes," she whispered. "Draevik is a monster."

Thoroughly disturbed by Risa's admission, Hetia added her own. "I did alert the people. I could no longer stand by either."

Risa wiped the wetness from her cheeks. "Can I help?"

"Do you have access to Dassius's roamer number?"

Risa raised a brow. "So you can warn him about Sidorn? I can try to get it for you."

"Yes, but not only that, I've sent a crew after Sidorn. My goal is for them to join forces with Dassius."

"I'm glad you told me that," Risa said, eyes shining. "I will try to collect the number from Draevik."

Hetia smiled, amazed Fresdin hadn't sensed Risa's dissent when it was so obvious. "Please do. And let's keep each other informed."

⟡

Draevik sat in his office, savoring that the end was near. Not for him but for the Archaics and Ceera Kestlyn. For himself, at the ripe old age of seventy, life was just beginning.

"I've confirmed it," a guard said, barging into the room.

Normally, this would be an insubordination, except the guard's expression told him the news was good. And Draevik was feeling rather uplifted and generous.

"Confirmed what?" he asked.

"The Archaics have lost their powers."

Draevik straightened. "Are you sure?"

"Yes, Luma failed to start a fire in the forest outside Semadon. She threw a fit, but even her anger did not enliven flames. Several Semions witnessed it."

Draevik leaned forward eagerly. "And the other two?"

"Baric no longer blends in with his surroundings. And the bay has been calm; none of the fishermen have com-plained lately."

"This has developed more smoothly than I expected," Draevik remarked as he rubbed his chin.

"What should we do?"

"Detain them."

The guard stared blankly.

"That's right. Round them up and take them to prison. I can't have their demise sullying public opinion."

"And if they resist?"

"With their powers dwindling, that shouldn't be a prob-lem now, should it? Especially with your new weapons."

"No sir," the guard said, though worry creased his face.

"Don't look so nervous about it. Did you ever think you would be in the position to seize an Archaic?"

"I didn't," the guard said, his gaze hardening.

"Neither did I. Let's hope they continue to deteriorate. Their downfall is society's gain."

The guard turned to leave.

"And one more thing. Have Mr. Rucien's roamer shut off. He won't be needing it much longer."

⚬

"I think a roamer could call a communication orb," Dassius told Ceera as they continued through a tunnel.

"Who told you this?" she demanded, annoyed he wouldn't drop the subject.

"No one. But new inventions are required to be compatible with existing ones."

"Fair point," she admitted. "But there's nothing you can do to make me want to call my father."

Dassius was silent as they neared a cliff. The drop off was many hundreds of feet beneath them.

"A dead end?" she asked. He had never misled her before.

"I've had my moments, but please have *some* faith in me," he retorted, pointing to where the tunnel continued across the abyss.

"You have more rope?" she asked, knowing he always did.

"That and more." Dassius removed the tightly wound cord from his pack along with a circular gadget. "This can attach itself to anything." He looped the rope through the gadget's side handle and pushed a button. The opposing side opened, revealing a blue, gooey substance.

"Stand back," he said.

She backed away as he swung the gadget over and above the abyss. With a squishy thud, it met with the stone ceiling and stayed attached. He tugged the rope to ensure the bond was secure, before beckoning her forward.

He looped the rope around their waists. "Ready?" he asked.

She wrapped her arms around him and half closed her eyes. "Yes."

Air brushed her face as they sailed over the abyss, and she was practiced enough not to look down. After landing on the opposite side, Dassius unwound the rope from their bodies and wedged its knotted end into a crack in the rock.

Crossing the abyss brought on a feeling of having crossed something within herself, as if all her emotions had finally settled into something solid yet at the same time gross and undesirable. She tried to ignore the unsavory feeling as she followed Dassius into what appeared to be another deep, dark passage.

Chapter Thirty

A FORCEFUL KNOCKING sounded on the CfNL's door. Desnia hurried over and swung it open. A large group of guards stood before her.

"How may I help you?" she asked, trying to soften the daggers forming in her eyes with pleasantry.

"Good evening, Ms. Marou. Sorry for our unexpected visit, but we're here on Draevik's orders."

Desnia raised an eyebrow. "Oh?"

"We have business with the Archaics. Please let us in."

"That depends," Desnia replied suspiciously. "Are these orders backed by all of High Service?"

"All Draevik's orders are backed by High Service," the guard said, smiling briefly. "They've given him absolute rule."

Desnia said nothing, continuing to stare.

"Ms. Marou? It would be best if you followed orders. I'd hate to make our business with the Archaics extend to you as well."

"What is *that* supposed to mean?" she demanded.

"You'll see once you let us in," the guard said, no longer sounding friendly.

"Very well." Desnia stepped aside and allowed the guards to enter.

They clomped past her and filed into the room of the statues.

Marvus was standing motionless in the room when Desnia entered. "What's this?" he asked, nodding at the passing guards.

"Guards sent by Draevik Warlyn," she responded bitterly.

"For what purpose?" he asked in a petrified tone.

"Business with the Archaics."

Marvus shook his head sadly. "And we just had the garden put back to normal."

The guards trooped out the door that led to the garden, followed by Desnia and Marvus. The Archaics were engrossed in an urgent debate down the path.

Luma was moving her arms theatrically, furious about something, though her hair and face didn't reflect her fiery persona. Baric sat against a tree with his arms crossed, contrasting sharply with the bark. Atmos appeared to be motioning unsuccessfully for the air to obey him, and Oc~ea stood without her usual sway.

Desnia hoped the guards wouldn't notice the change in their demeanor. It was unsettling and could put them at a disadvantage.

The Archaics' expressions turned deadly when the guards approached.

"Archaics," the head guard said as his crew encircled them. "Draevik Warlyn ordered your arrest."

Desnia pinched her lips together in distaste.

"Oh dear," Marvus murmured.

Without waiting for a response, a guard yanked Baric from the ground. The Archaics moved together while the guards closed in around them.

"On what grounds?" Baric asked, his commanding tone now gone.

"You've been charged with threatening High Service and harassing Semions."

"Harassing?" Luma spat out. "Don't tell me they haven't enjoyed every moment of my presence."

The guard blushed then cleared his throat. "Your indecency is unlawful."

A different guard grabbed her elbows from behind.

Luma shook with rage. "Let me go or I will kill you."

"You no longer have powers," the guard said. "You'll come with us."

Two guards seized Atmos. "Our luck has blown over," he said feebly.

"My powers are dammed," Oc~ea replied while being cuffed.

"Where are your children?" the guard demanded.

"I sent them home for misbehaving," she said absently. "I hope they don't drown." Tears trickled down her cheeks though her expression remained unchanged.

"This isn't necessary," Desnia said. "The Archaics are fine right here."

"Don't intervene," the guard said. "Or we'll have you arrested for conspiring with criminals."

Marvus tugged her sleeve. "Have trust, have faith," he begged.

"This must come to pass," Baric said. He headed toward the garden gate, which was covered in less vegetation than it'd been since their arrival. A guard rushed to catch up, cuffing his wrists and taking the lead.

"Oh you," Luma complained as a guard dragged her

away, "always content to let nature run its course. Look where that has gotten us."

"What happened to Ceera?" Atmos asked curiously as another guard forced him to start moving.

"Don't bother asking questions that we won't provide," the guard snapped.

"And if those children are still here," Oc~ea's guard said threateningly, "we'll find them."

Desnia and Marvus stared dejectedly as the Archaics were led out of the garden.

"What *has* happened to Ceera?" Desnia wondered aloud. "Is she dead?"

"I wouldn't put anything past Draevik," Marvus replied quietly. "He intends to rule over both nature and Semions."

With the Archaics now absent, the plants surrounding them seemed deflated as well.

Waive and Anemona watched from a heavily foliaged tree limb as the guards arrested their mother along with the rest of the Archaics.

Anemona sniffled, but thankfully or not, the sky was unaffected.

"Quiet," Waive whispered. "Don't draw attention to us."

He picked at the thick branch he'd broken off the limb when the guards had arrived. His breath rose and fell in strong waves.

Anemona sat as still as she could, frozen like ice atop the ocean near the poles. It was bad enough the water didn't listen to her anymore. And now this.

When the guard placed the shiny bracelets on their

mother's wrists, Waive's arm muscles tensed. Nostrils flaring, his fingernails dug sharply into bark.

Oc~ea did not even glance up at them when the guards led her from the garden. She did not respond when the guard said he'd come back to find them.

Once their mother was gone, Waive's branch crumbled within his hands and rained onto the lower limbs, lightly tinkling through the tree crown.

The funny man and woman remained below, flinging their hands about as they argued quietly with each other.

Frightened, Anemona asked Waive, "Should we go back home like mother said?"

"Haven't you been listening?" he said. "Our powers are gone. We could drown."

Sadness came over her, but only one meager tear slid down her cheek.

"Don't worry," he said. "I'll protect us."

Waive was acting more like an older brother than usual. His defiant expression, directed at something in the distance, didn't waver.

"What should we do?" she asked.

"Tonight, we'll go to the bay."

Anemona wondered why her brother made that suggestion when the water was no longer their friend.

"But water doesn't care about us anymore," she complained, resting her chin on her knees.

"It will remember us. Don't forget we have a father."

"Have you met our father?" she asked.

"I may have," he responded.

Anemona jabbed him in the ribs.

"Don't be a baby, and I'll show you how to talk to him."

"I've never met him," she mumbled.

"That's because you're too busy playing. And you never go into the deep."

He was correct. Anemona never felt compelled to go into the deep, for she could find depth in even the shallowest of waters.

⁂

Hetia was pacing inside her office, waiting to hear an update from anyone on the current state of affairs. She squeezed her roamer, willing it to hum, but it remained silent. Then the door burst open and Fresdin stood there, excitement on his face.

"It finally happened," he said.

"What has? Come in and shut the door," she hissed.

Fresdin obeyed and came toward her, bringing his face so close she thought he might kiss her. Her heart thumped in her chest, from desire or fear she did not know.

"The other officials are finally turning against Draevik," he said.

"I know. Risa approached me earlier."

Fresdin looked taken aback. "Risa?"

"She guessed I informed the public of Draevik's intentions with the weaponry. And she's joined forces with us."

Fresdin chewed his lip. "That's surprising. I almost can't believe it."

"She's not the one you came to tell me about?"

"No. Asfin and Leynin approached me. After a roundabout conversation in which I think they were testing me, they said they can no longer serve the people while staying loyal to Draevik. He's gone too far."

Hetia was now conflicted. "But Asfin snubbed me earlier. I tried to talk to her. She pretended to be distracted and walked away."

"They're afraid to be seen with you," Fresdin said sheepishly. "They think Draevik may sense an uprising if he sees us all together. You've developed…quite a reputation."

"I guess I'll have to look past the insult to find the positive in this," Hetia huffed, turning her back on him.

Fresdin placed his hand on her shoulder. "They've got a point. Is it such a bad thing?"

"It makes sense," she grumbled.

"But Risa?" he said. "Are you sure? Whenever I talked to her—"

"Fresdin," she interrupted, "Risa confided in me."

She relayed what Risa had told her about the sphere sevens.

"If she were truly appalled by it, she could have brought it up at a meeting," he said harshly.

"You know she's weak. The poor woman could hardly hold back her tears."

"She is weak," he said sourly. "Unlike you. But at least now when our crew succeeds, it won't be us against everyone else."

"That is a relief, although I think you and I could have taken them on."

Fresdin smiled. His arms twitched as if he wanted to hug her. Hetia wouldn't have minded, but she kept her expression impassive. There was no need to add flames to an already heated situation.

"When can we meet with the others?" she asked.

"About that," Fresdin said apologetically. "The others maintain you cannot be present."

Hetia had never felt so high and low during the course of one sentence. She nodded numbly.

"Do what you must," she said. "I cannot stand in the way of justice."

⁊

"Draevik will be speaking soon about the tornado," Baclus said, entering Glavin's office and interrupting him from a bout of heavy brooding. "Shall we go to the Aurora?"

The suggestion made his skin crawl in forewarning.

"No," Glavin said, "we'll watch."

They sat in silence as the time passed, all words in their defense having already been spoken. Glavin stared angrily at his ring, feeling as if its sun were shooting hot plasma through his veins.

Baclus turned on the global update.

Draevik came into focus on the screen, standing atop his perch with an expression that wasn't exactly seeking for-giveness. It showed concern but didn't exude the gravity one should have when relaying a tragic situation. Unsurprised, Glavin twisted his ring distastefully.

"Semions," Draevik began, "brave men and women lost their lives today in the devastation reaped by a vicious tor-nado. A settlement has also been tragically affected."

Sounds of anguish came from the crowd. Curious those sounds could be heard when they stood so far beneath the main speaker.

"Your pain matches my own," Draevik said.

Glavin bit back a scoff. Surely he was not the only one who could see through Draevik's disingenuous behavior.

"You may be wondering," Draevik continued, "how this tornado was able to wreak such havoc, when normally we evade tragedy. Let me tell you a little-known fact that the Caretaker of Ancient Affairs relayed to us before his recent retirement. The Archaics are responsible for the planet's aggressions, namely tornadoes or other events that would be termed 'natural disaster'."

Draevik bowed his head, feigning sorrow over the implications of his own words.

"Which is why we were quick to appease them by aiding Ceera in her quest. But this was not good enough for the Archaics. They stopped looking out for us, as evidenced by Atmos's use of time during the tragedy. He was antagonizing people instead of protecting them, a betrayal that is difficult to understand, but nonetheless true. Ask the survivors of the Eslan settlement, or the Semions who were harassed during their rally, how our wind deity chose to use the last of his powers. And yes, you did hear me say Eslan settlement, didn't you?"

"He wouldn't, would he?" Baclus said nervously.

Glavin saw no reason to respond.

"Originally the tornado was predicted to hit the Wakovian settlement, which is why we had the Wakovians evacuate to Eslan. The CfA assured us their weather enhancement project could save the Wakovians' homes from destruction. What they didn't say was that their method would redirect this environmental monster to the Eslan settlement, the very place we had sent our evacuees! This was unplanned, but mistakes are cobbled with good intentions.

"Their efforts failed"—Draevik's tone was light, accusing, unnatural—"with a startling and erroneous strategy that instead worsened the situation."

Baclus closed his eyes in embarrassment. Glavin took a long, deep, terrible breath.

"So the CfNL has been correct all along. The CfA's weather enhancement project was not adequately formulated. Or perhaps"—Draevik paused—"the fault lies solely with its leader."

Glavin trembled with rage.

"Could one man's incompetence be responsible for the failure of a project that has been progressing for years? I've imprisoned the Archaics for their transgressions, but I'll let you, the people, decide Glavin's fate through use of the vote.

"Just remember," he continued, "if a tornado plagues us today, then surely it could happen again. And who will protect us? As it stands, it won't be the CfA."

Sounds of discontent erupted on the lawn beneath Draevik, the target of the people's disapproval unclear.

"He planned this," Glavin said through clenched teeth.

"What do you mean?" Baclus asked glumly.

"He knew we wouldn't succeed. But this redirects the blame from him."

"One day he promises eternal life," Baclus said, "the next, he drags our council through the mud."

"This will be the last time he uses me or anyone from the CfA again."

"You won't be resigning?" Baclus asked.

"No," Glavin said. "He's been adding fuel to my fire for too long."

❧

Though Ceera thought she could manage another few hours of travel before bedding down for the evening, Dassius had insisted they rest. Especially, he'd claimed, since the creatures could probably not follow across the cliff, which meant he could finally nap with her. She had little desire to resist his suggestion.

The damp, cold passageways coupled with her new perception of reality were beginning to affect her. Not only was she growing more fatigued by the hour, but the endless dark gloom impacted her mood. Dassius's pitied looks told her that he'd noticed. And he stopped bothering her to call her father.

Everything now gnawed at her: the deceit, the unfairness of it all, how she was doomed from the start to carry out this task. Not to mention that there seemed to be a certain futility in dragging the relic into the planet's depressing dark interior. What could be the reason? And could she trust this was the correct decision anymore?

She'd thought the cave would enlighten her, but what she'd learned through her ancestor's writing had infected her with an empty feeling. Her mind thus lingered on bleak realities. The discovery of her father's lie was a betrayal that seemed irreparable. Her motivation, like her father, had officially abandoned her too.

What if she were playing the pawn of the wrong person? Could her ancestors be trusted? She couldn't trust the one who'd borne her. The Archaics were only helping for their own benefit. Even the relic seemed to have it out for her and had fully succeeded at wrecking her life. It had been a boring life, but at least she'd been safe. Could it kill her if it no longer existed? Perhaps its power would die with it.

"I'll destroy the relic," she whispered. "I'll destroy it before it destroys me."

The words felt good to say out loud, if only to herself. They gave her a strange sense of accomplishment. As if she'd changed something in the grand scheme, even if it were just her mindset or the acknowledgment that she did have a choice. But then her gaze drifted to Dassius asleep nearby, and disappointment at herself won over.

So she lay beside him, within the sleeping pad that did nothing to keep out the cold, and closed her eyes. Then she waded through the darkness, not trusting what could be found there.

⁓

Once dusk set in, Anemona and Waive slid down the trunk. Her brother moved with cool purpose, and she half ran beside him. More than once he pulled her behind a bush or parked travel pod when someone neared. His eyes gleamed like a shark in the moonlight while they huddled in hiding. His grip on her felt strong and protective.

When they finally reached the bay, Waive picked up shells and pieces of driftwood. Anemona copied his actions. When their arms were full, Waive gestured with his head toward the water. They laid the objects on the shore, watching as the waves drew the offerings into the water.

Waive knelt. "Father," he whispered. "We need your help."

The water was strangely still, as if it were listening. Anemona continued to watch her brother with wide-eyed wonder.

"Mother has been taken from us," he spat out bitterly. "Along with our powers."

The water rippled in response, but only near the sand.

"We need a place to hide," Waive pleaded.

Still nothing, just the subtle rippling. It washed a single shell to Waive's knees.

He scowled at the shell. Picking it up, he stood. "Father,"

he said angrily, throwing the shell into the distant waves. "Help us."

As the water receded, the ground shifted and rose, revealing a small cave. Anemona blinked in surprise.

"Thank you," Waive said. He winked at Anemona. "And you forgot we had a father."

And suddenly she had always known, she realized, as she followed Waive into their hiding spot. There had always been an unknown force lurking beneath the waves, watching over her. And he would continue to do so even now.

The woman was pacing again in Ceera's mind, beaded bag swinging, a lone spectral of light within the hazy gloom. Her movements were hurried, though less emphatic than before, as if she knew she must tread lightly to preserve the fragile, fleeting seconds. Each step exposed new light and space, and soon the hole in the dusky corner was visible. Only glancing into Ceera's consciousness this time, a tiny probing tickle, she pointed to the dim, inviting tunnel.

But Ceera's defiance dulled its lure. She resisted and did not enter. This woman was not welcome in her thoughts.

Go away.

The woman lifted her head as if she'd heard Ceera's command. Anxiety stole across the face that had once shown confidence. Ceera mentally batted the woman's emotions away and strained to thwart this presence from her mind.

The woman held strong and refused to be erased. She kept pointing to the tunnel, mouthing words Ceera refused to comprehend. Only anger, she soon realized, could rid her of this unwanted visual, and she had plenty of it to spend. Ceera's anger shrank the woman until she was reduced to a

tiny, barely blinking, star that winked out, no longer distinguishable amid the shades of black.

Ceera opened her eyes and tried to calm her breathing.
She curled closer to Dassius. He draped an arm around her.
She smiled, tried to find contentment in her rebellion, but
instead felt poisoned by her own spite.

CHAPTER THIRTY-ONE

A LOUD GRATING sound boomed deep within the planet, startling Ceera from her restless slumber. The wide tunnel encasing them quivered, as if the cave itself were cracking apart. Dassius jumped to his feet and lurched to the side as their world continued to shift, bracing himself against the tunnel wall. Ceera clung to unstable ground, her heartbeat magnifying the unsteadiness around her. The effect dwindled into tremors that were subtle yet insistent.

"What's going on?" she asked.

Dassius had no answer for her. "Let's get away from here," he said urgently. "Then I'll call High Service."

She put her shoes on while Dassius packed their belongings, trying not to dwell on what was happening. The surroundings blurred outside her immediate line of vision, and she refrained from telling him. Just like she'd decided not to mention her latest dream, when she'd forced the woman from her mind. He would tell her not to worry since it was only a dream, but she knew better. Her dreams were as real as the cave that trembled around her.

The thought made her dizzy, and she placed her palms on the ground to still her thoughts.

"Hopefully, High Service will have answers," Dassius

said, zipping his pack. "And according to the map, I think we'll make it to your destination today."

His words gave her little consolation. This meant she would have to make her choice. And after her recent dream, she didn't trust herself to make the right one.

Seeming to sense her negative outlook, he helped her stand, attached her pack to the one already situated on his back, and led her into the nearby passageway.

The deep resonant sounds, like stone rubbing against stone, followed them through the tunnels. It was disconcerting, an ominous insinuation that things were not right.

During a brief reprieve, Dassius pulled out his roamer to call High Service. He pressed the button to turn it on.

The roamer remained silent and unresponsive. Dassius shook it, as if this would trigger it to start working, but the device remained inactive.

"That figures," he muttered.

"What's wrong with it?"

"The power indicator light is on," he responded sullenly. "It's broken."

"Draevik gave us a faulty roamer?"

"You heard him; it's a new invention."

Ceera frowned. "Didn't Draevik say bringing it underground would be a test?"

"He did." Dassius gave her a rueful smile. "I just thought that it would work."

The cave shaking them from their slumber intensified Cafold's desire to do something. The crew had asked him for an explanation, and he suggested the rumblings were possibly side effects from a ground quake, which were rare.

Sidorn had pulled out his roamer to confirm, while Cafold had slipped away.

It was risky trying to trick someone with clairvoyant abilities, but he still hadn't the chance to make any calls. Sounds echoed, and he couldn't get far enough away. Nor had he found Hetia's roamer number. He had, however, been able to do something that required no sound at all. Now he'd have to see if his plan worked.

"Let's get going," Sidorn said, after ending his call.

"Wait," Cafold said.

The crew studied him, Sidorn's scrutiny the most intense.

"I think," Cafold said, his breaths quickening. "I think that's the wrong way."

"How would you know?" A guard sneered.

There was some grumbling from the others, but Sidorn ignored them. "Why do you think that?" he asked.

Cafold broke into a sweat. "I saw some items in the other tunnel. Dassius or Ceera must have dropped them."

The guards watched, waiting to see how this discovery would play out.

"Show me," Sidorn said.

Did he realize Cafold was attempting to fool him? That he had planted them there? Sidorn didn't let on he suspected anything. And what would happen if he became aware of this betrayal? Would they kill him? He made sure these fears stayed within his mental walls.

"This way." Cafold moved toward the passageway where he'd planted the evidence.

Sidorn and the men followed.

Cafold pointed to the scattered items: a writing utensil, a partial bar of soap, and a piece of paper displaying Draevik's roamer number.

He thought he'd done a good job of choosing from his meager supplies. Ceera was a scribe so she'd be carrying something to write with. The soap had been unnecessary since he'd had no chance to bathe and was surrounded by the other men's stench anyway. And it had been easy enough to write Draevik's number on the paper since it was programmed into his roamer.

Sidorn scanned their surroundings. Then his gaze rested on Cafold, who tried not to tremble. He felt Sidorn open him like a book and flip the pages, considering. Mentally, safely within the walls, or so he hoped, he imagined ripping the page indicating he was a traitor from the book. Or if not that, then perhaps it came down to the word 'traitor', which implied different people depending who you asked.

"How did you find these here?" Sidorn asked.

"I noticed them when I—" Cafold paused, frantically searching his thoughts. "I noticed them when I went this way for privacy."

Someone snickered, and Cafold flushed.

"So I could relieve myself," he added.

Sidorn continued to scrutinize him, but the other men didn't bother to hide their amusement. They found it funny he required privacy for such things, as they needed none.

"You know what I think?" Sidorn finally said.

Cafold waited nervously.

"I think these were planted here."

Sweat trickled down Cafold's face. He opened his mouth to deny the accusation.

"By them," Sidorn continued with a smirk. "I think they put these here to trick us."

Anxiety drained from him, relief that he wasn't being

incriminated. But it was replaced with a silent despair. He had failed. Ceera and Dassius continued to be at risk.

Sidorn strode past him. "Let's go."

The other men followed, leaving him standing alone. He trailed behind them. His mind raced to come up with another plan, though he was certain he would not have another chance to intervene. His remaining option would require desperate measures. He had a feeling he would not be getting out of this alive.

❧

Draevik stared out the window, disgusted at the sight on the lawn. The people had been protesting for days now, irrespective of his efforts to console them. He wasn't about to let them put a damper on his impending achievement.

He called his guard into the room.

"Have there been any acts of defiance by the people besides this shouting and sign waving?" he asked.

"Someone knocked down the statue near the walkway."

The marble statue portrayed a pair of officials holding seven spheres interlocked between them. As a symbol of High Service, its mistreatment could imply someone had initiated war against the government: a serious offense. And exactly what he'd been hoping for.

Draevik scowled. "Why was I not informed of this?"

"We set it back up. There didn't appear to be any damage—"

"I want you to arrest whoever did this. And anyone they associate with, arrest them too."

"But he acted alone."

"No matter. I want you to imprison anyone who defies

us. And if anyone uses force against you, treat them as an example and kill them."

The guard hesitated, looking uncomfortable.

"Don't forget," Draevik said carefully, "the importance of your allegiance, and what it will do for you and your family. You'll never have to worry for their safety again."

Determination came over the guard's face. "I will see that it is done." He left the room.

One more thing nagged Draevik, and he decided to end that too. He picked up his communication orb.

"Sci-Defense headquarters."

"This is Draevik Warlyn," he said briskly. "Is your superior available?"

"Yes, sir."

"Please put her on the line."

Dassius examined their map. Ceera sat nearby, arms wrapped around her knees. The relic was like dead weight on her chest. The cave no longer trembled, but the stillness now exaggerated that she felt unwell. Her surroundings remained fuzzy, and she still battled dizziness. Was she sick?

A stalactite dripped nearby, each drop leaving behind traces of its own image. This visual had nothing in common with the times she'd been sick before. Something else afflicted her.

The stalactite continued dripping. She imagined each drop to be a measure of time, each spatter the passing of a second. Then she figured out the problem. Time. They were running out of time.

"Dassius," she said, trying not to sound panicked.

He glanced up from the map. "You don't look well."

"We're running out of time," she said. How would she proceed in this state? How much farther did they have? Would she even get to make her choice? The possibility filled her with anger. At least she deserved to have that.

"Are you sure?" Dassius placed his hand on her forehead.

"I'm not sick." She shook her head then stopped when the dizziness worsened. "But I'm fading. We need to get moving."

He helped her stand. "You're trembling," he said.

Limbs shaking, she gave him a weak smile. A fake smile.

He swung both their packs over his shoulder. "Lean on me."

"Okay," she agreed, holding onto his arm.

The scenery blurred as they moved through it, despite their slow pace. Dassius's shoulders remained a fuzzy blob beside her.

"I thought we'd make it," she said.

"We will," Dassius assured her, although she didn't know how he could be so certain.

How fast would she deteriorate? Surely if she was already feeling the effects then it wouldn't be long. Would she even survive the day?

"If I fail—"

"Your mind has control of your body," he interrupted. "You won't fail."

"I don't want to be unrealistic."

"You're not," he insisted. "You're being determined."

"I wonder if Semions are cursing my name. They must know I'm failing them."

"It's not your fault High Service slowed you down," Dassius responded.

The dizziness bore down on her then, and she leaned against him even more. "I can do this," she said.

"You can," he agreed, then added coldly, "and if you don't then I'll personally pay a visit to Draevik Warlyn."

"You wouldn't!"

"I would," he said. "But don't worry because I won't need to."

"If I continue to deteriorate, would you carry me?"

"I would carry you now if you let me," he said.

"No," she decided, "then I might pass out. I need to keep moving."

The relic poked her chest as they moved awkwardly through the tunnel. She refrained from adjusting its strap, preferring to think that it was nudging her along.

CHAPTER THIRTY-TWO

HETIA TAPPED HER foot impatiently. Fresdin had been in meetings with other officials all morning, so she was forced to endure the stress alone. His absence made her prone to suspicion. And Risa had still not brought her Dassius's number.

Her roamer hummed. She fumbled before answering.

"Please report," she said with no preamble.

"It's me," Xyria said. "We've almost reached Sidorn. We've done all we can to keep up, have evaded the vermin, even crossed an abyss. We're running on adrenaline and no sleep. But the tornado motivated everyone. We fear for our families' lives."

Not wanting to reveal to Xyria that her family had not yet been found by the search party, Hetia asked, "Do you think you will reach them in time?"

"Our scout thinks we will. Timing is everything."

"You are worthy of the challenge. All of you. Take care and good luck."

"Thank you for your kind words, but I must know how the Eslan settlement is faring."

"I—" Hetia hesitated. Was it really her place to decide what another grown woman had a right to know? Of course it wasn't. "Will that motivate or discourage you?" she asked carefully.

Xyria gasped. "That depends, I mean…I must know."

Hetia closed her eyes, then said softly, "It's been devastated by the tornado. There are some survivors, but their identities are unknown."

She expected tears of despair, whimpers even. But Xyria surprised her.

"Then I must go," she said with the ghost of a devil in her voice, "for I have much to do before the day is done."

Hetia heard a click, and only a buzzing sound remained. She placed her roamer gently onto the table and hoped that Xyria would get her revenge.

She stood to gaze out the window, forgetting the Aurora's lawn was no longer peaceful. What she saw enlivened the despair within her, and she shook with rage. The ones who called themselves peacekeepers were lining Semions up, and she could guess what would happen next. Had she been an Archaic, her anger would have broken the Aurora's walls.

⁕

Cafold stood with the guards in the dark gloom as Sidorn set his trap in the passageway behind them. The Sci-Def member's intuition stretched in both directions, so he'd said, for he'd sensed they were being followed by an oppositional force. But Cafold considered Sidorn's discovery to be a mark of his own failure. He hadn't done his part in keeping Hetia updated. She must have sent reinforcements. And now there was nothing he could do to prevent Sidorn from stopping them.

The Sci-Def member had insisted rigging it in private since he was using a device that hadn't been revealed to the public. A bold claim since society was supposed to be forth-right. Yet after what Cafold had seen during the past few weeks, and ever since the inception of the Sci-Def team, this was believable. Not one man objected, not even Cafold within his mental walls.

Regardless, he was certain the Sci-Def member would succeed at crushing Hetia's forces.

Two choices dangled before him, neither very tempting. One involved him doing what Draevik wanted. That choice was the safer but viler of the two, though his conscience would undoubtedly suffer. Could he even live with himself thereafter? Not to mention forever, like Draevik aspired. The other choice involved endangering his life to ensure Ceera could finish her task. But physical strength had never been his strong point and likely never would be. He couldn't shake the feeling he'd be breathing his last breath underground.

Sidorn came around the bend with a satisfied grin. "Let's move," he said.

The planet's fissures swelled and widened, as if many mouths were opening all at once. These mouths called to the vermin, commanding them to take revenge on those who'd had the privilege of living comfortably on the surface, the life of which they'd been deprived.

They obeyed, ascending from the many underground tunnels beneath Semadon, eager to feast on raw flesh.

Inside the Archaics' prison cell, Baric sensed it happen-ing, for his internal sight was too deeply embedded to fade quickly. It felt like cuts in his skin breaking open, but instead of blood seeping, out came the creatures. Pus and infection.

Small, pale creatures slithered from the cracks and oozed

onto the planet's surface. Pathetic and withered versions of Semions, their twisted bodies hinted at what they once were. The sun did not deter them for their eyes had long closed over. They used the movements of plants and animals to gauge their whereabouts, the rhythm of the wind.

"They're coming," Baric said to the other Archaics, who sat with sullen expressions nearby. "The vermin."

"Yes," Atmos said softly, "I feel them too. Rancid bits of bad breath."

Luma sniffed. "Serves them right."

"I could drown them if the water would obey me." Oc~ea sighed. "But instead I will ask it to warn the children."

Once the vermin infiltrated the village, they used the tactics that had won them longevity in the cave. They prowled covertly until they sensed their prey. Attacking as one, their power came with numbers. The scent of blood excited speed in movement. Clawing and ripping, they chewed until their teeth hit bone. Afterward, the blood soaking their own bodies might inspire another feeding.

But there was no need, above ground, to feed on spoiled flesh.

Their ruthless attack on Semadon complicated an already stressed situation. Many Semions, the ones who hadn't locked themselves in their homes or escaped, protested with Aturin's citizens. Others sided with the current rule of High Service. So people of different and similar stations in life already feuded head to head. This third entity battled both without bias and fought deadlier than either side combined.

❧

Despite her failing senses, Ceera noticed a change in Dassius. His posture had stiffened and the concern on his face had transformed into anger. He hugged her waist even tighter, and she gasped from the pressure.

"What's wrong?" she asked him. Surely he wasn't wasting his energies sulking, not when he was being so encouraging and supportive of her.

"Don't worry about it," he muttered, hurrying her along.

"No one ever takes that advice," she said.

After a long pause, he said, "We're being followed."

She forced her steps to quicken. "The creatures again?" Could they outrun them in her weakened state?

"There's a group coming, but no, I don't think they're creatures," he said flatly.

"They've come to help?" she asked hopefully, dreading the answer.

"They've come to help someone, but not us."

Fear ripped through her, but it did not help her move quicker. Instead, she succumbed to the dizziness, fell to her knees, and retched.

Hetia fumed as she waited for the others to arrive in the meeting room. Ironically, her anger *had* seemed to shake the Aurora, for the trembling had caused her to stumble into the walls along the way. A ground quake was the likely culprit, but she was mad enough to credit the disturbance to herself.

Fresdin entered the room. "I was hoping it wasn't you."

"Have you looked outside?"

"Have you?" he responded. "The vermin are here. They arrived after the quake."

She rushed over to the window and cried out. The vermin were distinguishable right away, disgusting in their features, not to mention what they were doing to her people.

They swarmed what she could only assume was a body. Shoes poked out from beneath their wriggling mass. At first glance, the visual had the look of maggots on rot. But maggots didn't claw their food to death as these creatures were doing.

If it weren't for the partially picked clean skeleton nearby, she'd refuse to believe what she was witnessing with her own eyes.

"It's chaos out there, and the guards are somewhat controlling it. There will be no rebuking Draevik now. He even has Wyman guarding the back door to the Aurora."

Hetia shivered at the mention of the unsavory CfA member. He would be in good company with the vermin.

"You need to be patient and wait for news." Fresdin inclined his head toward her pocket, where she had tucked her roamer.

Other officials arrived, their faces grave.

Draevik entered. "Who dares question my decisions now? Semions are being torn up by those creatures, and my guards are armed and protecting who they can. Unlike the Archaics." He joined Hetia by the window before continuing.

"I've already commanded the global update to direct everyone to stay indoors and block the entry points to their home. My guards are escorting the unlucky ones home who were out in the streets."

"But not everyone has a home to go to," Hetia said, exasperated. "What about the people from the settlements?"

"You mean the ones who refused to use the AT cylinders to go back home?" Draevik's voice boomed. "The ones protesting against us in the streets? The vermin may help us solve a larger problem."

"You act indifferent to the death outside the window," Hetia said in a strained voice.

"Death can't be controlled until the relic is back in Semadon. Don't you see? That is why I sent Sidorn after it. If only you'd been so insightful, sphere three."

She refrained from opening the window and shoving him out the gaping hole.

"But maybe you are," he said. "After all, you did call this meeting, correct? So we could discuss these recent events? Please sit down."

Something in the tone of his voice killed the remainder of her spirit.

He gestured to where the sphere threes sat, and she numbly obeyed. Fresdin accompanied her, mumbling words that sounded like garble to her ears.

"Let's wait for the others, shall we?" Draevik said, his words portending her doom.

Properly shocked and discouraged, Hetia did as she was told.

Chapter Thirty-Three

DASSIUS'S CHEST WAS tight with worry. Ceera's condition, coupled with the motivation of whoever was following them, had him concerned about their safety in a way he'd never been before. But there was only one way to move forward at this point, and it pained him to the core.

"How are you holding up?" he asked, after they'd distanced themselves from where she'd gotten sick.

"Better," she said unconvincingly. "I feel stronger."

"Good, because they're gaining on us. I can ward them off, but you'll have to go the rest of the way by yourself." He helped her slide her arms through the straps on her pack. "You need to fulfill your duty regardless of what happens to me, got it?"

"Yes, but"—Ceera swayed unsteadily from the extra weight—"it won't be worth it unless you live to share the outcome with me."

"I'll be fine. Now please go, while you still have some strength." Dassius planned to catch up with her if fate allowed. And since he'd recently learned fate could be altered, as a member of the Sci-Def team, he'd do what he could to twist fate.

She nodded, blinking back tears. He bent to give her a slow, passionate kiss. "Take that with you," he said.

"Love is blind to many things," said a familiar voice from down the tunnel, "apparently even to foul breath."

Dassius spun around and closed his eyes momentarily, as if it would erase who stood before him. The guards in the background had weapons out and ready, unlike their leader, whose presence guaranteed the odds were no longer in his favor.

He caught one last look at Ceera as she stumbled away, knowing his adversaries had seen her too. And he cursed himself, remembering she had refused a knife.

"Sidorn," Dassius growled. "Nice to see you."

"Is it?" Sidorn asked, rolling up his sleeves. "I'm planning to kill you."

Dassius readied his stance to fight. "Plans don't shape reality."

The guards began to file past, but Sidorn held out his arm to block them.

"What's the hurry? Ceera can barely walk. Why not stay and watch the festivities? You may learn something. You"—Sidorn pointed to a slight, nervous-looking man not dressed in order patrol garb—"follow her and take it from her. I don't care what you do to her after that. We'll finish the job once we're done with Dassius."

The young man straightened and skittered away.

"I'll catch up to him"—Dassius pulled out his knife—"after I'm done with you."

Sidorn chuckled. "Get out your big boy weapon, Dassius. You're already at a disadvantage." With a flourish, he extracted a slightly curved, broad-bladed combat knife from the leather sheath aligning his hefty boot.

Blood pumping at his temples, Dassius rummaged in his pack and removed his skinny dagger from its case. Then he angrily flung his pack, spilling some of its contents across stone.

"That all you got?" Sidorn raised his blade. "I was savvy with my choice."

Dassius hunched over in a threatening manner. "You were always jealous it wasn't you."

Sidorn sauntered closer. "I don't wallow in petty emotions."

"Then why are you here?" Dassius took a jab that Sidorn blocked.

"Fulfilling my duty. I work for one man only." He swung his blade, barely missing Dassius's swerving shoulder.

"Draevik," Dassius spat out, "is evil." Hate swirled viciously inside, ruling him now. He would take revenge with one fitting, brutal act.

"Sometimes evil pays the bills," Sidorn retorted. "Sometimes evil's just a matter of opinion."

"It's clear to me," Dassius said darkly, "and should be to you too."

He lunged to thrust his dagger into Sidorn's heart.

"Your foresight's suffering down here." Sidorn flashed forward with a swivel to disarm him, slammed him against a slab of stone. His blade pressed against Dassius's throat. "Or maybe you saw this coming," he whispered grimly.

⁓

Once the seats in the meeting room were filled, Draevik hissed, "I'm onto you, Hetia. We all are."

Having regained her composure while the remaining officials arrived, she raised an eyebrow at him. "Excuse me?"

"Don't feign innocence with me."

"I don't need to feign anything."

"We know what you're doing."

"It's obvious what I'm doing. I'm attending a meeting."

"We know your secret."

She pushed back an uprising of fear. "What secret?"

"You're probably wondering why I haven't imprisoned you."

"I have no idea what you're talking about," she lied.

"You should have been an actress instead of an official."

"I think I'm doing fine as a sphere three."

"Enough," Draevik roared. "I know about your pitiful crew."

Hetia stood and fought her desire to flee. Several officials bowed their heads, Fresdin being one of them, though an angry glare permeated his features. Her trust wavered, but then he glanced at Risa, who stared at the floor. His intuition had been right about her. And Hetia had been too eager for allies.

"I have channels in every circuit," Draevik said. "You underestimated me."

"And you of me," Hetia retorted.

"Yet I'm the one who's winning, aren't I?"

"You may have bested me at this moment, but that's all the credit I will give you."

"Is that so? Guards!" Draevik's voice thundered. "Escort this traitor to the prison. Make sure she gets her own cell."

"Are you sure our prison isn't full?" Hetia asked condescendingly as the guards restrained her.

"There's about to be four new openings," Draevik said. "Now take her away."

The guard dragged her from the room and around the hall to the back door.

She caught a glimpse of Wyman's stooped figure when they shuffled past.

"The thrill of it all," he rasped with delight as they pulled her down the walkway.

Dead vermin littered the lawn, bleeding from gaping wounds in their withered chests.

The guards pushed her inside a parked travel pod, and one climbed in behind her. Then the pod began moving slowly around the orbit.

"I'm not the only one who deserves an award for my acting skills," she said as she fixed her mussed hair.

"Hetia," Nespi said, "not taking you to prison will endanger us. Our crew may not succeed, and we can't fight a losing battle."

Hetia looked out the window at the chaos—creatures swarming, shots, and so much blood—and knew that Nespi was right.

⁋

Ceera eased through the tunnel, shaking with both anger and disgust. The echoes of Dassius and Sidorn shouting grew quieter as she distanced herself. So he was a traitor. That she could bear, but if he were to outmaneuver Dassius then she may as well fall dead right here. For while disposing of the relic would keep her alive, what good would that do her if Sidorn killed Dassius after?

She clenched and unclenched her fist, trying to rid herself of the remembrance of his lips on her fingers when he'd tried to deceive her the day they'd met. Dassius said she'd been paranoid, but once again, his senses had slipped in her presence. He should have seen his friend's intentions were not noble.

And what of Litha? Had Sidorn had time to ruin her

before leaving Semadon or had his departure been too quick? He had undergone the same training as Dassius and could stay awake much longer than should be possible. And whoever was with him could be just as skilled. Equally disturbing was that Litha may never know what transpired. Sidorn would never admit he'd killed her friend.

The passageway forked ahead. Ceera mulled over her options. Sidorn would catch up to her regardless. She shuddered. Of course, she didn't want to be alive in a world without Dassius anyway. And hadn't he been the reason she'd decided against destroying the relic?

Ironic she'd die either way, regardless of her choice.

It was all she could do to refrain from going back to help. Like her female ancestor, who had chosen love over duty. And now she was in the same situation and again a product of this same choice. Yet she didn't go back, and she wondered whether that was because she was more like Rebial, who had chosen duty, however misguided, over love.

She glanced down at the relic. It had ruined her life, and now it was ruining her lover's. She could destroy it and get the final laugh over everyone. If she were going to die anyway, did it really matter? And hadn't Dassius given her the fire starter bundle? It would make short work of the pages. Perhaps his intuition, though faltering, had secretly foreseen even this.

But where would be the perfect spot to inspire flames? Certainly not here where the cave stretched high above her. She'd need to find a more enclosed spot. And if she were lucky, its fumes would finish pushing her through death's door.

She divided her attention between the two passageways. She had to choose one. The right-hand passage drew her, yet the left was bathed in shadows, thus more suitable for dark things. She stumbled toward it, her hands clutching the grooves in the wall alongside her.

No longer able to trust her own eyes, the shadows came forward to embrace her, and she faltered from the effects of the visual. Her shoe caught on a jagged protrusion in the stone, and she fell forward, banging her knees painfully when she landed.

She gasped for breath as blackness framed her vision. When her eyes refocused, the air moved like water, and the ground wavered beneath her. Her surroundings stabilized as the seconds passed, and when they finally stilled, she was left with nothing, her mind a vast cloud of emptiness. Was this death? Had it come for her? Strangely, it was not so terrifying.

The mystic's prophetic words floated into her mind.

On many planes and levels, existence is open to interpretation.

Images of herself and Dassius, existing together on this peaceful plane she now experienced, entered her thoughts. Inside her mind, this was better than the reality they had been chained to. If her ancestor had found a way to survive in some alternate realm with her lover so could she. In fact, she could feel his presence nearing by the second. His arms awaited her. Part of her was there already, content within his warm embrace.

Yet within that ideal, a tiny seed brimmed with the power of potential inside her gut. She still desired something before she died and persisted on this plane with Dassius, still had a need to fulfill before it was possible. Except what was it?

The need to trust someone, even if that person was only herself. The need to make the right choice. And she realized then what her flaw in logic had been. It was the same flaw she'd berated her ancestors for. She'd been blinded by it too, but that didn't mean she had to follow in their footsteps.

Both the woman and Rebial had acted on their feelings, hadn't trusted in the grand scheme of what was best for society. She, too, wanted to forgo all that and defy them both, let others suffer in retaliation of how her own life was panning out. But that wasn't the right thing to do.

She wanted to make the choice that was the best for everyone, not the one that would satisfy her spite. Even her father, whatever his motivations, had done what was best for him. Unlike them, she would do the right thing even if it meant sacrificing her own happiness.

Still on her knees, she unstrapped the relic from her chest. Renewed power emanated from its spiraling design. It had always matched her in spirit. This was clear to her. And now she would break the bond between them.

She stood on shaking legs, away from the mental fog that had almost seduced her into submission.

Someone scuffed the stone behind her. Was it Dassius? She swung carefully around.

The man looked nothing like who she hoped would be standing there. He was smaller, not broad shouldered, with a round smiling face. His nervousness showed in the sheen of sweat across his forehead, the way his hands twisted together. She stumbled backward and away from him.

"It's okay," he said softly. "I'm on your side."

The memory of Draevik telling her the same thing skimmed through her mental mist. She turned toward the right-hand passage, found her motivation, and ran.

Chapter Thirty-Four

"TRAITOR," DASSIUS SPUTTERED beneath Sidorn's blade. "You're going to kill me for a control hungry dictator and destroy my girlfriend."

"The only reason you're almost dead," Sidorn whispered gruffly, "is because she clouds your mind."

Dassius stared furiously into his traitorous friend's brown eyes.

"I told you to tell the trainers," Sidorn said, pressing his knife gently into Dassius's throat. "And now I'm here to prove that I was right."

Dassius winced from the pressure, before realizing the blade was broadside.

Sidorn, now looking amused, winked. "Just regular order patrolmen back there. Ceera shouldn't distract you so much that you can't help me defeat them."

Dassius felt the blood drain from his face as the realization came over him.

"Or we can put on a show, but you'd better be convincing if you want me to agree to that. Since I look about ready to kill you, that wouldn't bode well for my reputation."

He responded by taking a ragged breath.

"There's another crew coming up behind them, but they're on our side."

Dassius mentally pushed outward. Sidorn was right.

"They can clean up the mess." The corner of Sidorn's mouth twitched upward.

Dassius breathed another stilted breath. "What's the plan?"

"Friday's special."

Sparring day. His friend was bold. He tried to nod, but Sidorn's blade restricted his movement. Instead, he said, "I'm ready."

"Stop talking garbage and finish him off," someone shouted.

"No need to say that twice," Sidorn shouted back, tensing his arm and pretending to slit Dassius's throat.

With a surge of ruthless power, Dassius kicked his feet up and rammed them into Sidorn's chest. Sidorn sailed backwards and landed on his backside, but only long enough to use the impact to his advantage. He somersaulted backward, landed back on his feet, and staggered briefly from the force of it. Dassius was impressed he didn't drop his weapon.

"Dassius is an old friend," Sidorn said to his startled spectators. "And Draevik is my enemy. If any of you have second thoughts about your loyalties, now would be the time to switch sides."

Dassius stooped to retrieve his dagger and came forward to stand by Sidorn.

The guards looked nervously at each other and shuffled their feet. "Ah hell," one of them said.

"We outnumber you five to one," said a different guard.

Dassius glanced at Sidorn. With spirited smirks, they tossed their weapons into the shadows.

"Surrender," said another, "or we'll kill you."

"I like to keep my options more open than that," Sidorn replied.

"Immortality for all!" A guard swung his blade at Sidorn's head.

Sidorn crouched to dodge it. "Fighting to the death for immortality." He spun back up, smashing his boot into the man's face. "Ironic, isn't it?"

The man was down. Nine to go.

Dassius shifted to a fighting stance while the other men surged forward.

"I hoped I'd misread them. But nope." Sidorn grabbed a guard by the head and rammed his knee into the man's face. "Brainwashed. No helping a single one."

"What about that twerp you sent after Ceera?" Dassius asked, spinning out of a guard's reach. "Is he one of them?" His punch landed like concrete on the man's temple.

Eyes rolling back, the man wobbled and fell over.

"He pretends to be, but you can see right through him. Harmless as a slug." Sidorn crumbled a guard with a powerful kick to the shins and blasted another with his fist.

"Does he carry a weapon?" Dassius seized the man attacking from behind, rolled him over the shoulder, and slammed his dead weight onto an approaching guard.

"Just his integrity," Sidorn said as he finished choking out his victim. "You have nothing to worry about."

⁓

A dark entryway loomed ahead. Ceera ascended the wide, stone steps, knowing they led to her final destination. She held her arm out, almost afraid the arched entrance would vanish before she reached it.

She staggered through the entrance and found herself within a chamber so vast and elaborate, she no longer felt as if she were inside a cave.

Crystals hung from the ceiling, twinkling like stars. A large, stone formation jutted up, an intricate village, uneven over top but also curving and maze-like.

The relic had something to do with the formation, but what? The spiral design on the cover glowed brighter, no longer an interesting decoration, but an exact replica of the maze in which she would now be entering.

Someone cleared their throat behind her. "Can I help? I'm Cafold, Hegliod's apprentice. Remember?"

The name struck a chord in her memory. But the recollection caused her to feel imbalanced, and she slumped against the wall.

"I don't mean to be bossy," he said, taking a tiny step toward her, "but Sidorn is coming. You may want to hurry."

She pushed off the wall and teetered into a standing position. The relic, still glowing, emitted an energy she hoped would be enough to sustain her.

"I'm not sure who's more skilled, Dassius or Sidorn," he continued nervously, "but Sidorn does have the advantage with his men. I'd get moving," he added. "I'll protect you the best way I know how."

Even in her weakened state, Ceera knew the man was bluffing. He was not intimidating. Not even to her, now that she'd gotten a closer look.

"If they come then let me die," she said as she entered the spiraling maze.

Cafold shuffled behind.

∽

Hetia watched as the travel pod zipped around the orbits, dodging vermin and Semions alike. Twice now, they'd had to turn around and try the opposite direction. She had never seen such mayhem and bloodshed in all her life. If she were prone to tears, they would be falling, but instead she focused on what to do.

"What do you think Draevik meant when he said the prison was about to have four new openings?" Nespi asked as she leaned out the window to shoot the vermin approaching the pod.

Hetia winced at their animalistic cries of despair. "I don't know."

Draevik's comment had slipped her mind during her removal from the Aurora. Nespi had done a good job, almost too good.

Nespi relaxed her position, her steadfast gaze still focused outside. "I fear he meant the Archaics."

She gasped. Of course, Nespi was right.

"Can you find out if it's been done yet?" Hetia asked, feeling sick to her stomach.

"Yes, but I'll have to use your imprisonment as the reason for my inquiry. Which means at some point we'll have to take you there."

"Do it," Hetia said immediately.

Nespi pressed the roamer to her ear, visibly calm and well-trained in her duties. Hetia tried to stop shaking.

"Nespi with Patrol here. I have a prisoner and need to know if there are any open cells…I see. Do you have a holding cell we can use?…Affirmative. We'll be there soon. We're having difficulty navigating the pod." Nespi clicked off the roamer.

Hetia looked at her hopefully.

"They have not been executed yet. Draevik has our forces drained. They had to wait for some guards to return from the orbits. But it'll be done shortly."

Hetia's forehead creased. "We have to stop it from happening." The roamer in her pocket hummed, and she quickly answered. "Yes?"

"It's me."

Her expression changed. "I wasn't expecting a call from you."

"Ceera's about to do the deed. We're on our way to make sure she does."

"That's excellent. Thank you for the update. I will inform. Good luck." She thrust the roamer back into her pocket, eyes shining.

"What was that about?" Nespi asked.

"It was my secret collaborator."

"You have a secret collaborator?" Nespi asked.

"Yes, I finally do, and his timing is excellent. Take me to the prison. I'm going to release the Archaics."

The center of the spiraling maze drew Ceera. Though the path was wide, walking within its winding curve enhanced her dizziness. She moved unsteadily, her shoulders brushing against the edges. Stone rooms of inexact sizes and shapes, barely larger than closets, branched off to the side.

Cafold was careful to stay far enough behind so that he posed no threat. "Let me know," he said, "whether you want my help."

She continued without speaking. The pathway seemed longer than possible, and she realized it tilted downward, which accounted for the extra space. The farther she ventured, the more futility drained her motivation. She found it difficult to care about her own life when her lover had probably been killed. Sidorn's crew had not overtaken her yet, so there was still a small chance…

A chance Dassius could outwit a man he'd admitted was his equal? And his crew? These realities dashed her hopes like the naiveties they were. Plus, hadn't she already felt his presence when she'd brushed the other side? Anger pulsed within.

She would do what was best for her people, take her revenge against Draevik and dispose of the relic so he could not use it for his own selfish purposes. And she would dispose of herself after. A life without Dassius was hardly worth living. She couldn't return to Semadon. And even if she could make it to her father's settlement, he was not someone she could trust.

It would be best to have faith in the counsel of a mystic and not fear the end of her existence. And hopefully she hadn't missed her chance to join Dassius.

Suddenly the maze ended, and she walked into the center of a vast circular room. The relic illuminated what should have been a very dim space. The ground beneath her feet began shifting as the stones broke apart like pieces of a puzzle.

Cafold steered her to the outskirts of the room. "Let's wait here."

They watched as the stones fell away, revealing a dark opening that expelled a crushing heat, an impossible wind, and a sense of longevity, similar to the feeling one gets when confronted with the vastness of space. Sounds pierced her ears: strange, repetitive, as if the planet were screaming and singing all at once. Ceera assumed she'd be tossing the relic into this bottomless pit, and herself soon after, but then she knew something was coming. The wait was painfully quick but also wondrously long.

When the being came forth from the depths, an overwhelming sense of vitality came over her, like she was being born: the experience of emerging from the womb, once forgotten, now remembered. The being came closer, killing her elation with uncertainty. It was so perplexing and arresting, yet all encompassing, that she couldn't define it even to herself. It definitely was something, for it throve prolifically before her, but it was also too many things at once.

The more she focused the more ambiguous it became. A writhing mass of roots and white threads. Plants sprouting and withering into soil. This same dirt closing in on itself, as if to swallow. Flowers blooming into men and women intertwined. Colorful yet muted. An object breathing life. A plant that thought. An entity capable of destruction. Faces protruded and disappeared. Crystals sparkled, minerals streamed, fingers poked. Tendrils curled into eternal spirals. Eyes flashed in all directions.

Her own eyes wanted to look away and focus intently all at once. The visual was almost blinding, but she was too fixated to avert her gaze.

The emotions the being inspired within her were varied as well. Fear. Hope. Love. Hate. An overwhelming sense of being that was at once satisfying but also fleeting. Respect. Trust. But also uncertainty. Insignificance. The being examined her in the flesh and on the atomic level. She shone with beauty while rotting in ugliness. She held the relic and was both worthy and undeserving of that.

It was everything, and she was only Ceera. With or without Dassius, she was still a woman with a purpose. The time had come to relieve herself of that purpose. It had always been time.

"I don't know," Cafold mumbled, just a speck in her line of sight. "What that is…"

She wanted to run away from it and hide, but also longed for it to overtake her. Instead, she took a step forward that was both large and small. The tendrils came toward her. They were hands, slithering snakes, reaching roots. The spiral on the relic's cover, now glowing brighter than ever and swirling hypnotically, reached back. As they touched, the relic faded like a dream within the sound of clapping thunder.

"Take me with, I beg you," she pleaded, for she felt death's pull like a magnet, knew she'd desired it for some reason, yet was held back by the weakness in her own legs.

A mouth opened and spoke words too loud to hear. Flashing eyes again. Roots regressing. Then more swallowing, swallowing, until she felt her insides contracting, as if her stomach would consume her bit by bit and then spit her out again whole.

A soft weight on her shoulder pulled her downward.

"Come, look away." The voice buzzed her ear like a fly.

She complied, closed her eyes, and settled on the softness. Blackness encompassed her and lulled her to a place where thoughts went still.

Chapter Thirty-Five

HETIA WAITED IN the travel pod outside the prison with Nespi. They'd been discussing a strategy, and now that Ceera's success seemed imminent, Nespi was willing to take some risks. This entailed Hetia approaching the prison alone so the guards wouldn't know she was the prisoner Nespi was supposed to be taking to the holding cell. Instead, Hetia would tell the guards Draevik had ordered her to relay a final message to the Archaics.

Nespi would stay out of sight and ensure Hetia made it safely in the building.

Hetia placed a hand on the pod's door, wishing Sidorn would call with a final confirmation.

"Are you sure this secret weapon is fulfilling what needs to happen?" Nespi said.

"Yes," she responded. "He won't fail."

But it occurred to her that she had put her trust in someone who until minutes ago she had not known was her ally. It seemed careless after being wrong about Risa. Yet her hesitation to leave the pod and expose herself to outside forces would ensure the guards had time to execute the Archaics. And she couldn't allow Risa's betrayal to rule her instinct.

Hetia gave Nespi a nod of readiness and exited the pod.

She marched to the prison entrance and rang the bell. Nespi had stepped out as well but remained hidden behind the pod, weapon ready.

A guard answered the door and looked at her wearily.

"I am Hetia, sphere three," she said, "and I have a message for the Archaics."

"What for?" he asked skeptically. "They're about to be executed."

"It's confidential," she said, relieved it had not yet been done. "Draevik sent me."

"Draevik ordered their execution. This doesn't make sense."

The guard had not opened the door even a fraction wider. Hetia maintained her confident posture, despite the desperation brewing inside her.

Think, she told herself. *What are people on their death beds normally allowed?*

"I have a message from Oc~ea's children," she said. "They begged we share their final words of love."

Shots erupted behind her, presumably from Nespi's weapon, as the sounds were followed by the same animal-like cries she'd heard earlier.

The guard glanced up, his face tense, and yanked her inside.

"Draevik ordered us to find the children and kill them too," he said roughly.

Disgust at Draevik for crossing this last moral boundary tore through her. But instead of heaving, she found her strength.

"High Service has convinced Draevik that the killing of innocent children, deprived of their powers, is not something we want on our public record. Has he not relayed this yet?"

"He hasn't," the guard said suspiciously.

"Do you think your leader is so cruel that he wouldn't change his mind on such a sensitive matter?" Hetia grew more confident with each rebuttal. "He has, however, remained adamant that the children should not be allowed to relay the message themselves."

The guard exhaled in annoyance. He talked into his roamer, relaying what she'd told him to his superior. After shutting it off, he said, "You'll have to be escorted."

"Fine," she responded, "but I'll need privacy."

"That's against the rules."

Was she acting too soon? Or worse yet, could the Archaics' powers even be restored? There was only one way to find out.

"Come and listen then," she said. "But please give a mother about to be executed one last moment of respect."

The guard grunted something unintelligible. He led her past the front offices and into a dark hallway that bore resemblance to a cold, confining tunnel. Metal bars partially obscured men and women huddled on stone beds. She looked for the Caretaker but did not see him. The sight of so many detained distressed her. Prisoners watched her with accusing eyes. If only they knew what she had planned.

The Archaics were detained in a large cell at the end.

Baric sat cross-legged near a plant sliver that had worked its way in through a crack in the floor. Oc~ea stared lifelessly out the window. Atmos napped on a bed. Luma, who had been examining a blood red fingernail, looked up and scowled.

Seeing them together in one cell perplexed her. Hadn't

Draevik said she was deserving of her own? Besides that, it was apparent their powers had not returned. Which meant she would have to stall for as long as she could.

"Whose idea was this?" she asked the guard.

"What?" he asked.

"Stuffing them together into one cell?"

"What's it matter?" he said.

"It doesn't seem wise."

The guard tilted his head in the Archaics' direction. "Do what you came here for."

"I will," Hetia assured him.

The guard gave her a look that was intended to nudge her into action.

"Oc~ea," Hetia said loudly, hoping to rouse Atmos. "I have a message for you."

Oc~ea turned slowly. "Tell me," she said.

Hetia paused for effect, perhaps for too long.

"Hurry up," the guard said impatiently. "I was supposed to be taking them to the execution room, but instead I'm doing this."

"I need your full attention," she said.

Luma glared. "She doesn't have to give you anything."

"No," Hetia said, "she doesn't. But the message is from her children."

Atmos sat up and rubbed his eyes.

"They came to us last night, begging for their lives," Hetia said dramatically, feeling so empowered by her lie that she almost believed it herself.

Luma burst out laughing.

"No conversation," the guard snarled. "Say your message and get out."

"We conceded," she continued sadly, "for their condition moved us to pity them." She placed her hand upon her brow. Draevik was right, she would make a fine actress.

The Archaics stared now, unmoving, though Atmos had the presence to yawn.

"And now," she said slowly, "listen carefully to what they wished for me to tell you."

The guard squeezed Hetia's shoulder, signifying she had outstayed her welcome. "Are you sure you have clearance?"

"Your powers will soon be restored," she said bluntly. "Ceera is returning the relic as we speak."

The guard roughly grabbed Hetia's arm. "I need backup," he barked into his roamer.

"I was never on Draevik's side," Hetia said as the guard began pulling her down the hall.

Footsteps pounded their way.

"We checked into her claims," an approaching guard said. "She has no clearance from Draevik. In fact, she was supposed to be imprisoned. He authorized us to kill her."

Do something, Hetia pleaded with her eyes, *prove my timing wasn't wrong.*

"Then do it," the guard bellowed as he pushed Hetia toward him. "The rest of you, get ready. We'll have to off the Archaics right here in their cell."

The guard caught Hetia and tugged her backward.

The remaining order patrols joined the first. They eyed the Archaics nervously and took aim.

"Whoever shoots will expose themselves as the enemy," Hetia shouted.

Several weapons dropped from position.

"The Archaics will show no mercy," she continued.

"Don't listen to her," the head guard shouted. "They're behind bars. Blast them away!"

A ferocious outburst of wind blasted the metal bars into airborne shards, siphoning the weapon's projectiles along with them. The resulting debris flew into the guards' faces. Baric's plant enlarged forcefully and loosened the stone tile. Cracks branched out as it reached the ceiling, crumbling the floor beneath the guards' feet.

The guard wrestling Hetia away whirled around.

"Let go of her," Luma screamed, her hair a swirling mess.

The guard released Hetia, put his hands up, and fled.

"I must alert the children," Oc-ea murmured. She dipped her finger in a bowl of water that strangely had not tipped during the destruction.

A great mist swirled up and surrounded the guards, who were struggling to regain their footing on the uneven ground. Brief gusts sent them headfirst against the walls. Within seconds, they lay unconscious amid the rubble.

"Come," Hetia called out. "The vermin are here. And Draevik must be stopped."

The Archaics stepped over the broken metal nubs and trailed behind her. The prison walls shook as they proceeded, as if the building could barely contain the Archaics' powers.

Hetia began to lead them outside, but the anguish on the prisoners' faces stopped her. Some reached through the bars as she passed.

"You'll be released soon. Trust me, you don't want to be out there right now anyway," Hetia said.

"But we have children," someone protested.

Hetia's conscience wavered. "Fine then," she relented. "I will search for the keys."

∾

After receiving Nespi's call, Fresdin slipped from the room

where he'd gathered in secret with the other officials. They'd been discussing how to take back High Service, and he would leave them to that, for he had something important to do.

He headed toward the guards' headquarters inside the Aurora, so he could alert them to the game changer outside.

Entering the room without ceremony, he said, "I have news."

The large group, who'd been strapping on weapons, came to attention.

"The Archaics are loose," Fresdin said, "and their powers have been restored. We'll need every one of you out there to stop them from advancing on the Aurora."

The guards' demeanors changed quickly. Fear loosened their rigid postures and caused anxiety to ripple across faces. Not one of them hurried toward the door.

"How can we fight the Archaics?" one asked.

"Ah," Fresdin replied, "coming to your senses, are you?"

Still, not one guard moved.

"Would you defy your leader? Draevik Warlyn sits in his office, watches the proceedings with keen attention, but doesn't get his hands dirty, does he? Who wants to fight for such a man? Who will trade their life for his?"

Conflict now creased their faces.

"Are you betraying him?" asked a guard, feverishly holding his weapon. "He claims we're advancing society."

"He promised my family eternal life," said another, whose uniform was covered in someone else's blood.

"Society cannot advance when there's division among its people. If you wish to fight, go fight. If you wish to hide, run and do so. Either way, you will not be the recipient of Draevik's great rewards. High Service is divided, but not many stand on Draevik's side. Decide now which side you are ready to die for, and if it's Draevik's, know you put your life on the line so that one man and his chosen few can live forever."

Fresdin bowed and hurried from the room to rejoin the other officials. Not one footstep followed. He could have told them Ceera succeeded, that Draevik's ideal was now impossible, but after so much bloodshed, it would be more rewarding for them to make the right choice.

～

Cafold had prevented Ceera from collapsing once she'd handed the relic to that thing. He now sat on the floor, with her head in his lap. He stroked her hair, unsure of what to do next. Her face was soft and pretty. She had murmured Dassius's name seconds after passing out. When he'd reminded her he was Cafold, she'd flinched away.

And now, staring at her motionless form, he realized she may not be breathing. He placed two fingers firmly against the side of her neck.

"What have you done to her?" Dassius's voice imploded into his thoughts.

He raised his head. "I helped her," he said, recoiling from Dassius's wild-eyed look, then jumped when Sidorn came running up behind him.

"Take it easy on him, Dassius," Sidorn warned, and Cafold relaxed.

He should have known. That explained a lot. Namely the so-called strength of his mental barriers. Cafold wasn't insecure, just aware of his own capabilities.

"Is she dead?" Dassius asked, kneeling beside them.

"Her pulse is weak, but she's still alive," Cafold responded.

"Where's the relic? What was that sound?" Dassius asked.

"There." Cafold pointed. "Inside the hole. She gave it to the…thing that emerged."

"A creature?" Dassius asked.

"I don't know. It was everything. I can't explain…"

Sidorn leaned over to investigate the hole while Dassius gently picked Ceera up to cradle her in his arms.

"Yeah." Sidorn backed away from the opening. "This is weird. Let's get out of here."

"Now what?" Cafold asked.

"Back to the surface. We need to find out what kind of mess awaits us up there."

"That'll take days," Cafold said. "At least as many as it took to get here. And Ceera is unconscious."

"I'll carry her," Dassius said. "She won't slow me down too much."

"I have a feeling," Sidorn said, "that it will be quicker out than it was to get here."

"Why?" Cafold struggled to comprehend such an impossibility.

"Some passageways have opened up. I'm hoping we find one. In fact"—he winked—"I think it's highly probable we will."

CHAPTER THIRTY-SIX

THE ARCHAICS EMERGED into the orbits so powerful an entity that their natural inclination was to part ways. Luma and Oc~ea headed in one direction; Atmos and Baric proceeded to another.

"I can't wait to vent," Luma said with a gleeful twirl, the ends of her hair sending sparks into the grass near a building.

"You must be cautious," Oc~ea replied, sending rain on Luma's sparks with a flutter of her fingers, "or you will destroy the entire town."

"You're so smothering," Luma said. "They deserve it after what they did to us."

"But their leaders are divided. One of them even rescued us. The people have been tricked. They will amend their ways when this is over. Promise me you'll show mercy."

Luma's gaze grew distant. "I promise to find someone worthy to release my tensions on," she said slyly, then added, "but first I'll tend some bits of kindling."

She pointed to some vermin scrabbling toward a trio of roughened Semions peering around an AT cylinder. Knives out and ready, the Semions watched a violent encounter farther around the orbit, and thus were not aware of the impending invasion. Luma's blood red fingernail invoked flames. Fire embraced the vermin, charring skin with each lick, then extinguished itself on the blackened remains. The startled Semions fled.

Satisfied that her sister would obey her wishes, Oc~ea moved past for there were others to defend.

She walked calmly, drawing water from the sky. Condensation streamed toward her palms. She also called it from the bay. When the channel flowed toward her, she scooped it up as if it were a long-lost pet.

"My darling," she cooed.

She floated through the chaos with her ball of conjured water, searching for the right aggressor to unleash it on. It didn't take long to find him.

The guard was ordering a group of Semions with tattered clothes and grime-stained faces into a travel pod. Was he taking them to safety? Oc~ea's question was answered when he drew his weapon.

"Think you can hide in a High Service pod," he shouted angrily, "when you've been hounding us in the streets?"

It was time to turn the tide.

"Let them be," she ordered.

He looked at her and snarled, "Who let the myths out?"

Then he saw what she was holding. His eyes widened when she hurled the conjured water at him. It wrapped around his chest and knocked him down, streaming into his mouth and eyes. He gagged and choked as it gushed from his nostrils.

"Go ahead," she said to the shocked Semions. "It is safe now."

They stood unnaturally still, more fearful of her than the guard's weapon.

One man reminded her of Waive. "You," she said loudly, and he flinched. "Lead them."

He nodded, opening the pod's door and hustling the other men and women inside.

The guard still lay at her feet, gasping and choking.

"Do you believe in fairy tales yet?" she asked.

He sputtered yet managed to choke out, "Yes."

"You believed it all along, didn't you?" Her voice was stronger now, like a dangerous current. "And still decided to disregard those who had protected you all these years."

The man writhed on the ground, watching her with bulging, terror-stricken eyes.

"Those who disregard their past," she said passionately, "do not deserve to live inside the present."

The man twitched and cavorted on the ground as the water coursed through him.

"I made Luma promise to be kind," Oc~ea said softly, watching the man's eyes light up in hope. "Unfortunate for you, I have made no promises."

❧

"What do you mean some passageways have opened up?" Dassius asked.

"Apparently there was more at stake than just the fading of god figures."

"You mean demi-gods," Cafold interjected.

Sidorn raised his eyebrows before continuing, "And Ceera cut it pretty close."

"How close? My roamer broke yesterday."

"It didn't break. Draevik switched it off."

Dassius mumbled something rude, prompting a shrug from Sidorn, who said matter-of-factly, "I had to play along, or things could have turned out differently. The Archaics were losing their powers fast, and I didn't want to distract you."

"Why didn't you call me before he switched it off?" Dassius said defensively.

"Because I didn't know your number," Sidorn barked back just as defensively. "And besides, then I couldn't have proven my point as effectively as I did."

"Just because you're my friend, doesn't mean you're not a jerk."

"No one ever said I wasn't a jerk. Can you wake her up?"

The three men looked at her crumpled form in Dassius's arms. He gently shook her. She didn't stir, her condition seemingly impenetrable, but at least she was breathing.

"Must be some sort of side effect," Dassius said.

"It was an intense hand over," Cafold said. "I recommended she look away, but she was in some sort of trance."

"Can you carry her?" Sidorn asked Dassius.

"I can help," Cafold mumbled, "if you need me to."

"I already said I'd carry her. Let's go."

They wound their way back through the maze.

"I'll do my best to explain on the way," Sidorn said. "But we're looking for signs of light, or air flow, in hopes of finding a way out. So turn your senses on. If we miss them, we'll be traipsing back the way we came."

"How do we know there'll be an AT cylinder near where we emerge?" Dassius asked.

"We don't. We just hope. My roamer still works. I can pull up a map of all the cylinders."

They trekked the tunnels, Sidorn leading and Dassius carrying Ceera as if she weighed nothing. Cafold straggled behind, huffing and puffing, thinking he should work out more.

The battle room was an unsightly mess composed of blood splatters and battered men tied together in bundles. A few men were blinking, still dazed. Or perhaps they were just waking up. A small crew of unbloodied guards stood to the side.

"We found your note," said their female leader. "We tried waking them up, but we may need to send a separate crew later."

Cafold breathed a sigh of relief. No wonder Sidorn had wanted privacy when he'd supposedly set his trap.

"Yeah," Sidorn responded, "if the rats don't get to them first."

"We've seen more than rats around here," Dassius said.

"Get ready to see them again. Those things invaded Semadon."

The friendlies joined the group, and Sidorn led them into an alternate tunnel. He held a hand to his ears, motioning for them to listen.

There was that scrabbling sound again, coming from farther down the tunnel.

"I know what that is," Dassius said, turning to Cafold. "I do need your help. Hold her, gently, so I can fight."

The weight of her caused Cafold to stumble a few steps backward until his back met the wall. He stayed there, using the wall for support and hoped his straining muscles would hold up. Definitely needed to work out more.

"Here comes the cleanup crew," said Sidorn.

Cafold sputtered in protest.

Sidorn winked at him. "Nah, just kidding. We'll go back and get them."

Then the vermin poured from the tunnel, and the swishing of knives and the spray of blood was all that came after.

⁓

"The enemy of my enemy," Glavin mumbled, as he looked out his window, "is also…my enemy."

There was someone he needed to visit. The violence outside propelled him to undertake his most ignoble desire. He would obey this evil beckoning and do the deed.

His walk through the streets solidified his intent. Twice, he had to thwart the vermin from attacking him. Their blood made him want to draw more, but he was smart enough to realize this was an effect of violence. He would save his primal urges for the one most deserving of them.

A man stood outside the back entrance to the Aurora, his stature slight and stooped, but he wasn't whom Glavin was looking for. He tucked his knife away. "Where's Draevik?"

Wyman pointed his weapon at him with a sloppy smile. "It's you. My old grand master."

Glavin would not fall prey to dramatics. "As if that were ever the case. Though if you'd like to return to the CfA, you may want to point that thing elsewhere."

"Who says I want to return? This is my crowning achievement." Wyman cradled the weapon as if he revered it.

Unimpressed, Glavin said, "Where is he?"

"Inside."

Glavin placed his hand on Wyman's shoulder to nudge him away from the door, but Wyman jerked away. "I have strict orders to guard this door."

"Guard it from me?"

"From everyone and anyone."

Glavin stared at the unnatural looking man before him.

Months spent in solitude plotting how to kill had done the CfA member no good. It unsettled him to see someone so weak capable of such destruction, as if a powerful object could counterbalance what was lacking inside.

"You call this advancement?" Glavin asked, gesturing toward the weapon.

"Advancement works in mysterious ways."

"Along with everything else," Glavin said dryly. "Now I need to talk to Draevik."

"I'll tell him you're here," Wyman said, turning toward the door. "We'll see how high you are on his list—"

Glavin kicked Wyman behind the knees, expecting him to crumble to the ground. Instead, he rebounded back up when his knees hit the door.

"Is that how it's going to be?" Wyman raised his weapon to his shoulder. "You never used to have such bad ideas."

"I still don't," Glavin said, dampening his emotions with a sour expression. If he were going to die, he refused to die with fear permeating his face.

"Then why test your fate with me?" Wyman aimed his weapon now, signifying Glavin had mere seconds to live.

Words stayed locked inside Glavin's throat. He contemplated whether a snide retort would buy time or kill him faster, when a dark hooded figure stepped from the shadows alongside the building.

"I see you've brought a friend," Wyman said, slinking back a step so they were both within his weapon's range.

The dark figure gained proximity to Glavin in a freakish flash of movement. He broke into a sweat but dare not wipe the dribble from his forehead.

"Who wants to die first?" Wyman asked, his eyes glowing like a wild animal at night.

The tall figure's hood flipped backward, revealing feminine features that were vibrant and cutting.

Glavin's skin prickled with anger, relief, and something else. So far, he'd avoided the Archaics while they'd been in town, but this one refused to be ignored.

"Only one of us will die today," she said coyly.

"You…you," Wyman stuttered. "You should be locked up." His grasp on his weapon faltered, but not enough that Glavin felt it wise to intercede.

"Should I be?" Luma said condescendingly. She traced a finger across her blood red lips.

"Your powers are gone—"

"Are you sure I can't subdue you?" Luma took a step toward him.

"Not when I'm holding this."

Glavin bit back an insult.

Luma smirked. "Like your weapon, do you?"

"You can't take it from me," Wyman said, hugging it protectively to his chest.

"Keep it then," Luma said, but her assent contained an underlying threat.

Wyman apparently hadn't caught onto this. He aimed his weapon at them. His face turned a deep shade of red. Still holding the weapon, his hands trembled. A sickening sizzling sound grew in intensity. His mouth widened in terror, and he screamed. The weapon melted and dripped, encasing his hands and forearms in molten metal gloves. Looking at his blistering arms, Wyman howled in agony.

The smell of burning flesh pervaded the air. Glavin cupped a hand over his nose.

"I warned you," Luma said, but the damage had been done.

The liquid metal that had oozed onto his feet erupted. He began to run on glowing stubs, but the fire was already working up his body. He screamed again then tumbled headfirst onto the walkway.

Glavin watched the ex-councilman meet his fate within flames that blackened the terror on his face until he was just a scorched bundle on stone.

"And now you," Luma said, turning to him as if he were next. The blaze in the background, now subtle, gave her a sensual glow.

Glavin swallowed any words that might betray him, searched his brain for a safe retort. "You said only one of us will die today."

"That doesn't mean you still don't need convincing."

Her smoldering gaze sent shivers down his spine, but they weren't from fear. Never that. Still, an anger coursed through him that needed to be quenched. "Of what?"

"Of what I have to offer."

Was he being played? How did she know his inner thoughts?

"I can tell you're angry, that's why I'm so attracted to you," she said, running fingers down his arm.

Her touch was electric, left traces of desires he'd long forgotten, and suddenly what he'd originally set out to do had lost its luster.

⁊

Atmos was a drifter and thus had a natural inclination for travel. Spinning around the orbits at various speeds, restoring order with a gust here and a wisp there, he was able to impact the disorder quickly. These efficient outbursts were accompanied with a howling wind that alluded to amusement rather than fright, for Atmos did love the element of surprise his medium evoked.

Mist curled about the chaos, blinding Semions whose aggressions were misguided. Air blasted weapons from hands positioned on the wrong kill. Some were unable to move due to the wind's strong resistance and found themselves, quite literally, air locked.

Vermin fell to the ground, unaccustomed to these strong winds. Fascinated by this, Atmos rounded the vermin up, using individual gusts to blast each creature into an ever-growing group. His vortex spun around them, binding them together, and he pondered what to do with this disgusting, screeching mass.

He remembered Baric was not far away. He listened carefully for the breeze to tell him where and sent the verminous vortex spinning toward his brother. He only mastered the air. Baric would have to do the rest.

Baric deterred many a guard from opening fire on him with a flinty, omnipotent stare that sent them running like ants in the opposite direction. Trees plucked unsuspecting Semions from the reach of encroaching vermin, and ivy crawled to entangle these vermin in vegetative webs.

Within an inner orbit, mostly devoid of Semions now, he watched the vermin scrabble about and take whatever they desired. They squeezed food in small fists from fruit stands and stuffed it into their mouths like animals. They pounded on vacant storefronts; their insatiable hunger never quenched.

Baric liked animals, but it disheartened him to watch these pathetic creatures act in desperate ways. They needed to go back where they belonged.

When Atmos sent the mass of vermin toward him, he was ready.

He planted his feet firmly on the ground. Threads coursed from his soles into the soil. The ground cracked open and offset the vermin's footing, causing them to fall into the resulting crevices. Ivy pushed its captives neatly into these gaps. Pale, withered hands reached upward, but the soil closed over top of them and silenced any screams.

Soon shouts only came from the Semions farther around the orbit, still fighting amongst themselves, though with a growing indifference as they realized the vermin had disappeared and that order had prevailed. Baric stayed rooted to the spot, his feet itching as the nasty creatures descended back into the planet's cavities.

Chapter Thirty-Seven

DRAEVIK WATCHED WHAT was happening on the Aurora's lawn through the camera linked to his global update. The fighting was chaotic, and he couldn't tell which side was winning. Plus, those despicable pale creatures mucked up what could have been an obvious victory for his side.

He wondered whether he'd made a mistake when he'd ordered the remaining Sci-Def members to be locked into a never-ending Sim. They could be of better use outside, fighting the vermin along with his guards. But he hadn't had time to test their loyalties. And their loyalties would need to be tested now that Sidorn and Dassius were on opposing sides. In fact, Dassius should be on the other side entirely by now.

Which reminded him, why hadn't Sidorn called to tell him that Dassius was dead? He entered Sidorn's number on his roamer.

As it hummed, Draevik noticed a stream of long, blond tresses cascading past the doorway.

Who dare spy on a High Service official? He set the roamer down so he could apprehend the intruder. When he stepped through the doorway, he was not surprised to find the hallway empty. The intruder was careless though, must have been carrying a beverage, for they'd left a trail of water along the floor.

Feeling cleverly observant, Draevik followed the trail.

Around the hallway and yet another, he pursued, close enough to hear feet pattering away from him. When he rounded another curve, he was surprised to find a young girl standing there, unafraid and feigning innocence. She twisted a strand of flowing hair between her fingers.

Where had she come from? Children were not allowed at the Aurora. He had the impression that she knew this, deduced it from her smug expression, and stepped toward her.

"What are you doing here?" he asked sternly, noticing her appearance was different from most children.

Her skin had a bluish tint, and her dress was more costume than practical. A single green shell hung from her neck. She tugged on it absently as she appraised him.

Suddenly Draevik felt uncertain, not something he was accustomed to, especially in the presence of someone so small.

The child giggled, a lyrical sound that carried mischief on its notes.

Draevik was not about to be dominated by a child. He cleared his throat. "I asked you a question, girl. Explain why you think you have the right to use the Aurora as your play area. Where are your parents?"

Had they placed her here for safety? Draevik would have none of that. He would take this child back outside where she belonged. After all, she may be the enemy's offspring. Why cherish the youth with society now on the cusp of immortality?

The girl flicked her hair behind her shoulder, gave him a pert smile, and walked away.

Draevik was aghast. She was headed to the fountain room, bound to splash about and cause trouble. He had to stop her. Most importantly, he had to get back to watching what was going on outside the Aurora.

He entered the room and found her wading in the channel flowing around it, contaminating its purity with her grimy feet.

"Get out of there!" he shouted.

Where were the other officials and his guards?

Then Draevik noticed the boy sitting atop the sculpted statue of a sea creature, one of many that spat out the waterfall. His smug expression was more refined than the girl's. It came with hostility and a curled lip. Draevik stepped closer and stared disapprovingly. The boy stared shamelessly back at him.

Draevik pressed the communication panel on the wall. "Guards!" he called into it, wondering why something like fear now trickled into his chest.

The girl skipped inside the fountain, splashing around just as Draevik had foreseen and getting water on the floor. Then she did something strange. She closed her eyes, stretched her arms outward, and spun. The water rose. It lapped over the sides of the stone channel and gushed onto the floor.

"Stop that this instant!" he said.

An astonished look upward told him both the boy and the sea creature were gone. The sulky pre-teen was surely a vandal, had detached it from the fountain's wall, and needed some discipline.

Draevik wondered why his guards weren't coming. Water

now leaked into his shoes. In disgust, he turned to leave and find his guards, but found the door was locked.

That's what the boy had been doing while the girl distracted him. He jiggled the locked handle as the water reached his calves.

No reason to worry, he told himself, *his guards would be here soon.*

The girl slid down the sloping channel. She squealed with delight as she plummeted into the growing body of water.

"Get down from there!" he called.

An impossible amount of water flowed around him, now up to his waist. He backed up and almost fell. The boy was floating toward him, treading water perhaps for he seemed abnormally tall.

"Are you the babysitter?" he asked indignantly, noticing the boy was actually in his late teens.

The teen said nothing, sliding backward slightly when the sea creature he rode reared its scaly head.

It looked much like the one that had previously adorned the fountain. But this creature was not a mere fixture on a wall, it was alive.

How was this possible? Only a demi-god could give life to an inanimate object.

Draevik's eyes widened at the realization of who was pestering him. He scanned the room for the other Archaics. Assuming they'd escaped, they had to be nearby, readying to decimate him with their regained powers.

But only the girl and teen were present; the former still whirling about, and the latter floating toward him. Which meant this was nothing more than a game.

The teen glared malevolently, dug his fingers into the

sea creature's slimy neck. Draevik backed away instinctually, edging toward the window.

The teen dismounted the serpent. It dove to encircle them within a blur of scales. The dizzying maelstrom locked Draevik in place.

"Let me go," he commanded, but his voice had weakened.

The teen plunged his hands into the water. Lifted an orb of liquid to his chest. Draevik watched, mesmerized by the miniature tropical cyclone that spun within his palms. Then the young man raised his head, met Draevik's gaze, and focused like a predator.

The narrowing of his eyes triggered a deafening sound. A high-powered jet of water speared from the orb. It pierced Draevik's shoulder, burning as it moved through. He staggered backward, clutching his wound in both pain and astonishment.

"Stop," he whispered.

The teen narrowed his eyes again. Another ear-splitting sound accompanied a laser burst of liquid. It spiked through Draevik's other shoulder. He almost fainted as it shattered bone.

Arms now dangling, Draevik swayed from nausea. Desperation mingled with his pain. He was too close to life eternal to surrender now.

"Let me live," he said hoarsely, "and I'll build you a temple in Semadon. You and the girl."

The teen's muscles tensed. Water surged beneath him.

"We'll treat you both like demi-gods," he pleaded.

The young man rose upward within the clutches of a mighty wave. Or perhaps he commanded the billowing swell. Strangely suspended up high, water frothed ominously around him. He opened his mouth to speak.

"That didn't help my mother."

One final glowering look. The wave came crashing down.

Like the breaker that it was, it broke the rest of Draevik's body. Submerged now and unable to move, water's fingers flowed like rivulets to wrap around his throat.

Before he fell unconscious, laughter trickled into his ears and seized his lungs. As death took him, despair scratched his thoughts like fingernails across a coffin.

The game was over. And Draevik had lost.

❧

In Ceera's mind, two figures stood in the distance, illuminated by a brilliant white light. They faced each other and held hands. At first, she thought she'd finally been reunited with Dassius and waited for his kiss. But then, she realized with disappointment that she was detached from the visual and only watching from afar.

The female figure was the woman who had shown her the way. The other was Rebial, the man who had decided not to kill her. Gazing upon her ancestors like this made her suspect their reasons hadn't been so selfish. When they kissed, the brilliance engulfed them. Bits of light danced within her mind. Someone was shaking her. Probably Sidorn so he could kill her.

"Ceera, wake up."

Dassius's voice was enough motivation to open her eyes.

"You did it," he said. "We're done."

The sun shone behind him. When he kissed her, she knew life was about patterns. Events repeating themselves. Rising above tragedy and thus breaking the cycle. Starting fresh.

She had been exposed to everything as she'd handed over

the relic, but one thing stuck out the most, had changed her perspective on everything. She had experienced what it felt like to be hopelessly empty: a black hole devoid of meaning and purpose. She had also felt the fullness of life in its totality: a burgeoning plethora of meaning. No matter what, from now on, she would choose something over nothing. For both existed in this world, united as one. And not only had she accomplished what was intended for her, but also the path she had chosen for herself.

Chapter Thirty-Eight

HETIA WAS IN the best of moods. When she joined Fresdin in the backroom to wait for the sphere raising ceremony to begin, he smiled widely.

"You're lovely," he said.

Hetia sighed. "I'm a leader, not an object to admire."

"Perhaps you can be both?"

"I'm too busy to be both," Hetia retorted.

"Like anyone would consider you just an object to admire," Fresdin said. "Not when you challenged Draevik from the start."

This did cause Hetia to smile. "Thank you."

"No, I should be the one thanking you," he responded. "Thank you for persuading me to see Draevik's true colors. Thank you for persisting when I defended him."

"You're welcome," Hetia said. "Though I do wonder whether Draevik suffered from some form of dementia after his pneumonia. He wasn't always like that, which is why he was able to fool you and so many others."

"You're making excuses for him."

"Now that he's out of the picture, I have time to dwell on such things."

"The sphere sevens say his grief for his deceased companion caused him to turn."

The elder spheres had been released from Draevik's invasive rounds of testing once the orbits were safe. Only their pride had been harmed, but wisdom only falls prey to that wound for so long. They would be conducting the ceremony.

Risa and Karnen had been jailed. A judge would be conducting theirs.

"Promise me that my death would never turn you to such evil inclinations," Hetia said.

The death toll resulting from Draevik's actions was higher than Hetia would ever feel comfortable accepting. But she took consolation in the fact that Draevik's guards had saved more Semions from vermin than had been killed by them.

"It wouldn't. Though I would suffer from despair all the same."

"So would I," Hetia said, "but let's be done with such talk. They're ready for us to enter the ceremony."

Zivan stood near the doorway now and motioned them onto the stage. They entered and stood beside Sadra at the forefront of the room. She spoke both of their names in turn. The Caretaker clapped within the audience, along with their crewmates and the other officials.

Harnol held the shiny spheres that would soon be fastened to the three already dangling from each of their necks.

Hetia had been initially upset that she and Fresdin only went up one sphere level instead of two, but Sadra had kindly mentioned that though they were deserving of two, this would give them less time as active leaders. Hetia had accepted this explanation, saw the value in it.

As Sadra clipped a fourth sphere to each of their necklaces, Hetia felt relief for the first time since she'd defied the late sphere seven. Fresdin raised their clasped hands while the Semions in attendance cheered.

❧

When Ceera's father opened the door, he only stared. And she felt no need to greet him and pretend like she was merely there to visit.

"I know," she said, figuring the simplicity of her comment would speak its weight.

Her father squinted at her, scratched his head. Comprehension formed in his eyes. "How did you figure it out?" he asked softly.

She owed him nothing unless he confessed. "First, tell me why you lied."

He leaned against the wall, fiddling with the dirt-covered tool he still carried. "To protect you."

Ceera gave an exasperated sigh. "Forget it, I'm leaving."

"No wait." Her father held out a hand to stop her. "You came so you deserve an explanation."

"I know I do. But you've never been good at giving me what I need."

He frowned. "I deserve that. When I told you I sent you to Semadon to keep you away from the woods, that was the truth. Imagine how it was for me, watching all my family members go crazy and die. My mother, my sisters. My grandmother even. A cousin. All born with the same mark and nothing they could do about it."

Ceera crossed her arms over her chest. "But my mother wasn't one of them."

"No, she wasn't. But she still fell ill and passed. Another burden to bear. Another person I loved who went away."

"You told me the dreams made her crazy."

"I did, and I shouldn't have told you that. Because she wasn't the one who had them. But it was easier that way. I wouldn't have to have this conversation with you. And I'm a selfish man. If you went crazy like all the females in my family then we could blame it on your mother, and I wouldn't have any High Service officials snooping around to see if I'd go that way too."

"Do you have the mark?" she asked.

"No, solely a female thing, just like you've been told. And when you were born with it, I—" he pressed his fist to his mouth. "I didn't think I could bear to lose you too."

"So you got rid of me before that could happen."

He nodded. "A regret I can't fix. But I did try to warn you, when I found out the same thing was happening to you."

"But how did you keep the other family members' conditions a secret?"

"High Service keeps better records now. Back then, if you lived in a settlement, they didn't know much. They knew if you lived and if you died, but we kept the details of both within the family."

"My records in Drusilla's filing cabinet say I have a family history of mental illness."

"See then," her father said grimly, "they know more about you than they should."

"It would have been better for me to know the truth."

"Just know this. I didn't give you up because you weren't important. I gave you up because you were."

She cringed, hating how good his words made her feel. He should never have that kind of power over her again. Yet she couldn't resist asking, "And what am I now?"

"Skeptical," he said. "And rightly so. But you have your truth. You'll have to live with it. Just like I'll have to live with my regrets."

Draevik Warlyn met the death he had tried so hard to evade. He was found in the fountain room, drowned. Except he wasn't inside the fountain, but instead face down on the dry marble floor. Some thought he had drowned himself in the fountain, and that a guard had pulled him out after, yet no one would admit to that. And the Archaics had left Semadon after eliminating the vermin, not that interrogating them would have been comfortable for anyone.

His death was very mysterious, but Ceera was not one to overthink things any longer. Draevik had met the end he deserved, and that was all there was to it.

High Service, now functioning with their previous integrity, determined that Ceera needed rest, but instead of confining her to an institution, allowed her to stay at her dwelling. The repose was peaceful and relaxing. They did, however, insist she participate in Dassius's training sessions regularly to serve as a distraction for him to overcome. He had revealed that her presence hindered his clairvoyant ability, and this had been their solution. Of course, she was eager to help.

She also made a point to tell Hetia about the conditions at the institution, specifically about Garia and the machines. Hetia had adamantly promised that she would check into what was happening there and correct any wrongdoings. Ceera believed her.

Scribe work was still a possibility, but High Service insisted her future was hers to decide. Having never had that kind of freedom before, she felt a bit lost and wondered if her existence was still necessary.

"Don't be silly," Dassius said when she'd expressed this. "It's necessary to me."

He had given her a promise ring and came to her almost daily. They had their nightly meals together. And sometimes more than that.

Still an active member of the Sci-Def team, Dassius would soon embark on a mission. Space travel had been progressing slowly for many years, but there had finally been a breakthrough due to the collaboration of Hegliod Avatus and Cafold Brine. Soon Dassius would be whisked off for exploration, and she would be left alone for who knows how long. Sidorn had been recruited too. At least she would have Litha.

The love affair of Litha and Sidorn, though initially disturbing to Ceera, had seemed more natural once they'd all returned from the cave.

"I don't know how you do it," Litha told her one day. "All the knowing what you're thinking before you say it; it's annoying. Just once I'd like to say something and see a genuine reaction."

"Although," her friend had added slyly, "this whole merging together thing has its advantages in some areas."

Litha was referencing the method members of the Sci-Def team used to better read their environment.

She feigned ignorance, if only to fool her friend into thinking she had no experience with such a juncture. But perhaps Litha was learning things from Sidorn, because she'd said, "Like I can't see it on your face you know exactly what I'm talking about."

Ceera smiled then, glad her so-called innocent and vulnerable friend had the wherewithal to hide out with Drusilla in Mentoring Headquarters when the fighting broke out in Semadon. As for Drusilla, she'd told Ceera if she didn't return as a scribe, to be sure to come and visit. Ceera was still recovering from the shock.

So it was with great sorrow that she listened to Dassius tell her he'd be leaving. A date had been set. He would be gone in less than a month.

She counted down the days in agony, hoping Hegliod would have a lapse in logic to stall Dassius's departure. Except then the dreams came.

They were unexpected. And they had changed. No more forests or ancient relics. Now her dreams were composed of worlds she had not seen before. She'd thought her purpose was served, but no. She had a special talent that defined her now with nothing left to fear.

CHARACTER LIST

Ceera Kestlyn, *a scribe prone to daydreaming and stray visions*
Dassius Rucien, *Ceera's lover on the Sci-Defense team*
Sidorn, *member of the Sci-Defense team*
Cafold, *Hegliod's apprentice tasked to study the relic*
Rebial, *mysterious protector of the forest*
Dream woman (unnamed), *Ceera's ancestor that appears in her dreams*

Secondary Characters
Hegliod Avatus, *a grumpy yet genius inventor*
Drusilla Rune, *Ceera's scribe mentor*
Litha, *Ceera's scribe friend*
Caretaker of Ancient Affairs, *the expert of antiquity*
Bidlyn, Nespi, & Xyria, *guards on Hetia & Fresdin's crew*

Mystics, *enchanted entities that exist between the planes of reality*

High Service Members
Draevik Warlyn, *a corrupt sphere seven*
Jesra, *Draevik's deceased companion*
Karnen & Risa, *sphere six companions & Draevik's sidekicks*

Hetia & Fresdin, *sphere three companions who oppose Draevik*
Leynin & Asfin, *sphere five companions in charge of Wakovian settlement*
Zivan & Sadra, *sphere seven companions*
Harnol, *sphere seven*

Council Members
Glavin, *leader of the Council for Advancement (Cfa)*
Garia, *leader of CfA who resigned then disappeared*
Baclus, *CfA member tasked to study the relic*
Wyman, *CfA member in charge of Draevik's weapon program*
Falken Grihne, *the unlikable CfA member who Rebial killed*
Marvus & Desnia, *leaders of the Council for Natural Law (CfNL)*

Archaics
Atmos, *demi-god of air*
Baric, *demi-god of the planet*
Luma, *demi-goddess of fire*
Oc~ea, *demi-goddess of water*
Waive, *Oc~ea's son*
Anemona, *Oc~ea's daughter*

ALSO BY VELVET DAVIS

Immortal Roots

Short story series
Space Frivolity

Author's Note

Thank you for reading Dream Relic. If you enjoyed this book, please consider leaving an honest review. I appreciate any time you take to do this!

You can also join my email list at www.velvetdavis.com

Acknowledgments

I'd like to thank my family and friends for their unending support during the long process of writing a book. Thank you to my husband for his valuable input. He read every revision and motivated me to rewrite scenes until they were correct. Thank you to Jolivia Porter for her detailed notes and the insightful suggestion that a certain character needed to shine more. Thank you to Stephanie Vallez for pinpointing why one of my ending scenes wasn't satisfying the way I initially wrote it, and for mentioning that the vermin weren't frightful enough. Their help was wide ranging and non-inclusive to the specific points mentioned, and my book is better because of them. I'd also like to thank my beta readers for their helpful opinions. Lastly, I'd like to thank my parents and parents-in-law who continue to ask how my books are coming along and for their kind words of encouragement. Any remaining mistakes are my own.